A Class Act

Also by Gervase Phinn

THE TOP OF THE DALE SERIES
The School at the Top of the Dale
Tales Out of School

THE LITTLE VILLAGE SCHOOL SERIES
The Little Village School
Trouble at the Little Village School
The School Inspector Calls!
A Lesson in Love

THE DALES SERIES
The Other Side of the Dale
Over Hill and Dale
Head Over Heels in the Dales
Up and Down in the Dales
The Heart of the Dales
A Wayne in a Manger
Twinkle, Twinkle, Little Stars
A Load of Old Tripe
The Virgin Mary's Got Nits
Out of the Woods but not Over the Hill

POETRY
It Takes One to Know One
The Day Our Teacher Went Batty
Family Phantoms
Don't Tell the Teacher

Gervase Phinn

A Class Act

HODDER &
STOUGHTON

First published in Great Britain in 2021 by Hodder & Stoughton
An Hachette UK company

Copyright © Gervase Phinn 2021

A CIP catalogue record for this title is available from the British Library

Hardback ISBN 978 1 473 65070 1
eBook ISBN 978 1 473 65069 5

Typeset in Plantin by Manipal Technologies Limited
Printed and bound in Great Britain by Clays Ltd, Elcograf S.p.A.

Hodder & Stoughton policy is to use papers that are natural, renewable and recyclable products and made from wood grown in sustainable forests. The logging and manufacturing processes are expected to conform to the environmental regulations of the country of origin.

Hodder & Stoughton Ltd
Carmelite House
50 Victoria Embankment
London EC4Y 0DZ

www.hodder.co.uk

To Samuel and Elodie

A Class Act

I

Gerald Gaunt sat at his desk. He stared down at the letter of resignation, his pen poised to sign his name and he sighed, wondering for a moment if he was doing the right thing. He placed the pen down and gazed through the window, taking in the awesome view before him: silvered clouds stretching across a pale blue sky, undulating green pastures dotted with grazing sheep, bone-white limestone walls, tall pine woods and distant sombre peaks. He never ceased to be amazed by the breath-taking beauty of the scene; it never failed to fill his heart with a deep love of God's Own Country.

He had been the headmaster of Risingdale Primary School, the school at the top of the Dale, for over thirty years. It had been such a happy period in his professional life. As he often reminded himself, not everyone had such an untroubled existence and such a rewarding career. The children, on the whole, were biddable, friendly and tried their best at their studies; the teachers were amenable, got on well together and clearly had the interests of their pupils at heart, and the parents and the governors had let him get on with the job without undue interference. He loved his career in teaching and knew he would miss it greatly, but times in education were changing and, in his opinion, not always for the better. It had seemed so very simple in those post-war days when, as a new teacher, he had come straight out of college, keen and excited and full of bright ideas. There were none of the pressures then, none of the endless government initiatives and new Department of

Education and Science requirements, which came over the Dale like the Plagues of Egypt. In those bygone days, teachers had a great sense of freedom and could be creative and innovative. They were trusted to get on with the job at hand, but times had changed. He had tried over the years to resist such outside meddling and had had some degree of success, but now as the 1980s were coming to a close, he thought it was about time to call it a day.

The letter from the Education Office at County Hall asking him to consider early retirement had arrived out of the blue. It explained that there was to be 'a further programme of rationalisation' in the education service; several small village schools in the county were closing and, as a result, there would be a surfeit of teachers and several headteachers needing to be redeployed. All those over the age of sixty-two were being offered a generous package – a lump sum and a full, enhanced pension. It was rather too good a deal to pass up.

'Well, are you going to sign it?'

The speaker, a thin, slightly stooped woman with a pale, indrawn face, narrow dark eyes, and thick iron-grey hair cut in a bob, was the school secretary. Standing before the headmaster's desk, hands clasped below her bosom and staring over the top of her unfashionable horn-rimmed spectacles, she resembled an impatient teacher addressing a pupil.

'Yes, Mrs Leadbeater,' replied Mr Gaunt softly. His voice sounded wistful. 'I am going to sign it.' He tapped the pen on the desktop and looked thoughtful.

'You don't look all that sure,' she said.

'I'm sure,' he told her and quickly scribbled his name on the letter. 'There,' he said, 'that's done.' He placed down his pen and spread his hands on the desk. His fingers were smeared with ink.

'Well, if you were to ask me,' she told him, 'I think you should give it some more thought. I mean, you've got a few more years left in you yet.'

He chuckled. 'You make me sound like some old cart horse ready for the knacker's yard.'

She coloured. 'I didn't mean . . .' she began, unfolding her arms. 'I meant . . .'

'Yes, I know what you meant,' he told her, smiling.

'I meant that you're too young to be thinking about retirement.'

'I'm sixty-three, Mrs Leadbeater, hardly a spring chicken. I have thought long and hard about whether I should retire, and I think it is about time.' He drew in a breath. 'Everything in education these days moves at such a frantic pace and I'm rather too set in my ways to move with it.'

'Nonsense!' she snapped. 'You're in your prime.'

'Hardly,' he replied, leaning back on his chair. 'It's a far more demanding profession nowadays with all this constant change, the increasing pressures and paperwork, guidelines and strategies. It's about time I handed over to someone younger and better suited to it than I.'

'Well, you'll be greatly missed,' said the secretary. 'The school won't be the same without you.' She tried to control her emotions, but her voice betrayed the extent of her sadness.

'That's kind of you to say so, Mrs Leadbeater,' said Mr Gaunt.

'When are you thinking of going?' she asked.

'At the end of term,' she was told.

'So soon,' she said glumly.

'I thought of staying for another term but . . .' His voice tailed off.

'Do you think we will get one of these redeployed head teachers?' she asked.

'I should imagine so. Those head teachers who are losing their jobs must feel pretty miserable having their schools close. I know I would feel wretched if Risingdale ceased to exist.' He sat up in his chair and tried to sound more cheerful.

'Anyway, I'm sure the school will continue to thrive under new management and leadership. I know that whoever takes over will be fortunate to have a happy and committed staff and to have you as his or her secretary. We have worked well together, haven't we? I was thinking only yesterday that in all the years we have been together we have never had so much as a cross word.'

Mrs Leadbeater's eyes began to fill with tears. 'We haven't,' she agreed. 'Not a cross word.' There was a tremble in her voice. 'You've been the real gentleman, Mr Gaunt, and always appreciated what I have done. I just hope your successor is as considerate and appreciative as you have been.' She reached in her sleeve for a small lace-edged handkerchief and dabbed her eyes.

The headmaster regarded the tall, gaunt woman in her heavy grey skirt and prim blouse buttoned high at the neck who stood before him, her eyes full of tears. It was uncharacteristic of her to show her feelings in this way. To the teachers she had a brusque and direct manner and went about her business with a briskness and seriousness, rarely uttering a word she did not need to.

She reached for the letter with an expression of utter dismay on her face and, pushing the handkerchief back up her sleeve, said, 'I'll put this in the post this afternoon.'

'Oh, and Mrs Leadbeater,' said the headmaster, 'the Chairman of Governors is coming into school to see me this morning. I need to acquaint him with my decision before I tell the teachers and parents.'

'Sir Hedley? He's calling in this morning?'

'Yes, he will be here around eleven o'clock.'

'I had better get the best china out,' she said, 'and tell the teachers he's coming in.'

'I'm sure he wouldn't want you or the staff to go to any trouble.'

'I don't think he'll be best pleased to hear that you are leaving. It will certainly not go down well with the teachers either,' she predicted. 'You know how they hate any sort of change.'

'Maybe so,' agreed Mr Gaunt. 'Anyway, I should be grateful if you would not mention my leaving to the staff. I intend to tell them at the meeting at lunchtime.'

There was a sharp knock. Mrs Leadbeater opened the door to find outside a small boy of about seven or eight with grubby knees. A dewdrop trembled on the tip of his nose. He was dark and skinny with a soft crewcut, thin arms and gangly legs.

'Is 'e in?' asked the boy, sniffing.

The secretary gave a heaving sigh and stared down pointedly at the child with a severe expression.

'Nathan Barraclough,' she snapped. 'Where are your manners?'

'Where's mi what, miss?'

'I think you mean, "Is the headmaster available to see me, Mrs Leadbeater?"'

'Oh aye, miss,' replied the boy, wiping his nose on the back of his hand.

She grimaced. 'Well?'

'Is t'eadmaster havailable to see mi, Missis Leadbeater?' the child repeated.

'That's better,' she told him. 'Wait there and blow your nose.'

'I 'aven't gorran 'anky, miss.'

The secretary sighed again and shook her head. She reached into her sleeve for her handkerchief and then thought better of it. She turned to Mr Gaunt. 'Nathan Barraclough is here to see you,' she said. 'Shall I ask him to wait?'

'No, no, show the lad in.'

'He needs to blow his nose,' she said and departed with the letter, closing the door after her.

'Come along in, Nathan,' said Mr Gaunt, reaching into the top drawer of his desk and producing a box of paper tissues.

'Mi mam's sent thee a letter, Mester Gaunt,' said the boy. The dewdrop continued to tremble on the tip of his nose.

The headmaster reached over and passed the boy a tissue. 'Blow your nose,' he said.

The boy did as he was told. 'Mi mam's sent this letter,' re-iterated the child.

'Now, Nathan,' said the headmaster, adopting a mock stern expression. 'I have tried over the years to encourage children in the school to show good manners.'

The boy wrinkled his nose and looked perplexed.

'When you see someone first thing in the morning,' he continued, 'tell me what you are supposed to say to them?'

'I don't know, sir.'

'Let me give you a clue. What does your father say to your mother when he sees her first thing in the morning?'

The boy thought for a moment and rubbed his chin. ''E sez, "Will tha gerrup, Maureen, an' mek us a cup o' tea?"'

Mr Gaunt shook his head and suppressed a smile.

'I was thinking of "Good morning",' he said. 'So, shall we try again?'

'Oh, aye. Good morning, Mester Gaunt,' replied the boy, nodding and smiling.

'That's better.'

The boy handed him the used tissue and the letter. The headmaster deposited the former in the bin and began reading the latter.

'It says mi mam asks if it will be all reight fer 'er to tek me to t'dentist at lunchtime to 'ave a tooth out,' the boy informed Mr Gaunt.

'Yes, I can read, Nathan,' replied the headmaster, good-humouredly.

'I've got this wobbly tooth tha sees, an' it waint come out,' continued the child, wiggling a loose tooth with his index finger. 'Mi granddad tried to gerrit out an' tied a piece o' string around it an' tied t'other end around t'doorknob an' then slammed t'door.' His words spilled out in a rush.

'And I assume the tooth didn't come out,' said the headmaster.

'Tooth din't,' replied Nathan, 'but t'doorknob cum off.'

Mr Gaunt leaned back in his chair and laughed. 'Well, you run along and tell Miss Tranter I said it would be all right for you to leave the school at lunchtime.'

The boy scurried to the door and then turned, sniffed noisily, and wiped his nose on the back of his hand again.

'Good morning, Mester Gaunt,' he said, smirking from ear to ear. He gave a small bow. 'An' 'ave a nice day.'

When the pupil had gone Mr Gaunt thought on the school secretary's words. She was right, his resignation and the changes that would inevitably ensue with the arrival of a new head teacher would not be fully welcomed by the staff, certainly not by three of the four teachers. In truth, they were a motley trio. When Tom Dwyer, a newly qualified teacher, had joined the school the previous September, Mr Gaunt had taken the young man into his office to tell him about his three unusual colleagues.

'I guess they appear a pretty odd bunch to you?' he had told him. 'When I say odd, I don't mean that unkindly. Perhaps a better word might be "idiosyncratic". They do what is asked of them without complaint, work hard and the children like them. I have a genuine affection for them.'

He had told Tom that he did not interfere with what the teachers were doing, that they worked hard, provided the children with a good, sound education, treated their pupils with respect and related well to them; he did not see any need for him to get involved.

Mr Gaunt stood at his study window on that bright spring morning, surveying the panorama which stretched out before him. He wondered, as he awaited the arrival of the Chairman of Governors, whether the new head teacher would follow this practice and let the staff get on without unnecessary interference. The three teachers who came to mind were set in their ways and would, he guessed, not welcome any adjustment to their routine. They had taught in the school for many years and liked things as they were. Tom, enthusiastic and energetic, would, no doubt, take any changes in his stride – indeed, he had introduced a variety of initiatives and schemes since he had started at Risingdale – but the others were a cautious and conservative threesome. They did not possess Tom's flair and ability and might not take kindly to a head teacher who insisted on dictating what they should do in the classroom. Perhaps he was worrying unduly, he reflected. His successor would be an experienced head teacher who would, he guessed, know how important it was to take things slowly, gain the confidence and respect of the teachers and appreciate their efforts.

His thoughts were interrupted when he caught sight of the Chairman of Governors coming across the playground. Sir Hedley Maladroit – baronet, squire, landowner, Lord of the Manor, owner of half the properties in village and most of the land surrounding, controller of many of the residents' destinies, Justice of the Peace, Deputy Lord Lieutenant and Chairman of Governors – was like a character who had walked straight out of the pages of some historical novel. He was a portly, red-cheeked individual with a bombastic walrus moustache above a wide mouth, dark hooded eyes, prominent ears, and tightly curled hair on a square head. That morning he was dressed in a finely cut tweed suit and matching waistcoat with silver chain and fob dangling from a pocket. He wore a tightly knotted green bow tie and sported an expensive pair of brown brogues as shiny as conkers.

The caretaker and husband of the school secretary, a gangly man with dark, deep-set eyes and thick, wild white hair, saw the important caller striding purposefully up the path to the school. He scurried to meet him and, touching his forelock obsequiously, wished Sir Hedley, 'Good morning, my lord.'

The baronet was inclined to inform him that he was not, in fact, a peer of the realm, but he let it go.

'And a very good morning to you, Mr Leadbeater,' he replied jovially. 'Beautiful day, isn't it? Spring is with us at long last.'

'It is, indeed, my lord,' replied the caretaker reverently.

'I meant to have a word with you,' Sir Hedley told him.

The caretaker looked worried.

'It was good of you – and Mr Gaunt of course – to allow me to poach your assistant.'

'Beg pardon?'

'Mrs Gosling?'

The caretaker pulled a face. 'Oh, her.'

Sir Hedley had prevailed upon the cleaner at the school (although she preferred to be styled 'assistant caretaker') to become his housekeeper at Marston Towers, his stately residence near the village. She had taken little persuading to accept the position, happy to leave the job of cleaning at the school, which had proved an uphill battle. Mr Leadbeater and the teachers were glad to see the woman go, for she had made their lives a misery. Never a one to be backward in coming forward, Mrs Gosling had, since starting on the very first day at Risingdale, complained about all the work she was expected to undertake, the sloppiness of the teachers, the untidy classrooms, the messy staffroom, the lack of cleanliness and numerous other things that did not meet her very high standards of neatness and hygiene.

'I am sure she is a lot happier at Marston Towers,' said the caretaker tactfully and with a wry smile. I am certainly a lot happier without her, he thought.

He hurried ahead and opened the door to the school with a flourish before announcing in a thunderous voice, 'Sir Hedley Maladroit of Marston Towers!'

At the appearance of the distinguished visitor standing before her desk, Mrs Leadbeater patted her hair and adopted her professional smile and affected voice reserved for visitors who appeared a cut above the usual callers. She looked up at the Chairman of Governors and removed her spectacles.

'Good morning, Sir Hedley,' she said pleasantly before rising to her feet. 'Hif you would care to wait, I shall hinform Mr Gaunt that you have harrived. He is hexpecting you.' She turned to her husband, who was standing at the door. 'You may go,' she told him dismissively in a queenly voice.

'I hope I find you well, Mrs Leadbeater,' said the baronet jovially.

'Oh yes indeed, Sir Hedley, I'm very well, thank you,' she replied, smoothing down the creases in her skirt as if she were dusting away some crumbs.

'Such a beautiful day,' he announced. 'It makes one glad to be alive on such a day as this. This morning I heard the first chaffinch of spring.'

The secretary arranged her face with an appropriately sympathetic expression and lowered her voice. It was the first time she had seen him since the death of his son, and she hastened to offer her condolences.

'I was deeply sorry to hear about your son, Sir Hedley,' she said solicitously. She fingered the cameo brooch at her collared neck.

'Ah yes, James,' murmured the baronet, his manner suddenly changing. He breathed out long and slow. 'It was most unfortunate,' he nodded gravely. 'Thank you.'

'A terrible accident. It must have been—'

'Yes, yes, it was,' he cut her off. He did not wish to continue with this topic. 'Well, if you could tell Mr Gaunt I have arrived.'

As she went to tell the headmaster that his visitor was waiting, she considered the term used by Sir Hedley. 'Unfortunate' seemed to her a strange word to use by a father who had lost his only son in an horrific traffic accident some weeks before. 'Devastating', 'tragic', 'dreadful' seemed to her to be more apposite a description. It also occurred to her that he had seemed to be in particularly good humour that morning, considering the calamity that had happened.

Sir Hedley, of course, had been saddened by the death of his son but his relationship with James had been strained. The young man had the easy self-assurance that comes from growing up with money that you have not earned. He proved to be a huge disappointment to a father who had imagined great things of his son and heir. James lacked his father's steadfast spirit; he had been indolent and arrogant, indulged by his mother and disliked by all in the village. The car crash in which he had been killed was the result of his reckless driving while he had been under the influence of alcohol.

The headmaster's study was poky and dominated by a huge oak desk with brass-handled drawers, behind which was an antiquated swivel chair. On the desktop was an old-fashioned black telephone, a cup of half-drunk tea, now cold and grey-scummed, a leather-bound blotter, a large brass inkwell in the shape of a ram's head and an earthenware mug without a handle holding an assortment of pens and broken pencils. There were several books and a pile of untidily stacked papers and folders, on the top of which was a copy of Practical Poultry. There was not a space to be seen. A battered grey metal filing cabinet stood by the window next to a heavy dark wood bookcase crammed with more books and journals, magazines, and files. On one wall, a variety of children's paintings of various animals – black-faced sheep and prancing horses, grazing cows, and stout pink pigs on stubby legs – all executed in vivid colour, was displayed. On another was a faded cross-stitch sampler executed by a child of eight called Eliza Bentley, dated 1890, and titled John Wesley's Philosophy. It read:

> Do all the good you can,
> By all the means you can,
> At all the time you can,
> To all the people you can,
> As long as ever you can.

Propped up in a corner was the strangest-looking contraption: a long, wooden, trumpet-like instrument with a cup-shaped mouthpiece.

'Come in, come in,' said Mr Gaunt, rising from his desk when Sir Hedley was shown into the room. He removed a pile of folders from a small spindle-backed chair. 'I must apologise for the state of the place. I mean to tidy things up but have never got around to it. Mrs Leadbeater is always nagging me to do it. I am afraid it has got into a worse state since your last visit.'

The Chairman of Governors extended a hand, which the headmaster shook vigorously. 'Good morning, Gerald,' he said. 'Please don't apologise. If you want to see clutter, you only have to walk into my study at Marston Towers. Mrs Gosling is forever after me to tidy up the place but, like you, I like it as it is.'

'And how are things working out with Mrs Gosling?' asked Mr Gaunt.

'Oh splendid. Marston Towers has never been so clean and tidy, and she keeps me in order. She is quite a redoubtable character is Mrs Gosling. As I was saying to the caretaker, I am most grateful that you let her leave at such short notice.'

'Do take a seat,' said Mr Gaunt. He returned to sit behind his desk.

Sir Hedley sat on the hard, wooden chair, which creaked ominously under his weight, and fingered the silver watch chain. He smiled to himself as he ran his eyes over the headmaster. Mr Gaunt's indifference to convention was demonstrated by his rumpled jacket, which had seen better days, as well as his loosely knotted tie and shirt frayed around the cuffs. He looked more like a farmer than a head teacher with his lean, weathered face and thick crop of tousled greying hair that curled around his collar. Sir Hedley, like all those who came across Gerald Gaunt, found the man good-natured, unaffected, and easy to talk to. He had heard no one speak ill of him and over the many years he had been the Chairman of Governors, they had never disagreed. Of course, he had not had a great deal to do with the school in all that time. Governors' meeting were a rarity, for things at Risingdale ticked along happily and he and his fellow governors and parents saw no reason to interfere. He believed in the maxim that 'if the wheel is not broken, it does not require mending.'

'So how are you coping, Hedley?' asked Mr Gaunt.

'Regarding?'

'With the death of James. It was such a shock and—'

'Yes, yes,' replied the baronet quickly.

'You know that I am always here if you wish to talk to me about it. We've known each other a long time and I have thought of you as a good friend as well as a colleague.'

Sir Hedley nodded. 'I know,' he muttered. 'I appreciate that.'

'As you know, I was never blessed with children,' the headmaster told him, 'but had I been fortunate enough to have had a son, I would have found it unendurable to have lost him. Parents expect that their children will outlive them. It is a tragedy when this does not happen. I am deeply sorry for your loss.' His face was full of sincerity.

Sir Hedley's expression was grave. He scratched his neck and looked down at the floor and thought for a moment.

'I think it was common knowledge that James and I never got on,' he said at last. 'We never had anything to say to each other. I tried to teach him duty and honour, but it came to nothing. He was a wayward boy who wasted his time at school and went off the rails.'

Mr Gaunt was minded to say that children cannot pick their parents, and by the same token, parents cannot pick their children, but he said nothing and nodded staidly.

'Perhaps we were not the best of parents,' said the baronet thoughtfully. 'I often wonder if I had been too strict with James and expected too much and thereby inspired his excesses. I know that he felt that I was disappointed in him. I tended to place some of the blame for his behaviour on my wife, who I feel over-indulged the boy.'

'I take it that Lady Maladroit will not be returning,' commented Mr Gaunt. Following the funeral of their son and after venting her wrath on her husband, Sir Hedley's wife had left to live with her sister in London.

'No, no, Marcia has left for good. In fact, I received the divorce papers to sign only this morning. It grieves me to say it, but there was little warmth or attachment in our relationship. It is a sad fact that there was not much affection on either side.'

'I'm sorry that things have turned out as they have,' Mr Gaunt told him.

'Anyway,' said Sir Hedley, cheering up, 'I'm not here to discuss my family's concerns. You asked to see me.'

'Yes, I did.'

'Not a problem, I hope.'

'No, no, not a problem,' replied the headmaster. He examined his hands. 'I wanted you to be the first to know—'

He stopped mid-sentence when there was a knock. A moment later the door was opened by the small boy the headmaster had seen earlier. The school secretary entered carrying a heavy-looking wooden tray on which were a coffee pot, two thin porcelain cups and matching cream jug and sugar bowl.

'Thank you, Nathan,' she said. 'You can go back to your classroom now.'

The boy gave a small bow. 'Good morning, sir,' he said to Sir Hedley. 'I 'ope that tha're keepin' well. 'Ave a nice day.' Then he departed.

The baronet nodded. 'It's good to see children with manners,' he said.

Mrs Leadbeater exchanged a glance with Mr Gaunt and placed the tray on the desk. 'I thought you both might enjoy a cup of coffee,' she said with a smile.

'Thank you, Mrs Leadbeater,' said Mr Gaunt.

When she had gone, Sir Hedley gave the headmaster a hooded gaze. 'You were saying,' he prompted.

Mr Gaunt poured the coffee, added milk, and passed a cup to Sir Hedley. He then poured himself one and sipped his drink, seeming to need a pause before he could broach what he wanted to say.

'I asked you to come and see me,' he said at last, 'to let you know that I have decided to retire.'

'Good Lord!' cried Sir Hedley, nearly spilling his coffee.

'I've given the matter a deal of thought and decided to leave at the end of term.'

'Well, this is a shock and certainly not something I was expecting at all,' Sir Hedley told him, placing down his cup on the desk. 'Are you quite sure about this?'

'Yes, perfectly sure,' he was told. 'I have received this letter, which says that in order for the Education Authority to balance the budget, there is a need for what they call some "rationalisation". Some more of the small rural schools that are losing pupils and are no longer viable have been earmarked for closure.'

'Not Risingdale, I hope?' exclaimed Sir Hedley.

'No, no, not Risingdale. Our intake has remained steady over the years and next September we have an increase of pupils coming into the infants. We are in a healthy state. Anyway, over the next year the Education Department will either be making some teachers redundant or redeploying them. The head teachers of a couple of schools that are closing will need to be redeployed as well. I guess one of these will be given the post here at Risingdale. I have been offered an extremely attractive package to leave, which I have decided to accept. The fact is, I think I am a bit past it. I am finding it difficult to put up with the many changes in education and all these regulations, the mountain of paperwork, the unsolicited advice and petty directives. It's time I go.'

'Some regulations, in my book,' remarked Sir Hedley, brushing a hand over his bristly moustache, 'are written for the compliance of fools. As a farmer and landowner, who receives all the endless bumf from the Ministry of Agriculture and Fisheries, I know that only too well.'

'Maybe so, but I feel the time had come for me to finish. As you know, I have my smallholding which needs my attention and—'

Sir Hedley took a deep breath. 'I don't suppose that anything I can say will dissuade you. You seem to have made up your mind.'

'Yes, I have,' said Mr Gaunt. 'I shall of course write to the governors and parents to tell them of my decision, and I intend telling the staff at a meeting at lunchtime.'

'I will only say, then, that you will be sorely missed.'

2

When Sir Hedley told the headmaster that he would be sorely
missed, he was right. Gerald Gaunt was highly respected and
well liked in the community but few knew a great deal about
him, for he was essentially a very private man. He never said
much about himself, uttered a bad word about others or indulged in gossip. He had been a bright, studious boy from a
relatively poor farming background who had passed for the
grammar school with a county scholarship. After a spell in the
army he attended St John's teacher-training college, secured
a post in a school in a neighbouring village and returned to
Risingdale to be near his ailing mother and run the smallholding. His father had died the previous year. When his mother
passed away soon afterwards, Gerald Gaunt kept the farm on.
Promotion in education came fast and it was not long before
he was appointed headmaster at the village school in Risingdale, where he had stayed for most of his career. He could
have become the head teacher of a much bigger and more
prestigious school, but he had decided to stay in the village.

Gerald Gaunt was a thoughtful, gentle-natured, and modest
man. He was intelligent and widely read but never displayed
his scholarship, preferring to follow the precept he had heard
quoted by one of his college tutors. The eighteenth-century
Earl of Chesterfield had cautioned his son to be 'wiser than
other people if you can, but do not tell them so'.

Mrs Golightly, the teacher of the infants, had known and
worked for Mr Gaunt for many years but she knew little about

the headmaster apart from the few facts that he lived alone in a farmhouse inherited from his father and mother, that he tended a few sheep and cattle on his small farm, that he had never married and that he enjoyed long walks. It struck her as strange that he never wanted to socialise with his colleagues after school or involve himself in the various events and activities in the village. He was something of a dark horse.

Mr Gaunt enjoyed a quiet, occasional drink at the weekend but rarely frequented the local hostelry, the King's Head, knowing that if he did he would be cornered by parents wishing to discuss their children's progress at the school, seeking his advice or quizzing him about numerous educational matters. Instead he patronised the Black Pig in Urebank, where he had a certain anonymity and enjoyed his half pint of bitter undisturbed. As he sat in the corner of the public bar, he would often think of his grandfather who would have had a lot to say, seeing him in a public house. Nicholas Gaunt had been a direct-speaking and devout Methodist and had preached in the chapel about the demon drink, believing it led to neglect of duty, moral degradation, and crime.

When Tom came for the interview for a position at the school, he had been taken aback by the appearance of the headmaster. He had rather expected someone in a pristine white shirt, smart suit, college tie and polished black shoes and not a tall, lean man with the weathered face of a countryman, who sported a shabby trilby hat, green corduroy trousers, a thick tweed jacket with elbow patches and substantial boots. It took him no time at all to realise what a remarkable headmaster Mr Gaunt was: caring, supportive, approachable and with a generous honesty. He often wondered, as did his colleagues, why the headmaster had not married and had children.

None was aware that Gerald Gaunt once had a romantic attachment to the young vet in Barton-in-the-Dale. As a teacher, new to the profession, he had met Miss Moira Macdonald when he had called her out to look at one of his ailing sheep. He had watched the tall, red-headed young Scot with a homely face peppered with freckles and an engaging smile deal with the sickly ewe calmly and effectively. He had found excuse after excuse to call upon her services again: his sheepdog was off her food, a cow was out of sorts, the goat was not giving much milk. She was astute enough to guess why she was being asked to visit the farm so frequently when there was nothing really wrong with the animals, realising that the young teacher was interested in her.

He met her again at a dinner in aid of an NFU farming charity. He was plucking up the courage to ask her out when she surprised him by asking *him* out. They each enjoyed the theatre, music, walking, reading and farming, but neither of them seemed to want the relationship to get any more serious. They had been going out for a year when new job prospects had come up for both of them at the same time. Mr Gaunt, who was a deputy head teacher in Ruston by this time (the youngest in the county to hold such a senior position) was keen to apply for the headship at the village school in Risingdale, and Moira to accept a partnership in her native Glasgow. So, decisions had to be made. Should they get married? If so, who would do the moving? Which one would sacrifice job and career? Their relationship had been a strange one in that they were both so busy in their respective professions that they did not see a great deal of each other. Moira worked late and most weekends at the veterinary practice. Gerald was usually occupied at weekends either playing rugby, refereeing or taking school trips, and in the evenings marking books, planning lessons or rehearsing the school play. When they did go out to dinner parties together, they were not greatly enjoyable occasions. He would meet her colleagues from the veterinary practice and be bored by the constant discussion over the dinner table of animal ailments, diseases, operations and the latest developments in animal husbandry. When she met his colleagues from school, Moira was similarly wearied by the endless conversations about the curriculum and examinations, standards of education and difficult children. They both realised that their relationship could never survive the test of time. On their last evening together, they talked about things honestly and without quarrelling or recriminations and parted without rancour on either side, to pursue their own careers. That had been over thirty years ago. They had had little contact since then, save for the exchange of Christmas cards and the occasional postcard. He had often thought about Moira and wondered how her life had turned out. And then she had reappeared in his life.

In a recent conversation with Clive Gosling, a fellow farmer, Mr Gaunt had asked about the new vet in Risingdale.

'He's a decent chap, then?' he had asked.

'The new vet's not a man,' he had been told. 'It's a woman.'

Her name was Moira Macdonald.

Hearing this news, Mr Gaunt had wasted no time in paying Moira a visit and on an overcast Saturday morning he set off for the veterinary surgery in Clayton. He had made a real effort with his appearance that day, sporting a green silk bow tie, a finely cut sports jacket, stylish cord trousers and brown brogues.

Mr Vintner, the senior partner in the practice, a notoriously garrulous man whose conversation was almost exclusively about animal ailments, greeted him at the door of the surgery. He was an exorbitantly portly man with a full head of curly grey hair and bushy handlebar moustache. A leg was in an impressive plaster cast.

'Ah, my dear Gerald,' he said, standing at the door and leaning on a walking stick, 'I thought it wouldn't be very long before you showed your face here. I guess you have heard the news about the new vet.'

'Good morning, Michael,' replied Mr Gaunt. 'Yes. I heard from Clive Gosling.' He gestured to the leg. 'Whatever have you been up to?'

'This is care of John Fairborn's Cleveland Bay stallion,' he was told. 'I was treating the horse for a chronic lower respiratory disease and received this for my pains. Despite its age, the old stager gave me a fair old kick which has put me out of action for visiting the farms. That's why Moira has been such a godsend. I assume, by the way, that you are here to see her. Come along in.'

Mr Vintner hobbled down the hall ahead of his visitor, chattering non-stop.

In the parlour he slumped in a chair and stretched out his leg. 'I am afraid Moira is out at the moment. She's on a call to see one of Mr Olmeroyde's heifers It sounds like abomasal ulceration to me because there's been some gastric bleeding and perforation, which of course could be fatal. I have recommended—'

'About Moira,' interrupted Mr Gaunt.

'Ah, yes, of course,' said the vet.

'I wasn't aware that she was in Risingdale.'

'Oh, she's only been here a few days. I believe she did give you a ring a couple of times but you were out and of course she's been so remarkably busy taking on my workload and—'

'Is Moira here for good?' cut in Mr Gaunt again.

'Yes, I think she is. The thing is, Gerald, Moira has not been at all happy of late with things at the veterinary practice in Glasgow. I'm sure she will tell you all about it. She has had a series of set-tos with the senior partner, a rather strait-laced martinet of a man by all accounts, over the treatment of some animals and was looking to move. I met her a month ago at a conference in York, and suggested that she might like to come back to Risingdale and join this practice. As you are aware, she has worked here and knows the ropes and was very highly regarded. She thought it over and has decided to take up my offer.'

'Well, this is good news, indeed,' said Mr Gaunt.

'I'm pleased you think so.' Moira stood at the door. 'Hello, Gerald,' she said, smiling.

Over the weeks that followed, Gerald Gaunt and Moira Macdonald saw a great deal of each other.

*

The first staff meeting of the new term at Risingdale School took place that lunchtime. Mr Gaunt had asked all the members of the teaching staff to attend, so it was left to a disgruntled Mr Leadbeater to keep an eye on the children in the playground. He could be heard shouting.

'Put it down and stop laiking about!'

The four teachers gathered in the staffroom: Mrs Bertha Golightly, in charge of the infants, a plump, cheerful-looking woman with a round face and tiny darting eyes; Mr Owen Cadwallader, teacher of the nine-year-olds, a tall, straight-backed individual of military bearing, with silver hair, cropped short and neatly parted, and sporting a thin white moustache and Miss Joyce Tranter, the teacher of the seven-and-eight-year-olds, a striking-looking woman of indeterminate age with unnaturally shiny, raven black hair, startling, glossy red lips and large pale eyes. The last member of the teaching staff was Mr Tom Dwyer, teacher of the top juniors, a good-looking young man with a tanned face, long-lashed dark blue eyes and a winning smile.

'So, what do you think this meeting is about?' asked Joyce, casually filing a long nail.

'I don't know,' said Mrs Golightly, with a worried expression on her round face, 'but there must be a good reason why Sir Hedley was in school this morning. I saw him pacing down the path earlier today. I mean, he hasn't been in school for months. I reckon he's the harbinger of bad news.'

'I tend to agree,' said Mr Cadwallader, reaching into the biscuit barrel. He crunched on a custard cream. 'There's something afoot. I can't recall the last time we had a meeting so soon at the beginning of term – and at a lunchtime, too.'

'Mr Gaunt seemed miles away when I wished him "Good morning", and Mrs Leadbeater wasn't her usual self either,' added Mrs Golightly. 'I've never known them so quiet. You mark my words, those at the Education Office are going to close the school. I knew they'd get around to us before long.'

'I do wish you wouldn't go on and on about closing the school,' said Joyce, sighing wearily. 'Every time we have a staff meeting you always bring it up.'

'Well, it's a fact,' replied her colleague sharply. 'So many of the lovely little Dales village schools are disappearing. Skillington School has about the same number of pupils as us and is closing at the end of this term.'

'I am fully aware of that, Bertha,' retorted Joyce. 'You don't need to constantly remind us.'

'It's only a matter of time before it's our turn,' continued Mrs Golightly.

'It was to be expected,' pronounced Mr Cadwallader gloomily, reaching into the biscuit barrel again. 'We are in for the chop, make no bones about it.'

'You'll be all right, Tom,' said Mrs Golightly, turning to her colleague, who had been uncharacteristically quiet. 'You could return to the school where you trained. The school in Barton-in-the-Dale is flourishing, from what I've heard. I am sure the head teacher there would jump at the chance of having you back. Mr Gaunt was saying she thought very highly of you.'

It was true that the head teacher of Barton-with-Urebank Primary School would be more than pleased to have the young teacher back on her staff. Tom had made quite an impression during the short time he had been there as a student-teacher. In fact, he had been told by Mrs Stirling, the head teacher, that should a vacancy arrive, she would welcome an application. He had bumped into her when he visited his aunt in

Barton-in-the-Dale village soon after he had started teaching at Risingdale.

'If you were offered a permanent position at Barton-with-Urebank School, might you consider coming back?' she had asked him.

'I don't know,' he had replied. 'I've not been at Risingdale very long.'

'It's just that numbers in the school are increasing. With the closure of some neighbouring small schools, we have had an influx of children. We will be looking for a permanent member of staff, probably next term.'

'But won't you have to take another redeployed teacher?' Tom had asked.

'I have already appointed three redeployed teachers,' she had told him. 'I think this time I can persuade the Director of Education to let me advertise for a new position.'

'I see,' he had said thoughtfully.

Tom had loved his time as a trainee-teacher at Barton-with-Urebank School under the guidance of Mrs Stirling and the supportive members of staff. He had learnt a great deal, loved the company of young people, knew teaching was the profession for him and had gained his Certificate in Education with a distinction. Had there been a position at the end of his training, he would have jumped at the chance of staying at the school, but Mrs Stirling had been obliged to take a redeployed teacher.

'And I guess you won't have a problem finding another job either, Joyce,' stated Mr Cadwallader, perhaps unnecessarily.

'That's if she wants one,' said Mrs Golightly. 'I mean, she doesn't need to work.'

'That's true,' conceded Mr Cadwallader. 'She's very comfortably off now. I mean—'

'Would you mind not talking about me as if I weren't here,' Joyce cut in curtly.

Over the Easter holidays Joyce had married the owner of Smith, Skerrit and Sampson, the prestigious auction house in Clayton. Her new husband, a wealthy widower, was keen that she should give up teaching but, for her, it was not a question of money. She enjoyed her job and valued a degree of independence. She had explained to Julian on their honeymoon that she was not the sort of wife who would be content to sit at home twiddling her thumbs; she had a career. Then she had declared that she intended to retain her maiden name. Her new husband wondered whether he had taken on more than he could cope with.

'And you could retire, Bertha,' said Mr Cadwallader now. 'After all the years you've put in, you'd get your full pension. It is I who will miss out. I mean, coming into teaching late as I have, I can't afford to retire.'

'What about your army pension?' asked Mrs Golightly.

'Yes, there is that, but it's hardly sufficient for my needs. I suppose I'll be redeployed somewhere at the other end of the county.'

'Could we change the conversation?' asked Tom. 'It's all speculation that the school is to close.'

This discussion on the fate of Risingdale School came to an end with the appearance of Mr Gaunt in the staffroom.

'Thank you for staying,' said the headmaster. 'I won't keep you long.' He sat, crossed his long legs and stared for a moment at the faces before him. He would miss his colleagues. He had known and worked with three of them for many years and valued their support and friendship. 'There is just something I need to acquaint you with,' he said at last.

Mrs Golightly opened her mouth to speak.

'Now, before I start, let me assure you, and Bertha in particular, that Risingdale School is not closing.'

Mrs Golightly sighed with relief.

'Is it another school inspection?' asked Mr Cadwallader.

'If you will allow me to finish, Owen,' the headmaster told him, 'you will find out.' He paused and cleared his throat twice, then adopted a serious expression that did nothing to allay the anxieties of the teachers who sat before him with expectant looks on their faces. 'As you are no doubt aware, quite a lot of small schools in the county aren't viable any more with the decline in pupil numbers and they have had to close, with teachers needing to find other positions.'

'Are we to be redeployed?' asked Mrs Golightly anxiously.

'I might have guessed,' added Mr Cadwallader shaking his head. 'We're in for the chop.'

'Perhaps you didn't hear what I just said, Owen,' said Mr Gaunt irritably, 'so let me repeat it. Risingdale School is not closing and there is no question of any of you being redeployed. The reason I wished to speak to you is to tell you that I have decided to retire.'

'Good gracious!' exclaimed Mr Cadwallader. His three colleagues were lost for words.

'I have given the matter a great deal of thought,' the headmaster continued, 'and I have decided that it is time for me to finish. I am a bit long in the tooth, to be honest. A very generous offer has come from Ms Tricklebank, the Director of Education, an offer it would be foolish to refuse, and I have decided to accept. I shall be leaving at the end of this term. That is all I really have to say.'

Before anyone else could respond to what they had heard, there was a loud knock.

Joyce got up to answer the door to discover Nathan Barraclough standing outside in the corridor wiping his nose with a finger.

'Sorry to disturb you, miss, is t' 'eadmaster havailable to see me?' said the boy, sniffing and recalling his earlier conversation with Mrs Leadbeater outside Mr Gaunt's study concerning good manners.

'We are in a meeting at the moment, Nathan,' she told the boy. 'Is it important?'

'No, not really, miss,' replied the boy. 'I just wanted to tell t' 'eadmaster that it's come out.'

'What has come out?' asked the teacher, intrigued.

Nathan held up the tooth. 'I don't need to go to t'dentist any more. I'm purrin it under mi pillow toneet fer t'tooth fairy.'

'And how old are you, Nathan?' asked the teacher, raising an eyebrow.

'Eight, miss.'

'Rather too old I should imagine to believe in the tooth fairy, don't you think?'

The boy gave a wide toothless grin, sniffed, and ran a finger under his nose again. 'Oh, I don't believe in all that rubbish, miss,' he told her, 'but I'd believe that pigs could fly if it meant me gerrin a quid under mi pilla.'

'Said like a true Yorkshireman,' observed Mr Cadwallader, who had been listening to the exchange with interest.

*

Tom stood at the window of his classroom later that lunchtime watching the children playing in the yard; they were running, jumping, chasing, skipping, darting, and dashing, hardly stopping to draw breath. It is amazing, he thought, how energetic the young are. He smiled. It was not so long ago when he was a professional footballer and captain of Clayton United, that he was as active as his pupils. Injuries meant he had had to give up that career. He never regretted leaving the game behind for, having trained as a teacher, he felt he had found his vocation. He would not change his present profession for the world.

His thoughts turned to the recent meeting in the staffroom. Mr Gaunt's decision to retire had been a bombshell; he had

given no indication that he was thinking of stepping down
as headmaster. Tom predicted that the arrival of a new head
teacher would mean a great many changes in the school, most
of which would not be welcomed by his colleagues. He had
only known them for less than a year, but it was long enough
to appreciate that they were rather fixed in their ideas and
were likely to find adjusting to anything new unpopular and
difficult. This had been clearly demonstrated when a computer had arrived at the school the previous term and had
been housed in Tom's classroom. All three of his colleagues
had declined the invitation of Ms Babcock, the county's newly
appointed Information Technology Adviser, to attend a
training course on 'computer literacy' and they had remained
unimpressed despite Tom's enthusiasm for the new technology. Mrs Leadbeater had turned up her nose when she had
been offered a computer to replace her typewriter, telling Mr
Gaunt that she had no intention of using some 'new-fangled
contraption'. Mr Gaunt too had expressed no interest.

Tom felt some real misgivings about the change in the
school leadership. A new head teacher would no doubt want
to stamp his or her identity, feel the need to alter things and
innovate and take a more active part in what was being taught.
Mr Gaunt had never been one to prescribe what the teachers
did in their classrooms. He was fully aware of what happened
in the lessons and he trusted the teachers and saw no need for
detailed curriculum guidelines. Tom recalled the conversation
he had had with Mr Cadwallader soon after he had started at
the school.

'You will find our headmaster,' he had told Tom, 'is not the
most energetic of men but he likes the children, and they are
very fond of him. He is very supportive of his staff and is a
thoroughly decent sort who thankfully does not interfere with
what we are doing.' Yes, thought Tom, things would change.

'Penny for them, Mr Dwyer.'

Tom turned to find one of his pupils, a plain-looking, thin little individual with a wide mouth, dark eyes, large ears, and tightly curled hair.

'Oh, hello, Charlie,' he replied, smiling.

'You were miles away, sir.'

'Yes, I guess I was.'

'"In vacant or in pensive mood".'

'Pardon?'

'It was in the poem we read – the one about the daffodils.'

'Ah, yes, that was in the Wordsworth verse, wasn't it?'

'Am I disturbing you, sir?' asked the boy.

'Not at all, but you should be outside with the others getting some fresh air.'

'Oh, I get enough fresh air, Mr Dwyer, when I go for my walk on Saturday. I came in to finish my story.'

Since first meeting Charlie Lister, the teacher had warmed to this bright-eyed, enthusiastic, and affable little boy with the ready smile. Tom had been driving to the interview for the post at Risingdale when he had very nearly knocked the child down. Charlie had leaped over a wall of greenish-white limestone and darted across the road directly in front of the car, trying to escape from a larger boy who was chasing him. Tom had screeched to a halt, missing the child by inches.

'That was a very silly thing to do,' he had said, approaching the little scallywag.

The boy had grinned widely and shrugged. 'Sorry, mister,' he had said.

Later Tom, newly appointed teacher at the school, was to learn that the boy was a pupil in his class. He soon found out that Charlie was keenly interested in all the work he undertook, had a quick mind and a cheerful disposition. He discovered the boy was a bit of a loner, a free spirit, and spent a deal of his time walking in the countryside or down to the public library at Clayton, or just sitting by the duck pond, reading.

During the visit of the school inspector, he had charmed the HMI, chatting about the books he had read, his interest in history and astronomy, how he liked to cook, play the ukulele, was interested in wildlife and enjoyed taking long walks in the outdoors. The inspector had been duly impressed by this highly intelligent, confident, articulate ten-year-old, and with the standard of the work he had produced.

Charlie lived with his mother in one of the tied cottages on the Maladroit estate. He had often asked about his father, but his mother had always been evasive when he raised the matter and had told him that when he was older and able to understand she would explain. She had finally decided it was time to tell him who his father was, that he was a kind and decent man and very clever, but circumstances meant that he could not live with them because he was married. She swore him to secrecy, explaining that if those in the village found out who his father was, it would be difficult for him, for her and for Charlie.

By chance, Tom had discovered the identity of Charlie's father, having met him one evening coming out of Mrs Lister's cottage. It was Sir Hedley Maladroit, the squire.

'So, what are you reading at the moment?' asked the teacher now.

'*Great Expectations*,' replied the boy.

'Another Charles Dickens. Are you enjoying it?'

'Oh yes,' replied Charlie. 'It's really exciting, but I am a bit puzzled.'

'In what way?'

'Well, at the beginning of the novel the escaped convict, Magwitch, frightens the boy Pip into stealing a file so he can cut off the leg-iron around his ankles.'

'And?' asked Tom.

'But how had Magwitch managed to swim from a prison ship with massive iron chains fastened around his ankles? He would have sunk.'

'Yes, I see.'

'And a file is not a great deal of use in cutting through heavy iron shackles. He would need a hacksaw.'

The boy had the wise expression of a child well beyond his years.

'It looks as if the great novelist seems to have overlooked that, doesn't he?' said the teacher.

'It's a mystery,' said the boy.

'You know, Charlie,' said Tom, 'you never cease to surprise me.' The boy grinned. 'Well, I can hear that the bell has gone. You can finish your story at afternoon break.'

There were fifteen children in Tom's class of ten-and-eleven-year-olds – a mixed group of individuals but on the whole interested, good-natured and well behaved – the kind of youngsters all teachers dream of teaching. Tom loved their company and found a genuine pleasure in sharing his knowledge with them. He felt some satisfaction that he had made a positive difference in the lives of his pupils since he had started at the school.

He watched as the children filed into the classroom chattering excitedly as they took their seats, and thought to himself how lucky he was to have fallen on his feet to teach at Risingdale. Most voluble of his pupils was Vicky Gosling, a large, ginger-headed, good-hearted child but of a bossy disposition and strident voice, who, like her grandmother, former cleaner at the school and now housekeeper at the big house, had a great deal to say for herself. In contrast were Holly and Hazel Wood, the twins, shy and unobtrusive little girls, both talented musicians and two of the best readers. There was Judith, the thoughtful child with the long black plaits and rosy cheeks, the quietest pupil in the class. Then there were the farming experts: Carol Midgley, the pretty girl with the mousy-brown hair and pink glasses who knew more about sheep than anyone in the Dale; George, whose only conversation seemed to be about sheep and cattle and the make of tractors, and Andrew, the lean,

bespectacled boy with a thick mop of tawny hair, who knew
how to build a dry-stone wall, dig a dyke, chain harrow a field,
tickle a trout, snare a rabbit and name a bird by a faded feather.
All three sat by the window and were often found staring out
over the landscape, probably wishing they were out of doors instead of stuck behind their desks. There was Matthew, the stur-
dy, sharp-faced pupil with the untidy curls and his pal, Simon,
the heavily freckled boy with a head of shiny copper-coloured
hair, both stars of the school football team. In the corner of
the classroom sat Christopher Pickles, a large, ruddy-complexioned boy with a runny nose, a boy who seldom smiled and
never laughed. Tom regarded David, one of his success stories.
He was the pupil who had made the greatest progress over the
two terms. A small, underconfident, gangly boy with a notice-
able squint, he could barely string two sentences together in his
writing and used the most bizarre spellings. He had come on
by leaps and bounds since Tom had become his teacher. At the
front desks sat Marjorie Olmeroyde, the little, pixie-faced girl
and her friend Angela, two of the brightest in the class. Tom
had been most pleased in the change that had taken place with
a once sad and angry boy, who at first was rude and difficult
but, when his talents in art had been discovered and he came to
understand that Tom was genuinely interested in him, he had
changed his attitude. Now Colin Greenwood was well behaved
and more sociable. And, of course, there was young Charlie
Lister, whose eager smile made people feel like smiling back.

'Right everyone, look this way, please,' Tom told the children, clapping his hands to gain their attention.

Vicky was not only the loudest pupil in the class, she was
also the most vocal. She waved her hand in the air like a daf-
fodil in a strong wind.

'Mr Dwyer, Mr Dwyer,' she shouted in a high and hectic
voice, 'what were the staff meeting about at lunchtime? All the
teachers looked dead miserable. Is there something up?'

'The meeting was teachers' business,' replied Tom, 'and doesn't concern you.'

'Are they going to close the school like Skillington?' she persisted.

'No Vicky, they are not going to close the school.'

'Because my gran says that—' the girl began.

Tom raised a hand. 'That is quite enough,' he said, adopting a stern expression. 'Let us get on with the lesson. Now, would you all sit up smartly and eyes this way. This morning we are going to hear me read a poem.'

There was a groan from the corner of the room.

'Is there something you wish to say, Christopher?' asked the teacher.

'Do we have to do poetry, sir?' asked the boy. 'It's all la-di-da and flipping daffodils.'

Tom noticed that Charlie gave a small smile, perhaps recalling the earlier conversation they had had about Wordsworth's verse.

'No, it is not always about la-di-da and flipping daffodils, as you say,' said Tom. 'Poetry can be about anything; it can be funny, sad, powerful, touching, gripping and a whole lot more. Today's poem is a ballad and an extremely dramatic piece of work with a real sense of atmosphere, lots of action, colourful characters, rich and vivid imagery, and wonderful descriptions of the natural world. It is called "The Highwayman" by a poet called Alfred Noyes. Now, you will remember last term when we were talking about legends, Marjorie recounted the tale of Gentleman Jack Joiner, a story told to her by her grandfather. It was said that he was a local highwayman who held up coaches passing through Bloxton and Skillington. Perhaps you could remind us, Marjorie?'

'Well,' said the girl, standing up and clearing her throat noisily, 'it's the story of Gentleman Jack who robbed the coaches and then he galloped off on a grey mare called Lady, to

Risingdale and counted his swag at the King's Head. He was finally captured and hanged at Snig Hill.'

'This poem is similar in many ways,' said Tom, 'and it may be that Alfred Noyes, the poet, had heard the folktale of Gentleman Jack and told the story in this narrative poem. It opens on a blustery night with the highwayman riding into town. Listen carefully, particularly to the descriptions.' The teacher began to read:

"'The wind was a torrent of darkness among the gusty trees.
The moon was a ghostly galleon tossed upon cloudy seas.
The road was a ribbon of moonlight over the purple moor,
And the highwayman came riding –
Riding – riding –
The highwayman came riding, up to the old inn door.'"

The children listened attentively as he continued to read the poem in a deliberately theatrical manner – of how the highwayman visited Bess, the landlord's daughter whom he loved, and how the jealous ostler betrayed him to the King's soldiers who set a trap to catch him by tying up and gagging Bess with a musket pointing at her heart. Tom reached the climax when the landlord's daughter fires the musket and kills herself to warn the highwayman.

"'Her eyes grew wide for a moment; she drew one last deep breath,
Then her finger moved in the moonlight,
Her musket shattered the moonlight,
Shattered her breast in the moonlight and warned him – with her death.'"

'Oh no!' cried Vicky, slapping her hand over her mouth. 'She shouldn't have done that.'

'Listen!' said Christopher excitedly. His face was aglow with interest. 'I want to hear what happens.'

Tom continued reading the poem, telling how the highwayman rode off unaware that Bess had killed herself to warn him and save his life and how, when he finds out, he returns to the inn where he meets his death.

> '"Back he spurred like a madman, shrieking a curse to the sky,
> With the white road smoking behind him and his rapier brandished high.
> Blood red were his spurs in the golden moon; wine red was his velvet coat;
> When they shot him down on the highway,
> Down like a dog on the highway,
> And he lay in his blood on the highway, with a bunch of lace at his throat."'

'Oh no!' cried Vicky, 'not him as well.'

Tom read on:

> '"And still of a winter's night, they say, when the wind is in the trees,
> When the moon is a ghostly galleon tossed upon cloudy seas,
> When the road is a ribbon of moonlight over the purple moor,
> A highwayman comes riding –
> Riding – riding –
> A highwayman comes riding, up to the old inn door."'

There was a silence in the class.

'So, Christopher,' said the teacher at last, 'not all poetry is about la-di-da and flipping daffodils, is it?'

'No, sir,' replied the boy quietly.

There followed a lively discussion about the character of the highwayman, how he was handsome, charming, and elegantly dressed and although a robber, someone we admire for his bravery and his love of Bess. This moved on to the villain of the poem – the resentful and envious ostler whose betrayal leads to the deaths of the highwayman and Bess.

'So, how would you describe the ostler?' Tom asked the class.

'A nasty piece of work, if you ask me,' grunted Vicky.

'He was jealous because he loved Bess,' said Marjorie, 'and that's why he gave the highwayman away.'

'What do we call somebody who informs on another?' asked the teacher.

'A snitch,' said Carol.

'A grass,' volunteered Colin.

'A traitor,' said Vicky.

'A collaborator,' added Christopher.

'I was thinking of a word beginning with the letter "b",' said Tom, having the word 'betrayer' in his mind. 'Any idea, Simon?'

'A bastard?' asked the boy.

3

Tom and Joyce were on yard duty at afternoon break, enjoying the warmth of the spring sunshine. Joyce looked striking in a stylish cream coat and silk, lilac-coloured scarf. Across the playground they could hear the shrill voice of Vicky Gosling berating a boy who had interrupted her skipping.

'Do that again, Christopher Pickles,' she was bellowing, 'and I'll wrap this skipping rope around your scrawny neck and throttle you!'

'That girl could stand on a cliff and warn shipping,' remarked Joyce. 'Her voice is like a foghorn.'

Tom grinned. 'I once told her that I had heard quite enough of her loud voice and she replied, "You should hear my gran".'

'Well, I can believe that,' said Joyce. 'Her grandmother was a nightmare when she cleaned at the school. She was one person I was heartily glad to see leave. How Sir Hedley puts up with that virago I shall never know. And, speaking of leaving, what about Mr Gaunt? That was a turn-up for the books and no mistake.'

'Yes, it was.'

'I mean, he gave no indication he was about to retire.'

'No, it was quite a surprise,' Tom admitted.

'So, you didn't know?'

'I had no idea.'

'I wonder what the new headmaster will be like,' she said. 'I hope he will fit in.'

'Or she.'

'Pardon?'

'It could be a woman.'

'Yes, yes, of course. I cannot say that I am looking forward to having a new head teacher. I just hope he – or she – is as understanding as Mr Gaunt.'

'I hope so.'

'And I can't see Owen and Bertha welcoming the change, or Mr and Mrs Leadbeater for that matter.' She thought for a moment. 'The thing is, Tom, this news has put the cat amongst the pigeons at home as far as I am concerned.'

'In what way?' he asked.

'Well, it will give Julian more ammunition to try and persuade me to hand in my resignation, like Mr Gaunt. He has been on at me to give up teaching and help with the business. As soon as we got back from honeymoon, he brought the matter up again. He'll probably say that it's a good time for me to finish when he hears that Mr Gaunt is to go.'

'So, how is married life?' Tom asked now.

'Oh fine,' she replied, not sounding overly convinced. 'I mean, Julian couldn't be more attentive and generous and he's very protective, it's just that having lived alone for so long we have both become rather set in our ways and have definite views about things. I am afraid we do not always see eye to eye. He had read somewhere that before getting married each one should write down all the things that irritate them about the other person, the idea being that it clears the air and avoids arguments later on. He suggested we should do it.'

'And did you?'

'I did not!'

'I should think so too,' said Tom.

'We both just need time to get to know each other, I suppose,' Joyce confided. 'He wanted me to change my name when we were married but I was determined to keep it, and as for giving up my career – well, I have thought about it, but decided that I really don't want to. I like teaching and I think I'm good at it, and what's more I value my independence. I certainly do not want to work at the auction house and I'm not the sort of woman to stay at home cooking and cleaning and twiddling my thumbs.'

'I see,' said Tom.

'I really shouldn't complain,' Joyce continued. 'I mean, after my last disastrous experience of married life this is a match made in heaven.'

Tom was not so sure.

Joyce's previous marriage had indeed been a catastrophe. Her ex-husband had been a controlling and abusive individual who treated her very badly and undermined her confidence. Eventually she summoned up the courage to leave him, but he had turned up like a bad penny. The previous term he had arrived at the school, parking his motorbike on the road outside and waiting for her to set off home. The harassment had started again. In a way, things worked out well for Joyce but not for her bullying ex-husband. After a heavy downpour, driving a motorbike at speed on a wet and muddy road, he skidded on a sharp bend and hit the car driven by James Maladroit head on. Both drivers were killed outright.

As they strolled around the playground that afternoon, Tom pondered if his colleague had got herself into another controlling relationship. He recalled Joyce telling him before her marriage that her husband had insisted on arranging everything. He had chosen her dress and her shoes, picked the cake and even selected the bouquet she would carry. He had also booked their honeymoon without discussing it with her. Tom, who had been asked to be the best man at the wedding, was annoyed that Joyce's husband-to-be had spent a deal of time explaining to him what his duties were and then he had asked to vet his speech to make certain that nothing risqué would be included. Tom wondered now if Joyce had become involved with another domineering man.

'And how is your love life these days?' she asked.

Tom hesitated, thinking about the last few months. He had fallen for the daughter of a prominent local farmer, Miss Janette Fairborn, she of the jade-green eyes and mass of red hair. He found he had fallen in love with her and had been under the impression his feelings were being reciprocated. He discovered he was wrong. When he had told her how he felt about her, she had made it plain that she did not share his feelings. She was fond of him, of course, but had said there was no future in any relationship. She had left the village to take up a new job in Nottingham. Soon after her departure, Tom had become fascinated with an artist and the parent of one of his pupils. Amanda Stanhope had moved into Risingdale and he became smitten by this tall, elegant woman of strikingly good looks with a wave of bright blond hair, a streamlined figure and eyes as bright as blue polished glass. When he had told her how he felt, he had been rebuffed again. 'Of course, I have feelings for you,' she had told him. 'I'm very fond of you. You have become a dear, dear friend but if you are telling me you thought there was something more than friendship, Tom, then I must tell you, you were mistaken.'

'Come along, Tom, spill the beans,' Joyce persisted now.

'I'm afraid there's nothing to tell,' he said. 'I just seem to be unlucky in love. Women don't seem to fall for me.'

This, of course, was untrue, for he had never had to make much of an effort where members of the opposite sex were concerned; they took an immediate liking to him. He had had several girlfriends who had wanted their relationship to become serious and had hinted at marriage, but he had not felt the same way. He had thought that perhaps the beautiful artist who had so charmed all in the village (particularly the men) was the one woman with whom he could settle down and marry but soon after Amanda had left for London to pursue her artistic career, Tom had realised his had been more of a crush than love and that he still had the deepest feelings for Janette after all.

'Aren't you and Miss Fairborn an item again now she has moved back into Risingdale?' Joyce asked.

'Not really,' he replied. 'I would like—'

Before he could answer, their conversation was interrupted by three of the girls in Tom's class, who approached arm-in-arm. Vicky, who was in the middle, was cackling.

'Something's amused you three,' said Joyce.

'Christopher Pickles pinched our skipping rope, miss,' Marjorie told the teacher.

'I'll have a word with him,' Tom said.

'You don't need to, Mr Dwyer,' said Carol. She giggled. 'It's sorted. He got tangled up in it and fell over.'

'With a little help from Vicky,' added Marjorie.

'And he hit his head,' said Carol with a smile on her small face.

'Is he hurt?' asked Tom.

'Just his pride,' replied Vicky, sounding like her grand-mother. 'It'll teach him not to spoil our game.'

'I like your coat, miss,' Carol told Joyce.

'It's really nice, miss,' added Marjorie.

'Thank you, girls,' replied Joyce, smiling.

Vicky scrutinised the teacher for a moment and then announced, 'I bet you were dead pretty when you were young, miss.'

Tom turned away to hide his smile.

*

After school, as Mrs Golightly and Miss Tranter were putting on their coats ready to depart, Mr Cadwallader, who had been supervising the children onto the bus, entered the staffroom.

'I don't know what has got into the children this afternoon,' he complained. 'They were in a very silly mood, giggling and snickering as they got on the bus.'

His two colleagues stared at him for a moment and then Joyce spoke. 'I think it may have something to do with the front of your trousers.' She pointed.

'What?' he asked. He looked down to see a wet patch.

'Has someone had a little accident?' asked Mrs Golightly playfully.

'My goodness!' cried Mr Cadwallader, reaching into his trouser pocket. He produced a plastic water pistol. 'This wretched thing must have been leaking. I confiscated it from Jimmy Brogan this afternoon. I'll swing for that boy!'

*

Sir Hedley stood by the window in his study at Marston Towers, looking out at a clamour of rooks. They wheeled in the clear blue sky above a green sward of parkland which had not changed for over a hundred years. Far off came the grating call of a partridge and the chug-chug of a distant tractor. He had grown to love this rich and diverse landscape and the wild creatures that inhabited it. He thought for a moment of the person who would one day inherit the estate. He felt sure that he would see himself as a caretaker of this land and know that he would benefit from the diligence of his ancestors to preserve it so that his own descendants would be able to continue to live and work here and manage the land properly.

As Mrs Leadbeater had observed the day before, Sir Hedley was in good humour. Since his wife had left there had been so many moments of solitude, of stillness, of regret, of relief, where thoughts rose unbidden, but of late his world had become clearer somehow, more vivid and filled with opportunity and optimism. The divorce papers had arrived from his wife's solicitor the previous day and all he needed to do was sign them and he would be free of the woman forever. Of course, he should have divorced Marcia before. He had considered it, but then decided that it would be such a bother and, of course, a costly business with half of his estate disappearing with her. Best just to put up with it, he had thought, keep my head down and see as little of her as possible. This arrangement had suited Lady Maladroit, who was quite content that her husband made himself scarce. Over the years there was hardly a moment of peace or calm at Marston Towers. To her, the marriage had become a sham, an empty shell, nothing more. Things, however, came to a head with the death of their son. Lady Maladroit had entered the study the day of James's funeral and had given vent to her feelings about her husband, feelings that she had harboured for many years. She had stood before the desk with a vulturine face that made Sir Hedley think that at any moment she was about to pounce upon him. Her thin hands had been clasped before her.

'I'm leaving you,' she had informed him. 'The only reason I stayed in this godforsaken place and put up with you all these years was because of James. He was the only thing we had in common.'

As a final cruel riposte, she had told him that she had never loved him and only married him for the lifestyle and the title. Then she had left to live with her sister in London. So, at last I will be rid of her, Sir Hedley thought now.

Since her departure, the house had been blissfully peaceful. There were no more arguments, weary sighs and simmering silences. As soon as his wife had left, Sir Hedley had prevailed upon the former housekeeper to return to Marston Towers. Mrs Gosling had been wrongfully accused by Lady Maladroit of stealing a necklace and had been sacked. Later it was discovered that it was James who had taken the jewellery to sell at the auction house in Clayton, where it was purchased by Miss Tranter. Mrs Gosling, hearing that Lady Maladroit was no longer at Marston Towers, had been overjoyed to be reinstated.

Sir Hedley sat at the heavy mahogany desk. He bridged his fingertips together and thought for a moment. Then he dipped his pen in the impressive brass inkwell in the shape of an eagle with outstretched wings and he signed the papers with a flourish. He reached into a drawer and took out a cigar, lit it and blew out a cloud of smoke. Then he leaned back in his chair and thought about the future. After the divorce and a suitable period, he told himself, he would marry the woman he had loved for twelve years.

Sir Hedley had met Christine Lister one lunchtime at the Clayton Golf Club. He had escaped from his wife after another bout of acrimonious bickering and had been sitting at the bar nursing a glass of whisky. He had begun chatting to the woman who had served him. She was pale-complexioned with violet eyes and an abundant explosion of curly black hair and a lovely smile. After that first propitious meeting he had started to spend more and more time at the golf club, not to play golf but to see the woman with whom he had fallen helplessly in love. Sir Hedley had courted her, she had become his mistress and he had installed her in a cottage a convenient distance from his home at Marston Towers. After a year, she had given birth to his son – Charles Edward Lister. An older married man with a young woman as his mistress and a child born out of wedlock would have caused quite a scandal in the village, so they had been very careful to keep their liaison a secret – or so they had thought. He had been surprised that his wife had known all along about the affair.

There was a knock at the door and a moment later the housekeeper bustled in, carrying a tray on which stood a fine bone china cup and matching milk jug and teapot.

'I've brought your afternoon tea, Sir Hedley,' she said.

'Ah, thank you, Mrs Gosling,' he replied, placing his cigar in an ashtray, taking the tray from her and putting it on his desk.

'The decorators have arrived and are making a start with the master bedroom, so I have put you in the guest room. I have told them that I don't want them messing the place up, leaving paint all over the floor and putting marks on my walls. I've warned them to be careful of all the antiques. I shall be keeping a close eye on them.'

'I have no doubt of that, Mrs Gosling,' said Sir Hedley.

The housekeeper was a small, plump woman with darting, judgemental eyes and handsome features buried in a broad face. Her tightly permed hair was dyed the colour of brown boot polish. When she was the cleaner at the school her usual garb consisted of a startlingly pink nylon overall beneath which was a thick knitted cardigan and a red and white gingham frock. Since becoming housekeeper at the big house again, she had felt it necessary to change her attire to suit her elevated position and now sported an iron-grey pleated skirt and an elaborately frilly white blouse. She wore large artificial pearl earrings and a rope of very yellow beads around her neck.

The indomitable Mrs Gosling was a law unto herself. She had no conception of status, rank or position in the world and treated everyone exactly the same, usually like naughty children. This attitude had greatly annoyed the teachers at the school and Mrs Leadbeater, who thought she should know her place. The caretaker found the woman insufferable; he had been driven to distraction by her interference, unsolicited advice, and constant criticism. They all breathed a great sigh of relief when she left. Because she was such an excellent cleaner who vacuumed and dusted, wiped and polished, scoured and scrubbed with a vengeance and took such a pride in her work, Sir Hedley tolerated her blunt manner and the way she often made pronouncements, offered suggestions and sometimes gently took him to task. She reminded him of the nanny he had had as a child.

Mrs Gosling sniffed in the smoky air with disapproval and surveyed the room. Displayed on the walls were oil paintings showing different animals: grazing cattle, fat black pigs on stumpy legs, bored-looking sheep, leaping horses and packs of hounds and a set of hunting prints. There were also dark portraits of the baronet's ancestors, staring pompously from the frames. In a glass dome on a marble-topped console table was a variety of stuffed hummingbirds hovering around a branch. Other stuffed exhibits included the head of a snarling fox mounted on a wooden plaque on the wall, a stoat with a rabbit in its jaws and a falcon perched on a branch, the last two creatures displayed in a glass-fronted cabinet. The house-keeper had remarked to her son that the room was like a zoo and said it was the devil's own job to keep it clean and tidy.

'Is there something troubling you, Mrs Gosling?' asked Sir Hedley. He placed the cigar in an ashtray.

'Now you mention it,' she told him, screwing up her face. 'I can't say that I like these stuffed animals. Nasty, dusty creatures they are, with staring glass eyes and sharp beaks.'

'They were bought by my grandfather,' the baronet told her. 'He was very keen on wildlife.'

'Well, there's not much life in them now and that's for sure,' retorted the housekeeper. 'They're dead.'

'Indeed, they are,' admitted Sir Hedley.

'They will all have to come out when the decorators come in here.'

'Perhaps it is about time I got rid of them,' Sir Hedley told her.

'Well, I'd be grateful if you would. They give me the creeps.'

'I'll get Mr Greenwood to dispose of them next week. Perhaps the museum might be interested.'

'Young Mr Dwyer at the school had a lot of stuffed animals. I told him I was not keen on them. He's put them all along the windowsill in his classroom and uses them for the children to write about and draw.'

'Then perhaps he might like them,' suggested the baronet.

'If you ask me, I wouldn't encourage him. He's got quite enough without adding to the collection.'

'If you say so,' replied Sir Hedley.

'By the way, you might get another tray,' said the housekeeper, looking at the crudely made object of cheap wood with misshapen handles and clumsy joints. 'It's seen better days.'

'My son James made that at boarding school,' she was told. 'It was the only thing he ever produced.'

'Oh, I'm sorry, Sir Hedley, I didn't know. I didn't mean to speak out of turn.'

He gave a small, sad smile. 'He spent three years at a top independent boarding school and left passing just the one exam – woodwork. I think I will keep the tray. Considering the amount I paid in school fees, the tray is worth its weight in gold.'

'Well, I'll let you get on,' she said. 'Oh, I meant to ask, will you be staying in for dinner tonight?'

'No, I shall be dining out.' He had arranged to meet Mrs Lister.

When Mrs Gosling had gone, Sir Hedley re-lit his cigar and stared at the tray. He wished his relationship with his son had been different. As he had mentioned to Mr Gaunt, perhaps he had expected too much of him. Maybe he had been too critical of his son and not spent enough time with the boy. It was a sad fact, he reflected, that being related is no guarantee of love. That was all water under the bridge now. He drew on his cigar and blew out a cloud of smoke. There was something that his son had left, for which his father would be grateful: James's fling with Leanne, the barmaid at the King's Head, had resulted in the young woman becoming pregnant. Sir Hedley was to become a grandfather.

James Maladroit, a regular frequenter of the King's Head in the village, had spent many an hour propping up the bar chatting to the daughter of the landlady. Leanne was a large, healthy-looking girl with curly brown hair, large, watery grey eyes, and prominent front teeth. She was a gullible and un-sophisticated young woman and, flattered by the attentions of the son of the Lord of the Manor, had agreed to go out with him. The one-night stand had resulted in the young woman becoming pregnant. As her mother, the redoubtable Mrs Mossup, had explained to Sir Hedley when she acquainted him with the circumstances, 'It happened after the Young Farmers' barn dance. They both had had a bit too much to drink and one thing led to another.' Sir Hedley had sat open-mouthed and was completely lost for words. Now was added another misdemeanour to his errant son's list of wrongdoings – he had taken advantage of a naïve and impressionable young woman. When the baronet had let the news sink in, his reac-tion surprised the landlady. He did not appear unsettled or embarrassed hearing that his son was to be a father and there was no question of keeping things under wraps. He had been angry with James, of course, but the prospect of becoming a grandfather did not displease him and he hoped that he could play a part in the child's life. To Mrs Mossup's satisfaction, Sir Hedley had insisted on covering any costs and making one of his cottages available for the mother-to-be. This arrangement would not have been well received by Lady Maladroit, but she was in no position to object for, by this time, she had packed her bags and departed.

Before going out that evening Sir Hedley went in search of the housekeeper. He found her in the kitchen energetically rubbing the surface of the black leaded kitchen range.

'Ah, there you are, Mrs Gosling,' he said. 'Hard at work I see.'

'"The devil makes work for idle hands", Sir Hedley,' she told him.

'Might I have a word with you?' he asked.

The housekeeper stopped buffing. She looked perturbed.

Her face stiffened. 'I hope there's nothing amiss,' she said, immediately feeling defensive.

'No, no, not at all,' Sir Hedley reassured her. 'I have been more than satisfied with your work since you returned to Marston Towers. The place has never been so pristine.'

'More what?'

'Very clean and tidy. You are doing a splendid job, Mrs Gosling.'

'Oh, well, that's good to hear,' she said, mollified. There was a pleasant gleam of inward satisfaction in her eyes.

'The thing is,' continued the baronet, 'I have a couple of people coming to see me tomorrow afternoon. I wonder if I might prevail upon you to arrange for some afternoon tea?'

'Of course, Sir Hedley. I've just this morning made an orange and lemon cake.'

He thought for a moment and rubbed his jaw. 'The visitors are Mrs Mossup, the landlady of the King's Head, and her daughter.' He gave a throaty cough. 'You are aware, as indeed are all in the village by now, that Leanne is to have my late son's child in the near future.'

'Yes, I did hear.'

'I know that this news has not been well received by some of the residents and it had caused a deal of gossip and disapproval. I do hope that when my visitors arrive that you will treat them with—'

'If I might stop you there, Sir Hedley,' cut in Mrs Gosling, a gentle reproof in her voice. 'I have an idea what you are about to say. Let me be plain. I take folk as I find them. I always have and I always will. I have always found Doris Mossup and Leanne to be good-hearted and friendly enough and I would be the last person to judge. To be honest, I feel sorry for the lass bringing up a kiddie all on her own. So, there is really no need to tell me to be agreeable to them if that is what you are about to tell me.'

'Of course. I'm sorry, Mrs Gosling,' said Sir Hedley. 'I didn't mean to give any offence.'

'None taken,' she replied.

4

The following afternoon, Sir Hedley's visitors arrived at Marston Towers. Mrs Mossup, a round-faced, cheerful-looking, middle-aged woman with elaborately coiffured, dyed blond hair, stood with her daughter below the stone steps leading up to the great entrance door. It was the first occasion they had been invited to the big house.

'I'm dead nervous, Mam,' said Leanne Mossup. She was wearing a tight-fitting flowered dress which emphasised the considerable pre-natal bump on which she rested her hands.

'Don't start all that again, Leanne,' admonished her mother. 'If I've told you once, I've told you a thousand times, there's nothing to be nervous about. Sir Hedley is a real gentleman, and he has been particularly good to you, sending you money, paying your bills and setting you up in one of his cottages. He could have reacted very differently, my girl, when he was told you were having his son's baby. He might have denied it and said he wanted nothing to do with it. You want to be thankful that he has been so understanding.'

'I know that,' replied Leanne, petulantly, 'but I'm still dead nervous.'

If truth be told, Mrs Mossup, usually so self-confident and determined a woman and a formidable presence behind the bar of the King's Head, felt a twinge of nerves too. After all, Sir Hedley not only owned most of the land around Risingdale, but he was also a man with weight, authority, and considerable influence.

'I wish you'd have dressed a bit more modestly,' said Mrs Mossup. 'I mean, you're sticking out like Blackpool pier in that dress.'

'It's what pregnant women wear these days,' retorted her daughter, pouting. 'It's all the fashion.'

'It's not my idea of fashion,' her mother told her.

'Yes, well, you're not wearing it, are you?' replied Leanne.

'In my day we had maternity smocks that covered everything up.'

'Yes, well, times have changed.'

'More's the pity.'

'Are we going to stand here all day?' asked her daughter. 'My back hurts.'

'I'm not surprised, wearing those high heels.'

Leanne puffed out her cheeks.

'Now, remember,' said Mrs Mossup, dusting a bit of fluff off her daughter's shoulder, 'be polite, smile and don't speak until you're spoken to.'

'I'm not going for an interview,' said Leanne with a sullen expression.

'You might not think so,' replied her mother, 'but you are, so be on your best behaviour. You need to make a good impression. And don't look so mardy.'

'And I'm not a child either, so you don't need to speak to me as if I am,' her daughter answered back.

Mrs Gosling greeted the visitors with a warm smile and ushered them into the imposing entrance hall with its intricate marble floor so shiny one could skate on it.

'So how are you keeping, Leanne?' asked the housekeeper cheerfully.

'She's doing fine. Thank you for asking, Mrs Gosling,' answered the girl's mother before her daughter could reply. 'She has a few cravings but that's to be expected. I had the same when I was expecting. It was pickled onions with me.

I couldn't get enough of them. And her appetite. I do not know where she puts all the food she consumes. She has—'

'I'm eating for two, Mam,' cut in Leanne.

'Way you eat, I reckon you're having more than two. You've got off lightly when I think of what I went through having you – swollen ankles, vomiting, cramps, headaches, constipation.'

Leanne pulled a face and sighed but didn't say anything.

'Sir Hedley's asked me to show you into the drawing room,' said Mrs Gosling, quickly. She was not inclined to hear any more about Doris Mossup's morbid gustatory conditions. 'So, if you would like follow me.'

The visitors were shown into a large room lavish in its decoration. The highly polished antique cabinets, the heavy, plum-coloured velvet curtains and thick Persian carpet, the delicately moulded lattice-work plaster ceiling and the deep armchairs and magazine-laden tables conveyed a comfortable opulence. Two walls, lined with fixed mesh-fronted mahogany bookcases, were set between tall sash windows overlooking a vast parkland. Above the impressive carved white marble fire-place, bearing the Maladroit coat of arms, a huge, gilded Chip-pendale-style mirror caught the light from a chandelier. The room had a mingled smell of old wood and beeswax polish.

'I'll inform Sir Hedley that you've arrived,' said the house-keeper, and hurried out.

Mrs Mossup picked up a photograph in a silver frame pad-ded with red velvet. It was of a severe-looking, bewhiskered man with large, hooded eyes and protuberant ears.

'I hope your child doesn't turn out like him,' she ventured, turning the photograph around so her daughter could see it. 'He's got a face like a smacked bottom.'

'Whatever my baby looks like it will be loved and wanted,' her daughter replied loudly and with a rare flash of defiance.

'I know that,' said her mother, replacing the photograph and turning her attention to a large decorative porcelain vase, which stood on a highly polished walnut inlaid table. She went for closer inspection. 'Look at this ugly great thing. I wouldn't give it houseroom. I've not seen anything like it.'

'It's Rockingham china,' came a voice behind her.

Both his visitors jumped as if poked with a cattle prod.

Sir Hedley stood in the doorway.

'It was given to my grandfather by Lord Fitzwilliam,' he said. 'I am told there are only three vases like it in the country. Bit too fancy for my liking.'

Both women stared like strangers meeting him for the first time. Neither said anything.

'I was just saying how nice it was,' lied Mrs Mossup, when she found her voice. Her face reddened.

'Do sit down,' said the baronet, gesturing to a chaise-longue before seating himself opposite in a dusky-pink upholstered chair. He folded one leg over the other, rested his hands on his stomach in a relaxed way and gave a kindly smile.

His visitors sat awkwardly on the edge of the sofa. Mrs Mossup leaned forward. She wanted to say something but restrained herself.

'Thank you for coming to see me,' he said.

'It's very good of you to ask us, Sir Hedley,' Mrs Mossup replied. 'Isn't it, Leanne?' She dug her daughter in the side with an elbow.

Leanne swallowed nervously and licked her lower lip. 'Yes. Thank you, Sir Hedley,' she said, refusing to meet his eyes. Her voice trembled a little. She was wondering what her mother had meant saying that this was some sort of interview.

'And how are you keeping, my dear?' asked the baronet, retaining a sympathetic smile.

'Oh she's—' began Mrs Mossup.

'Fine, thank you, Sir Hedley,' said Leanne quickly before her mother could take over.

'And are you settled in at the cottage?'

'Yes, thank you, Sir Hedley.'

'Nothing you need?'

'No, nothing, thank you, Sir Hedley.' She gave a limp smile.

'And how are you getting on with your neighbour, Mrs Lister?'

'Oh, very well, thank you, Sir Hedley.

'And her young son?'

'He's been very helpful, Sir Hedley.'

'Charlie's a nice young man,' said Mrs Mossup. 'Would that all children were as considerate and well behaved. He helped Leanne move in and has been tackling the garden. Mrs Lister has been very friendly and brought around an apple pie,' and then she added as an afterthought and glancing at her daughter, 'which didn't last long.'

'That's good to hear,' said the baronet.

'It was very generous of you, Sir Hedley, to let her have the cottage,' said Mrs Mossup. 'She's an incredibly lucky young woman.' She nudged her daughter again. 'Aren't you, Leanne?'

'Yes, Mam,' said Leanne, giving a small sigh. 'Thank you, Sir Hedley.'

'It's the least I can do,' he answered.

There was a small silence.

'Of course—'

'What I wanted—'

Mrs Mossup and Sir Hedley started to speak at the same time.

'After you, Sir Hedley,' she said.

'Thank you. Firstly, I wish to reiterate what I said to you both when I heard the news of the baby. I am thrilled and will take care of any costs you might incur.'

Leanne smiled shyly, eyes averted.

'Now, let me tell you the reason I have asked you both to come and see me. This is a delicate matter and I feel you should be aware that—'

He was interrupted with the appearance of Mrs Gosling who entered pushing a trolley on which was a big silver teapot, strainer, bone china cups, saucers and matching side plates, an antique creamer, silver spoons, sugar bowl with doilies. There was also an orange and lemon cake with thick icing on the top.

Leanne eyed the confection like a cat hungrily watching a tankful of goldfish.

There was no conversation as the housekeeper served and gave each of the visitors a cup of tea and a wedge of cake.

'Thank you, Mrs Gosling,' said Sir Hedley.

When the housekeeper had gone, he looked down at his cup for a moment, as if he needed a pause before he could broach what he wanted to say. Mrs Mossup drank her tea in little bird-like sips. Leanne took a substantial mouthful of cake.

'You will be aware,' began Sir Hedley, 'that my wife has left me.'

'Yes, I was sorry to hear about that,' said Mrs Mossup. She was not the slightest bit sorry, for she disliked the woman intensely.

'To be frank, neither of us was unhappy about a parting of the ways,' said the baronet. 'Sadly, it was not a favourable marriage. We rarely saw eye-to-eye. I am sure that those in the village realised as much. The death of our son brought things to a head. Lady Maladroit has gone to live with her sister in London and I manage here quite well on my own, with Mrs Gosling's help. Yesterday I signed the divorce papers.'

Mrs Mossup took another furtive sip of her tea and wondered why she was being vouchsafed this information.

'I guess you are wondering why I am telling you this,' said Sir Hedley.

'It's really not for me to say,' said Mrs Mossup. She frowned as she caught sight of Leanne, who, having devoured the cake in quick time, was now licking her fingers.

'I am to tell you this, Doris, if I may call you that, because now your daughter is to have our grandchild, I guess we will be seeing much more of each other. You and Leanne and, of course, the child will become part of my family and always be welcome here at Marston Towers.'

Mrs Mossup swelled with pride, basking in his attention. She thought of how her customers at the King's Head would react were she to repeat what she had just heard.

'Let me explain,' continued the baronet, 'but before I do so, I would ask that what I am about to tell you is kept in strictest confidence.'

'Of course, Sir Hedley,' said Mrs Mossup, a smile nailed firmly on her face. 'I wouldn't dream of repeating anything.'

He turned to her daughter. 'It will not have escaped your notice, I'm sure, that I have been a regular visitor to the cottage next to yours – Mrs Lister's cottage.'

Leanne, who having wolfed down the last of the cake, licked her lips and cast a bemused glance at her mother.

'I have been seeing Mrs Lister for quite some time,' Sir Hedley told her. He leaned forward in his chair and cleared his throat. 'Indeed, we have been in a relationship for nearly twelve years.'

It was as if a bucket of icy water had been tipped over Mrs Mossup's head. She jerked up in the seat and nearly dropped her cup. Her eyes widened in shock. There was nothing to say that could adequately express her feelings, so she remained silent. Leanne, for her part, gaped like a fish on a fishmonger's slab.

The baronet continued. 'We have been very discreet over the years and only a very few people are aware of our liaison and that does not include Mrs Gosling. She will learn in due course, as indeed will those in the village.'

'My lips are sealed, Sir Hedley,' Mrs Mossup reassured him, regaining her composure, and trying not to show how shocked she was. The revelation reduced her voice to a whisper. 'And Leanne won't breathe a word either.'

'I won't say a thing,' said her daughter.

'When the divorce is finalised,' he carried on, 'I intend to marry Mrs Lister and she and our son will come and live here at Marston Towers.'

Mrs Mossup sat open-mouthed, too stunned to speak. She and *their* son, she thought. Young Charlie Lister was his son? She was, as they say in Yorkshire, 'gobsmacked'.

'So, there it is,' he said. 'I asked to see you to acquaint you with the facts and to assure you that the welfare of my son's child will be guaranteed. Leanne, you may remain in the cottage for as long as you wish, and all expenses will be settled by me. On my death the estate will pass to Charlie, with ample provision for my grandchild. I wanted to set your mind at rest that your child, Leanne, will in no way be ousted. I will be setting up a trust fund, which will ensure he or she is well provided for. I wanted to make you aware of this and, as I have asked, I hope this will remain hush-hush – for the time being at any rate. When I marry, of course, it will become common knowledge and then, had you been unaware of what I have just said, you would no doubt have wondered where Leanne's child would stand in the scheme of things.' Sir Hedley paused, appearing to expect some sort of reaction to his words, but none was forthcoming. 'Is there anything you wish to ask me?' he said.

'No, nothing,' muttered Mrs Mossup, trying to come to terms with what she had just heard.

'Is there anything you wish to ask me, Leanne?'

'Well, yes, there is, Sir Hedley,' she replied.

Her mother stared at her daughter reprovingly.

'What is it, my dear?' asked Sir Hedley.

'Do you think I could have another piece of the orange and lemon cake, please?'

*

It was lunchtime on a gloriously sunny day in early May. Joyce stood by the window in the staffroom, looking out over the playground. She smiled as she saw the headmaster, surrounded by a knot of happy children; they were laughing and chatting. It was Mr Gaunt's custom to spend his lunch hour in the playground, something his staff appreciated for it relieved them of supervision duties.

'He loves the company of children,' she said thoughtfully.

'Who does?' asked Mrs Golightly.

'Mr Gaunt. He will certainly miss them when he retires, and they will miss him.'

'I'll certainly miss him,' sighed her colleague.

Mr Cadwallader crunched noisily on a biscuit and looked across the room to where Mrs Golightly had stopped knitting. 'We will all miss him,' he said, spilling crumbs down his jacket. 'Of course, he'll find it difficult to adjust to living by himself after such a hectic life and with not much to occupy his time.'

'He's got his farm,' said Tom. 'That will keep him busy.'

'Maybe,' said Joyce, 'but it will be a lonely existence, living all alone in the middle of nowhere with only the animals to talk to.'

'Well, he might not be living all alone for much longer,' remarked Mrs Golightly with a mischievous gleam in her eye.

'What do you mean, Bertha?' asked Tom.

'He's got a lady friend.'

'Mr Gaunt?' cried Joyce.

'I was told by Mrs Midgley in church last Sunday that he's walking out with the new vet – that nice Scottish woman with the red hair. They were seen coming out of the Methodist chapel and she had her arm through his. Evidently, he knew her in his younger days and was keen on her and they've—'

'Shacked up?' interjected Mr Cadwallader.

'I wouldn't put it quite so crudely,' said Mrs Golightly.

'Well, good luck to him,' said Joyce. 'He deserves every bit of happiness and he's fortunate to have found someone at his age to share his life with.'

'You are rather jumping to conclusions,' said Tom. 'They're probably just friends and enjoy each other's company. You two have got them practically married off.'

'From what Mrs Midgley told me,' confided Mrs Golightly, 'they looked more than friends. They were very intimate.'

'I, for one, am pleased for him,' said Joyce. 'He won't be so lonely now when he retires.'

Mrs Golightly gave a long, weary sigh such as she might produce when one of her infants has had (as she termed it) 'a little accident in the downstairs department'. 'His leaving certainly focuses the mind,' she pronounced. 'I've not stopped thinking about it since he told us he had decided to go. I just hate change, and you mark my words, everything will change when he goes. I am in two minds whether or not to finish myself. Like Mr Gaunt, I have had a very tempting offer from the Education Office to retire on a full pension and with a generous lump sum. I'm thinking seriously about accepting it.'

'Yes, well, I can't afford to retire even if I wanted to,' grumbled Mr Cadwallader. He peered into the empty biscuit barrel and pulled a face.

'Don't you start thinking of leaving, Bertha,' said Joyce, ignoring him and staring again out of the window. 'It's bad enough Mr Gaunt leaving without you following suit.'

'It's just that when Mr Gaunt said that he was long in the tooth, it got me thinking,' replied her colleague. 'I just wonder if I'm past my sell-by date. I have been teaching a long time and I am feeling my age of late. I was listening to Freddie Bowman in my class reading to me yesterday and he stopped and looked up from his book and told me, "Oh I do like the smell of old age, Mrs Golightly." I felt ancient.'

'That's just the lavender water you wear,' Joyce told her. 'His grandmother probably uses the same scent.'

'Exactly,' said Mrs Golightly. 'Grandmother – an old lady.'

'I think you are very well preserved for your age, Bertha,' remarked Mr Cadwallader tactlessly.

'Well preserved!' she exclaimed. 'You make me sound like one of the stuffed animals in Tom's classroom.'

'You don't want to listen to what children say, Bertha,' said Tom. 'Everyone over thirty is old to the young.'

'Jimmy Brogan in my class asked me last week what it was like in the trenches in the First World War,' declared Mr Cadwallader. The boy had had a mischievous half-smile on his face.

'He was just being facetious,' announced Joyce.

'He's got far too much to say for himself, that boy,' said Mr Cadwallader, thinking of the noisy, unappealing boy who had been squirting children in the playground until his water pistol had been confiscated. 'Mind you, I have to admit age is creeping up on me. You certainly know when you're growing old. I mean, everything hurts and what doesn't hurt doesn't work. You feel like the morning afterwards, but you've not had the night before.'

'And your back goes out more than you do,' added Mrs Golightly.

'Getting old has its advantages,' remarked Tom. 'What about vintage wine and seasoned wood? Some things get better with age. My Auntie Bridget reckons the older you get, the better it gets,' said Tom.

'Unless, of course, you happen to be a banana,' quipped Mr Cadwallader.

Tom shook his head.

'I know why you're grinning like a Cheshire cat, Tom Dwyer,' said Joyce, having turned from the window and caught sight of the amused look on the face of her colleague.

'Well, I have to admit, I did smile,' he answered.

'About what?' asked Mr Cadwallader. 'Do tell.'

'He's thinking of that garrulous girl in his class—' began Joyce.

'Glamorous girl?' said Mr Cadwallader.

'Garrulous,' corrected Joyce. 'Are you going deaf, Owen?'

'That's another sign of growing old – losing your hearing,' said Mrs Golightly. 'Then your eyesight starts to go, and you need your glasses to find your glasses.'

'Joyce is talking about Vicky Gosling,' Tom enlightened him.

'She came up to me in the playground and told me that I must have been pretty when I was young,' said Joyce. 'That made me feel my age, I can tell you.'

'This conversation is getting increasingly depressing,' said Tom. 'None of you are in your dotage yet.'

'Well, you know what they say,' said Mr Cadwallader, '"Men are as old as they feel; women are as old as they look".'

The stare his two women colleagues gave him could have frozen soup in pans.

*

That afternoon it was an art lesson in Mrs Golightly's infant class. It was always a messy activity and frequently had been the cause for much complaint from the former cleaner. Mrs Gosling had taken the teacher to task on many an occasion about the state of the infant classroom but had been particularly critical after the art sessions.

'I teach the children to paint, Mrs Gosling,' Mrs Golightly had told her, bristling at the censure. 'It is an essential part of the work they undertake, and their artistic efforts were mentioned most favourably when we had the inspection from the HMI. They do not use felt-tip pens, coloured pencils, and crayons in my classroom. I encourage the children to mix and use paint and to have an appreciation of the different shades.'

'Yes, well, they don't need to make such a mess,' countered the cleaner.

'I am sure that Monet or Degas left a deal of mess after completing a masterpiece.'

'That's as may be, Mrs G,' the cleaner had retorted, 'but this Moneyordayga, whoever he may be, didn't teach in this school and if he did, I would have the same thing to say to him about the mess.' With that she had marched off, clutching her feather duster like a baton, and grumbling to herself.

That afternoon Mrs Golightly equipped each child with a small apron, a large sheet of white paper, a brush, a plastic cup of water and several small pots of paint. She demonstrated how to mix the colours. The small children were soon splashing away with enthusiasm and abandon, and many soon had more paint on them and their aprons than on the paper. The teacher was pleased to see how earnestly the children took to the task and that they were producing pictures of very pleasing quality. The school inspector had indeed complimented her on the children's bold and brightly coloured efforts – 'so fresh and spontaneous' – and had mentioned that it was good to see art playing such a prominent role in the early years' curriculum.

Most of the children that afternoon painted figures of their families – great round, pink faces showing massive smiles and bright blue eyes with spiderlike lashes atop fat bodies with long arms and fingers like twigs. Some had added tummy buttons and nipples. They applied the paint with unrestrained confidence, not concerning themselves with perspective or detail.

Mrs Golightly approached a massively freckled boy with spiky ginger hair that stood up like a lavatory brush. He had painted a large multi-coloured smiling figure with a great black lump attached to the side of the face.

'Who is this, Freddie?' asked the teacher.

'My grannie, miss,' answered the child.

'She looks happy.'

'She is. She's always smiling and smells like you, miss.'

Mrs Golightly pulled a face. 'Yes, you did mention it.'

'It's a nice smell, miss – like the flowers she has in her garden.'

The teacher was somewhat mollified. 'What's that big lump on the side of her face?'

'It's a grenade, miss.'

'A grenade,' repeated the teacher, looking at the painting with a puzzled expression.

'My grannie has a grenade in her ear,' explained the boy.

'Why has she got a grenade in her ear?' asked the teacher.

'To help her hear, miss. She's going deaf. It's an ear grenade.'

The teacher, making a serious attempt to control her laughter. 'I see,' she said, '"a hearing aid".'

Over the years the teacher had always been amused by how this tricky and troublesome language can confuse young children and by their innocent attempts to get to grips with difficult words and phrases. She remembered the time that an infant had told her that their new baby brother was poorly and was in an 'incinerator' at the hospital and the occasion when another child had informed her that his granddad was 'a drunken vegetarian', meaning a Dunkirk veteran. She recalled the assembly given by the vicar, Mr Pendlebury, who had visited the school. In preparation for Palm Sunday he had asked the children what the people waved in the air to welcome Jesus as he approached Jerusalem. He had been thinking of palms.

One child had shouted out, 'Prawns'. Once, a child had told her that he knew what they called two men who loved each other. She had thought, on hearing this, that she would have to deal with this observation with a degree of tact. 'They are called Christians, miss,' the infant had announced before she could respond. One morning, when she had been on play-ground duty, one of her young charges had run up to tell her that another child had used a very rude word. When asked what the rude word was, the child had answered, 'I'd rather not repeat it, miss, but if you say all the rude words you know, I'll stop you when you come to it.'

Sometimes the children's use of language was, to say the least, surprising. There was the memorable occasion when the children were painting. One child, a serious-minded and precocious little girl called Imogen, had drawn a picture of a group of figures, all of whom had bright purple hair, green faces and red hands. Mrs Golightly had been worried that the child might be colour blind, so she had put her fears to the test. 'If I were in a wood,' she had told the girl, 'where the trees were green, the bushes were green, and the grass was green and I was wearing a green coat . . .' Before she had complet-ed the sentence, the infant had piped up, 'No one would see you, miss, because you'd be completely camouflaged.' When Mrs Golightly had enquired of the child why all the people's features in the picture were painted in such bright colours, the little girl had told her, 'Because I'm using my imagination, miss.'

Mrs Golightly revelled in the company of her small chil-dren. They were so open, uncritical and curious. She encour-aged them to share their feelings, tell her about their interests and to ask questions, which she endeavoured to answer calm-ly, honestly and in a matter-of-fact manner. She was fascin-ated by the preoccupations of her young charges. 'Why are holes empty?' 'Why do we have to die?' 'What does God look like?' 'Why do people sometimes cry when they are happy?' 'Why does it rain?' 'Why are bananas bent?' 'What's at the end of the sky?' 'What happened to the dinosaurs?' and the perennial, 'Where do babies come from?'

That afternoon, the teacher approached a little girl with wide, cornflower-blue eyes and a mass of blond hair, which was gathered in two large candyfloss bunches. She had painted a picture of four people: two men both holding the hands of a woman and a small child standing in front of them. All had great wide smiles on their round pink faces.

'This is Mummy and Daddy and Uncle Eric and me,' explained the girl. 'Uncle Eric only comes to stay with us when my daddy is away.'

'I see,' said Mrs Golightly, deciding not to ask any questions. She moved on.

One of the pictures she examined concerned her. The young artist, a sad little boy called Stevie, had a grubby face, a small, tight mouth and a crewcut. His skin looked unhealthily pale. He said little in class but was as sharp as a tack and one of the best readers. His painting showed three figures all depicted in black. There was not a trace of any colour. Mrs Golightly recalled that at college the art lecturer, Mr Bowden, had explained that pictures painted by small children often revealed a great deal about their state of mind. It was unusual, for example, for paintings of people drawn by small children to have sad faces and not be bright, bold, and colourful. Mr Bowden had told them that there was something significant if a child used a deal of black paint. It could be an indication that the pupil found the world a dark and depressing place. This child's effort was unlike any other in the class. Perhaps, thought the teacher, this depiction revealed some psychological problem or difficulties at home. She was aware that the boy was from a one-parent family and his mother had difficulty making ends meet. One winter morning the child had arrived at school with a thin coat. At the end of school, snow had settled on the ground. Mrs Golightly had wrapped the child up in her own scarf and gloves before he set off home.

'This is an unusual painting, Stevie,' she said. The boy gazed up at her sadly with large, dark eyes. He remained silent. 'Who are these people in your picture?' she asked encouragingly.

'Mum and my baby brother Daryl and me,' he told her.

'I see you've not used any colours,' remarked the teacher.

'No, miss.'

Mrs Golightly thought for a moment. Then she put her hand on the boy's arm and rested it there. She leaned forward. 'Is everything all right at home, Stevie?' she asked in a low sympathetic voice.

'Yes, miss?' He stared at her blankly.

'Are you sure?'

'Yes, miss.'

'There's nothing troubling you?'

'No, miss.'

'What about school? Is there something worrying you about school?'

'No, miss, I like school and I like having you as my teacher.'

'And I like having you in my class,' said Mrs Golightly, putting on a sympathetic smile. 'Could you tell me why Mummy and baby Daryl are painted in black rather than in any other colours?'

'Yes, miss.'

'Why is that?'

'Because I've spilled all the pots with the coloured paints in, miss,' he replied.

*

At the end of the school day, when the children had gone home, Mrs Golightly displayed their paintings on the walls around the classroom and sat at her desk, thinking. The children had been particularly keen and well behaved that afternoon and she had been touched by what Stevie had said about how much he enjoyed having her as his teacher. Before he went home, he had given her a hug. She decided that she would not make a hasty decision to retire. How many people, she reflected, got up in the morning and anticipated going to work as she did? She was very fond of her colleagues, enjoyed the company of the children, loved the job and derived great satisfaction from what she did. And what is more, she was successful. No child left her classroom unable to read, the children knew the key words, could draw and paint and were good little early writers. They could add up and subtract; some could divide and multiply and all could recite some of their tables. What would I do, she asked herself, if I retired: sit watching television all day, knit a few more jumpers, learn to play bridge, flower arrange? That sort of existence was not for her; it would make her lonely and unhappy, having no life beyond work and lacking the company of her colleagues. No, she would retire when she was good and ready.

5

On Tuesday morning the weather was perfect; it was one of those bright late spring days when there was a warmth in the sun and the air was alive with bird song and the scent of blossom. Tom, as was his custom, was at school at just after eight o'clock. He arrived early so he could prepare his lessons for the day and mark the children's work. He had asked his pupils to write an account based on the poem about the highwayman he had read, summarising the narrative, and giving their views on the theme and the characters. The children's efforts varied greatly. Marjorie's and Angela's essays were, as always, neat, competent and clearly written; Christopher's effort was short and to the point; George managed to include a tractor in his account and Colin dwelt rather too much on the death of the landlady's daughter, whose ending was described in gruesome detail. Charlie had produced the best account – accurate, imaginative, and thoughtful, the work of an accomplished writer, skilled well beyond his youthful years. The boy had been critical of the verse. He took issue where the poet had depicted the highwayman as an attractive and romantic figure and the soldiers as villains.

'Of course, the soldiers acted wrongly in tying up the landlord's daughter,' he had written, 'and her death was tragic, but one should not forget that highwaymen were not starry-eyed rascals but lawbreakers. They were violent thieves who terrorised passengers and left them fearing for their lives.'

Tom was so engrossed in reading the accounts that he failed to notice the figure who had appeared at his classroom door until the smell of cigarette smoke made him look up from his books. An elderly woman with thin, bloodless lips, a fuzz of white hair and an amazingly wrinkled indrawn face was watching him, a half-smoked cigarette dangling from the corner of her mouth. A heavy woollen coat enveloped her small frame.

'Good morning,' said Tom cheerfully. 'May I help you?'

The woman removed the cigarette and stared at him for a moment.

'I'm Mrs Wellbeloved, the new cleaner,' she told him, without a trace of a smile. She then replaced the half-smoked cigarette between her lips, drew in a mouthful and blew out a cloud of smoke, wheezing loudly in the process.

Tom closed the book he had been marking, got up from his desk and approached the woman. He detected a curiously pervasive odour of mothballs mixed with the cigarette smell.

She nipped the end of the cigarette and dropped the stub in the wastepaper basket by the side of the desk. There was another hacking cough. 'Where is everybody?' she asked.

'The caretaker and school secretary arrive at eight thirty,' Tom told her, noticing with distaste that the woman's fingers were stained yellow with nicotine. 'Mr Gaunt, the headmaster, and the teachers usually get here about a quarter to the hour and the children turn up for nine o'clock or thereabouts.'

'I thought there'd be somebody here to meet me,' she said crossly. 'I've come a long way. I had to get the early bus from Clayton and was stuck at the bus stop for twenty minutes before it arrived. It's in the middle of nowhere up here. Mr Nettles at the Education Office never told me that.' She studied Tom for a moment. 'And who are you?' she asked.

'Mr Dwyer,' he replied, taken aback by her abrupt manner. 'I'm the teacher of the top juniors.'

'I hope the kids are well behaved. I can't be doing with misbehaved children.' Before Tom could respond she continued. 'Is this your classroom?'

'Yes, it is.'

'I don't like them stuffed animals,' she said, pointing to the menagerie of wildlife displayed on the windowsills. 'I hope I'm not expected to dust them. They are probably full of fleas. And I can't say I'm all that keen on cleaning all them old wooden desks and chairs,' she added, coughing. 'They'll be full of splinters. At the other school they had plastic-topped tables and chairs that were easy to wipe clean.' She glanced down. 'I hate these varnished wooden floors, as well. They're the devil's own job to polish.'

Tom drew in a breath. He had considered offering the woman a cup of tea, but he was irritated by her sharp manner and thought better of it.

'I guess you would like to make a start,' he said, 'so I won't detain you.' He returned to his desk and went back to his marking.

'I don't know where anything is,' she said irascibly.

'Cleaning materials are kept in the cupboard at the end of the corridor,' he told her. He returned to the books on his desk. His colleagues complained about Mrs Gosling, but wait until they meet Mrs Wellbeloved, he thought.

The woman pursed her lips and, muttering to herself, she left the room. Glancing out of the classroom window a moment later, Tom saw her heading down the path. Thank goodness for that, he thought. He hoped that this would be the last sight of Mrs Wellbeloved. Come back, Mrs Gosling, all is forgiven.

At half past eight Mr Leadbeater poked his head around the classroom door.

'Has the new cleaner arrived yet?' he asked.

'She came, she saw, she departed,' Tom replied.

'Eh?'

'She's gone. She took one look at the school and then left.'

'Blood and sand,' muttered the caretaker.

'Somehow,' Tom told him, 'I think we are better off without her. She would not have fitted in.'

'So, I'm back to square one,' complained Mr Leadbeater. 'What do I do now?'

'Look, Bob,' said Tom, 'the next time I visit my aunt in Barton-in-the-Dale, I'll get the shopkeeper there to put a card in the window advertising a vacancy here. With several of the small schools closing there is sure to be a cleaner looking for a job.'

The caretaker retained his lugubrious expression. 'I'm not keeping my fingers crossed,' he replied morosely, and departed, jangling his keys.

The second visitor to Tom's classroom later that morning was Dr Merryweather, curator of the Clayton Museum. She had telephoned Tom the week before to ask if he would like her to visit the school and speak to the children about the results of the excavation she had been undertaking with a team of archaeologists at the ruins of the nearby Marston Castle. She offered to talk about what they had discovered about the stronghold and show the children some of the artefacts that they had unearthed.

Tom had first come across Dr Merryweather when he had taken his class, accompanied by Mrs Gosling to help with the supervision, on an excursion to the Clayton Museum and Art Gallery, where she had given them a guided tour. He had met her again when he had arranged a visit to see the excavation of the site at the ruined castle and she had promised to call into the school after the dig had been completed and talk to the children about the team's findings. At that first meeting Tom had been pleasantly surprised to find that the museum's custodian was a young woman with a flawless complexion, grass-green eyes, and long blond hair. She had had a look on her face of someone quite aware that she was being admired.

'She's a bit of all right, that curator, i'n't she, sir?' George had remarked after a tour of the museum. He had winked.

'Yes, George,' the teacher had replied. 'I have to agree with you there, she is.'

It was clear to the children (and to the eagle-eyed Mrs Gosling) that Dr Merryweather had taken quite a shine to Tom, with his handsome black curls and long-lashed blue eyes. It was the way the woman watched him. The attraction had been obvious.

Dr Merryweather arrived at morning break. Tom, assisted by two of his pupils, helped her unload a rusty sword, a knife, two helmets and a leather-bound box from the boot of her car. They carried them into the classroom and displayed them on a table at the front.

'Now, everyone, sit up smartly and look this way,' said Tom to the class. 'You all remember Dr Merryweather when we visited the site of the castle, don't you?'

'Yes, sir,' the children chorused.

George looked at his teacher and winked.

Tom stared back at the pupil with the expression which said, 'Behave yourself.'

'We are lucky this morning,' he said, 'because Dr Merryweather has kindly agreed to come into school and talk to us about what she and her team have discovered at the castle.'

'Good morning, children,' she said.

'Good morning, Dr Merryweather,' responded the class.

'Now, you may recollect, children,' she said, 'that I told you that Marston Castle was once a great majestic fortress of solid stone dating back to the twelfth century, which towered over the surrounding area. Can anyone remember who built it?'

Several hands went up. She pointed to a girl with mousy-brown hair and pink glasses. 'Yes?'

'A Norman nobleman called William de Burgh, miss,' Carol answered.

'That's right, and then I told you the castle eventually passed to another rich and powerful family.'

'The D'Arbours, miss,' said Judith.

'They were supporters of King Henry VIII,' added Andrew.

'Who was really fat and when he died all the gases inside him built up and he exploded,' said Matthew.

'And pieces of him were scattered all over and dogs ran off with bits of him,' added Vicky gleefully.

'That's right,' said Dr Merryweather. She did not wish to hear this particular story again. 'I mentioned that—'

'Charlie told us,' said Matthew. 'It's called internal combustion.'

'Yes, he did, which is something a lot of people don't know.' She moved on quickly. 'I told you there was a siege at the castle at the time of the English Civil War. Now I have brought in to show you some of the things we found when we were excavating. I'm afraid we didn't find anything quite as valuable as the coins your father discovered, Colin.'

The children all turned to look at Colin Greenwood.

'I'm sure you are all aware that some extremely rare and interesting coins were discovered, which are now on show in the York Museum.'

When Mr Greenwood had owned the land on which Marston Castle had been built, he had dug up a Charles I silver shilling and an exceptionally rare coin called a Scarborough siege piece minted at the time of the English Civil War. They fetched a considerable amount of money at auction.

'We did,' continued Dr Merryweather, 'find something of interest.'

'Skeletons!' cried Vicky.

'No, not skeletons,' she replied. She held up a small silver band. 'This is a medieval ring and inside is engraved the words, "O mi hart is yours". It was probably a love token given by a young man to his sweetheart. I wonder to whom it belonged and how it came to be lost.' She turned to the teacher. 'There's a story there, Mr Dwyer, isn't there?' Tom nodded. 'History is full of stories, children – that's what makes the subject so fascinating.'

'Is it valuable, miss?' asked Vicky.

'I'm afraid not. Just a few hundred pounds.'

'Not to be sniffed at,' commented George.

'The sword, the knife and the helmets we didn't find at the castle,' Dr Merryweather continued. 'They are from the museum, but they will give you an idea of the weapons used in the seventeenth century and some of the armour worn at the time of the siege.'

The children gathered around the table to view the artefacts and listened intently as Dr Merryweather showed them shards of glass and fragments of pottery, a rusty sword and a knife and a silver belt buckle, a collection of old coins and several corroded nails. Then she turned her attention to the two helmets. One was in immaculate condition; the other was rusty and full of dents and holes. She turned to Charlie and asked him to look at the helmets.

'One of these is an original helmet and the other is a reproduction,' she told him. 'Would you like to have a guess which is which?'

Charlie tapped the top of the old rusty one.

'This is a copy,' he said. 'The other is the original helmet.'

Dr Merryweather was surprised.

'Why do you say that?' she asked.

Charlie gave a grin. 'Well, I guess most people would pick the other one because it looks old and damaged,' he said. 'I'm guessing this was a bit of a trick question.'

Dr Merryweather put a hand on the boy's shoulder.

'You're right,' she told him.

'He always is,' remarked Vicky under her breath.

At lunchtime the children, except for Vicky and George who volunteered to help carry the various objects to the car, thanked the visitor and left the classroom.

'That was a really interesting and enlightening session,' Tom told Dr Merryweather.

'It was a pleasure,' she replied, 'and by way of thanks, you might like to take me for a drink.'

'Ah,' said Tom, rather taken aback by the request. 'Er . . . I'd like that, but I'm afraid I can't, I'm on yard duty.'

Not one to give up, she persisted. 'I'm sure one of your colleagues could fill in for you just this once.'

He couldn't really refuse. 'Well, er . . . yes . . . I suppose they could.'

'Good, that's settled then. Why don't you go and ask them while I take these things to the car?'

As Tom left to go to the staffroom, Dr Merryweather collected the artefacts together. While she had been talking to Tom, George had donned one of the helmets and was stabbing the air with the knife.

'I'll take charge of those, thank you, young man,' said Dr Merryweather. She put the items in the boot of her car.

'He's dead nice, our teacher, isn't he, miss?' asked Vicky as they loaded the car.

'Yes, he is,' she replied.

'He's dead dishy,' said the girl. 'Before Mr Dwyer came, we had Miss Cathcart as our teacher. She was dead old and crabby.'

'We learnt nowt, wi' 'er,' added George.

'Miss Cathcart fell in the river and drowned,' said Vicky.

'Yes, I remember you telling me that when you visited the castle.'

'My gran said she probably had too much to drink and lost her footing,' said the girl.

A real little gossip is this one, thought Dr Merryweather. 'Well, that seems to be everything,' she said. 'Thank you for your help. You can both run along now.'

Neither of the children moved.

'Are tha married, miss?' asked George. There was a mischievous glint in his eye.

'No, I'm not married.'

'Mr Dwyer's not married either,' said Vicky. A slight smile pulled at the corners of her mouth.

'Really?' said Dr Merryweather sounding unconcerned.

'My gran reckons—' began Vicky.

Dr Merryweather cut her off when she saw Tom emerging from the school. 'Thank you, Vicky and George,' she said. 'You have both been a great help. Now, off you go.'

The two children remained where they were and watched as their teacher climbed in the car. They both exchanged a glance, then nodded and smiled.

*

The King's Head was an inhospitable country hostelry in the centre of the village, a dim and stale-smelling place, frequented largely by the local farmers of the village who gathered in the evenings and at Sunday lunchtimes to argue about sport, politics and farming and to put the world to rights. Arranged on the grey flagstone floor was an odd assortment of uncomfortable and unstable spindle-backed chairs and wobbly stools. To the side was a shabby horsehair bench. The walls, once white, were now the colour of sour cream and displayed several faded hunting prints, a dark oil painting of a horse and some sepia photographs of farm workers of centuries past. Arranged on two shelves was a variety of dusty Toby jugs, Staffordshire pottery dogs, some tarnished silver sporting cups and a collection of old tankards. Along the old black beams was a line of horse brasses and two copper fox-hunting horns. One attractive feature of the hostelry was the large and old inglenook fireplace, which took up most of a wall.

'I'm sorry I couldn't take you to a more salubrious place,' said Tom to Dr Merryweather as they entered the inn. 'It's just that I must be back at school in an hour and this is the nearest pub.'

'This is fine,' she replied, resting a hand on his arm. 'It has a certain "olde worlde" charm. It has probably remained unchanged for many years.'

'I'm sure you're right. I gather that when the brewery suggested the place needed refurbishing, there was an outcry from the regulars, who threatened to take their custom elsewhere if any attempt was made to make changes. They were supported by the landlady, who is quite a forceful woman. I soon discovered when I came to Risingdale that there is strong objection to any kind of change in the village and this applies to the village school. I agree with the locals; I do like the King's Head as it is. It is only a stone's throw from where I live and is convenient. It means I don't have to drive when I come in for a drink on Saturday night.'

'I remember coming in here to meet you when I told you the good news about the coins found up at the castle.'

Mr Greenwood, who had found the coins at Marston Castle, had agreed with Tom that the find should be examined and valued. Dr Merryweather had been consulted and she had enlisted the help of a coin expert. She had met Tom at the King's Head later when she revealed the startling news that the discoveries were rare and valuable.

'Thank you for coming into school today,' said Tom. 'The children were fascinated.'

'Oh, I love taking about history,' she told him. 'I shall be giving a lecture on the excavations at the museum in a couple of weeks' time. I hope you'll come along.'

'Yes, I'd like that. So, what would you like to drink?' he asked.

'Just an orange juice, please.'

Tom went to order the drinks. Propping up the bar was one of the nosiest and most vociferous (and meanest) of the local farmers – a grizzled old man with a wide-boned, pitted face the colour and texture of an unscrubbed potato, a long beak of a nose with flared nostrils and an impressive shock of white hair. He was unpopular among his fellow farmers and with the landlady and known as a parsimonious, self-opinionated know-all, who had never been known to buy anyone a drink and was forever on the cadge to get someone to buy his. The farmer was dressed in his usual working attire consisting of a grubby, long-sleeved, collarless shirt, a waistcoat which had seen better days and threadbare corduroy trousers.

'Mr Croft,' Tom said, coming to stand next to him.

'Aye, that's me,' replied the man. There was the fresh peaty smell of the country about him. 'Are thee all reet?'

'I'm fine, thank you. How about you?'

'Mustn't grumble,' he grunted.

'That'll be a first, Toby Croft,' observed the landlady, coming to join them. 'You're forever grousing and griping. How your poor wife puts up with you, I cannot fathom.'

'She's a truly fortunate woman is my missis,' Toby told her. 'While I'm slavin' away on t'farm, she's allus out wi' WI, flower-arrangin' group, Countrywomen's crowd an' church cleanin' an' I don't know what else. She only sees me fer an 'our a day.'

'Well, I'm sure the hour soon passes for her,' said Mrs Mossup.

The farmer blew his cheeks out but before he could respond, she turned to Tom. 'Now then, Mr Dwyer,' she said smiling, 'what can I get you?'

'Just a couple of glasses of orange juice, please, Doris,' he replied.

'Not a pint?' she asked.

'No, no, I don't want to smell of beer when I'm back at school.'

'What's tha doin' in 'ere at this time o' day, anyroad?' questioned Mr Croft. 'Tha should be teachin' them kids instead of 'angin' abaat a pub.'

'It's my lunch hour,' Tom answered.

'You don't need to justify anything to *him*,' chided Mrs Mossup, looking at the farmer. She was in no hurry to get the drinks. 'Anyway, Toby, why aren't you up at the farm instead of hanging about a pub?'

'I'm hentitled to a bit of a break, tha knaas,' he told her, holding an empty beer glass ostentatiously before him. He hoped that Tom might take the hint.

'So is Mr Dwyer,' she told him.

'Teachin' kids in a classroom in't same as working on a farm,' grumbled the old farmer. 'I've been up wi' t'lark this mornin', feedin' t'beeasts, doin' some wallin' an' 'edgin' afore 'e gor out o' t'bed.'

'You can always tell when Toby Croft is spinning a tale,' remarked the landlady. 'His mouth moves.'

'I shall hignore that comment,' said Toby. 'I'm dog-tired an' my mouth's as dry as a camel's arse in a sandstorm.' He tilted his glass again, displaying a set of yellowing teeth.

'The drinks, Doris,' Tom reminded her.

Mrs Mossup ignored him and smirked. 'Since your Dean's left,' the landlady told Toby, 'you've had to bestir yourself for once in your life. Poor lad used to run your place. He never had a moment's peace. You had him working all hours and for a pittance.'

The man's son, after the altercation with his father, had left the farm and become the assistant gamekeeper for Sir Hedley. He had not looked back.

'I'll have you know—' the old farmer began.

'And from what I hear, he's doing very nicely for himself.'

'I was abaat to say—' began Mr Croft again.

'I also hear,' she butted in again, 'that you can't get anyone to work on your farm, you're so bad-tempered and cantankerous.'

'Now look 'ere, Doris, I don't come in 'ere to be hinsult-ed. If you don't mind yer manners, I shall tek mi custom to t'Black Pig.'

'Well, as I've told you before,' she retorted, 'you are very welcome to take your custom elsewhere. I shall not get rich on the amount you spend on beer and I'm weary with your griping and grousing. Anyway, I can't stay arguing the toss with you.' She finally went to get the drinks.

Tom chuckled. 'And you had better get a pint for Mr Croft,' he shouted after her. 'It might cheer him up a bit.'

'That's one of the great pleasures you have in life, Toby Croft, isn't it?' remarked Mrs Mossup, shouting from down the bar. 'Drinking at someone else's expense.'

'That's very decent of you, Mester Dwyer,' said the farmer, paying no attention to the landlady but fixing her with a malicious glare. He lowered his voice. 'I'll tell you this, t'landlady's changed since she learnt 'er Leanne was hexpectin' t'squire's grandchild. Full of 'ersen, she is, and wi' a tongue as sharp as two pair o' braces.'

Tom decided not to continue the conversation. He knew that any comment he might make would soon be repeated.

'I thought you'd be in a better frame of mind now that spring is here,' he said instead. 'Clear skies, sunny days, a world teeming with new life. Isn't lambing the best time of year for farmers?'

'Best time o' year?' echoed the farmer gloomily. 'There's never a best time o' year. You don't know t'alf on it. I've 'ad 'edges want cuttin', walls want repairin', leaks want fixin', gates want mendin'. It's one thing after t'other. An' as for lambin' bein' best time o' year fer farmers, I can do wi'out it. There's no best time o' year. I've 'ad sheep daan wi' ovine grass staggers, rattle belly, scour, black bag – you name it, my yows 'ave 'ad it. Then there's feed bills an' t'exhorbitant fees charged by t'vet. All I need now is a bloody plague of locusts.'

With the appearance of Mrs Mossup with the drinks, Tom managed to extricate himself and returned to the corner table.

Dr Merryweather watched Tom as he sat down and placed the drinks on the table. There was no doubt he was a strikingly good-looking man, she thought.

'I'm sorry about that,' he apologised. 'I couldn't get away. That old farmer likes the sound of his own voice and once he gets started there's no stopping him.'

She took a sip of her drink. 'You clearly love teaching,' she said.

'I do,' he replied. 'I don't think there's any job to compare to it. I really do believe, you know, that teachers change children's lives.'

'But not always for the better.'

'Do I gather from that comment that your experience of school was not all that good?' he asked.

She thought for a moment. 'I wasn't that happy at school,' she told him. 'Because I was bright, I was put up a year to a class with pupils older than myself, which was a mistake. I made no friends so immersed myself in my schoolwork. Most of the teachers were just about adequate. They lacked enthusiasm and a real interest in the students. Their heart wasn't in it. Some were sarcastic and others cynical. There was one teacher, though, who inspired me and gave me a love of history. Miss Frith was a bit of an eccentric, with a strange high-pitched voice and false teeth that wobbled when she talked, but she brought the subject to life. She wore long, pleated tweed skirts, thick brown bullet-proof stockings and brogues and had her hair scraped back into a tight little bun. Of course, some of the girls made fun of her behind her back but I really liked her and enjoyed her lessons. I would sit open-mouthed as she told us wonderful stories of the past, of the kings and queens, the great battles, and voyages of exploration. I remember one lesson in which she described the death of Mary, Queen of

Scots, how she ascended the scaffold at Fotheringhay Castle to face her executioner seemingly without a trace of fear and full of grace and majesty. The queen was dressed in a black cloak which, when it fell from her shoulders, revealed a dress of brilliant scarlet – the colour of the Catholic martyr. That must have been quite a scene. When the executioner held up her severed head, it fell from his hands. The beautiful auburn hair, for which she was famed, was a wig. When I moved to North Yorkshire, I visited Castle Bolton where she had been imprisoned. It was quite an eerie feeling, standing at the window of the room in the which she spent six months of her life, looking sadly out over Wensleydale and thinking of the life she had lost.'

Tom laughed. 'You are quite the romantic,' he said.

'Yes, I suppose I am.' They were quiet for a moment. 'Anyway, what about you?' she asked.

'I wasn't always a teacher, you know,' he told her.

'Really?'

'I was a professional football player.'

'That's quite a change from teaching.'

'Yes, quite a change,' he agreed.

'So, why did you give it up?' she asked.

'I had a few nasty accidents on the pitch and with age creeping up, I couldn't really continue. I enjoyed my time as a footballer, the camaraderie of the other players, the cheering crowds, the travelling and some of the notoriety which came with the position, but I have no regrets. I trained as a teacher and realised that I had at last found my true vocation. I landed on my feet when I was appointed to Risingdale School.'

'I have heard rumours that more small village schools are about to close,' she said. 'I hope Risingdale isn't on the list.'

'It's not, as far as I know.'

'I shouldn't imagine you will find it hard to get another position if the school does close,' she said.

Gervase Phinn

'That might not be so easy,' answered Tom. 'There are teachers at the schools that are closing who will need to be redeployed. Teaching jobs in the county will be hard to come by.'

'You love it at Risingdale, don't you?'

He nodded. 'I do,' he said. 'We have just heard that the headmaster is to retire at the end of term so I guess there will be a few changes in the offing.'

'Look at "love's young dream",' observed Mr Croft, stopping the landlady as she walked down the bar.

'Who?' she asked.

'Yon young starry-eyed schoolmester in t'corner,' said the farmer. ''E din't let grass grow under 'is feet, did 'e? I mean 'e 'ad 'is sights set on John Fairborn's lass until she cleared off to Nottingham an' gave 'im t'old 'eave-'o. Then there were Missis Stan'ope, that fancy artist from London what 'e took a shine to. It din't tek 'im long to shack up wi' that woman from t'museum – 'er in t'corner canoodlin' wi' 'im. Mind you, when I went up to see what were 'appenin' up at t'castle wi' hexcavation, I could see she were settin' a cap for 'im, wagglin' 'er 'ips and flutterin' 'er eyelashes. 'E wants to watch 'is step. Women want nowt but 'usbands but when they gerrem, they want heverything.'

'One of these days, Toby Croft,' the landlady told him, 'you might have something nice to say about somebody.'

6

The following Saturday evening, the King's Head was crowded and noisy. The main topic of conversation among the farmers was the auction at Northfield Farm, which had taken place earlier that day. The land, farmhouse, outbuildings and a stretch of woodland had been purchased by the Maladroit estate, the livestock and farm machinery bought by local farmers.

The landlady was in conversation with Sir Hedley's gamekeeper, Richard Greenwood, and his assistant, Toby's son, Dean. The young man had asked how Leanne was keeping.

'She's as fit as a flea,' Mrs Mossup told him. 'Thank you for asking.'

'She must be near to 'avin' t'babby,' said Richard.

'Any time now,' said the landlady.

'Give 'er my best,' said Dean.

'Aye, an' mine,' added Richard.

Toby Croft, perched on a stool at the end of the bar, was holding forth vociferously, giving his opinion to the one farmer who was prepared to listen to his usual griping and grousing. His companion was a small, wrinkled individual with wisps of wiry white hair combed across his otherwise bald pate, pendulous ears, rheumy eyes and a dimpled, veined nose.

'That's another farm gone to t'wall, Percy,' remarked Toby sagely. 'At this rate t'squire will own 'alf o' Yorkshire t'way 'e's goin' on, buyin' up heverythin', purrin 'ard-workin' families out o' theer 'omes to mek way for 'is grouse shootin' an' 'oliday lets. I mean 'e's gor enough land wi'out adding more hacreage. It's a disgrace, that's worrit is.'

'I'll pass on yer comments to Sir 'Edley when I next see 'im,' came a voice from down the bar. Richard Greenwood had overheard.

'Tha needn't bother,' replied the old farmer. 'An' anyroad, tha shun't be listenin' in to a private conversation.'

'Three words – "pot", "kettle", and "black" – come to mind, Toby Croft,' observed the landlady, looking in his direction. 'You miss nothing. Ears like an elephant. You could hear a feather falling on a piece of cotton wool.'

'Tha should be out tryin' to catch poachers instead o' ear-wigging an' proppin' up t'bar suppin' ale,' said the farmer, ignoring her words and pointing at Richard.

'Biggest poacher is sitting at t'end o' bar on thy stool,' said the gamekeeper.

'Don't thee gu castin' haspersions, Dick Greenwood,' said Toby.

'So 'ow's life up at t'farm, then, Dad?' asked Dean. Of course, it was a rhetorical question, for he was well aware of the situation. He had learnt on his visits to see his mother, that things were far from good. Then he had been stopped in the village by several farmers who told him that matters at the Croft farm were going from bad to worse. Since he had left his father's employ, where he had shouldered most of the work, got little thanks for doing so and received a derisory wage, Toby hadn't been able to keep any employee for more than a couple of days. His curmudgeonly attitude and inclination to avoid any exertion himself, added to the poor wages, had put people off.

'Never thee mind,' his father told him angrily. 'It's nowt to do wi' thee.'

'T'way it's goin',' teased Richard, 'thy farm might be t'next on Sir 'Edley's 'it list.'

Before the old farmer could respond, Leanne appeared from the parlour at the back of the inn. She waddled to the counter, gripped the top with both hands, drew in a deep breath and then exhaled long and slowly. She felt the clench of a contraction, winced, and then placed her hand protectively on the curve of her stomach.

'I think it's coming, Mam,' she whispered to her mother.

'What?' hissed Mrs Mossup.

'The baby, I think it's on its way.'

'Are you sure?'

'I think so,' replied her daughter. 'My waters have broken and I'm getting lots of contractions.'

'Oh, my goodness,' said the landlady. There was panic in her voice. 'Go . . . go back into the parlour and sit down. I'll call for an ambulance.'

'I don't think there's enough time,' said Leanne composedly. She stroked her stomach. It felt as tight as a drum.

Dean rushed down the bar and held Leanne's hand in his. 'Try and keep calm,' he said with real concern in his voice.

'I am keeping calm,' she replied peevishly, 'which is more than can be said for my mother.'

'Oh, dear me,' cried Mrs Mossup. She turned to Mr Greenwood. 'Richard, could you do me a big favour and run our Leanne and me to the hospital?' she pleaded.

'I'm sorry, Doris,' he replied. 'I can't. Dean an' me 'ave walked daan toneet an' t'pick-up's at Marston Towers. Anyroad, I've 'ad a couple o' pints an' I'm in no condition to drive.'

'An' it's no good lookin' in this direction,' remarked Toby Croft who had been eavesdropping, 'unless o' course she wants to ride on t'back of mi tractor.'

'What about thee, Wayne?' said Percy, nodding in the direction of the spotty-faced barman. 'Tha could 'appen run t'lass to t'ospital.'

'I'm on my motor bike,' the barman replied.

'I could dash back up to Marston Towers an' get t'pick-up,' said Dean. 'I've not 'ad that much to drink.'

'That'll tek too long,' answered Richard.

'Oh, dear me,' groaned Mrs Mossup. 'Whatever are we to do?'

Leanne, remaining unruffled, looked at her mother. 'Will you calm down, Mam,' she said snappily. 'You're not helping by getting all worked up. You're making me all jittery.'

Mrs Mossup was about to ask if there was anyone in the room who would be willing to take her daughter to the hospital, when Tom walked in. His arrival could not have been timelier. As soon as he reached the bar and the situation was explained to him, he shot off to get his car. Ten minutes later the mother-to-be was strapped in the back seat and on her way to Clayton Royal Infirmary. Leanne had persuaded her mother not to accompany her.

'I can't be doing with you fretting and fussing, Mam,' she had told her mother. 'You're getting me all jumpy. I don't want you coming with me. Tom will call you as soon as there's any news.'

'I'm coming,' Mrs Mossup had announced, firmly. 'I'll get my coat.'

'Mam!' Leanne had snapped, as she headed for the door. 'I don't want you to come.'

'Don't worry, Doris,' Tom had assured the landlady, 'I'll take good care of her. We had better get moving.'

'Could you drive a bit faster?' Leanne asked as they headed out of Risingdale and trundled along a country lane.

'We're getting to that bad bend in the road,' he told her, 'so I need to take things easy. I want to get you and the baby to the hospital in one piece.' He made a great effort to keep his voice calm. Another reason for his snail pace was that he didn't want to hit at speed a few bumps in the road that might bring the baby on. 'I wish you had let your mother come with us,' said Tom. His stomach was churning with nerves.

'She would have only started nagging me and getting all worked up and in a state.'

I'm getting all worked up and in a state, and that's for sure, Tom said to himself. He peered at the surface of the road ahead, trying desperately to avoid breaks and potholes.

Leanne suddenly started to make moaning noises in her throat and gripped the back of the driver's seat. Her face was wet with perspiration.

Tom slowed down, his foot hovering over the brake. 'What's wrong?'

'I don't think I can hang on much longer. Can you speed up?'

Tom put his foot down.

They soon arrived at the hospital. At the reception desk in the Maternity Unit, Leanne explained her condition and was wheeled off with Tom following. A nurse came to meet them.

'If you would like to wait,' she told Tom, 'I will tell you when the baby is on the way. I guess you will want to come in and see the birth.'

'No, not at all,' he spluttered.

'Most fathers these days like to see the baby being born,' she said.

'Oh, he's not the father,' announced Leanne. 'He's just a friend.'

Tom sat waiting in the corridor next to a tall, wiry youth with stringy hair, a long thin face, and small black eyes. He had the air of a condemned man who was about to meet his fate and wrung his hands anxiously.

'Is this your first?' he asked. His voice trembled slightly.

'Well, yes, I suppose it is,' replied Tom.

'It is mine.' The youth was quiet for a moment, then examined his watch, bit his bottom lip, and scratched his thin neck. 'I hate this waiting.' He glanced at Tom with a faintly puzzled expression. 'You're dead calm,' he said. 'I'm dead nervous. I've smoked a packet of fags, been sick and nearly wet myself.'

'I'm sure everything will be all right,' Tom reassured him.

'I hope so,' muttered the man. He swallowed hard and then took to biting his nails.

When he was told the birth was imminent, Tom went off to call Mrs Mossup with the news. He had just got off the telephone when he was informed that the baby had been born and was shown into a small side ward. Leanne, sitting up on the bed, rosy-cheeked and beaming, was nursing a tiny bundle.

'It's a boy,' she said.

Tom bent and looked at the baby. The child had a round moon face, papery skin as white as milk and a down-turned little mouth. It was clear to him that this was James Maladroit's son, for the child bore a strong resemblance to the father.

'He's a cute little chap,' said Tom, stroking the baby's cheek.

'That was one of the easiest births I've seen,' the midwife told Tom, 'and your wife did really well.'

'He's not my husband,' Leanne informed her.

'I'm sorry, your partner,' the midwife corrected herself.

'He's not my partner either,' Leanne said. 'He's just a friend.'

The midwife raised an eyebrow. 'I see,' she said.

It wasn't long before Mrs Mossup and Dean arrived. Leanne's mother was handed the baby.

'It's a little boy, Mam,' Leanne said triumphantly.

Mrs Mossup kissed the baby's cheek, and her eyes began to fill up.

'He's beautiful,' she said. She touched the little face. 'Hello, little man. This is your grannie.'

'And I guess *you* are the father,' said the midwife, turning to Dean who stood like a spare part by the door. 'I'm afraid you missed the birth. Would you like to hold your son?'

'I'm not the father,' Dean told her quickly.

'He's just another friend,' said Leanne.

A moment later Sir Hedley arrived.

'I hope I'm not intruding,' he said, popping his head around the door. 'I'm afraid I couldn't resist seeing my new grandchild.'

'Come in,' said Leanne. 'It's a little boy.'

Sir Hedley was passed the child. 'He's a handsome fellow,' he said, peering at the baby, 'and a healthy size too.'

'Nearly nine pounds,' announced Leanne proudly.

'And are mother and baby doing well?' he asked.

'They are both fine,' the midwife told him.

'He's a fetching-looking little boy and no mistake,' said the baronet. The baby grasped a finger with a tiny fist. 'And strong, too.'

'Now, I'm afraid you will all have to leave,' the midwife said. 'The new mother needs to rest.' She took the baby from Sir Hedley. 'Could I ask you and your wife and the two young men to say goodbye.'

'Oh, this good lady is not my wife,' he replied.

'They're just friends,' explained Leanne for the fourth time that evening.

'I see,' said the midwife, raising an eyebrow again. The old Yorkshire expression – 'There's nowt as queer as folk' – came to mind.

Outside, Sir Hedley suggested that they all retire to the King's Head to celebrate the birth and the party set off back to Risingdale in high good humour.

When they arrived at the village inn, Tom was greeted with handshakes, pats on the back and clapping. Before driving Mrs Mossup to the Maternity Unit, Dean had informed those gathered in the bar that Tom had got Leanne to the hospital on time and the baby was on the way. This news had been greeted with loud applause.

Sir Hedley now raised a hand as if stopping traffic.

'If I might crave your attention for a moment,' he said. 'I am delighted to report that Leanne is in excellent health and her baby boy of eight pound and nine ounces is a champion little chap, as they say in Yorkshire.' The landlady gave a small, self-satisfied smile. 'Mrs Mossup and I are, of course, both overjoyed to be proud grandparents and we would like to invite you all to help wet the baby's head by joining us in a drink – on me of course.'

Toby Croft, leaning over the bar and catching the young barman's attention, was the first to order a pint and double whisky chaser.

'But before that,' continued Sir Hedley, giving the old farmer a searching look, 'I should like to give a very special thank-you to Tom Dwyer who managed to get Leanne to hospital in the nick of time.' There was more clapping.

Toby, who stood next to John Fairborn and his daughter, rubbed his bristly chin. 'I've sed it afore an' I'll say it agen, yon young schoolmester dun't let t'grass grow under 'is feet. Only been in t'village less than a year an' 'e's runnin' t'school, bought 'issen a nice little cottage, got well in wi' t'local MP an' vicar an' now 'e's local squire's blue-eyed boy. That lad could fall under a cow's arse in a coal mine an' climb out wi'out a mark on 'im.'

Janette looked over with amused affection to where Tom was standing in the middle of a crowd of noisy people. He was the centre of attention and laughing at something Sir Hedley was saying. How handsome he was. She now so regretted what she had said to him in this very room before she left for Nottingham, that she was fond of him but that there was no future for them. She knew now that it had been a mistake to leave the village; it had been a mistake to accept the manager's job in Nottingham and it had been a mistake to tell Tom that she was wanting more out of life, more challenge and more excitement, and that any sort of relationship would not have worked out. How true was the old proverb, she reflected, that 'absence makes the heart grow fonder'.

'An' now 'e's after courtin' that young lass from t'museum,' remarked Toby, breaking into her thoughts.

'I'm sorry, Mr Croft,' said Janette. 'What were you saying?'

'I was sayin' that Mester Dwyer's gone an' got hissen a new girlfriend, that good-looking lass from t'museum. They were in 'ere yesterday ovver in yon corner table carrying on like nob'dy's business.'

'Oh,' murmured Janette, with a sinking heart.

'Really?' said her father.

And on cue, the very person to whom Toby Croft was referring walked into the bar. Dr Merryweather waved at Tom before going to join him. She kissed him lightly on the cheek.

*

The following morning was mild and bright. Sir Hedley, in pensive mood, stood by the window in his study looking out over the vast parkland that stretched before him. Beyond were a scattering of grey farmhouses and hillside barns, endless criss-crossing dry-stone walls shining silver in the sunlight and two dark antique oaks of great size, gnarled by age. Patches of white cloud moved across the azure sky casting shadows on the ground below. He smiled on seeing a fox loping unhurriedly across the grass, his brush down and snout up, unafraid, unconcerned.

He had never felt quite so contented with life. The birth of his grandson had brightened up his world. He brushed a hand over his bristly moustache and felt happy to think of the future that lay ahead for the child and the future that lay ahead for him with Mrs Lister and his son living with him at Marston Towers. After the unhappiness he had endured in his married life, the rancour and arguments, he now felt a real sense of optimism. There was one thing, however, he had to do that day. He turned to his desk, picked up the receiver and telephoned Marcia's sister.

'Hello, Daphne Coulson,' came the strident voice down the line. 'May I help you?'

'It's me,' he said.

There was a short silence. 'I thought I made it clear to you, Hedley, the last time you telephoned, that Marcia does not wish to speak to you. Any communication should be through her solicitor. The last time you called it was very upsetting for her and put her in the most dreadful frame of mind. She wants—'

'I'm calling to let her know that she is a grandmother,' he broke in. 'Leanne had a baby boy last night. Eight pound and nine ounces. Mother and baby are doing well.'

'Oh.' There was a pause.

'I thought she might like to know,' he said.

'I'll tell her, not that I think she will be interested. The whole episode of James getting mixed up with a barmaid and the prospect of an illegitimate child has caused her a great deal of distress.' Sir Hedley decided not to respond; he knew it would be fruitless. 'Are you still there?' she shouted down the telephone.

'Yes, I am still here.'

'I shall tell her.' With that, she thumped down the receiver.

*

When the housekeeper brought in the morning coffee, she was all smiles.

'Congratulations, Sir Hedley,' she said, putting down the tray on his desk. 'I only heard the news from my Clive this morning before I came out of the house. Fancy, a little boy. He said Mr Midgley, who was in the King's Head when Leanne was rushed off to the hospital, told him she only got there in the nick of time, thanks to Mr Dwyer. I bet you are over the moon.'

'I am indeed over the moon, Mrs Gosling,' he said, getting up from his desk, 'and I am most grateful to Mr Dwyer for coming to the rescue.'

'And how are things?' she asked.

'The baby is a grand little lad and mother and baby are doing fine.'

'I shall have to get cracking with the knitting needles,' said the housekeeper. 'My sainted grandmother, Martha Gosling, God rest her soul, was a famous knitter and known as "the demon knitter of Risingdale". She started knitting when she was only four. Her Fair Isle gloves were the talk of the Dale and in great demand. They were extremely popular with the gentry. Your grandmother the old Lady Maladroit, God rest her soul, would not wear any others.'

'Yes, I recall she spoke highly of your grandmother's work. Now, I have something to tell you, Mrs Gosling,' said Sir Hedley. 'Would you take a seat, please?'

She did so and clasped her hands on her lap.

Sir Hedley returned to sit behind his desk and, pushing the tray to one side, rested his hands on the surface.

'You might have wondered why I asked Mrs Mossup and her daughter to visit me the other day. It was to tell them something that I have kept a secret for some time. Since Lady Maladroit left, my life has changed, and I felt it was about time that they needed to know. I think you should know too. It will soon become the talk of the village. I wanted you to be amongst the first to hear.' He studied his hands. 'This will, no doubt, come as a bit of a shock to you but, the thing is, I have been seeing Mrs Lister for quite some time now. In fact, I have been in a relationship with her for twelve years. We have been very discreet and only a very few people are aware of our liaison. It is my intention, when my impending divorce is finalised, to ask Mrs Lister to marry me and for her and our son to come and live here at Marston Towers. Charlie, by the way, is my son.'

Mrs Gosling remained quiet for a moment. 'I knew that, Sir Hedley,' she replied, unable to help sounding a little smug.

'You . . . you knew!' he gasped.

'Sir Hedley, I've known about you and Mrs Lister for don-key's years. My cottage is opposite hers in Rattan Row and I've seen you coming and going most Saturday nights.' What was the point, she had thought, of living in the centre of the village in a terraced cottage if she couldn't have a healthy curi-osity about her neighbours? 'And as for young Charlie,' she took up again, 'why, he looks just like you. The resemblance is obvious to those with eyes to see.'

'You have known all this time and said nothing?'

'Why should I say anything? I do not deal in tittle-tattle, Sir Hedley. You have treated me well. I like working for you and have always found you to be a decent and approachable employer who appreciates what I do. You are a real gentleman. I am certainly not going to spread any gossip about you. It's nobody else's business but your own.' Her words were ful-some but the tone and expression on her face were sincere.

'I'm very heartened to hear you say that,' he told her. 'You have been supremely tactful. I am most grateful. Thank you, Mrs Gosling.'

'You should drink your coffee, Sir Hedley,' she told him, adopting an almost wifely tone, 'it's getting cold.'

*

On leaving her husband, Lady Maladroit had gone to live with her sister Daphne in Chiswick. The flat was small, cramped, and cluttered and soon the two women found they were under each other's feet and both had become increasing-ly short-tempered with each other. Marcia's sister, who had lived quite happily alone since her divorce, found, after a few weeks, that another woman moving in with her came as an unwelcome change in her life. She had soon become exasperated with Lady Maladroit, who was melancholy company most of the time, forever complaining about her lot in life and how she had been treated so heartlessly. Since moving in, her sister took little care of her appearance and would rise late in the morning and come downstairs in her dressing gown, her hair hanging down loose and unbrushed. Furthermore, she was lazy and untidy and rarely lifted a finger to help around the apartment. Added to this was the galling fact that she was not paying for her upkeep. For her part, Lady Maladroit found her sister irritating with her constant grumbles about the messy state of the place and the cost of everything.

'Who was that?' Marcia asked now as she came down the stairs, still in her dressing gown. She had heard her sister speaking on the telephone.

'It was Hedley. He rang to ask me to tell you that the girl James got pregnant, that barmaid, has had a child, a baby boy.'

'Did he want to speak to me?'

'No, he just thought you needed to know. Anyway, I told him it would be of no interest to you.'

'And why did you tell him that?' demanded her sister loftily, looking squarely and urgently into her sister's eyes. Her voice was high and accusatory.

'Well, you have made it patently clear, on many occasions I may add, that you want nothing to do with the girl or her baby and you do not wish to speak to Hedley should he phone.'

'I should have spoken to him,' Lady Maladroit said abruptly.

Her sister rolled her eyes and sighed theatrically. 'You told me that if he called again you didn't want to speak to him.' She made a great effort to keep her voice calm. 'I do wish you would make up your mind.' Marcia opened her mouth to speak but her sister continued talking. 'And you ought to get dressed, it's gone ten in the morning.'

'I shall get dressed when I see fit,' her sister replied with undisguised coldness. 'I am not used to being given orders.'

'No, I guess not,' responded Daphne. 'As the Lady of the Manor I am sure you were used to giving orders rather than receiving them and having everyone cleaning up after you.' There was more than a hint of sarcasm in the tone of her reply. She was of a mind to add that she was not the Lady of the Manor in this flat but resisted the temptation.

Lady Maladroit went into the kitchen to make herself a drink, leaving Daphne standing by the window, irritated beyond measure. I shall have to say something, her sister said to herself. This situation could not continue.

'I like that special French blend of coffee,' came a voice from the other room. 'There's only that dreadful instant variety in here.'

Daphne gritted her teeth. Her reaction was one of incredulity and rage. She went into the kitchen and was about to suggest that her sister buy her own bloody coffee, but she thought better of it and bit her tongue. She breathed deeply to calm herself. 'Now look, Marcia—' she started.

'We are nearly out of milk,' her sister informed her. 'You will remember I only drink semi-skimmed. Oh, and could you get some marmalade – thick cut – when you next go shopping.'

'Now look, Marcia,' Daphne began again, 'this is not working.' She placed her hands on her hips. 'I assumed, when you asked me to take you in, that you would be staying with me for a few days and not setting up home here. Living together is not working out. Neither of us finds the situation at all satisfactory. You are treating my home like a hotel and me as one of your servants. Well, I cannot put up with it any more. You never lift a finger; you rarely leave the flat and do nothing with your days but sit and gaze blankly through the window sighing or complaining with a miserable expression on your face. Furthermore, you haven't offered to pay me a penny for your upkeep. I think you should look for somewhere else to stay.'

Marcia pressed her lips together in a tight thin line. 'You are throwing me out?' she said. 'I should have thought that my own sister would show a little more understanding and sympathy over what I have been going through.'

Daphne stiffened then drew a deep, exasperated breath.

'You perhaps have forgotten that I too have been through an acrimonious divorce,' stated her sister, 'but I have learnt to get on with my life and put all that behind me. You seem to enjoy being the victim.'

'That is most unkind. You can see how unhappy I am.'

'You are one of those people who cannot be happy any-where,' said her sister. 'Look, Marcia, I just think you should get a place of your own.'

'And pray how am I supposed to do that on the pittance Hedley allows me?' Her face was as hard as a diamond. 'When the divorce comes through, I shall be in a position to buy a place, but until then—'

She was cut off. 'Then I suggest you speak to your husband and explain the situation,' her sister told her. 'I am sure he will increase your allowance if you ask, certainly enough to rent a place. Hedley may be many things, Marcia, but he could never be accused of being ungenerous.' Before her sister could respond she headed for the door. 'Now I am meeting friends for coffee – ordinary variety, I may add – so I must go.'

When her sister had gone, Marcia wandered restlessly around the room, then stood at the window looking out at the jungle of rooftops on the cramped, miserable-looking houses that crowded around the flat. Below was a yard no bigger than a couple of doormats, some dead flowers in cracked pots and a line of dustbins. How different was this view from the drawing room at Marston Towers, she thought, with that vast panorama of parkland and fields. She had to get out of this claustrophobic apartment and decided, on a whim, to take a trip into the city. She smartened herself up and ordered a taxi (not wishing to travel on a crowded underground) and arrived at the art gallery where she had once worked as the personal assistant to the owner.

The exterior of Poskitt and Placket Fine Arts had changed little over the years. There were the same shiny burgundy window frames and the heavy door with the brass knocker. Marcia frowned with disapproval as she saw the large, framed watercolour in the window. It was a panoramic study of a Yorkshire dale by Amanda Stanhope, the artist who had spent some time in Risingdale and who had been commissioned to paint some views of the village and the surroundings. She had met the painter and had formed an instant dislike, finding her cold and stand-offish. The feeling was mutual, for Mrs Stanhope had found the Lady of the Manor 'frightful'.

The interior of the gallery had been refurbished and was now a minimalist space, bare save for a modern sculpture of an odd-shaped reclining figure and several contemporary prints and paintings displayed on the off-white walls. Behind a glass reception desk stood a smartly dressed young woman in a grey suit and cream silk blouse. She was fine-boned and petite.

'May I help you?' she asked pertly as Marcia stood before her. There was no trace of a smile. Her voice was as hard as crystal.

'I should like to see Mr Poskitt,' she was told. Marcia tilted her head back a fraction and looked down her nose.

'Have you an appointment?' She observed the visitor without blinking.

'No, I do not, but he will see me. Please tell him it is Lady Marcia Maladroit who wishes to speak to him.' She was surprised to feel that her heart was beating fast. She suddenly felt apprehensive over the coming reunion.

The young woman disappeared into an office. A moment later the owner of the gallery emerged. The years had been kind to Rupert Poskitt, for he had changed little. He was still the good-looking, trim figure with the full head of hair, now streaked with white, that Marcia remembered. He was taken aback at the sight of his visitor. His brow rose in surprise.

'Hello, Rupert,' she said.

'Marcia.' They stood for a time staring at each other. My goodness, he thought, how she has changed. His narrowed eyes examined her. She looked so gaunt; the lines on her face had hardened and those once bright eyes were now sunk further into their sockets. He gave her hand, which was extended, a perfunctory shake. 'You had better come through,' he responded awkwardly, giving an unconvincing smile. He turned to his assistant. 'Hold any calls, Araminta.'

'You won't forget you have Mr Constantine coming to see you this afternoon, Mr Poskitt,' the young woman at the reception desk reminded him.

'No, I haven't forgotten,' he replied.

'And that you are due at the Strand Gallery later for the opening of the Victoria Doherty exhibition.'

'Yes, I have remembered,' he told her. There was a tell-tale tightness in his voice.

In the office, Marcia sat in a soft leather chair, placed her handbag on her lap and crossed her legs. He took a seat behind his desk, shifted uncomfortably, and twisted a pencil in his fingers. The obviousness of his embarrassment served to embarrass his visitor. Neither spoke. Marcia stifled her disappointment at this cool reception.

'It's been quite a time,' he said at last.

'Yes, it has,' she agreed, looking into the green-grey eyes she remembered so well.

'Are you in London long?' he asked.

'I live here now,' she told him. 'I'm staying with my sister at the moment, but I intend to buy a place of my own once the divorce comes through.'

'Divorce?'

'Yes, I have left Hedley. I knew the marriage was a mistake after the first few weeks.'

'And yet you have stayed with him for over twenty years,' he remarked.

'It was convenient for me to do so,' she answered. 'We have both led separate lives.'

'So, what has decided you to leave him now?'

'Our son was killed in a car accident. It brought things to a head.'

'I'm sorry,' he said.

She was inclined to tell him that by 'our son' she meant his and hers, but then thought that this was not the time nor the place.

The receptionist poked her head around the door.

'Mr Constantine is here, Mr Poskitt,' she informed him.

'I'll just be a minute.' He got to his feet. 'You will have to forgive me, Marcia,' he said with the indication of bringing the visit to a close. 'I'm afraid your visit has come at an inconvenient time. This is a most important client, whom I really must see.'

She remained seated. Despite feeling disappointed and irritated by the cool reception, she managed a faint smile but there was a pained look in her eyes. 'Yes, I can see you are in demand as ever,' she said. 'Perhaps you may care to take me for lunch one day this week and we can catch up on old times.'

'Ah, er . . . that would be difficult,' he told her. 'I am so massively busy at the moment. Up to my eyes, in fact.'

'I'm sure you could spare one lunchtime,' she replied in a taut, artificial voice.

'The fact is, my diary is chock-a-block, I'm afraid,' he told her untruthfully. The flat tone of his voice indicated that he was keen for her to leave.

'I see,' she said coldly. The smile froze. 'Well, I must say that I expected a rather better reception.'

'Look, Marcia, I don't think meeting for lunch after all these years is such a good idea. Things have moved on for both of us. I feel we should let sleeping dogs lie. After all it's over twenty years since . . . since we . . .' His voice tailed off.

'You don't need to say any more, Rupert,' she interrupted, getting to her feet. 'You have made your position quite clear.'

The receptionist reappeared. 'Mr Constantine is getting impatient, Mr Poskitt,' she said.

'One minute,' he told her sharply. He ushered Marcia to the door. 'It is good to see you again,' he said unconvincingly. He shook her hand, hoping his clumsy lie was not too obvious. The smile was faked. She recognised a fake smile when she saw one. Those green-grey eyes – now appearing cold and distant – gave it away. 'I hope things work out well for you,' he added. With a jerk of her chin Lady Maladroit departed without replying.

When Marcia had gone, he returned to his desk, stretched back in his chair and folded his arms behind his head. He puffed out his cheeks and exhaled noisily. The last thing he wanted was this woman, with whom he had had a brief and unexceptional dalliance over twenty years ago, back in his life. He stood, straightened his silk tie and went to meet the client with a practised smile on his face.

'Do come in, Mr Constantine,' he said breezily.

*

Later that day, Marcia sat at a corner table in the café watching the people rushing by on the pavement outside. Her coffee remained untouched. She realised it had been a mistake to get in touch with Rupert after so long. She had not imagined for one moment that he would welcome her with open arms and that their momentary affair of years past would be re-kindled, but she had expected a warmer welcome. She had thought about him often over the years and had had an urge to see him again, but it was evident he did not wish to see her. Clearly unsettled and embarrassed by her appearance, he had made it obvious he wanted nothing to do with her. She re-called the time she had worked as Rupert's personal assistant, the position now occupied by the hard-faced Araminta, and had met her future husband. Sir Hedley Maladroit had come into the gallery to purchase a picture by an up-and-coming young artist. She noticed how deferential her employer was to this favoured patron and learnt later (having made it her business to find out) that this client was unmarried and was a wealthy and titled landowner with a large estate in the north of the country. When Sir Hedley made a return visit to the gallery, she turned on the charm, fluttering her eyelashes and exuding warmth. He had asked her to dine with him at one of the capital's most exclusive restaurants. This was the first of many assignations. She was flattered by his attentions and could tell he was clearly attracted to her. Of course, she told herself, she could never love this large, fleshy and red-faced man with the gloomy hooded eyes and protuberant ears, but the idea of a future of living in a stately home as a titled lady with a retinue of servants and every creature comfort, had an undeniable appeal. When the baronet asked her to be his wife, she wasted no time in accepting his proposal.

After the marriage, Marcia soon found living in a village in the middle of nowhere was not what she had expected. Ris-ingdale was so cloying and provincial and full of nosy, gossipy people. In no way could Marston Towers be described as a stately home. It was oppressive – cold, damp, and draughty

– and full of glowering portraits of the baronet's ancestors and a collection of stuffed animals. There was no retinue of servants, merely an ageing housekeeper whom she found ill-mannered and truculent. Her husband proved to be a great disappointment. He was boring company and preoccupied with estate matters in which she had no interest. The marriage went downhill. Life was full of endless arguments and recriminations and at times she couldn't stand the very sight of him. How different it was from her previous life. London had been so hectic and exciting – all the champagne receptions and stylish exhibitions, the parties, plush restaurants, and sophisticated people she met day-to-day. This had all ended when she married Sir Hedley and moved to the back-of-beyond in Yorkshire.

She had returned for a visit to London soon after her marriage and met up with her former boss. Rupert had invited her back to his stylish apartment in Chelsea and she had stayed the night. Nine months later their son had been born. She had often wondered if Hedley realised that the child was not his. After all, the boy bore not the slightest resemblance her husband.

Sitting now at the sticky-topped table in the café, she contemplated the empty, lonely days which lay ahead of her. She had no friends in London and it was unlikely that her sister would have time for her after their heated disagreement. The life at Marston Towers seemed to her preferable to this existence. Her thoughts were interrupted when a young waiter approached her. He had noticed this sad old lady at the corner table with the cold cup of coffee in front of her, staring vacantly out of the window. She had been there for nearly an hour.

'Are you all right, madam?' he asked, fingering his tight collar, and fiddling with his cuffs.

Marcia looked up. 'No, not really,' she replied.

7

At Monday morning break, Tom sat on the low wall that bordered the school. The sun shone brightly, and the air was alive with bird song. He stared at the vast landscape of rolling hills and rocky outcrops and watched two crested lapwings wheel and plunge in an empty blue sky. A proud pheasant strutted along a dry-stone wall. In neighbouring fields, lazy-looking sheep with slanting yellow eyes grazed, and lambs twitched their tails and jumped high in the spring sunshine. From a distant farmstead a corkscrew of smoke curled in the air. What school, he thought, could be set in such a beautiful environment as this?

His reverie was broken into by Carol, who jumped up to sit next to him. She dangled her thin legs before her and began swinging them backwards and forwards.

'Are you enjoying the view, Mr Dwyer?' she asked.

'Hello, Carol,' replied the teacher. 'I am indeed enjoying the view.'

'Them's our sheep,' she told him, pointing to the nearby field. 'We've done really well with lambing this year. It's been a record. My granddad's dead chuffed.'

Tom had met the girl's granddad when he had been out for a run one day and had liked the old farmer immediately. Mr Midgley was a short, thickset man with a face the colour and texture of leather which had been left out in the rain. He was inordinately proud of his granddaughter and had told Tom that she knew more about sheep than some graduate with a fancy degree from an agricultural college. Tom, in his various conversations with the girl had discovered this already.

'I've been busy helping my granddad with the birthing and marking and tagging the lambs,' said the girl. She nodded. 'I love this time of year.'

'And how's Lazarus?' he asked.

Lazarus was the oldest sheep in Mr Midgley's flock. The ram had been buried in a snowdrift and thought to be dead, but the ancient tup had, by some miracle, survived – hence his name. Most of the creature's teeth were missing and his eyesight was poor but, as Carol's granddad had explained, the old fellow was far from being past it when it came to tupping and in his time had served over a hundred ewes and produced some of the best lambs he had ever had.

'Lazarus is still alive and kicking,' the girl told Tom now, 'and has fathered a good few lambs this year and all of top quality. As I said, Mr Dwyer, granddad is well chuffed.'

'Lazarus is getting a bit long in the tooth, isn't he?' observed the teacher.

'Not at all, Mr Dwyer,' replied the girl. 'Granddad says it's the oldest oven that gets hot the fastest.'

Tom laughed. 'And what about that sheepdog of yours?' he asked.

Carol's grandfather had bought a collie from Mr Gosling. Toby Croft had bought the dog first, but he took her back reckoning she was no good. Trained by Mr Midgley, however, she had become a fine working sheepdog.

'She's champion is Meg,' answered the girl. 'My granddad reckons she's the best we've had. There isn't a wall she can't jump or a beck she can't cross or a hill she can't climb, and she rounds up the sheep a treat.'

'I suppose for a collie all this is second nature,' remarked Tom.

'Oh no, Mr Dwyer,' she said. 'Every sheepdog has a different temperament – a bit like people, really. Some collies are too keen, others are too lazy, some get jealous of other dogs and become snappy and others just don't take to shepherding at all, but Meg is the best.'

'She certainly sounds it,' said Tom.

The girl thought for a moment. 'Mr Dwyer,' she said at last, 'could I ask you something?'

'Yes, of course,' Tom told her.

'Have you a girlfriend?'

'That's a very personal question, Carol,' replied the teacher.

'Well, have you?'

'If you must know, I don't.'

'Why?'

'Because I haven't met the right young woman yet. Now no more questions.'

The girl was not dissuaded. 'Well, you're not that bad look-ing and you have quite a nice personality,' she said.

Damned with faint praise, thought Tom, smiling.

'That's kind of you to say that but—' began the teacher.

'That lady who came from the museum to talk to us, she liked you a lot,' announced the girl. 'Everyone in the class could tell.'

'Ah, there's George,' said Tom, seeing one of his pupils heading his way. It was a good opportunity to put an end to Carol's interrogation. 'Now, run along young lady and no more personal questions.' The teacher called out to the boy, 'Could I have a word with you, George?'

Tom was joined on the wall by the boy. The pupil had a hangdog expression on his face and his hands were dug deep into his pockets.

'Are you all right, George?' asked the teacher. 'You were noticeably quiet in class this morning.'

The boy removed a hand, pushed back the black curls from his face and sighed as if the weight of the world was on his young shoulders.

'I'm not that champion, Mester Dwyer, if truth be telled,' he replied, shaking his head.

'Trouble at the farm again?' he was asked.

'Aye, summat like that,' replied George.

The previous term the boy's father had bought a fine-looking Belgian Blue bull they called Sampson, perfect, or so he thought, for breeding. Unfortunately, the massive creature had, as George had explained to Tom, 'been firing blanks' and ended up at the knacker's yard. Now there appeared to be a further problem.

'I'm sorry to hear that you have had another setback,' said the teacher. 'Do you want to tell me what's happened?'

The boy gave a careworn, spontaneous sigh. 'We lost a calf last week. Mi dad reckoned it would 'ave been a reight good milker an' all, good udder texture, but it were dead inside o' t'cow.'

'Oh dear.'

''E 'ad to call t'vet to gerrit out. Mi dad wun't let me go into t'barn to see it. 'E said it wun't be a pretty sight. T'vet sed cow 'ad to be given what she called "a fetotomy" an' be removed piece by piece.'

'Piece by piece?'

'Aye, chopped up like.'

Tom gave a shudder and drew his breath through his teeth making a sort of hissing noise. 'I see,' he muttered. 'I can see it wouldn't be a very pleasant thing to see.'

'Well, tha knaas, Mester Dwyer, there are lots o' things on a farm townsfolk wun't want to see but farmers 'ave to deal wi' 'em. That's t'way it is.'

'Yes, I can appreciate that,' replied Tom.

'An' as I sed to mi dad, if I'm gonna tek over t'farm one day, I need to know abaat these things.'

'I suppose so.'

'Anyroad, I did see it.'

'You did?'

'Aye, I did. There were a knot 'ole in t'barn an' I peeked through. It were reight interestin'.'

Not a word which readily springs to mind, thought Tom. 'Gruesome' might be a more apt adjective.

'T'vet used this piece o' wire wi' sooart o' teeth on,' continued George, 'an' sawed off t'dead calf's 'ead an' then—'

Tom cut in. 'Too much information, George,' he told the boy. 'I think I've got the idea without you carrying on.'

'T'dead calf weren't t'end to it though,' continued the boy.

'Oh yes,' said the teacher, preparing himself for another grisly account.

'We lost two sheep yesterday. One of 'em ramblers must 'ave left yat oppen in t'top field an' two o' t'yows gor out an' ended up in t'beck an' both of 'em 'eavy wi' lambs. It were me what found 'em. Drowned they were, floatin' on top o' t'water. Then one of our cows 'ad a torn teat an' we 'ad to send for t'vet. Aye, as mi dad sez, it's been one thing after t'other lately.'

'That's dreadful, George,' said Tom. 'Your father must be distraught.'

'Aye, 'e were none too chuffed, if truth be telled,' said the lad, 'but as 'e allus sez when things gu wrong, there's nowt tha can do abaat it, thy 'as to tek rough wi' t'smooth, it's no use cryin' ovver a calf we never saw. It dun't 'elp to gu mitherin'.'

'Well, that is a very admirable attitude to take,' Tom told the boy.

'That's what t'vet telled 'im. She reckoned 'e were tekkin' things very well, considerin'.'

'She was right,' granted Tom.

The boy sucked in his bottom lip and thought for a moment. 'Aye, when things gu wrong mi dad dun't mek a fuss abaat it. 'E sort o' shrugs. "Shit 'appens," 'e sez.'

'Yes,' said Tom. 'I guess it does.'

During the time the teacher had lived in Yorkshire he had come to appreciate and admire the resilience of the farmers and their stoical acceptance of the setbacks which they frequently had to face. He had also become accustomed to the farming children's blunt turn of phrase.

*

'I want to see the headmaster,' barked the visitor crossly. He was a short, thick-necked individual with a nose as heavy as a turnip and large, heavy-lidded eyes. He had marched through the office door and glared down at Mrs Leadbeater.

The school secretary, who was mid-way through typing a letter, slowly removed her unfashionable horn-rimmed spectacles and stared up at the visitor with a glacial expression.

'Would you mind lowering your voice,' she told him. 'I do not have a hearing problem.'

'Eh?'

'I am not deaf.'

'I said I want to see the headmaster,' repeated the man, his voice surly and impatient.

'I heard you the first time,' she replied, retaining her stony countenance.

'Well, can you tell him I want to see him?'

'No, I can't.'

'What?'

'He's out.'

'When will he be back?'

'I don't know.'

'Then I'll speak to Mr Dwyer.'

'He's in a lesson.'

'I need to see him.'

'Not when he's teaching.'

'Look, I need to see him.'

'What about?'

'That's no concern of yours,' the man told her, his eyes bulging beneath the heavy lids. 'I'm not discussing a personal matter with *you*.'

Mrs Leadbeater replaced her spectacles and examined the half-typed letter on her desk. She breathed out audibly. 'Then I suggest you call back another time when Mr Gaunt will be available to speak to you and I advise you to make an appointment. Now, I have work to do.'

The bell sounded for afternoon break. The man stormed out of the school office in search of Mr Dwyer. He found the teacher halfway down the corridor on his way to the staffroom.

'Hang on!' the man shouted, 'I want a word with you.'

Tom turned around. 'Mr Pickles,' he said. 'What can I do for you?'

'I've come in to see you about what you told our Christopher last Friday,' said the parent, raising his voice. 'He come home after school in a right state. He said you won't let him play football in the match next Saturday.'

'That's right,' admitted Tom calmly.

He had come across this belligerent parent before when he had arrived at the school to complain about Colin Greenwood giving his son a bloody nose.

'Well, it's not on!' shouted the angry parent. 'He has his heart on playing in that match.'

'I presume Christopher told you why I have banned him from playing?'

'Something about not doing his homework.'

'That's right,' said Tom, remaining unruffled. 'It was the second time your son has come to school without completing his homework,' Tom told him. 'He was warned that should it happen again, he would miss the next football match. It was to teach him the lessons that he cannot continue to disobey me and that I mean what I say. I hope that explains things.'

Tom had retained his composure during his response. He had learnt from the head teacher of the school where he had trained, and from Mr Gaunt, that the best method for a teacher to deal with an antagonistic parent was to simply remain calm and agreeable and appear most attentive until the person had got things off his or her chest and became silent. It was a clever and disarming technique and a powerful way to overcome hostility. However, it did not seem to be working that afternoon, for the man was far from mollified. He became redder in the face, continued to raise his voice, and then started stabbing the air with a stubby finger.

'The lad forgets to do a bit of work,' he shouted, 'and you punish him by stopping his football. It's over the top. As I said, it's just not on.'

'Christopher was given a warning, Mr Pickles, and if he chose to ignore it, then he must suffer the consequences.'

'So, you're not letting him play?'

'No, I am not.'

'Now look—' began the parent.

At this point Joyce appeared from the staffroom. She was dressed in a red and black tight-fitting dress, black stockings, and ridiculously high-heeled patent leather shoes. Her make-up was flawless. She approached the two men, her high heels clacking on the floor.

'There's an awful lot of noise down here,' she said, fluttering her long black lashes. 'Whatever is the matter?' She looked at the parent. 'Is there something wrong, Mr Pickles?'

The man's expression changed. It was like a miracle. All the belligerence had seeped out of him. His face softened and his bluster disappeared.

'Oh, Miss Tranter,' he said, lowering his voice. 'I was speaking to Mr Dwyer about Christopher not being allowed to play in the football match next Saturday. I think it's very unfair.'

'Unfair?' repeated Joyce, with another flutter of her eye-lashes.

'And I was telling Mr Pickles that it was a punishment for his son for not doing his homework,' explained Tom.

Joyce moved a little closer to the parent. He could smell the expensive perfume. 'You know, Mr Pickles,' she said, 'it really is so important that the pupils do their homework. If they do not, it holds back their academic development. I am sure you want your son to do well at school.'

'Well, yes I do but—'

'Now, when Christopher was in my class,' she continued, 'I recall that he had ambitions to become a vet.'

'A vet? I didn't realise that,' said Mr Pickles, sounding genuinely surprised.

'I know he has a strong rapport with animals,' said Joyce.

'Has he?' asked the boy's father. His son had never shown much interest in animals, in fact he frequently complained about having to help his father with the cows and sheep on the farm.

'Of course,' continued Joyce, resting a hand on the parent's arm, 'Christopher would need the necessary qualifications to go to university, which I gather have to be of a very high standard for him to study veterinary science. I am afraid that if he does not apply himself to his schoolwork there is little chance of him realising his dream. I appreciate that he is keen on his football, but he has to learn a lesson, Mr Pickles, that if he does not complete his studies then there will be consequences.' She fluttered he eyelashes again. 'I am sure you agree.'

During this monologue, Tom had remained silent with an open mouth.

'Well, if you put it like that, Miss Tranter,' said the parent, 'I can see the sense in what you say. I suppose I was overreacting a bit. He wants to be a vet, does he?' He nodded. 'I never

knew that.' He looked at Joyce. 'Well, I reckon his football will
have to take second place to his schoolwork.'

'I so agree,' said Joyce.

'Thank you, Miss Tranter,' he said. 'I'll wish you good
morning,' and, ignoring Tom, he left the school.

'That was quite a performance,' Tom told his colleague.

'I am a trained actress, after all,' Joyce told him. 'May I offer
you a bit of advice, Tom?'

'Yes, of course.'

'If you wish to make confrontational parents pay attention,
don't raise your voice.'

'Actually, I didn't—' he started to say.

'In my experience,' his colleague continued, 'speaking
quietly to stroppy parents like Mr Pickles is a sure way of
commanding their attention.'

Tom shook his head and smiled.

'And what's this about Christopher Pickles wanting to be
a vet?' he asked. 'It's the first I've heard about it. He's always
complaining that he hates it on his father's farm.'

Joyce gave a small shrug and raised a carefully plucked eyebrow.

'Yes, it was the first time I had heard he wanted to be a vet
as well – until a few minutes ago when I thought of it,' she
said.

*

The following day Joyce was not in such a good mood. Tom
was always the last to leave the school at the end of the day
but that afternoon, as the children made their way home, he
discovered his colleague at her desk looking vacantly through
the classroom window.

He popped his head around her classroom door.

'Penny for them,' he said.

'Oh, hello, Tom,' she replied, turning to him. Her face was etched in an expression of anguish, giving the impression that she had received some bad news.

'You're usually away by this time.'

'Yes, well, I didn't feel like going home at present.'

'Something wrong?' he asked.

'You could say that. Julian and I have had a bit of a falling out.'

'I don't think it's unusual for a married couple to have a few disagreements,' he tried to reassure her. 'Marriage is not all plain sailing – or so I've been told. I'm sure it will soon blow over.'

'I wish I were that sure,' she replied.

Mr Leadbeater appeared at the classroom door. He jangled a heavy bunch of keys. 'Are you two ready to get off home?' he asked. 'It's just that I want to lock up. I've got a darts match tonight.'

'Thanks, Bob,' Tom answered. 'We're just about ready. If you could just give us a minute.'

The caretaker sighed, made a sort of grunting noise, and departed.

'Look, we can't talk here,' Tom told Joyce. 'Would you like to come back with me for a cup of tea and get things off your chest?'

'Yes, I would,' she answered. 'I need to talk to somebody about it otherwise I'll go mad.'

Tom, with the help of a loan from Mr Gaunt, had bought Roselea Cottage from Mrs Golightly, who wished to down-size. She had moved into the apartment block on the Clayton Road where Joyce had lived prior to her marriage. When he heard the property, five minutes' walk from the centre of the village, was up for sale, he imagined a small country cottage in honey-coloured stone with a yellow thatched roof, roses around the door, the sort one sees on picture postcards or on the front of tins of biscuits. He was soon disabused when he saw the rather unattractive red-brick building with the sagging roof, which had clearly been neglected. There was much to do to get it into some sort of shape. However, the spectacular vista from Roselea won him over and he bought the place. Over the weeks, Tom had partly refurbished the interior and tamed the garden.

The sitting room of the cottage could hardly be described as cosy. The dispiriting cream-coloured walls were bare save for prints of the castle at Oranmore and a view over the Burren in Galway and two watercolours by Colin Greenwood of Marston Castle and the barn at Bentley Beck, gifts from his pupil. There was an old pine bookcase, the shelves stacked with paperbacks, a rather shabby chintz-covered sofa with mismatched cushions, an old leather armchair, faded plum-coloured brocade curtains, a threadbare kilim rug and a dark wood occasional table. On the mantelpiece were a few photographs and a couple of matching brass candlesticks. An ornate, gilt-framed mirror propped up against a wall looked incongruous.

'I can see that this is a single man's house,' said Joyce when she glanced around the cottage sitting room later that afternoon.

'I'm afraid I'm not that good at interior design,' Tom called from the kitchen, where he was making the tea, 'and anyway, I can't afford anything more stylish for the present. Some of the stuff was left by Mrs Golightly but most of it I got from charity shops. My Auntie Bridget gave me the mirror and Father Daly the old leather chair.'

'I live in this huge house full of heavy, overbearing antique furniture, thick velvet drapes at the windows, dusty rugs and stacked with antiques,' Joyce told him. 'It's like a museum. It hardly gets any light. I wish Julian and I could get somewhere like this, but he won't consider moving.'

Tom brought in two mugs of tea and placed them on a small table. Then he sat with Joyce by the widow.

She stared at the panorama that stretched before her.

'It's such a lovely outlook,' she said. 'I'd love a view like this.'

'That's what persuaded me to buy the cottage,' he told her.

They sat a while in silence.

'So, what's the problem at home?' Tom asked.

'Stanley,' said Joyce, picking up a mug. She cupped her hands around it and took a sip, then put it back on the table.

'Stanley?'

'Julian's nephew.' She shook her head and heaved a sigh. 'He's come to live with us, and I cannot put up with it. My dear husband is wishing to wind down and, without asking if I agreed, decided to invite his nephew Stanley to help manage the business and for him to live with us. I arrived home last week to find this . . . this . . . cuckoo in the nest installed in the drawing room with a glass of whisky and his feet on a footstool, looking like he was part of the furniture.' She pictured the barrel-shaped, paunchy little man with the receding chin, thin plastered-down carrot-coloured hair over a bald pink scalp and watery-blue eyes, who had made himself at home. He reminded her of a Russian doll with six smaller versions of himself inside each other.

'You mean this nephew is going to live with you permanently?' asked Tom.

'I sincerely hope not,' Joyce lamented. '"Well," said my husband, "this is a big house with plenty of rooms and it seems sensible to have Stanley stay here with us rather than him having to rent a flat or stay in a hotel." I was livid. The appearance of his nephew has cast a shadow over my relationship with Julian. He obviously assumes that I will do the cooking and cleaning, the washing and ironing not just for him but for his nephew as well, in addition to holding down a full-time job. What would suit him, of course, is that I give up my career and help with the business or be the little woman who stays at home and deals with all the domestic duties. I guess that is what his last wife had to put up with. Well, I am not going to fit in with what Julian wants. My first husband tried to control me; I am certainly not going to let my second go down the same path. I do not intend any man to manipulate me again. Do you think I am overreacting?'

Tom gave a hollow laugh. 'Overreacting! Not at all. You've only been married a few weeks and you get a lodger. It is totally unreasonable.'

'Well, I think so, but when I raised the matter with Julian, he said it was me who was being unreasonable. He was quite sharp with me last night.'

'I'm so sorry, Joyce,' said Tom.

'What do I do?' she asked.

'In my opinion, for what it is worth,' he said, 'I should make the nest in which the cuckoo has established himself not quite as agreeable as he would like. I think you should put your foot down about the washing and ironing, cooking, and cleaning. I am not suggesting you be unpleasant or difficult but make it clear that you are not prepared to be the skivvy. You were a professional actress and are a spirited and independent woman, as well as a well-regarded and experienced teacher. I'm sure you can adopt the appropriate role.'

'You're right,' she said, looking a whole lot more cheerful. 'I shall start as I mean to go on.' She smiled at her colleague. 'You know, you would be good as a marriage guidance counsellor.'

Later that evening, when Joyce had gone, there was a knock on the cottage door. Tom found Dr Merryweather on the doorstep. She was dressed in a stylish pale green linen suit with cream silk scarf tied neatly round her neck. She looked particularly attractive. There was the fragrance of perfume in the air.

'Oh hello,' he said.

'May I come in?' she asked.

'Yes, of course.'

'I hope you don't mind me calling unannounced. I thought I would drop off the ticket for my lecture next week.'

The ticket could have been left at the door of the museum to be collected on the night, thought Tom, but he didn't say as much. It had been a tiring day at school, and he was not keen on visitors. He had been looking forward to a quiet evening in with a book.

He gestured to a chair. 'Do sit down.'

She sat on the sofa. 'It looks very neat and tidy in here,' she said, thinking what a plain and uninviting environment it was with the old furniture, faded curtains and bare walls.

'There's still much to do,' he replied. 'As I was saying to a friend, I'm afraid I'm not the best person in the world to know anything about interior design.'

'What you need is a woman's touch,' she told him, tilting her head to one side and smiling.

'You may be right,' he replied.

'Don't you have a television?' she asked.

'No, I've not got around to buying one yet. In fact, I might not bother. I don't miss a TV. There seems so little on I want to watch – programmes about antiques and cooking, game shows and police dramas.' He changed the subject. 'So how did you find out where I lived?' He sat opposite her in the leather armchair which had seen better days.

'I called in at the King's Head,' she told him. 'There was an elderly gentleman at the bar who was most helpful. He gave me directions.'

'That would be Toby Croft,' Tom said.

'I didn't get his name, but he was most informative. He told me all about you.'

'Yes, I bet he did,' Tom muttered.

'He said you have made quite an impression in Rising-dale since you came to live in the village and teach at the village school. He told me you had caught a gang of thieves red-handed trying to steal lead from the village church—'

'It was two men, actually,' corrected Tom, 'and I didn't catch them, I just happened to see them and contacted the police.'

'And didn't you come to the aid of the local MP when his car ran out of petrol?'

'Anyone would have done the same.'

'And you got into a fight with the son of the local squire – the one who was killed.'

'Just a bit of a misunderstanding.'

'And you also saved the day, didn't you, by taking that young woman who was about to give birth to the hospital? You were quite the hero.'

Tom held up a hand. 'I think I've heard quite enough about my exploits,' he said. 'Toby Croft is a great gossip and a story-teller. He seems to have given you a blow-by-blow account of my life.'

'It sounds a very interesting life,' she said. 'Well, now I am here, I thought we might go for a drink in the King's Head.' She looked at him with pleasurable anticipation.

'Ah . . . no . . . I can't I'm afraid,' he told her. 'I have to pre-pare my lessons for tomorrow, and I have a stack of marking.'

'I'm sure you can leave that for an hour,' she persisted.

'No, really I can't. I have so much to do.'

'Are you sure I can't tempt you?'

'Yes, quite sure.'

'Oh well,' she said, 'perhaps we can go for a drink after my lecture next week.'

Tom stood. 'Yes, that would be . . . er . . . nice,' he replied.

She got to her feet, leaned towards him and kissed him lightly on the cheek.

'I'll hold you to that,' she said, smiling.

When Dr Merryweather had gone, Tom slumped into the chair and ran his fingers through his dark hair in an exasperated gesture. It was clear she had designs on him. He rested his head on the back. 'Oh dear,' he said aloud. 'How do I get out of this one?'

8

When Joyce arrived home later that afternoon, she found her husband and his nephew in the drawing room. They were laughing. She winced as she heard Stanley's high-pitched nasal voice. His presence was like a sharp stone in her shoe, irritating and impossible to ignore. Having hung up her coat, she studied herself in the hall mirror, arranged her hair, adopted a fixed smile, and went to join them.

'Something has amused you both,' she said, entering the room.

'Oh, there you are, Joyce,' said Julian. 'We were wondering where you had got to.'

She noticed the nephew was comfortably installed in an easy chair with an infuriating half-smile on his round face. He held a glass of whisky.

'I had lessons to prepare and books to mark,' she fibbed. 'So, have you both had a fruitful day at the saleroom?'

'Yes, indeed,' said her husband, sitting up in his chair and becoming animated. 'Stanley here is a natural when it comes to auctioneering.'

'Really?'

'He has managed to sell a particularly ugly oak dresser that we have had on display for a few months with no takers. It had not reached its reserved price in previous auctions but at today's sale Stanley knocked up the bidding like a seasoned auctioneer, outlining its desirability and explaining its provenance. We were laughing about the sale when you came in. Poor man has been on his feet all day.'

'Yes, so have I,' said Joyce indignantly before sitting down.

'I don't know how you put up with a load of screaming kids all day,' remarked Stanley, stretching back in his chair. His pudgy face creased into a grin. 'I know I certainly couldn't do it.' He took a mouthful of his drink.

Joyce maintained a blank expression, making a great effort to hide her irritation. 'No, I guess not,' she answered. 'It takes a certain sort of person to teach. As for a load of screaming kids, the children in my class are very well behaved and amenable. Indeed, when we had a school inspection, the HMI applauded the good behaviour of my pupils and commended me on my excellent class control.'

'I have suggested that Joyce might like to give up teaching,' Julian told his nephew, hardly listening to what she had said. 'I mean, it's not that we need the money and—'

'And as I have told your uncle,' cut in Joyce, looking at Stanley, 'I have no intention of doing so. I enjoy my job and intend to continue in it. I'm not the sort of woman to stay at home all day.' She stroked an eyebrow.

'An independent woman,' chortled Stanley.

'Yes, I am,' agreed Joyce. She turned to her husband. 'May I have a drink, please, Julian?'

'Yes, yes, of course,' he said. 'I'll get you a sherry.'

'Something a bit stronger, I think,' she told him. 'I've had a hard day. A gin and tonic, please. Make it a large one, will you, darling.' She directed her attention back to Julian's nephew. 'But enough about me; tell me about yourself, Stanley.'

'About me?'

'Yes.'

'There's not a lot to tell,' he replied, placing down his whisky.

'Oh, I am sure there is.' She took her drink.

He gave a vapid smile. 'Not really.'

'You are not married, I take it?' asked Joyce, taking a sip.

'No, no, I never got around to it,' he answered, sitting up.

'Never found the right woman,' she said.

'Something like that,' he replied. He rotated his thumbs slowly around one another and stared into space. His demeanour had changed from the relaxed and grinning figure Joyce had seen when she had first come into the room. He felt uncomfortable.

'You will discover it will be a big change up here in the middle of the country compared to life in buzzing London,' Joyce remarked before taking another sip of her drink. 'None of the night life, the fancy restaurants, the museums, and the theatres. We are rather parochial and set in our ways.'

'Oh, I'm sure I shall be very settled here,' he replied. 'To be honest, I got increasingly tired of living in the capital with all the hustle and bustle and I'm not a theatre person anyway or one for the night life. Dusty museums don't interest me either. The commuting really got me down, crammed like sardines onto a tube train without a seat with an armpit in your face and people blowing down your neck. And it was full of foreigners. Sometimes you never heard a word of English. I shall not miss London and shall enjoy breathing the fresh country air instead of petrol fumes.'

'Julian was telling me you used to work for an investment firm in the City,' she said. 'It sounds an extremely exciting and challenging job.'

'Yes, er . . . that's right, something along those lines,' he answered.

'Financial director, that sort of thing?' He did not respond. 'And now you have moved up here, have you sold your house in London?'

'Oh, I don't have a house,' he told her. 'I have a flat in the east of the city.' He shifted uneasily in the chair.

'So, you have sold your flat, then?' Joyce enquired.

'Actually, I rented it,' he replied. He thought for a moment of the damp and poky ground-floor apartment he had not been able to afford.

'I should have thought that someone in high finance in London would have invested in a property.'

Julian, feeling embarrassed with the interrogation of his nephew, rose from his chair and rubbed his hands.

'Well, I think we might have another drink prior to dinner,' he said.

'That would be nice,' said Joyce, a smile fixed upon her face. She took a gulp of her drink and passed him her empty glass.

At dinner, Joyce maintained the role of the sociable and entertaining hostess, chattering away inconsequentially and continuing to smile. The more she probed about Stanley's life in London, the more ill at ease he became and the more he evaded revealing very much about his life. She soon had the measure of him. He was no financial whiz. He was just a dull, ineffectual, self-important man who imagined working for his wealthy uncle would be to his advantage.

Joyce had prepared a lasagne the evening before and prior to calling Julian and Stanley to the table, she sprinkled salt and pepper liberally over half of the dish. When sharing out the pasta, she was careful to give herself that part of the meal free of condiments but served her husband and his nephew a generous salty portion. She watched with satisfaction as they both tried to consume the inedible concoction.

'This was one of the dishes Julian's first wife used to cook,' said Joyce gleefully. 'I do hope mine has come up to scratch.'

'I think I need a glass of water,' said Stanley, spluttering, as he got up from the table.

'It's very tasty, my dear,' Julian told his wife tactfully, moving the pasta around his plate with a fork, 'but just a tad on the salty side, don't you think?'

'I do tend to overdo the condiments,' admitted Joyce blithely. 'For my part, I am partial to spicy food. Wait until you sample my curry.'

Having finished her meal, leaving an empty plate, she dabbed her lips on a napkin and rose from the table.

'Well, I have my preparations for tomorrow,' she said. 'I am sure you both have lots of business to discuss so I will leave you to it. Perhaps you might like to load the dishwasher, Stanley.' She turned to her husband. 'Oh, and by the way, darling, I shall be out tomorrow night and will get a bite to eat in Clayton. I have the auditions for the next production I am directing at the Civic Theatre.' She looked at Julian's nephew. 'Unlike you, Stanley, I love the theatre. I was a professional actress in an earlier life.' She felt pleased with her performance that evening. 'You will find plenty of food in the fridge or perhaps you might rustle something up. I guess living by yourself, you must have become something of a dab hand in the kitchen.'

Joyce felt a little guilty about adopting such a stratagem but then, as she told herself, such measures were necessary to induce the cuckoo to take flight and leave the nest.

'I don't think Stanley feels all that settled here, my dear,' said Julian to his wife later that evening in the bedroom. He sat on the edge of the bed and watched her at her dressing table busily applying cold cream to her face.

'Oh,' she said, sounding deliberately surprised and not turning to face him. 'Has he said something?'

'Not in so many words, but I am sure he feels you aren't entirely happy about him staying with us.'

She turned to face her husband. 'Well, as I told you when you asked him to stay – without consulting me – I am not *entirely* happy about your nephew living with us. How would any wife feel if a lodger moved in after just a few weeks of her marriage?'

'Stanley is not a lodger, Joyce,' retorted Julian. 'He happens to be my only blood relation.'

Tension built up in the room.

'I have been most accommodating and not said anything disagreeable to Stanley – or has he said otherwise?'

'No, no, not at all. It's just that I have this feeling that you don't like him,' said Julian. 'I thought that your cross-examination of him was rather pointed.'

'I was merely trying to get to know him,' she answered indifferently.

'It appeared to me that you resent his presence.'

'I think I need to make things clear, Julian,' she told him with a touch of steel in her voice. 'I *do* resent his presence and I will add, I do not intend to clean and cook, wash and iron for your nephew as well as for you. I am not a domestic appliance. I have a career that I like, and I am not giving it up to be a house servant.' She turned back to the dressing table and began removing the cream.

'I see,' he murmured.

'I'm pleased you do,' she replied with a hint of triumph in her voice.

*

Mrs Sloughthwaite, the proprietor of the Barton-in-the-Dale village store, was a round, red-faced woman with a large, fleshy nose, pouchy cheeks and a great bay window of a bust. Like a squirrel hoarding nuts she would seek out and store any interesting titbits from those who patronised her shop. Thus, she knew everything that there was to know in the village and gathered gossip with the speed of light. Those wishing to keep up to date with the news and rumours only had to call into the shop to receive a detailed and colourful account of the latest happening or hear a fascinating fact about someone's personal life. Mrs Sloughthwaite was utterly incapable of holding her tongue on any subject of general interest so the locals who patronised her shop were very selective in

what they told her, aware that she was a walking encyclopae-
dia of gossip.

The shopkeeper stopped mid-sentence when Tom walked
through the door on Saturday morning. She was in an animated conversation with a smartly dressed, elderly man of
military bearing with red cheeks, a bristly moustache and
greying short-cropped hair. At the sight of the young teacher,
she raised her substantial bosom and chubby arms from the
counter where they had been resting and her face lit up.

'Well, well, look who has walked in,' she said amiably. 'We
were just talking about you,'

'Good morning, Mrs Sloughthwaite,' said Tom. 'Good
things, I hope.'

'Beg pardon?'

'I hope you were not taking my name in vain,' he told her
pleasantly.

'Beggar the thought,' she replied. 'I was just telling the
major here about the new incompetent at St Christopher's
who's upset half his congregation.'

'Incumbent,' corrected the major. 'Mr Cherry is the incumbent, not the incompetent. An incompetent is someone unable to perform his function.'

'Well, a lot of people think he is an incompetent,' she said. 'He's
banned people throwing confetti at weddings, told Mrs Fish, the
church organist, to speed up when she plays the hymns, and her
with arthritical hands and a bad hip, cut down on the Sunday
services and he's stopped the kiddies playing in the graveyard.
And they say his sermons could put a glass eye to sleep.'

Mrs Sloughthwaite was a woman famous for her memorable malapropisms and amazingly inventive non sequiturs.
When the vicar in Barton-in-the-Dale was elevated to the
position of archdeacon, assuming the designation of the
'venerable', to the amusement of her customers she referred
to the cleric as the 'venereal'.

'I've been told people call him the incompetent,' retorted Mrs Sloughthwaite. 'And it seems to me that it fits the bill from what I've heard.'

'I think you do the reverend gentleman a grave disservice, Mrs Sloughthwaite,' retorted the major. 'In my dealings with Mr Cherry, as a fellow governor at the village school, I have found him to be highly literate, most intelligent and always most congenial.'

'That's as may be, but he wants to smarten himself up,' said Mrs Sloughthwaite. 'When Reverend Atticus was the vicar, he was always well turned out. Mr Cherry wants to get his hair cut and stop wearing that crumpled hassock.'

'Cassock,' muttered the major.

Tom, finally managing to get a word in, turned to the customer. 'Good morning, major.'

'And a good morning to you, Mr Dwyer,' the man replied.

'So, what has the new vicar got to do with me?' he asked.

'I was mentioning you earlier to Mrs Sloughthwaite with regard—'

'Course, you know Major Neville-Gravitas, don't you, Mr Dwyer?' the shopkeeper stepped in. 'He was Chairman of Governors, here at the village school where you trained as a teacher.'

'Yes, of course, we know each other,' the customer told her testily. He turned to Tom. 'I was mentioning you earlier to Mrs Sloughthwaite—' he began again.

'And you did very well when you were training to be a teacher, didn't you, Mr Dwyer?' she cut in. 'You ended up matriculated and fully certified.' She glanced at the major. 'Everyone at the school said it was a crying shame you weren't offered a permeant position.'

'Well, of course, we should have really liked to have offered Mr Dwyer a *permanent* position,' said the major, with a growing sense of irritation in his voice, 'and indeed the head teacher was most enthusiastic about appointing him, but we were constrained by the Education Department to employ those teachers who needed to be redeployed from the schools which were closing. In that matter our hands were tied. I am sure that Mr Dwyer is fully aware of this.'

'I'm sure if you, being Chairman of the Governors, had put your foot down and precipitated, they would have agreed,' she told him.

The major closed his eyes briefly, looking pained. When he opened them again a twitch had appeared in the right eye. He decided not to respond. Later, when he recalled the conversation, he kicked himself for having felt it necessary to justify things to the shopkeeper. It was really none of her business, he thought, but of course, being the inquisitorial woman she was, she made it her business like everything else that happened in the village.

'Actually, things have turned out for the best,' Tom came in quickly, before Mrs Sloughthwaite could get in another word. 'I'm very happy at Risingdale School.'

'That is good to hear,' said the major. 'Now, meeting you this morning—'

'Mind you, it's a bit out of the way up there insulated at the top of the Dale,' said the shopkeeper, 'I should have thought—'

'Now, meeting you this morning,' repeated the major, butting in and raising his voice, 'is quite fortuitous, Mr Dwyer. You may be aware that I have a son who lives in Germany. He has a young son, Hans, my grandson, who is eleven, and the boy is coming to spend a fortnight with me next week. His father is keen that while he is in England, Hans should improve his English and, with this in mind, he has asked if it might be possible for him to spend a few days in a school. I did approach the head teacher of the village school here in Barton-in-the-Dale but Mrs Stirling pointed out that Barton-with-Urebank is heavily over-subscribed and the classes overly large and that it might be better if Hans could attend a little school and join a smaller class of children his own age. She mentioned that Risingdale would be a good option. She spoke very highly of you and said you might be willing to have Hans join your class. I believe you are the teacher of the top juniors there so, if you are agreeable, my grandson could join you. What do you think?'

'I should be more than happy for him to come,' replied Tom.

'That's very kind of you,' said the shopkeeper.

The major heaved a sigh. 'Yes, indeed, it is very kind of you,' he said, irritated by the interruption. 'Perhaps Hans could spend a couple of days with you. I could drop him off in the morning and collect him after school.'

'That will be fine,' replied Tom.

'I shall, of course, contact the headmaster at Risingdale and clear things with him,' said the major.

'There's really no need to do that,' Tom told him. 'Mr Gaunt is very easy-going and rarely interferes with what the teachers do. I can have a word with him. I am sure he will be agreeable.'

'That's settled then,' said the major. 'My son tells me that Hans is a bright and interested young man, a little serious perhaps and rather old-fashioned in many ways. His father thinks he may be a touch autistic.'

'I was never any good at art at school,' remarked Mrs Sloughthwaite, not wishing to be left out of the conversation. 'Miss Pratt, my teacher, took one look at my work and said it resembled a car crash rather than the painting on the ceiling of the Sixteenth Chapel in St Peter's.'

The major sighed with weary sufferance. He had a sudden urge to throttle the woman. 'I did not say artistic,' he retorted, 'I said autistic. It's a condition that . . . oh, never mind.' He looked at his watch. 'I must make tracks. Thank you for your help in this, Mr Dwyer. Could we say next Wednesday for me to drop my grandson off at Risingdale?'

'Yes, of course,' replied Tom. 'I arrive at school just after eight so if you would like to bring your grandson along before the children arrive, I can meet him and settle him in.'

'Splendid,' said the major. 'I will wish you both good day.'

When the customer had gone, Mrs Sloughthwaite resumed her posture on the counter.

'He gyrates on my nerves, does major double-barrelled,' she said, pulling a face. 'Likes the sound of his own voice, he does, puffed up with his own importance like a Christmas turkey.'

'I called in,' Tom said, 'to ask if you might place this card in the shop window for me.'

'Course, you know the story about the son in Germany, don't you?' the shopkeeper told him, ignoring his request, leaning over the counter and lowering her voice conspiratorially.

'No,' replied Tom, 'I can't say that I do. I never realised that he was married. The card, by the way, is to advertise—'

'Oh, he's not married,' she said. 'After the War, he was posted to Germany and had a fling with a German woman. He came back to England and left her in the family way. It was only when the woman was at death's door that she told her son who his real father was. After his mother had breathed her last, the son came over from Germany and into my store looking for the major. Very striking-looking man, he was, in a camel-hair overcoat and kid gloves.'

'About the card—' Tom began.

'It's all very well the major pontifificating about the carryings-on of the young when he has a secret love child of his own.' She scowled. 'Them who live in glass houses shouldn't be chucking bricks. What were you saying?'

Tom slid the card across the counter. 'I wonder if you might place this in your window. We are short of a part-time cleaner at the school and we thought someone here in Barton might be interested?'

'Well, I don't think you'll have any luck,' she told him. 'We had the housekeeper of the big house up at Risingdale asking me to do the very same thing, some time back. She works for the local squire and big wig, Sir Hedley Maladroit. You've no doubt come across him. His son was killed in a car crash and then his wife up and left him. He was another one who played fast and loose and had a "by-blow", as my mother used to say.'

'A "by-blow",' said Tom, puzzled.

'It's a fancy way of saying an illegitimate child,' she told him. 'I don't wish to use the other word. Anyway, I said to her, the housekeeper – Mrs Gosling was her name – I said to her, "You're a bit off the beaten track, at the top of the Dale, I can't see as how anybody would be interested travelling right up there, particularly in the winter." I don't think there was any interest. I'll pop the card in the window, just the same, and I'll mention it to those who call into my store.'

Tom took out his wallet.

'You don't need to pay me,' she said.

'Thank you,' said Tom. 'That's kind of you.' Before the shopkeeper could detain him any longer, he made for the door. 'Now I must dash. I'm meeting my Auntie Bridget in town.'

*

In a head-to-head with Mrs Sloughthwaite to decide which of the two women was the most loquacious, Mrs O'Connor could give the proprietor of the village store a good run for her money. Like many of her race, Tom's aunt had the gift of the Blarney and embellished the English language with the most colourful expressions and amusing observations.

Tom had left Ireland to live with his Auntie Bridget in Barton-in-the-Dale when he was in his teens. At first, like many an adolescent, he was moody, uncommunicative and could be short-tempered, but his aunt recognised that at heart her nephew was a good-natured boy with a strong moral sense and a generosity of spirit. He came to rely on her and value her opinion, which was always wise, measured and invariably peppered with the axioms of her old Irish grandmother, who had a caustic comment, a saying or snippet of advice for every occasion. It was through her support that he followed his dream and became a professional footballer. It was through her encouragement that, when injury forced him to give up the game, he studied to become a teacher. He had much to thank his Auntie Bridget for. That morning he was in need of her counsel on a matter that had been on his mind for some time.

'And how are you keeping, Auntie Bridget?' asked Tom later that day when he called into his aunt's cottage.

'All the better for seeing you, so it is,' she said, giving him a kiss. 'Now, come and sit down and tell me what's on your mind?'

'And how would you know there is something on my mind?' he asked.

'Sure, I don't need to lift the lid to see what's in the pot. It's written all over your face that there's something troubling you.'

Tom sat on the edge of a chair and thought for a moment. 'It's a woman,' he said, leaning forward and resting his hands on his knees.

'Ah, I might have guessed,' she said, shaking her head. 'Is it about the attractive girl with the red hair?'

'It is,' he said.

'Sure, I might have guessed. It's as clear as day that you are keen on her, so what's the problem?'

'It's complicated,' he told her. 'There is someone else. Her name is Sandra Merryweather and she's pretty and clever and personable and it's obvious that she likes me – in fact, I think she likes me rather a lot.'

'And?'

'She's a bit . . . how can I put it . . . she's a bit persistent. Sandra is nice enough but she's not Janette. It's Janette I'm keen on. I realise that more than ever now and no matter how hard I try, my feelings for her just never seem to go away. I can't stop thinking about her.'

'You're in love with her.'

Tom nodded. 'Yes, I guess I am.'

'You've got it bad, so you have,' said his aunt. 'It's said that true love binds without a cord. You seem to be well and truly attached. If you love her and she makes you happy, then what's the problem?'

'I'm not sure she feels the same way about me. The last time I told her how I felt, she said there was no future in any relationship. She said she wanted more challenge and more excitement in life and that's why she moved to Nottingham.'

'People change.'

'I'm not sure she has. I guess she thought I was pretty boring.'

'You're the least boring person I know,' said his aunt.

'Perhaps not to you. Anyway, it was like a smack in the face for I thought she really cared for me.'

'But she's come back,' said his aunt, 'so I guess Nottingham was not all that challenging and exciting. Perhaps she missed you. People do change their minds. "Absence makes the heart grow fonder." There's a lot of sense in the old proverbs.'

'Well, I do get the impression that since she's returned to live in the village her feelings might have changed. I'm just not sure.'

'You should tell her how you feel. "Fortune favours the brave."'

'I'm just a bit cautious about doing that.'

'Caution in love will never lead to happiness, Thomas. You should ask her again.'

'Yes, I think you might be right,' he said. 'My problem is Sandra. I know that she has made it obvious that she likes me and is keen for me to ask her out. She's the curator at the Clayton Museum and came into school to talk to the children about the excavations at Marston Castle. She has invited me to a lecture she is giving at the museum next Saturday evening. I couldn't really refuse. Anyway, she suggested I take her for a drink afterwards. I was put in a difficult position. I said yes because I didn't want to hurt her feelings but if I do go out with her it might give her the wrong message and then if Janette sees me out with another woman . . .'

'You have always been a bit of a softie, so you have,' said his aunt. 'Since you were a boy you never wanted to hurt people's feelings. Sometimes, though, it is best to be honest with people, even if it means upsetting them. I think you should tell the young woman that there is someone else who has captured your heart.'

Tom nodded.

Mrs O'Connor rested a hand on her nephew's arm. 'You love Janette and I think, from what you've said, that she probably loves you. Tell her. It's so hard to find a good, generous love, Thomas. Grasp the nettle and tell her what you feel.'

*

The following Wednesday morning the weather was wet and overcast. A ragged grey curtain of cloud hung from a pewter-grey sky and a fierce wind drove the rain at a sharp slant against the windowpanes in Tom's classroom. There was a sudden growl of thunder and a snap of lightning. Then the rain began to fall in earnest. Great drops drummed on the roof, snaked down the windows and formed puddles in the playground.

Tom caught sight of Major Neville-Gravitas and his grand-son running in the downpour across the playground. He went to meet them.

'What a dreadful morning,' said the major, ushering the boy before him into the school entrance. He brushed the water from his coat and ran a hand over his short-cropped hair.

'Yes, it's not the best of days,' Tom acknowledged. 'Come along in.' He glimpsed at the small figure: a serious-faced child with deep-set, intense eyes magnified behind large, heavy, black-rimmed glasses. The boy wiped his shoes vigorously on the mat by the door, stroked a strand of blond wet hair from his pale face and studied the teacher with a penetrating gaze. There was not a sign of a smile or a trace of nervousness.

'You must be Hans,' said Tom warmly.

'That is right,' replied the boy giving a slight bow. '*Guten Morgen*, Good morning, Mr Dwyer. Thank you for letting me come to the school.'

'It's a pleasure,' said Tom, smiling.

'Not too early, I hope?' said the major.

'Not at all,' replied Tom.

'It is the early bird that catches the worm,' said the boy suddenly.

'I'm sorry,' said the teacher, 'what did you say?'

'It is the early bird that catches the worm,' repeated Hans. 'My teacher in Germany, Frau Schneider, she teaches us all the English proverbs. I know many of them.'

'Ah, I see,' said Tom. He had to stop himself chuckling. 'I'm sorry that you've arrived in such an awful downpour, Hans. The weather is very changeable up here at the top of the Dale. We sometimes get heavy rain.'

'It never rains but it pours,' announced the boy, brushing water from his sleeve.

'Very true.' Tom exchanged a look with the major.

'But every cloud has the silver lining,' said the boy.

'It does indeed,' agreed Tom. 'Now if you would like to come along with me to my classroom, Hans. The children will be arriving presently.'

'Presently?' The boy looked confused.

'They will be here soon,' explained Tom. 'I think you'll find everyone here is friendly.'

The boy turned to the major. 'You may go now, grandfather,' he said, like a grandee dismissing an underling.

'Righty-ho,' said the major. 'I'll collect you at three thirty. Now you be a good boy and behave yourself.'

Hans stared at his grandfather through the thick-rimmed glasses with a faintly puzzled expression. He clearly resented the patronising air. 'Of course, I will,' he answered, sounding peeved.

True to his word, the young visitor was exceedingly well behaved and demonstrated a politeness and consideration rarely seen in one so young. His manners were impeccable. Tom expected the boy to be rather shy and reticent on joining his class, but Hans appeared calm and relaxed and was not afraid to raise his hand and ask a question when something puzzled him. He appeared to the teacher to be a serious child, mature beyond his years. He didn't laugh and he seldom smiled but he listened intently to what was being said with the trace of a frown on his young face. The teacher was pleased that the youngster soon made friends with George, who sat next to him and chatted away nonstop. During the two days he was at the school the boy took a real interest in the lessons and volunteered answers and observations that usually included a proverb taught to him by Frau Schneider. Tom was also pleased to see that the children in the class were friendly and welcoming, but it was clear they found the staid little boy odd and intriguing.

The frequent mention of proverbs from the young visitor gave Tom an idea. There was potential here for him to explore with the class the origin of idioms and sayings in the English language and he set the children some homework.

'Now, there are hundreds of proverbs in the English language,' he told the class, 'some of which Hans has used.' The boy nodded and there was a rare trace of a smile on his lips. 'Tonight,' continued the teacher, 'I want you to ask your parents and grandparents if they know any unusual proverbs, and I'm sure they will know plenty, and tomorrow we will compile a list and in the next lesson we can decide what they mean and the advice they give us.'

The following day the children arrived at school with their list of proverbs, keen to share what they had discovered. They took it in turns to show the results of their research.

'"Good things come to those who wait",' said Marjorie. 'That's my gran's favourite, especially at Christmas. Another is, "When sorrow sours your milk, make cheese".'

Tom noticed that Hans was making notes.

'"About as wise as Waltham's calf that walked a mile to suck a bull",' said David. '"Better to turn your back on a gale than press your face against it".'

'Good advice,' said Tom.

'"The cock crows the loudest on his own dunghill",' Colin shouted out, 'and "Don't bite the hand that feeds you".'

'My gran knows loads of proverbs,' announced Vicky with breathy enthusiasm. 'I couldn't shut her up once she got started.' She consulted a list on her desk '"No one knows where the shoe pinches but them who has to wear it", "Fretting and cares make grey hairs", "A fool and his money are soon parted", "Better to be the head of an ass, than the tail of a horse".'

'Thank you, Vicky,' said Tom. 'I am sure—'

'Oh, there's lots more, Mr Dwyer,' the girl told him. '"It's the quietest pig that eats more from the trough", "Little fish should not spout at whales", "Many a good cow has a bad calf".'

'That's really good,' the teacher told the girl, managing to get a word in. 'Several proverbs there I have never heard before.'

'I think my gran makes them up,' said Vicky.

Tom sometimes wondered if his Auntie Bridget invented some of the proverbs she was wont to use and frequently puzzled over what she meant. 'You should never bar the door with a boiled carrot', was one such adage. 'If life throws a clutch of lemons at you, then make lemonade', was another. 'Never let your mother comb your hair after an argument', was a favourite saying. Such aphorisms rattled off her tongue like melted butter off a knife, as she herself might have remarked.

'Shall I tell you some more, sir?' asked the girl.

'Let us give others a chance,' Tom told her. 'Judith, what about you?'

'"Practice makes perfect",' said Judith. 'That's what my clarinet teacher is always telling me.'

'My granddad says, "A petted lamb makes a cross tup",' volunteered Carol.

'"It is not always the clock that ticks the loudest that keeps the best time",' volunteered Charlie.

'That's very true,' said the teacher. 'All these proverbs are full of wise advice on how to behave. I remember Mr Pendlebury telling me that in the Bible it says, "Acquaint thyself with proverbs, for of them thou shalt learn instruction".'

'Some proverbs give you daft advice, though,' announced Matthew. 'There's one where it says, "Barking dogs seldom bite", well Mr Croft's Jack Russell terrier barked like mad and then it bit me. It got its head stuck down a rabbit hole and they had to dig it out.'

'There's another one about a dog,' said David. '"Beware a silent dog and still water".'

Hans raised his hand.

'We have many proverbs in German about dogs,' he said. '"*Schlafende Hunde soll man nicht wecken*", which means "Do not disturb a sleeping dog".'

'"Let sleeping dogs lie",' said Tom. 'That's an old English proverb too, but I guess that many proverbs say much the same thing in many languages. Have you a proverb we haven't heard yet, George?'

'Aye, I 'ave, Mester Dwyer,' replied the pupil. 'It's what mi dad says when 'e's done summat what turns out to be a waste o' time. 'E says, "I might as well 'ave been fartin' agin thunder".'

There was a titter from the class.

Hans raised his hand. 'Mr Dwyer, what is this farting?'

'Shall I tell 'im, sir,' asked George.

'No, not at the moment,' said Tom.

'My teacher, Frau Schneider, never told us this proverb,' he announced. 'I shall tell her when I am back in Germany.'

'It's not one I'm familiar with either,' admitted the teacher.

At home time on the Thursday afternoon, the pupils gathered around Hans and said their goodbyes.

'Tek care o' thissen,' George told the boy, 'an' watch 'ow thee gu's. Mebbe if tha cums an' visits us ageean, I can tek thee round our farm an' show thee some of our beeasts.'

'That would be champion,' replied Hans, using one of his newly acquired words.

When the children had gone, Hans approached the teacher's desk.

'I see my grandfather is waiting for me in the car,' he told Tom, 'so I must be departing but I would like to thank you for letting me come to the school, Mr Dwyer. It has been interesting, and I have learnt many words that I have not heard before. I think my teacher, Frau Schneider, will want to know about them. I would have liked to have stayed longer. It has been good here, but "*Ost und West, danheim das Best*".'

'East and west, home is the best?' asked Tom.

'*Ja,*' said the boy with the hint of a smile. 'You have learnt some German.'

'It's been a pleasure having you with us, Hans,' replied the teacher, 'but as the proverb says, "All good things must come to an end".'

The boy laughed. It was an easy laugh, one the teacher had not expected to hear from such a serious child. 'Ah, *ja,* I know that one. There is a German proverb too which is like that: "*Alles hat ein Ende, nur die Wurst hat zwei*".'

'I'm afraid I don't speak that good German,' he was told. 'You will have to translate for me.'

'It means everything has an end, only the sausage has two,' said the boy. He gave a small bow and held out a hand, which Tom shook. '*Auf Wiedersehen*, Mr Dwyer,' he said.

9

On Saturday, Tom went for his usual early-morning run. The sun was high in a clear blue sky and the air fresh as he jogged through the village, passing the King's Head inn, the village green, and the duck pond. He came to a row of pretty, rose-coloured stone cottages with mullioned windows and blue-slate roofs and the squat, grey-stone former Primitive Methodist Chapel. He passed by the Norman church with its spire spearing the sky and the adjacent imposing Victorian vicarage built in shiny red brick with its broad gravel drive curving through an overgrown garden. Turning by the ancient oak tree with its gnarled branches, he ran up a little-used narrow path which snaked steeply uphill. Dodging nettles and thistles, sheep droppings and cow pats, he paused to catch his breath and perused the vast green landscape below. A wood pigeon cooed in a distant wood, a skylark hung in an azure sky and the fluttering wings of a linnet winked in the morning sun. Lazy-looking, black-faced sheep observed him in a field and rabbits stopped cropping the grass and scuttled to their burrows. He loved the clear cool mornings, a soft breeze blowing in his face waking him up.

When he had breasted the hill, Tom stopped and stood as still as a statue, staring at the scene before him. A hare, fawny-gold in colour with its long, lean body and great erect ears, lolloped across the field. It stopped, sensing something, then rose high on its hind legs and sniffed the air before darting off at an amazing speed. Last March he had witnessed the most extraordinary behaviour of two hares on one of his early-morning runs. He had watched fascinated as two bucks, jumping vertically for seemingly no reason, had punched and pummelled each other. The expression 'As mad as a March hare' made sense. When he shared this experience with his pupils, Charlie had informed him that the animal's name came from 'Hara', an Anglo-Saxon word meaning 'jump' and that it was the Romans who introduced the animals into Britain.

Soon Tom arrived at the imposing ruin of Marston Castle, its huge corner towers and half-destroyed walls towering over the landscape. It was here that the recent excavations had taken place. Tom paused again and thought of the evening that lay ahead when he was to attend Dr Merryweather's lecture. He really did not want to go out for a drink with her. That would give her the wrong idea. He regarded her as a friend, that was all, a pleasant companion with whom he could talk about history. It was Janette he had feelings for. Perhaps I should call the museum and say I'm ill, he considered, but it was not in his nature to lie. He needed to be honest with her and explain that, romantically speaking, he had no interest in her but to do so that evening in a public house was not the time nor the place.

Back at his cottage, Tom had a shower, changed and sat down for his breakfast. The telephone rang.

'Neville-Gravitas here,' came a throaty voice down the line.

'Good morning, major,' said Tom.

'I just wanted to thank you for letting Hans join your class,' said the caller. 'He apparently had a most er . . . stimulating and instructive couple of days with you.'

'I'm glad he enjoyed it,' said Tom. 'He was a very polite and interested boy. I hope he learnt something from his visit.'

'Oh yes, he learnt a great deal.'

'That's good. He must spend a bit longer with us the next time he visits.'

The major was silent for a moment, pondering what to say. He coughed. 'Ah, well, I'm not so sure about that, Mr Dwyer. Of course, I'm very grateful to you for agreeing to have him join your class but some of the English he had learnt is . . . how can I put this, it's a little colourful, if you follow my drift? I guess his teacher back in Germany will not be greatly impressed with some of the words he has picked up.'

'I see,' said Tom.

'On our way home,' said the major, 'I had a bit of trouble with the car. I had a puncture. I became rather exasperated and short-tempered waiting for quite a while for the break-down people to come. Hans just shrugged. It didn't seem to bother him at all. "You must calm down, grandfather," he told me. "Getting upset is like fartin' agin thunder. Shit happens."'

'George,' said Tom, under his breath.

*

The museum was crowded that evening. Dr Merryweather's lecture had certainly generated a great deal of interest. Gath-ered in the entrance of the museum, Tom recognised many familiar faces from Risingdale. Toby Croft, smartly dressed for a change, had cornered Richard Greenwood and was stabbing the air with a bony finger, no doubt complaining about something or other. There was Mrs Gosling shielding her granddaughter from seeing a rather revealing seven-foot naked statue of some classical male figure, which left little to the imagination. The vicar, Mr Pendlebury, was in animated conversation with Mr Cockburn, the Methodist minister, be-neath a large portrait in oils in a glowing gilt frame of some worthy. Mr Gaunt and Moira, standing before a glass case of wildly colourful exotic stuffed birds, were chatting with Sir Hedley and Mrs Lister. It appeared the baronet was making no secret of his association with his companion. Joyce stood in earnest conversation with members of her amateur theatre group. She waved and smiled. Then Tom saw Janette with her father. She looked lovelier than ever. He took a deep breath, swallowed nervously, and went to join them.

'Good evening,' he said.

Mr Fairborn, his face expressionless, nodded and grunted. There was a slight raise of the eyebrow and brief lift of the chin. Janette's father presented a daunting figure: a stocky man with a rugged, creased face the colour of an overripe russet apple, a complexion no doubt derived from his working all day in the outdoors in all weathers. His features gave him a grave and threatening look. He wore a loud tweed suit and tan brogues.

The reason for Mr Fairborn's brusque manner was that he believed the teacher who stood before him like an anxious schoolboy in front of the head teacher, had treated his daughter shabbily. After Janette had left to work in Nottingham, Tom had telephoned to speak to her. The over-protective father did not consider the young schoolmaster good enough for his daughter and, without mincing his words, he had told Tom so.

'I don't mean this unkindly,' he had said to Tom, 'but I think you're wasting your time with my daughter. I know that she likes you, but that is as far as it goes.'

It became clear to him, however, that his daughter, on returning from Nottingham, had really missed Tom Dwyer and there was more of a liking on her part. She seemed love-struck. Her father, seeing Janette so miserable and learning why she was so unhappy, decided to speak to Tom and explain.

'She's fallen for you in a big way,' he had told him as they sat in the King's Head one evening. 'She only realised it when she was in Nottingham.' He had looked into Tom's eyes. 'She misses you. I don't want Jan to know that I've seen you and told you all this. Let's keep this conversation to ourselves.' He had reached in his pocket and produced a scrap of paper, which he had placed on the table in front of him. 'This is Jan's number,' he had told Tom. 'I imagine you will want to give her a ring.'

But Tom did not give Janette ring. Mr Fairborn's hope that his heart-to-heart would bring the two young people together was misguided, for Tom had, at that time, had his sights set on another. While Janette had been away, he had tried to banish her from his thoughts and his affections had changed. There was now someone else in his life. Mrs Stanhope, the artist who had moved into the village, was clever and confident, with a tender heart and an enchanting personality. This tall, elegant woman of strikingly good looks with a wave of bright blond hair and a streamlined figure had captivated Tom. He had been smitten. Later when he had thought about his attachment, he realised his had been an infatuation rather than love. He still had the deepest feelings for Janette.

Mr Fairborn, hearing that his daughter had been 'passed over', as he termed it, now had little time for the fickle young man who he felt had trifled with her affections.

*

So now here they were at the museum, Tom and Janette, two young people in love with each other but both too hesitant to show their real feelings.

'Hello, Tom,' said Janette coyly. She inclined her head gracefully and smiled at him with large, almond-shaped green eyes. He could not take his eyes off her face. He reached for her hand and held it for a moment longer than was necessary. This made her colour slightly and for a moment they stood in silence, both of them blushing.

'I'll get the tickets,' grunted Mr Fairborn before departing.

'It's nice to—' Tom began.

'I'm afraid—' she started.

They stopped nervously as if they were meeting for the first time.

'After you—' she said.

'No, no, after you,' he replied.

'I was going to say that my father is not much of a conversationalist, unless, of course, he gets on to farming. Then there's no stopping him.' How handsome Tom was, she thought, with his luxuriant black hair, fine skin, large dark eyes and lean body. She longed to tell him what he meant to her.

'I was about to say that it's good to see you,' said Tom.

'And I you.' She could feel the heat rise in her neck, but she held his gaze.

'I've not seen much of you lately.'

'Late nights at the bank,' she told him. 'I can't complain. I was fortunate to get the manager's position back at the Clayton branch.'

'You don't miss the bright lights of Nottingham then?' he asked.

'Not a bit. It was a mistake to go there,' she replied.

'You said you wanted more excitement and challenge,' he reminded her.

'Yes, I remember what I said,' she replied. 'I didn't get any excitement and challenge though, just more worry and stress. I said a lot of things I now regret. I am glad to be back. I didn't realise how much I would miss.'

'Your horse, for one.'

'Not just my horse. I missed other things, other people.' She wanted to say that she missed him and that she had not realised her true feelings until she was away.

'Well, they say that "home is where the heart is",' said Tom, thinking of a proverb one of his pupils had mentioned in the lesson.

'That's true enough,' she said.

For a moment there was an awkward silence. He licked his lower lip nervously.

'I was wondering—' he began.

'I thought that maybe—'

They both laughed.

'After you,' he said.

'No, no, after you,' she replied.

'Well, I was wondering whether, if you are not doing anything—'

The sentence remained unfinished, for Dr Merryweather came hurrying up, her face lit up in a smile. She was wearing a close-fitting charcoal-grey suit with a narrow chalk stripe and appeared very businesslike.

'Oh, there you are, Tom,' she said breathlessly. She looped her arm through his, stood on tiptoe to kiss him lightly on the cheek. 'I've reserved a seat for you down the front.'

He looked uneasy. 'Oh hello, Sandra,' he said. 'Let me introduce you. This is Janette Fairborn.'

'Oh, hello,' said Dr Merryweather curtly, giving Janette a quick glance. She turned back to Tom. 'Look, I must hurry you. I am about to start. Come along, I'll show you where you're sitting. You are down at the front. I've reserved you a seat. I'll see you afterwards. You haven't forgotten our date; remember you are taking me for that drink after the lecture.'

Tom gave a weak smile.

*

Dr Merryweather's lecture was very well received. She was in her element in front of an audience: confident, entertaining, informative and in full command of the subject. She gave a fascinating account of what had been discovered at the castle, illustrated with slides and artefacts, and answered questions adeptly and with assurance.

At the end of the talk, as people crowded around her to congratulate her and ask further questions, Tom got up quickly. He needed to speak to Janette. He saw her heading for the door and edged his way past people making for the exit. His path was blocked by Toby Croft.

'Nah then, Mester Dwyer,' he said.

'Not now, Toby,' snapped Tom, pushing past him.

The old farmer grasped his arm and held him back. 'She's certainly got what it teks, that girlfriend o' thine,' he said, chuckling.

'What?'

'Doc Merryweather,' Toby told him, winking. 'She's a grand lass an' no mistake. Clever as two pair o' clogs an' twice as 'andsome.'

'She is *not* my girlfriend,' replied Tom, nudging him out of the way.

By the time it took him to get to the exit, Janette was nowhere to be seen. He hurried into the car park to see a large four-by-four vehicle pass him with Mr Fairborn at the wheel. In the passenger seat sat his daughter. Tom waved. Janette stared back but did not return the wave. The sadness on her face matched his own. He felt his heart sink like a lead weight into the mud. He set off for home.

Tom had only just arrived back at his cottage later that evening when the telephone rang. It was Sandra.

'Where were you?' she asked. 'We were supposed to be going for a drink after my lecture.'

'Ah, Sandra,' replied Tom. 'I'm really sorry but I had to dash.'

'Why, was there something wrong?'

'Er . . . I was feeling unwell,' he said, which was not really a lie in that he did feel in poor spirits and couldn't face an evening in a noisy public house.

'Oh, I'm sorry to hear that. I saw you rush away. I wondered why you disappeared in such a hurry. Are you all right?'

'Yes, I feel a lot better now, thank you,' he said, 'but I think I'll get an early night and sleep things off.'

'Well, you take care of yourself. When you feel better, give me a ring and we'll fix up that date.'

It was not a date, he thought. I was just a drink. He determined to have a word with her next week and clear things up. He had been weak-willed and should have made it clear to her from the start that he had no amorous interest in her. He quickly changed the subject. 'Your talk was excellent, by the way.'

'Yes, it was well received,' she replied. 'I was surprised how many people came along. Now, don't forget to ring me.'

'Good night,' he said.

'Good night, Tom.'

He put down the receiver, then picked it up again, took another deep breath and dialled the number.

The telephone was answered by Janette's father.

'John Fairborn,' came the gruff voice down the line.

'Good evening. This is Tom Dwyer. May I speak to Jan, please?'

'It's late.'

'I won't keep her long.'

'I'll put her on,' he said abruptly.

A moment later Janette answered.

'Hello.'

Tom could feel his heart beating in slow thumps.

'I tried to catch you at the end of the evening,' he said.

'Oh, yes.'

'I wanted to ask you if you would like to go out with me one night.' There was silence. 'Are you still there?'

'Yes, I'm still here.'

'So, would you like to?'

'And what would your girlfriend say?' she asked.

'I haven't got a girlfriend.'

'What about Dr Merryweather?'

'Janette, she is not my girlfriend. She's just a colleague.'

'She seemed rather more than a colleague tonight.'

'There is nothing going on between me and Sandra . . . Dr Merryweather. That is the honest truth. Now, will you go out with me one night or not?'

'I shall have to think about it, Tom,' she replied. 'My feelings are all over the place at the moment.'

'Fine,' he said, irritated by her answer. 'Well, let me know if you would like to. Good night, Jan.' He placed down the receiver.

*

Since Lady Maladroit's departure, Sir Hedley predicted many more quiet evenings with the woman he loved and saw no reason now to be so circumspect about his relationship with Mrs Lister. Indeed, he felt a great relief at not having to be so secretive. Let people gossip if they wished; it would not bother him. He longed for the time when Christine Lister and their son would live with him at Marston Towers.

After Dr Merryweather's lecture, Sir Hedley had driven his mistress back to her cottage. He now sat with her on the sofa in the sitting room. Charlie was upstairs in his bedroom.

'I saw quite a few inquisitive eyes looking in our direction tonight, Hedley,' said Mrs Lister, sounding uneasy. She had noticed that their departure from the museum had not gone unobserved.

'Really?'

'People seemed more interested in us than in the lecture. I guess they were speculating why we were there together.'

'Let them speculate, my dear,' he said. 'I really couldn't care less. Very soon they will have nothing to speculate about.'

'Nevertheless, perhaps it might be better to keep things as they are for the time being.'

'Nonsense!' he exclaimed. 'Once the divorce comes through—'

'You will make an honest woman of me,' she interposed, smiling.

'And I will tell you this, Christine: if I hear anyone speculating about you and me in my hearing, they will feel the edge of my tongue. I will not have anyone being disrespectful to you. People in the village know on which side their bread is buttered and they know not to get on the wrong side of me.'

'You had better be going,' she said, smiling.

'I could stay the night.'

'I'd rather you didn't,' she replied. 'Let's take things slowly and wait until your divorce is settled.'

'If you wish.' He leaned over and gave her a kiss on the cheek. Then he put his arm around her shoulder and drew her close. 'You know I love you, don't you?'

'Of course I do,' she replied.

'Since Marcia upped and left me I have never felt so contented,' he said. 'It's such a relief to know that she is out of my life forever.'

*

When Joyce arrived home later that evening, she found her husband and his nephew in the sitting room. It irritated her to see Stanley ensconced in the most comfortable armchair with what was now the usual whisky clutched in his hand. His fat fingers stroked the side of the glass. He will have to go, she said to herself.

'Ah, here she is,' said Julian, rising from his chair. 'Do come and join us, my dear, and I'll get you a drink.' He was being particularly solicitous. Joyce sensed there was something in the air. 'Have you eaten? he asked.

'Yes,' she replied. 'I joined some of my friends from the theatre group after the lecture and we went to the new Indian restaurant by the station.' She sat down. 'We should go there sometime, Julian.'

He handed her a large glass of gin and tonic. She took a mouthful. 'Yes, that would be nice,' he said, sitting down. He crossed his legs. 'And how was your day?'

'Busy, as usual,' she replied.

'Stanley cooked us a very palatable tuna bake,' Julian told her. 'We did save you a portion but since you have eaten . . .'

'I'm afraid tuna doesn't agree with me,' said Joyce, with rather splendid indifference. She took another sip of her drink. That evening she had enjoyed a seafood curry.

'And how did the lecture this evening go?' asked Stanley.

'It was fascinating,' Joyce told him. 'Dr Merryweather was excellent.'

'He is the curator at the museum, is he not?'

'He is not,' replied Joyce. 'Dr Merryweather is a woman and she certainly knew her stuff and how to put it over. I can never understand why some people think that only men have doctorates. She had the audience eating out of her hand. You should have come along, Stanley, you might have enjoyed it.' Then she added, 'And learnt something.'

There was a snort of laughter. 'I'm afraid history doesn't interest me,' he replied, ignoring the barbed comment. 'I was turned off the subject at school. All those facts and dates bored me to tears. I found the lessons mind-numbing.'

And no doubt his teachers found you a tiresome and bumptious pupil, thought Joyce.

She finished her drink and went to get another. 'I should have thought that as someone who is dealing with so much from the past in an auction house, you would be fascinated with history,' she said, pouring herself a generous quantity of gin and tonic.

'Speaking of the auction house,' said Julian, 'Stanley has suggested some changes we might make.'

'Changes?' said his wife.

Julian turned to his nephew. 'Perhaps you might like to enlighten Joyce.'

Stanley sat up in his chair, downed the whisky in one gulp, placed the glass on a side table and leaned forward, his eyes bright with enthusiasm. He wore the facial expression of the school sneak.

'Yes, of course,' he said. 'Well, the thing is, I have been giving the business a deal of thought since I arrived, and I have mentioned to Uncle Julian a number of ideas for making it move with the times, so to speak. Smith, Skerrit and Sampson tends to be a bit passé. There is so much that is dated, outmoded and unfashionable.' Three words which meant the same thing, thought Joyce. 'Coming new to the company and with some experience of successful businesses in the capital city, I've been in a position to see things with fresh eyes and with a new perspective and—'

'I thought the business was doing well,' interjected Joyce, looking at her husband.

'Oh, it's ticking over,' Stanley hastened to say, 'but there are a few developments I have suggested to Uncle Julian that I think might improve the service we offer. He seems quite interested.' His face betrayed his naked ambition to take control of the business.

'Such as?'

'Stanley is suggesting we have a café,' Julian told her. 'I think—'

'Rather more than a café, Uncle Julian,' Stanley cut in. 'You see, Joyce,' he carried on, attempting a jocular tone of voice, 'sometimes the auctions take all day and people do need refreshments – a cup of coffee in the morning, something to eat at lunchtime, tea in the afternoon. At the moment, when we have a pause in the sales, the bidders have to go into Clayton to have a drink or a meal. A small, high-class restaurant on the premises, however, would offer a welcome service for our customers and in addition generate more income. It would also attract people who would not normally visit the auction house. It could be a little gold mine. What do you think?' His face revealed a smiling slyness.

'There is the Ring o' Bells a few hundred yards away,' she said. 'Do you think there is room for another café?'

'Oh, I wasn't thinking of a poky little greasy spoon with plastic tables, uncomfortable chairs and steamed-up windows,' he told her excitedly.

'Have you been in the Ring o' Bells?' asked Joyce.

'Well, no, not really,' he replied.

'Actually, it's a rather charming little café, not at all like a greasy spoon.'

'What I envisage is more of a bistro than a café,' Stanley told her, 'something stylish and sophisticated, a tasteful tearoom with starched tablecloths and silver cutlery and smartly dressed waitresses. The annexe to the saleroom, which faces the main street in Clayton, is hardly used at the moment and could be renovated.'

'So, what do you think, Joyce?' asked her husband.

'I've never got involved in your business, Julian,' she replied. 'I have quite enough on with my job.'

'So, you don't like the idea?'

'I didn't say that. I suppose this project does have some merit in it.'

'You think so?' He sounded surprised.

'Yes, I do.'

Stanley exchanged a glance with his uncle. He looked pleased with himself.

'Perhaps you might consider giving up teaching,' said Julian, 'and run the bistro. Keep things in the family, so to speak.'

Joyce was taken aback by the suggestion. She regarded him with a flat, unblinking stare. Then came her reply; it was steady and controlled, which concealed her anger. 'I have not spent three years at drama college and a further stretch in teacher training to become a waitress in a bistro, or whatever you care to call it.' She met his eyes without the trace of a smile but with an intense and overpowering gaze.

'No, no, n–not a waitress,' stuttered Stanley. 'You would be the manager. You would be in sole charge.'

'It is out of the question,' Joyce replied firmly. Her face was a mask.

He pushed his luck. 'You might wish to think about it,' he said.

'There is nothing for me to think about,' she said with finality. 'The answer is "No".' She looked indignantly at her husband. 'I have told you repeatedly, Julian, that I do not intend to give up my career. I don't know how many times I have said this.' She finished her drink in one gulp, placed down the empty glass and rose from her chair. 'And since Stanley seems to be a dab hand with the cooking,' she declared, 'perhaps he might like to manage the bistro himself. Now, I have had a tiring day so I will wish you both a good night.'

IO

The visitor arrived at Marston Towers on the Monday morning.

Mrs Gosling opened the door to find her nemesis standing on the doorstep, her face as blank as a figurehead on the front of a ship. She pursed her lips and tucked her hands under her bosom, which was secured underneath an unyielding grey nylon overall. Her face was a mask of indifference. At the sight of the housekeeper, Lady Maladroit's countenance changed to one with unmistakeable disdain. Her eyes were as hard as enamel.

'Oh, it's you,' she said, in a voice sharp and clipped. Her features were set in a rictus of distaste. Having swept past and into the spacious entrance hall, her shoes clacking on the polished liver-and-pink-coloured marble floor, she glanced around before removing her coat and scarf and placing them on a highly polished inlaid Regency mahogany centre table. On his visit to Marston Towers, Mr Sampson of Smith, Skerrit and Sampson Auction House had noted the particularly fine quality of this item of furniture. It was one of the many rare and valuable pieces owned by the baronet. She had missed the opulence of the house. The more she thought about her sister's flat – cramped, furnished with modern, tasteless furniture and cluttered with bric-a-brac – and Daphne's unreasonable attitude, the more determined she was to leave.

'I see that you are back,' she said, turning to face the housekeeper and arching her brows. Mrs Gosling maintained a robust silence and remained tight-lipped; her expression was as stony as a dry-stone wall. She did not deign to reply. 'Inform Sir Hedley that I have arrived,' Lady Maladroit instructed haughtily. 'I shall be in the drawing room. You might fetch me some tea.'

Go put your head in a pot, said the housekeeper to herself, walking away without a word. She was no longer taking orders from that harridan. She could whistle for her tea.

Mrs Gosling found Sir Hedley in his study, poring over the estate accounts.

'Yes, what is it?' asked the baronet, looking up from his papers.

'You have a visitor,' she replied, her face showing a distinct sourness. 'She's in the drawing room.'

'Who is it?'

'Lady Maladroit.' She was inclined to add, 'who has appeared like the wicked fairy at the christening', but she held her tongue.

Sir Hedley rubbed his forehead and sighed. 'Now what does she want?' he muttered. He stood and thought for a moment that he might join her but then reconsidered. Let her come and see him; he was not inclined to be at her beck and call. 'You had better tell her I'm in my study,' he said.

If she comes back to this house, thought Mrs Gosling, as she headed for the door, I am out of here.

A few minutes later, Lady Maladroit entered the study. She was wearing a severe, high-necked dark blue linen dress. Her eyes ran over the room before she sat in the chair in front of the desk. She crossed her legs and folded her hands slackly in her lap.

'Hello, Hedley,' she said. Her husband did not get up. 'I see you have changed things around in here and got rid of all those dreadful stuffed animals. It's a great improvement.' She tilted her head and glanced at two dark oil paintings, one of a racehorse in the manner of Stubbs, the other of a liver-

and-white German pointer holding down a dead partridge with its paw. Her eyes seemed bright in the pale, pinched face. 'I think those ugly pictures should go as well. I never liked them.'

Her husband's face betrayed neither surprise nor anger; his features were as immobile as the marble bust of a bewigged ancestor which sat on a small table in the corner of the room. He studied his wife for a moment and noticed that she still wore the wedding ring, which bit into her flesh. She looked strained and worried, the furrows on her cheeks had deepened since he had last seen her, drawing the corners of her mouth even more downward. Her hair was pulled back tautly. A vein pulsed in her temple.

'What is it you want, Marcia?' he asked. She sensed his restrained impatience.

'Not a very warm welcome, Hedley,' she said. She raised her hand which was slightly trembling and pushed back a stray strand of hair which had fallen over an eye.

'What did you expect?' he replied.

She didn't respond. She had determined not to make the meeting rancorous, for she hoped the proposition she had in mind would be acceptable. They sat for a moment in grim silence.

'I see that the Gosling woman has inveigled herself back here,' she remarked at last with an arrogant tilt of the chin.

'I asked Mrs Gosling to return, as a matter of fact,' her husband answered. 'I thought it very decent of her to do so considering the way she had been treated. She is still smarting at being accused, quite wrongfully, of being a thief and, I might add, receiving no apology from you for the false allegation you made.'

'Oh, don't let us start going over all that again, Hedley,' she said dismissively. 'The matter of the necklace is all water under the bridge.'

'For you, maybe,' he responded, 'but not for Mrs Gosling, and for that matter not for me. May I ask you again
what is it you want? As you wished, the divorce papers have
been signed so I cannot see there is anything else for us to
discuss.'

Lady Maladroit shifted somewhat uncomfortably in her
chair and considered what she would say next. Then she lifted her chin sharply.

'While I have been staying with my sister,' she told him, 'I
have had some time to think of the situation in which we find
ourselves.'

'Which is?'

She avoided answering the question. Her head was lowered
and her chin drawn in. 'As you are aware, the death of James
had a traumatic effect upon me. I recall what the vicar told us,
that to lose a child is the most devastating blow that no parent
should ever have to face.'

'I am at a loss, Marcia,' said Sir Hedley. 'What is it you
want?' He was barely managing to hide his irritation and frus-
tration.

Again, she deflected the question. 'I think you will own that
after our son's death we both of us said things we now regret.'
Her face was set hard and she held herself rigid.

'I don't regret anything, Marcia,' answered her husband.
'As I recall, it was you who said so many hurtful things, telling
me that you had never loved me and admitting that you only
married me for the title and for the lifestyle. I remember that
I said very little.'

'I was in a dreadful state of grief,' she began. Her face
twitched from the effort of self-control. She had determined
not to argue with him.

'You told me our marriage was an empty shell.' He said
this without bitterness or accusation but quietly with a slight,
bewildered shake of his head.

'That was in the heat of the moment,' she countered, 'and emotionally I was going through an extremely bad patch. I had just lost my son and was near to having a nervous breakdown.' Her lips pressed into a narrow line. 'We all say things that we later regret.'

Sir Hedley sighed. A long-suffering expression appeared on his face. 'Marcia,' he said, 'let us be honest. We both of us soon discovered that our marriage was a mistake. It became patently clear that we were incompatible. Our life together was a battlefield of silences, angry glances, arguments and recriminations. We should have separated long ago.' When James was born the baronet thought that things might have got better in the marriage, but they had got worse. Everything and nothing proved reason for a dispute. As his son grew, the acrimony and arguments increased. Family life, such as it was, ended forever.

'You never appreciated how difficult I found it to adjust to my life up here after London,' she told him, 'to live in this insular and claustrophobic village, rife with gossip, where everyone knows one's business. I was never accepted. I was always the wife of the squire, not a person regarded in my own right. You see, you have always seen yourself as the very centre of everything, with the world revolving around you. I was just a spare part, the wife of.' This was said in a more subdued tone of voice.

'What is it you want, Marcia? Why are you here?' There was a growing sense of impatience in his voice. He had heard this so many times before.

'As I have said, I have been giving our present situation a deal of thought and I have a mind to return.' A little spasm touched her face.

'What!' he cried. 'Come back to Marston Towers?'

'Please don't raise your voice, Hedley,' she said. 'I am trying to have a civil conversation with you. I am willing to come back but there would be certain conditions.'

Her husband gave a wry smile, then leaning back in his chair gave a dry and humourless laugh. 'Conditions,' he echoed.

'Yes.'

'And what might these conditions be?' He was intrigued. He sat up.

'Firstly, the Gosling woman has to go. I found her rude and disrespectful when I was here. I cannot have her in the house. There would have to be a new housekeeper. Secondly, we agree to continue to lead separate lives. Of course, to keep up appearances, we will for all intents and purposes still be Sir Hedley and Lady Maladroit. You will be free to pursue your interests and I will pursue mine, which will involve my regular visits to London where I could have a flat.'

Sir Hedley leaned back in his chair again and felt a touch of unaccustomed pity for this sad and embittered woman. Did she really think that she could return after all she had said? He shook his head and said without any asperity, 'No, Marcia, this just won't do.'

'Won't do?' she repeated. She leaned forward with a dull and perplexed expression on her face. She felt a tremor of despair.

'We are far better off apart,' he told her temperately. 'Were you to come back, we would inevitably resume the animosity and quarrelling. I think it best if we go our separate ways. I know how you missed your life in London. You told me frequently how miserable you were in Risingdale, how life up here is tedious and the people unfriendly. And you told me, as I recall, that our marriage was a sham, nothing more.'

'I admit I might have said those ill-considered things,' she answered after a pause, her voice dropping lower as she spoke. 'I now regret saying what I did. I was not thinking straight. I was worn out both physically and emotionally and devastated by James's death.' She swallowed and looked down. Tears came into her eyes, but she blinked them away. 'I should like to come back, Hedley,' she said almost inaudibly. There was an element of pleading in her voice.

'No, Marcia,' her husband told her. 'That is not a good idea. It just wouldn't work.' There was a note of tenderness in his words.

She twisted the ring on her finger, hardly able to breathe. When she raised her eyes there was a deep unhappiness in her face and the corner of her eyes were again pricked with tears.

'We could try and make it work,' she said.

He closed his eyes in a weary gesture and shook his head. 'It is too late for that,' he told her. There was a certain tragic dignity in his words. 'I shall buy you a flat in London and you will be well provided for,' continued Sir Hedley. 'After the divorce and the financial settlement, you will be comfortably off – more than comfortably off. I am sorry it has ended like this, Marcia, but your returning to Marston Towers is not on the cards.'

'There's nothing more to say, then,' she replied stiffly, getting to her feet.

Sir Hedley stood. 'I am sorry that things have turned out as they have, Marcia,' he said softly. 'I am sorry for you in more ways than you might perhaps imagine.'

'I am not looking for pity, Hedley,' she told him, recovering her self-possession. 'I hate that in a person. I can get on with my life very well without you.'

'While you are in Risingdale, do you wish to see our grandchild? I can arrange it if you wish.'

'Our grandchild?' She stifled a snort of derision.

'James's son.'

'No,' she replied, 'I don't wish to see the child.'

'We are to have the christening in a couple of weeks,' he told her. 'It would be a generous gesture on your part were you to attend. I am sure that Leanne—'

'I'm sorry, Hedley,' she cut him off. 'It might appear heart-less to you, but I want nothing to do with the child or his mother. The whole episode and James's relationship with the young woman has caused me great distress. It is something I wish to put behind me.'

'He's a bonny little chap and the spit and image of his father,' said Sir Hedley.

'I must go,' she said, not wishing to discuss the topic fur-ther. She walked to the door where she stood and thought for a moment, wondering if she should enlighten him. She could have told him that the infant was not, in fact, his grandchild, for James was not his son. To reveal that piece of informa-tion, she knew, would hurt him unimaginably. She opened her mouth to speak but then closed it. Lady Maladroit was many things: a snob, a bearer of grudges; she was narrow-minded, self-righteous and opinionated; she was often wrong but with the supreme confidence that she was always right. But she was not that vindictive.

'Was there something else, Marcia?' asked Sir Hedley.

'No,' she replied, 'nothing else.'

*

At lunchtime on Friday, Mrs Leadbeater popped her head around the classroom door.

'This is for you, Mr Dwyer,' she said, waving an envelope in the air 'It's from Germany.'

'Thanks, Beryl,' he said. The letter was from Hans:

Dear Mr Dwyer,

I am thanking you for letting me kindly spend time with you in your class. I had a good time, and I learnt many new words. I put them in my book. My teacher in Ger-many, Frau Schneider, had not heard some of these words.

She would like to know what is a *cakeoil* and a *cooatook*, a *mardyarse* and a *clartead*. She cannot find *nobbut*, *laikin* and *chuffineck* in her English dictionary. Could you write and tell us what they mean? Thank you.

From Hans

Tom, keen to impart the contents to his colleagues and for them to share his amusement, headed for the staffroom. He found Miss Tranter and Mrs Golightly in heated discussion so thought this was not the best time to read the letter. Clearly the two teachers were not in the right frame of mind to be entertained.

'You are perfectly entitled to your opinion, Joyce,' Mrs Golightly was saying, 'but I disagree with you. In my classroom we do not use baby language. We use the correct English. We call things by their proper names. We do not have moo-cows and bow-wows and chuff-chuffs and gee-gees. As I told Mrs Bowman when she asked me to oversee her son going to the lavatory because he "gets his little nipper caught in his zipper", we do not use terms like that. I teach the proper names for those parts of the body and do not encourage the use of ridiculous euphemisms. It is just prudery. There is nothing crude or vulgar about referring to the correct medical terminology.'

Joyce rolled her eyes. 'We have had this conversation before, Bertha, you don't need to rehearse it again.'

'You brought the matter up,' reported her colleague tartly.

'No, I did not. You were telling Owen, before he went on yard duty, what was going on in your lesson. I could not help but overhear.'

'Then you shouldn't have been eavesdropping,' announced Mrs Golightly. There was a wary, resentful look in her eyes.

'I couldn't very well ignore what you were saying, you were speaking so loudly. And while we are about it, you might spend a bit more time teaching the infants to speak properly. Andrew Johnson in your class ran up to me when I was on duty in the playground last week and told me, "Freddie Bowman's just cracked me across mi lug-oil for nowt!" Now, what sort of language is that to use?'

'Don't lay at my door the way children speak,' replied Mrs Golightly, her voice hardening. 'You're the drama specialist, so it's more in your province than in mine to teach the children to speak correctly.'

The exchange, which had continued to go back and forth like a game of shuttlecock, was getting more intense, so Tom intervened.

'So, what were you saying, Bertha?' he asked.

'Oh, do I have to hear it all for a second time?' Joyce sighed again.

'I was telling Owen,' said Mrs Golightly, addressing Tom, 'that each Friday morning I do some vocabulary work and to get the children in the mood, to blow away the cobwebs and get them to concentrate, I start the lesson with "I Spy".'

'I can't see there is anything so controversial about playing, "I Spy",' remarked Tom.

'There isn't, but Joyce seems to think otherwise,' said Mrs Golightly, giving her colleague a sharp look.

'I did not say there was anything unsuitable in playing "I Spy",' countered Joyce. 'You are twisting my words. It was what followed which I considered to be inappropriate.'

'I wish you would tell me,' said Tom, intrigued.

'Well, if I might continue without repeated interruptions,' said Mrs Golightly, 'we were playing "I Spy" and it came to Gareth Lomax's turn. I said, "I spy with my little eye, something beginning with 'T'." "Teacher," he replied. "No," I said, "not teacher." "Tie," guessed Gareth. "No, not that either," I told him. So, I gave him a clue, by looking down at his trainers.

"You have two of them," I said, "but I don't have any" and he replied, "Testicles".'

Tom put a hand over his mouth to smother his laughter.

'I can't see there is anything funny,' said Joyce. 'I think the child was being impertinent. One wonders where he's heard such a word.'

'His elder brother is George,' Tom told her, thinking of the young farming expert who no doubt knew a great deal more words concerning anatomy. 'I guess he's heard the word from him.'

'That may be so,' said Joyce, 'but Bertha should have left it at that and not gone into details as to what the word meant.'

The interruption was ignored by the teacher.

'Then Bethany pipes up,' continued Mrs Golightly, 'and informs everyone that octopuses have eight of them. "No dear," I told her, "those are tentacles." "Is it a rude word?" asked Andrew. I told him that it wasn't,' said Mrs Golightly. 'Of course, Freddie, who always has something to say for himself then told the class his dog has them. Then Marigold asked me what the word meant.'

'And she told her!' exclaimed Joyce.

'I did not go into any details. I merely said that boys and girls, men and women, are different and that boys and men and male animals have what are called testicles which are below the stomach and girls and female animals do not.'

'You should have moved on and told the child that she would find out when she is older. It was not the time nor the place to go into that sort of thing.'

'If children ask something,' said Mrs Golightly, stung by the criticism, 'I believe that teachers have a duty to answer honestly and not evade the question. Anyway, most of the children come from farms. You are not telling me that they are unaware of parts of the male body surrounded as they are by bulls and tups.'

'Well, I think there is an age when children should be taught the medical terminology,' persisted Joyce, 'and it isn't at the age of six. Words like . . . like that . . . should be introduced when they are in the top juniors and not before.'

The teachers glared at each other like a pair of angry cats.

Joyce turned to Tom. 'Don't you agree with me?' she asked.

'I am sure Tom agrees with me,' said Mrs Golightly.

Tom looked at his watch. He was in the middle of a rock and a hard place and felt it politic not to give his opinion. 'Oh,' he said, 'look at the time. Lunchtime is nearly over.' With that he hurried from the staffroom.

*

If Tom thought the staffroom discussion was closed, he was soon disabused.

'Well, I must say that Bertha surprised me allowing young children to use such terms,' Joyce told him as the two teachers wandered around the playground at afternoon break. 'They need to know about such things when they are a lot older.'

'To be fair, I don't think she allowed the boy to use the word,' said Tom. 'Gareth just came out with it. Children are open and honest and say all sort of things that surprise adults and ask questions that are sometimes a bit unsettling. You know that, Joyce.'

'I think you will allow that I know a little more about children than you do, Tom,' she told him. He could hear the reproach in her voice. 'I have been a teacher for a lot longer that you have. I think the child was being impudent.'

'I don't think Gareth was being cheeky,' said her colleague. 'I remember when I was at junior school, I asked what a virgin was in all innocence. We had been learning about the Virgin Mary. The nun thought I was being impertinent and told me not to be so bold, which in Ireland means "naughty". I merely wanted to know. Later when she spoke about something called "the immaculate conception", I kept my hand down and my mouth shut. I had no idea what she was talking about. Surely it's best to be candid with children and answer their questions truthfully?'

'Yes, but I believe that explaining some things to children should be left until they are older when they can better understand,' she replied.

'So, when a small child asks where babies come from, you say the stork brings it or it's found under a gooseberry bush?' asked Tom.

'Of course not.'

'I am sure that the parents of the children who live on farms, such as Gareth's mum and dad, make no bones about explaining the facts of life,' said Tom.

'That is the parents' prerogative,' Joyce told him. 'It is not for teachers to explain the facts of life.'

'I disagree,' began Tom. 'Some parents are too embarrassed to broach the matter. Mine certainly told me nothing. Like many youngsters, I picked up the wrong idea about sex from other children.'

'Look, Tom,' she said, 'I do not wish to fall out over this. Let us not discuss it further.'

Both fell silent, and they walked around the school yard. 'How are things at home?' Tom asked at last.

'A great deal better, I'm pleased to say,' replied Joyce, her tone now warmed with pleasure. 'Julian and I had a heart-to-heart and he has accepted that I do not intend to give up my career and that I have quite enough on with a full-time and demanding job without having to do all the household chores as well. He has been very thoughtful and arranged for two young women from a professional domestic cleaning company to come in once a week to do the housework and a laundry service to deal with all the washing and ironing.

"Connoisseur Cuisine of Clayton" stock up the freezer each Saturday, which saves me having to cook so often. It's such a weight off my mind.'

'And Stanley?' asked Tom.

'Oh, he's still with us, more's the pity, and he's as self-important as ever. Thankfully, he goes out quite a bit in the evenings, which suits me. Anyway, enough about that. What about you?'

'Nothing much to tell, really,' replied Tom.

'I saw you at the museum lecture talking to Janette Fairborn. Do I take it that you two are now back together?'

'Back together?' he repeated. Chance would be a fine thing, he thought. 'We never were together in the first place.'

'You're very keen on her though, aren't you?'

'Yes, I am.'

'And what about Dr Merryweather?' she asked.

'What about her?'

'She seems pretty smitten. She could not take her eyes off you at the museum. It looked like she was giving her lecture to you alone, the way she kept staring at you and smiling.'

'Well, I'm not interested in her,' he replied. He changed the subject. 'Actually, I do have a bit of good news. Leanne has asked me to be the godfather of her baby. The christening's the Sunday after next.'

'I think you'll make a brilliant godfather,' said Joyce. 'Julian and I have been invited to the christening and the reception afterwards. He has dealings with Sir Hedley in a business capacity.'

'And are you going?'

'Of course, we're going.'

'You surprise me,' he said. 'I thought you had little time for Sir Hedley and the fiefdom. I recall you telling me that country squires ruling the roost are a dying breed and the sooner they are extinct the better, that people like the Maladroits are a walking mass of out-dated values.'

'I did say that, and I've not changed my opinion,' she answered. 'These titled landlords with their vast estates have driven half the farmers out of their homes and acquired their land. They think they're still Lords of the Manor and are living in the 1880s and not in the 1980s. If it were up to me, I wouldn't go to the christening, but Julian thinks it is good business sense for us to attend. He reckons that when Sir Hedley's divorce comes through, Lady Maladroit will take him for every penny he's got and that he will have to put a lot of his things into auction to pay the alimony. Julian says there are some exceptionally fine pieces of antique furniture at Marston Towers and rooms full of valuable objets d'art. He hopes that he will be asked to deal with selling them. Since Julian has been so understanding regarding the household chores, I felt I should be equally accommodating, so I have agreed to go with him. I just wish he would do something about Stanley. He really is—'

She stopped when she saw Mr Gaunt striding across the playground in their direction.

'Ah, Tom, there you are,' said the headmaster. 'There's a call for you. It's Dr Merryweather from the Clayton Museum. She wishes to speak to you.'

Joyce raised an eyebrow and tried to supress a smirk.

*

Joyce arrived home later that evening after a particularly tiring day. After school she had driven into Clayton, eaten a quick meal at the Ring o' Bells café and gone on to the Civic Theatre to direct a rehearsal of the new play that was to be staged the following month. She found her husband in the drawing room.

'Oh, are you still up?' she asked.

'Yes, I wanted to have a word with you,' replied her husband. 'Do come in and sit down and I'll get you a drink.'

He poured a large sherry from the decanter on the dresser and placed the glass in her hand and then sat next to her on the sofa.

'Where's Stanley?' she asked.

'He's out.'

'You look very serious, Julian,' said Joyce, taking a sip of her drink. 'Is there something wrong?'

He let his breath out very slowly and knitted his brows. 'Yes, I'm afraid there is,' he muttered.

'Well, what is it?'

'It's Stanley,' he told her.

'Has he had an accident?'

'No, no, it's what he's been doing.'

'What has he done?'

'Quite a deal, by all accounts,' he said. Sudden anxiety darkened his face.

'You had better tell me.' She placed down the glass and slipped her arm through his.

'As you know, I've been winding down of late and not been such a frequent visitor to the office at the auction house. In fact, I didn't go in at all last week. I called in this morning and sensed there was an atmosphere. I couldn't put my finger on it, but I could tell things were not right by the way people were behaving. Smith, Skerrit and Sampson has always been a happy environment in which to work, where the staff get on well together, but the mood seems to have changed. There was no sign of Stanley and when I asked where he was, they were evasive and uncommunicative. I questioned the General Manager and Mr Cavill explained. He said he was meaning to come and see me, but I had pre-empted matters.'

'And has this to do with Stanley?' asked Joyce.

'I'm afraid it has,' her husband concluded gloomily.

'I thought you were pleased with him. Didn't you say he was a natural when it comes to auctioneering?'

'He did make a promising start, but I have to say that clearly he is not a natural when it comes to relationships. He has been treading on a lot of toes. I was told he is most ill-mannered with the staff and offhand with Mr Cavill. Evidently, he has been setting up all sorts of things without consulting me or the General Manager – meeting clients, making changes, interfering and reorganising systems that have been in place for many years.'

'He's not in a position to do that, surely,' she remarked.

'No, he is not,' agreed her husband tetchily. 'His actions have caused a great deal of upset and have bothered me greatly.'

'Oh dear,' said Joyce. Her eyes betrayed a sly satisfaction. Julian finding fault with Stanley pleased her no end. 'I'm sure it can be sorted out,' she said softly, seeing how tormented her husband had become. She edged closer, reached for his hand and squeezed it. 'You need to have a word with him, Julian.'

'Oh, I had it out with him when he came in this evening. I don't know where he'd been all day and I didn't ask. I was straight with him and repeated what I had been told but, at first, he brushed this off, saying the staff had been uncooperative, that they disliked him and took exception to the changes he was making. He claimed that Mr Cavill was envious of him and resented his presence. I'm afraid that I lost my temper at this point and explained that Mr Cavill had been with the firm for over twenty-five years, that he is a man of great integrity and honesty and, as the General Manager, it is he who is in charge and makes the day-to-day decisions.'

'And what did he say?'

'That his intentions were to make the firm more efficient and improve the way things were done but he apologised if he had caused any upset, rather half-heartedly I may add. He agreed that from now on he would discuss any ideas he might have with Mr Cavill and me and make no further changes unless we are consulted. We shall see if he keeps his word. I am afraid that this episode has changed my view of Stanley. I thought perhaps that he could take over the firm when I pass on, but I am now of the opinion that the management of an auction house is not his forte after all and perhaps he should seek another position, perhaps back in finance where he would be more at home.'

'That might be the best thing to do,' agreed Joyce. She was unable to keep the satisfaction from her voice. At the corners of her mouth were the beginnings of a smile, which she tried to suppress. She finished the sherry in one swallow.

'Well, it's well past your bedtime,' said Julian. 'You've had a long day and I am sure you must be very tired.'

'Not that tired,' she said with a touch of coquetry.

II

The following Monday morning Joyce, her face pink with pleasure, was in an exceptionally good mood when she arrived at the school gate. She paused for a moment and inhaled deeply. The sun was shining, the birds were singing, and everything seemed right with the world. Her conversation with Julian the previous Friday evening had cheered her greatly. From what her husband had said, his nephew could say goodbye to any expectation that he would one day be taking over the running of the auction house. Stanley was no longer in his uncle's good books, which filled her with a great sense of relief and pleasure. At breakfast that morning the atmosphere between Julian and his nephew had been decidedly cool. She could predict that it would not be long before Stanley was given his marching orders and the cuckoo would take flight and leave the nest.

Joyce found Tom in the school office, his ear pressed to the telephone receiver. Mrs Leadbeater was in the headmaster's study occupied with filing away some documents, so he had the place to himself.

'Good morning,' said Joyce jauntily.

Tom nodded and gave a polite if somewhat forced smile.

In the staffroom she found two of her colleagues. Mr Cadwallader was reading the paper, crunching on a biscuit and dropping crumbs on the floor. Joyce approached Mrs Golightly, who was standing at the sink waiting for the kettle to boil.

'I owe you an apology, Bertha,' she said.

'About what?' she asked.

'I'm sorry I got a bit on my high horse on Friday. I must have sounded priggish and narrow-minded. I didn't mean to be so judgemental, and it was wrong of me to criticise you.'

'Oh, it was a small difference of opinion, that's all,' replied Mrs Golightly, surprised by her colleague's volte-face. 'I'm not going to fall out with you over that. Actually, I think I got a bit hot under the collar myself.'

'Well, we will leave it at that,' said Joyce, 'and put the subject to rest.'

'A good idea,' agreed Mrs Golightly.

'What was this small difference of opinion?' enquired Mr Cadwallader, looking up from his paper. 'It sounds most interesting.' He posted the remains of his biscuit in his mouth with an air of finality.

'Nothing of importance,' Mrs Golightly told him, 'and will you go steady with the Garibaldis? You ate a full packet last week.'

Mr Gaunt entered the staffroom.

'Good morning, everyone,' he said, rubbing his hands together vigorously. 'Beautiful day, isn't it? It makes one glad to be alive. Now, I've had another communication from Mr Nettles.' He held up a square of paper.

The teachers groaned in chorus.

Mr Nettles was an education officer based at County Hall. He was a man intoxicated with the sound of his own voice and obsessed with burying schools beneath a snowstorm of paperwork. Each term the headmaster would receive questionnaires, memoranda, guidelines, initiatives, policies, directives, programmes of study, schemes of work and other documents from him, most of which were ignored and consigned to a file in Mr Gaunt's study marked FIFI ('File It And Forget It'). Mr Nettles was an elusive and ineffectual man. On the few occasions when he had telephoned the Education Office at County Hall, to see if a cleaner for the school had been found, Mr Gaunt had been informed by the snappish clerical assistant that 'Mr Nettles is tied up at the moment. He'll get back to you.' Of course, he never did.

'I shall pin this document on the notice board,' Mr Gaunt told the teachers, 'and you can read it at your leisure – if you are so inclined. It concerns yet another new initiative.'

'It's a pity that that silly man has nothing better to do than bombard schools with such bumf,' observed Mr Cadwallader.

'While I tend to agree with you, Owen,' said Mr Gaunt, 'I am obliged to bring it to your attention. Actually, this is one initiative agreed by the Education Committee, which, I feel, has some merit. It's worth taking a look.' He consulted the paper. 'It says here that each head teacher in the county has been asked to nominate what it calls "a named person" in the school who will co-ordinate the teaching of this subject, attend the awareness-training afternoon and develop this programme. As you are aware I have asked Tom to co-ordinate the teaching of English, computer science, games and PE in the school, Bertha to be in charge of reading development and Owen to lead on mathematics and science teaching, so I thought perhaps you might be happy to take this on, Joyce. It seems to me that it's right up your street.'

'Well, what is the initiative called?' asked the teacher.

'"Sex Education in Primary Schools",' he told her.

The expression of Joyce's face could have curdled milk.

'I'll make the tea,' said Mrs Golightly, a slight smile on her lips.

In the school office, Tom was wondering how best to respond to the caller. On the previous Friday, when he had been summoned from the playground by the headmaster to answer the call from Dr Merryweather, the conversation with her had been rather stilted. He had explained that he was fully occupied on yard duty at that moment and could not speak for long. He agreed that he would be in touch to arrange the promised drink. This he had failed to do. He now felt he had to grasp the nettle. It was only fair-minded of him to be honest with her.

'So how are you feeling now?' Dr Merryweather was asking.

'Er . . . a lot better, thank you,' he replied. He thought of the kindest way of saying what he needed to tell her and cleared his throat with a small cough. 'Look, Sandra, I don't really know how to say this, but er . . . you need to know.'

'This sounds intriguing,' she said.

Tom took a deep breath. 'I'm sure you know that I am fond of you – I mean that I like you.'

'And I'm fond of you, Tom, and I like you too,' she replied.

'You have become a good friend and been really helpful and supportive coming into school to talk to the children and letting us visit the castle to see the excavations.' He struggled to find the right words.

'It was a pleasure. I'm always delighted when I see children taking such an interest in history. For many it's a dry and dusty subject and—'

'Sandra,' Tom stopped her mid-sentence, 'if I might continue.'

'Yes, of course,' she replied. 'You were saying how fond you are of me.'

This is a nightmare, he thought. He tried to think of the best way of breaking things to her, but his mouth just would not seem to form the words he wished to say.

'Are you still there?' Dr Merryweather asked.

'Yes, yes, I'm still here. I'm just finding it difficult to say what I need to tell you.'

'You're not ill? I thought you said you were feeling a lot better.'

'No, no, I'm not ill, nothing like that.'

'Well, what is it?'

'It's just that I have an idea that you . . . er . . . maybe . . . think there could be . . . that there might be something . . . oh dear.'

'For a man whose profession is words,' she told him, 'you are surprisingly inarticulate. What is it, Tom, you wish to say?'

'I think you may be under the impression that our . . . relationship, our . . . connection that is, is perhaps more than friendship . . . if you see what I mean. I wouldn't want you to get the wrong idea.'

'The wrong idea,' she repeated.

Tom wondered if he had heard a chuckle in her voice.

'I might have got the wrong end of the stick,' he continued falteringly. 'Forgive me if I have. I just want you to know it would cause a bit of a problem going out with you.'

'Going out with me?'

'You see, I've fallen for someone.'

'Oh.'

'As I said, I like you, I like you a lot as a friend, but that's as far as it goes. I don't have any stronger feelings. Does that make sense?'

'Yes, I see,' she replied. Then there was a strange noise down the telephone.

'Are you all right?' he asked. He couldn't tell whether she was laughing or crying.

'Oh, Tom,' she said, giggling, 'I never thought of you as anything but a friend. It is so hard for me to find someone with whom I am able to share my passion for history, another person who feels the same way as I do about the past and is keen to enthuse children. I saw, when you first visited the museum with your class, how interested you were in the exhibits and what I had to say. I found in you a sort of kindred spirit. I certainly had no romantic expectations, that we would walk off into the sunset together hand in hand.'

'You didn't?'

'Of course not.'

'I seem to have made a bit of a fool of myself, haven't I?' he said, feeling a great sense of relief.

'Yes, I think you have,' she replied, 'but we can still be friends.'

'We can still be friends,' Tom repeated.

'And I see no harm in us going for that drink.'

Tom was about to say, 'It's a date,' but he stopped himself in time.

*

Sunday lunchtime at the King's Head was unusually quiet on the day of the christening. Many of the regulars: local land-owners such as John Fairborn and Ernie Sheepshanks; tenant farmers like Arnold Olmeroyde and Clive Gosling; Dick Greenwood and Dean Croft and other employees of Sir Hedley's, were all attending the christening reception at Marston Towers. They were joined by Gerald Gaunt and Moira; Mr Pendlebury, the vicar; Mrs Lister and Charlie; Julian Sampson and Joyce; and Tom Dwyer. Janette Fairborn had also been invited.

In the King's Head Toby Croft, moody and resentful, was hunched like a sulky monkey on a stool at the end of the bar with his long-suffering companion, the small, wrinkled man with the veined nose and putty-coloured teeth.

'It's quiet in 'ere today,' observed Percy airily, looking around.

'Aye it is,' agreed Toby, grimacing. 'Most o' t'village are up at t'big 'ouse drinkin' an' scoffin' an' carousin' after t'christenin'.'

'Tha weren't hinvited then, Toby?' needled the old farmer, knowing full well what the reaction to his words would be.

'Was I 'ellus like!'

'Your Dean were,' said the old farmer, smirking. It was a carefully and cleverly aimed provocation and had the desired effect. 'I saw 'im 'eadin' up to t'big 'ouse, spruced up wi' a spring in 'is step.'

'Don't thee talk to me abaat our Dean. I've done wi' 'im. Left me to run t'farm all on mi tod after all I've done fer t'lad. I'll tell thee this, Percy, there's nowt as cruel as an hungrateful child.'

'Tha should 'ave tret 'im better, then 'e wun't 'ave left.'

The old farmer spoke the truth, for Dean had done most of the work on the farm when he lived with his parents with little recompense and no thanks. Toby Croft's meanness was legendary and so was his aversion to labour. As one local observed, 'He's as lazy as Ludlum's dog, which has to lean against the barn door to bark, it's so idle.' He would watch the boy, giving him orders, commenting and criticising at every turn, but rarely stirring himself to lend a hand.

'Don't thee tell me 'ow to run mi farm,' Toby answered defiantly. 'Kindly keep thy remarks to thissen an' save yer breath to warm yer porridge.'

'From what I've 'eard, thy farm's not doin' all that well, now that Dean's gone,' remarked Percy, persisting in his mischief. 'People are sayin' it's goin' daan'ill like a greased pig.'

'It's doin all reight,' lied Toby.

'Anyroad, 'e fell on 'is feet bein' med a gamekeeper on t'Maladroit estate.' Percy knew how this would infuriate his companion.

'Assistant gamekeeper!' snapped Toby. 'Fancy title fer one o' t'squire's lackies. 'E'll soon come runnin' back wi' 'is tail between 'is legs when 'e meks a pig's ear o' t'job an' Sir 'Edley sacks 'im.'

'From what I've 'eard, lad's med a reight good himpression at Marston Towers,' remarked Percy, much enjoying his companion's discomfiture. 'They say t'squire's dead chuffed wi' 'im.'

'Anyroad, I wun't 'ave gone to t'reception if I'd 'ave been hinvited,' grumbled Toby, ignoring the comment. ''Obnobbin' wi' t'gentry is not my cup o' tea.'

'I 'eard that t'church were full to burstin' fer t'christenin' service,' said Percy.

'Aye, it were,' replied Toby. 'There were Missis Mossup smilin' like a Cheshire cat what 'ad got t'cream, sat in t'front pew dressed up like a dog's dinner. Clive Gosling's mam were there an' all, lookin' like Lady o' t'Manor hersen, wi' this big red 'at wi' feathers stickin' up. An' who should cum in an' sit daan t'front but Tom Dwyer. I could 'ave been knocked daan deead when I saw 'e were godfather. 'E's gorris finger in hevery pie in t'village. Bloody golden boy 'e is. Not been in Risingdale above a few months an' 'e's gorrin wi' t'local MP an' vicar an' landlady, buying a cottage, runnin' things up at t'school an' 'as lasses chasin' after 'im like nob'dy's business, an' now 'e's godfather fer Sir 'Edley's grandson. An' I'll tell thee summat else—'

'Oh, shurrup, Toby,' Percy jumped in, wearying of the constant complaining. 'Thy're like a bloody gramophone record. T'lad's done nowt to thee. 'E's a decent young man is Mester Dwyer an' allus furst at t'bar, as thee well knaas. Good luck to 'im.'

'Then Missis Lister waltzes down aisle to t'front pew and sits hersen daan next to t'squire, as large as life, an' twice as natural,' Toby carried on. 'She were t'godmother. Mind you, I weren't that surprised. 'Er an' squire were carryin' on at t'lecture at t'museum. 'E din't let t'grass grow under 'is feet, I'll say that fer 'im. Soon as t'wife were out o' t'door, 'e teks up wi' Missis Lister. I reckon it waint be long afore she's gorrer feet under t'table up at Marston Towers.'

'She's a nice woman,' said Percy.

'An' it were a reight carry on in t'church,' continued the old curmudgeon. 'T'vicar rambled on, tellin' everyone it were a joyous occasion but as soon as 'e gorris 'ands on t'babby, it lets out this scream what'd wake t'dead. Like a bloody screech owl it were. Then it started to wriggle an' kick an' thrash abaat like summat possessed. When he put watter on its 'ead, it were more like a hexorcism. I tell thee, Percy, it's a bad omen when a babby carries on like that at a baptism. I reckon it'll turn out like that ne'er-do-well of a father. I'm not superstitious but it's bad luck fer a babby to act like that at a christening.'

Percy, tired of being subjected to such unremitting gripes and grumbles, had finally had enough. He finished his pint in one great gulp and slammed the glass down on the bar. 'Tha wants to give that gob o' thine a rest,' he cried. 'One of these days, Toby Croft, tha'll surprise heverybody an' say summat nice abaat somebody.' Then he strode out of the inn.

Toby drained his glass and called down the bar. 'Are tha servin' down 'ere, Wayne, or purrin roots daan?'

The young bartender approached. 'Pint is it, Mr Croft?' he asked.

'Aye, an' I'll 'ave a whisky an' all. Mek it a double.'

'All by yourself today, then?' asked Wayne.

Toby glowered. 'I like mi own company,' he said.

'I thought you'd be at the christening reception up at the big house like everyone else.'

If looks could maim, the bartender would have been on crutches.

*

The Sunday-lunchtime reception was held in the drawing room at Marston Towers. The crystal sparkled, the silver shone and vases of freshly picked roses filled the room with their fragrance. Several bottles of vintage champagne were opened; a caterer, supervised by an eagle-eyed Mrs Gosling, served a large selection of hors d'oeuvres.

'Thank you all for coming to this special occasion,' said Sir Hedley, speaking to the invited guests who had grouped around him. A great smile enveloped his whole face. 'I wanted you, my dear friends, to help Leanne, her mother and me celebrate the christening of Marcus Hedley Mossup.' He looked tenderly at the baby, who was whimpering in his mother's arms. The child was wrapped in an electric-blue and pink knitted blanket, a present from Mrs Gosling. Not knowing what gender the child would be, she had opted for a combination of the two colours. 'I cannot put into words the great feeling of pleasure I have at having a grandson,' continued the baronet. When considering what he might say, Sir Hedley had thought he might mention that, although he had not got on all that well with his son, he was sorry that James was not present to see his baby boy, but then decided against it. 'I know,' he went on, 'that Marcus Hedley will grow up to be a fine young man, loved and cherished by his mother and by his grandparents.' The baby stopped crying and lifted a chubby arm and tiny, curved fingers. The nails shone like tiny translucent seashells. Sir Hedley glanced for a moment at Mrs Lister, who was standing at the back with Charlie. 'I now look forward to a more auspicious and happy future. I have asked the godfather to say a few words, but he tells me that he is unaccustomed to public speaking.' He chuckled. 'I find that hard to believe from a teacher and an Irishman and from someone, if I may be so bold, who is not, as they say in Yorkshire, "backward in coming forwards".' There was a ripple of laughter. 'But to be serious for a moment, I know that with the baby's mother and godmother, Tom will encourage the child to be kind and considerate towards others, standing against things in the world that cause injustice and suffering. They will pray with us that the child will grow up healthy, happy and loving.'

'Well said, Sir Hedley,' the vicar called out.

At the sound of Mr Pendlebury's voice the baby started twisting and struggling, perhaps recalling the frightful experience at the font and the memory of being dunked in cold water. He arched his back and his little arms and legs worked like pistons, and with a screwed-up mottled face of livid pink, he let out the most ear-splitting scream. Leanne began rocking the child, whispering in his ear and stroking the curve of his tiny cheek, but to no effect. The child continued to squirm, open-mouthed, then after taking great shuddering breaths, he began shrieking again.

'Now, as I have mentioned,' said Sir Hedley, raising his voice above the bawling baby, 'the godfather is not inclined to speak, but he has agreed to read a poem of his own choosing, suitable for the occasion. So, Tom, if you would like to do the honours.'

'Thank you,' said Tom, joining the baronet and raising his voice too. 'This is called, "The Irish Blessing for the Christened Child."'

Suddenly the baby stopped crying and grew still. He didn't shut his eyes but stared unblinkingly instead at Tom, seeming to anticipate the words which were to be read. Leanne bent to kiss the child's head, breathing in the delicious smell of the baby.

Tom cleared his throat and recited the poem:

'"May the strength of the wind and the light of the sun,
The softness of the rain and the mystery of the moon
Reach and fill you.
May beauty delight you, and happiness uplift you,
May wonder fulfil you, and love surround you,
May your step be steady, and your arm be strong,
May your heart be peaceful, and your word be true,
May you seek to learn, and may you learn to live,
May you live to love, and may you love always."'

There followed a small silence and then exuberant applause.

Tears appeared at the corners of Sir Hedley's eyes as he thought of James – lazy, egotistical and arrogant, a boy indulged by his mother and disliked by all in the village. Would that he had lived up to the sentiments expressed in the poem.

'Without further ado,' he announced, rubbing his eyes, 'I would ask you to raise your glasses, and toast my grandson: Marcus Hedley Mossup. Happy days!'

Mrs Gosling left the room, reappearing a moment later with a large, iced cake, which she had made especially for the occasion. She placed it down and then went quickly over to Sir Hedley, who was in conversation with the vicar.

'Might I have a word, Sir Hedley?' she asked in a hushed voice.

'Yes, yes, of course, Mrs Gosling. What is it?'

'There's that woman on the telephone again. She called last night. I left a message on your desk. She asked you to call her back.'

'I'm afraid I didn't see your message,' he told her. 'Do you know what it was about?'

'No, but she said it was important.'

'Will you tell her I'll give her a ring later?'

'She said it was urgent.'

'Did she say who she is?' he asked.

'Her name's a Mrs Coulson, Lady Maladroit's sister.'

Sir Hedley turned to Mr Pendlebury. 'I had better go,' he told the vicar, putting down his glass. 'Please excuse me.'

When he had left the drawing room, Janette approached Tom, who was standing by the window staring out over the expanse of parkland.

'Breathtaking view, isn't it?' she said.

'How the other half live,' he replied.

'Money doesn't bring happiness,' she said.

'That's not what one would expect to hear from a bank manager.'

'It's the truth.' She touched his arm. 'I liked the poem by the way. You read it really well.'

'Look, Jan, when I spoke to you after the lecture at the museum,' he brushed the compliment away. 'Sandra Merryweather and I are not an item. She's . . . well . . . she's—'

'Keen on you.'

'Not in the way you think,' he replied. 'Honestly, I have given her no encouragement. There is nothing going on between the two of us. I like her but nothing more. She is just a friend. Now, you can choose to believe me or not, but it is the truth.'

'I see.'

He was vacillating between longing and desire; longing to tell her how he felt about her and desire to hold her in his arms and kiss her.

'So, will you come out with me one night?'

She smiled. 'What about this evening?' she asked.

*

Sir Hedley went to his study to answer the telephone. He sat at his desk for a moment before picking up the receiver, then he closed his eyes and breathed deeply. It was clear to him why Marcia's sister was getting in touch: to persuade him to let his wife return to Marston Towers. This he could not countenance. Finally, he answered the call.

'Hello,' he said. His voice was slightly slurred and impatient.

'Oh, at last,' came an agitated, breathless voice down the line. 'It's Daphne Coulson here. I left a message yesterday for you to contact me. I did say it was urgent.'

'I'm afraid I never saw it,' he replied. 'I was out last evening, and I have been rather preoccupied today. It's the day of the christening. We are in the middle of the reception.'

'Oh, I see,' she replied, sounding mollified.

'I did ask Marcia if she would like to come to the christening, but she told me she preferred not to. I guess your call concerns her.'

'Yes, it does. She—'

'Let me stop you there, Daphne,' he interjected. 'I imagine that you are contacting me to persuade me to take Marcia back. I could have predicted that it would not work out, her coming to live with you. I made it quite clear to your sister when she visited Marston Towers that her returning is not possible. We would—'

He was now cut off.

'It's not that at all, Hedley,' she said. 'It was to tell you that Marcia has had a dreadful accident.'

'An accident?'

'Yes. I cannot tell you what a terrible time it has been these last few days.'

'Oh, I'm sorry, I imagined—'

'She was rushed to hospital, dangerously ill.'

'What happened?' he asked.

'She caught her hand on a rose bush in the garden and a thorn got embedded. It went septic.'

'Is she all right?'

'No, Hedley, she is not all right,' she answered.

'So, how is she?'

'If you would allow me finish. As I have mentioned, she caught her hand on this rose bush and a thorn got embedded. I was not aware that thorns from roses are poisonous, but evidently they are. Anyway, her hand became swollen and infected. She would not go to the doctor, despite my efforts to persuade her. You know how stubborn she could be and—'

'Daphne, could you tell me how she is?' he asked. 'Is it serious?'

'She died, Hedley.'

There was a moment's silence before he spoke. 'She died?' he repeated.

'She developed septicaemia, and something called cellulitis and sepsis. It was blood poisoning.' She heard him draw a deep breath. Then there was silence. 'Are you still there?'

'Yes, I'm still here.'

'There was really nothing they could do,' she told him.

'Good God.' He was quiet for a time. 'You may not believe me, Daphne, but I am deeply saddened. Poor Marcia.'

'Yes, it was all so sudden. She was taken into hospital last Wednesday and then everything happened so quickly. I've been at my wits' end.'

'It must have been dreadful for you,' he sympathised.

'I'm afraid that things didn't work out when Marcia came to live with me. There were constant arguments. She could be very difficult and demanding and became snappy and fractious. I said things to her that I now regret. After coming back from seeing you and hearing that you did not want her to return, she became very quiet, full of self-pity and paranoia. Perhaps I wasn't as sympathetic as I could have been. As I said, I did try and get her to see a doctor when she had the accident, but she would have none of it. It was almost as if she didn't want to get better, that she had given up. In a way, I feel partly responsible for what happened.'

'I am sure that's not the case,' he told her. Sir Hedley thought for a moment. He wanted to choose his words carefully. 'I don't think it is at all helpful to apportion blame for what has happened. Marcia was a sad and rather mixed-up woman. I'm so sorry that things did not work out for her in London. I'm sorry that things have ended for her like this and that she didn't at last find some happiness and her place in the world.' He changed the subject. 'Now, is there anything I can do?' he asked.

'Well, yes, there is. I wanted to discuss with you where we go from here. I can arrange the funeral if you wish. I feel

certain she would not want it to take place in Risingdale. As
you know, she never really took to the place. I could see to the
arrangements. I think she should be cremated. It seems to me
more fitting to have her ashes scattered on our parents' grave.
I just wanted to run this past you before doing anything.'

'I'm sure what you suggest is the right thing to do,' he said.
'I will, of course, cover all the costs.'

'That's generous of you,' she said. 'The other thing I need to
discuss is what to do with all Marcia's possessions. I can arrange
for them to be sent back to you, if that is what you wish. I would
ask one favour. May I keep the peridot and pearl necklace?'

'Ah, the necklace.'

'It belonged to our grandmother and has great sentimental
associations.'

'Of course. You may keep everything, including all Marcia's
jewellery with the one exception. I should like the emerald
and diamond ring that belonged to *my* grandmother. That too
has great sentimental associations for me.'

'I'll arrange to send it,' she said. 'I know that you and I did
not get on, Hedley. I made no secret of the fact that I thought
the marriage was a mistake, but I have never accused you
of being parsimonious.' She thought for a moment. 'And I
do know how difficult Marcia could be. You have been very
generous. I shall let you get back to the reception. I hope the
christening went well.' She placed down the receiver.

'Poor Marcia,' muttered Sir Hedley again.

*

Mrs Lister sat with Sir Hedley in the drawing room at Marston Towers that evening, listening as he related the details of
the telephone call from Marcia's sister. The guests had departed, the caterers had packed up and gone and Charlie was
in the kitchen helping Mrs Gosling tidy things away.

'We should be going,' she said.

'Stay for a while,' said Sir Hedley, taking her hand in his. 'It's such a comfort to have you here.'

'Well, maybe for a bit longer,' she replied, 'but Charlie has school tomorrow so I can't be too late.'

'It's been an eventful day,' he said. 'One that I'll not forget in a hurry.'

'How are you feeling?' she asked.

'Oh, rather bewildered, to be honest.' He sighed. 'It was such a happy occasion and then I heard news of Marcia. I take no satisfaction in the news of her death, you know,' he said. 'She was an unhappy and troubled woman. I would not wish what happened to her on anyone.'

'I know that, Hedley,' she said gently.

'We both knew early in the marriage that it was a mistake,' he continued. 'When she left me, I thought we could both open a new chapter in our lives – her in London where she always wanted to be and me here in God's own country with you and Charlie.' He sighed. 'Well, it wasn't to be – not for Marcia, anyway.'

They sat for a moment in companionable silence.

'The christening was a great success,' said Mrs Lister, wanting to lighten the mood.

'Yes, I thought so. Mr Pendlebury did extremely well when the baby put up a struggle as he tried to baptise the little chap. He's certainly got a good pair of lungs.'

'I liked the poem Mr Dwyer read,' said Mrs Lister.

'So did I,' said Sir Hedley. 'I've asked him for a copy. I thought I might have it framed and give it to Leanne with a silver christening cup as a memento.'

'You're a good man, Hedley,' she said, and lightly kissed his cheek.

During this conversation, in the kitchen Charlie was helping put the cups and plates away in the cupboard.

'Go steady with that china,' warned Mr Gosling, 'it's very old and very valuable. I don't want any accidents.'

'I will,' he replied.

'So, how's school?' she asked.

'It's good,' the boy replied. 'I never used to like it when Miss Cathcart was my teacher but since Mr Dwyer came, I really enjoy it.'

'He's a good teacher is Mr Dwyer,' stated the housekeeper, 'and unlike some I could mention, kept his classroom neat and tidy. Mind you, I could have done without his stuffed animals.'

'Nothing's neat and tidy since you left,' Charlie told her. 'There's lots of dust and the toilets aren't as clean.' Mrs Gosling gave a smug little smile. 'Do you think he'll get married and have a baby?' asked the boy.

'Who?'

'Mr Dwyer.'

Mrs Gosling chuckled. 'I suppose he might one day, when he finds the right woman.'

'I think he *might* have found the right woman,' said Charlie.

'And what makes you say that?'

'They spent most of the christening together.'

'Who did?'

'Mr Dwyer and Miss Fairborn. They were as thick as thieves.'

'My goodness, Charlie Lister, you do come out with some expressions. Wherever did you hear that one from?'

'I heard Mrs Mossup telling Leanne,' he told her. 'Mrs Mossup said that Mr Dwyer and Miss Fairborn make a nice couple.'

Mrs Gosling nodded. 'Yes,' she said, 'I reckon she's right.'

*

Back at his cottage after the reception at Marston Towers, Tom was at a loose end. He couldn't concentrate or sit still and abandoned the things that usually occupied his Sunday afternoons, namely preparing the week's lessons and marking the children's books. He kept thinking about his date with Janette that evening, and his feelings were mixed: elation, excitement, nervousness, anxiety.

Tom arrived early at the Fairborn farm and stood hesitantly on the doorstep. He looked forward to the evening with a certain amount of apprehension, picturing all sorts of awkwardness and embarrassment when faced with Janette's father. He knocked. Mr Fairborn opened the door. He was a forbidding figure.

'Oh, it's you,' he said brusquely. 'You had better come in.' He pointed to a door off the hallway. 'Go through.'

The sitting room was bright and tastefully furnished. There were deep-cushioned sofas and chairs, a richly patterned Indian carpet that covered most of a polished oak floor and beige-coloured drapes hanging before long sash windows. A longcase clock with a gleaming brass face ticked reassuringly in a corner and a collection of photographs in silver frames was arranged on an antique oak dresser. One of the photographs was of a striking-looking woman dressed for the hunt in black jacket and white cravat and posing before a large chestnut horse. She bore a remarkable resemblance to Janette. Another was of Mr Fairborn, handsome and smiling, holding a silver cup and a rosette and standing next to a huge double-muscled bull. Several of the photographs were of Janette, some when she was a little girl, another in her school uniform and one showing her in a mortar board and academic gown. Curled up on one of the easy chairs was a plump, lazy-looking ginger cat with large green eyes and long whiskers. At the sight of Tom, it jumped from the chair, ambled towards him and, meowing loudly, began to rub its fat body against the visitor's leg. Mr Fairborn scooped up the animal and deposited it in the hall before closing the sitting-room door.

'You had better sit down,' said Mr Fairborn, nodding in the direction of a chair. 'Janette's not ready yet.' He went to stand before an elaborately carved mantelpiece and stared fixedly at his visitor.

'I am a little early,' said Tom, sitting on the edge of the chair.

'Aye, you are.' For a moment there was an awkward silence. 'I won't offer you a drink because you're driving,' Mr Fairborn informed him. 'It's the cause of many an accident, is drink driving. It was on the road out there that Jamie Maladroit was killed. *He'd* been drinking.'

'Well, I won't be drinking tonight,' Tom assured him.

'And it was there that you came off the road, as I recall, travelling too fast and nearly knocking Janette off her horse.'

Tom took a deep breath. On his way to the interview for the post at Risingdale School, he had indeed nearly hit Janette and her horse.

He had driven a bit too fast around the bad bend as she was crossing the road and he had nearly run into her. She had given him a real earful. It was not the most propitious start to a relationship. The near accident had been the talk of the village for some weeks. The story, suitably embellished by Toby Croft in the King's Head, was now something of a legend in Risingdale. When will I hear the last of it? thought Tom now.

'You won't be back too late?' said Mr Fairborn. This was more of an instruction than a question.

'No, not too late.' There was another silence. 'It's been a lovely day,' Tom said at last.

'It bloody hasn't!' snapped Mr Fairborn. 'I've been out all afternoon trying to round up Toby Croft's sheep. The times I've told the dozy good-for-nothing to repair his dry-stone walls. He's taken not the blind bit of notice. Half his sheep got out of the field and into mine and the rest took off down the road. It's been the devil's own job rounding them up. It was left to me to do it. I went round to tell him, and he just

shrugged and said he'd see to it later. That farm of his is a disgrace. Since that lad of his has left, place is going to the dogs.'

'I'm sorry,' said Tom, his words sounding feeble.

'So, then,' said Mr Fairborn at last, 'Mr Gaunt is leaving.'

'That's right.'

'He'll be greatly missed.'

'He will.'

'Salt of the earth, is Gerald Gaunt.'

'He is,' agreed Tom.

'It'll take a big man to fill his shoes.'

'It will.'

'You're not very talkative, are you?' asked Mr Fairborn.

'I'm nervous,' replied Tom.

'Do *I* make you nervous?'

'Yes, you do.'

'Happen I make a lot of people nervous.'

Tom prayed that Janette would hurry up.

'Now look here, Tom,' said her father, resting his hand on
the mantelpiece. 'I'm sure that you've been in Risingdale long
enough to realise that Yorkshire folk are direct and say what
they think. I am a plain-speaking sort of chap and I do not
beat about the bush. I say what I think. Sometimes the truth
isn't always welcomed. Now, I want to ask you and I would
like an honest answer. Are you playing fast and loose with my
Janette?'

'What!' cried Tom, jumping up from the chair like a puppet
that has had its strings pulled.

'It's not gone unnoticed that you and the young lass from
the museum are on very friendly terms. I hope you're not
playing the field, having another young woman in tow.'

'Certainly not!'

'Because if you are two-timing, I'm not best pleased. Janette is very precious to me. I won't see her hurt. I know she
thinks I've been over-protective since her mother died and

maybe a bit interfering at times, but that's because she means the world to me.'

'Mr Fairborn,' replied Tom, trying to keep calm, 'I take exception to what you have just said. There is nothing between Dr Merryweather and me except a professional relationship and I resent the insinuation that there is anything more. And as regards Janette, your daughter means the world to me too. I would do nothing to hurt her.' His face was flushed with anger. 'As for playing fast and loose, as you put it, or playing the field or having some other woman in tow, I don't know from where you've got these ridiculous ideas but I can tell you they are nonsense. I have the greatest respect for your daughter.' He took a deep breath. 'I hope I make myself clear.'

'By gum, you've got a lot to say for yourself when you get started,' said Mr Fairborn, smiling for the first time that evening. 'I'll give you that.'

Footsteps could be heard on the stairs and a moment later Janette, all smiles, came into the room.

'Have you two been having a nice little chat?' she asked.

12

Mr Leadbeater, leaning on a sweeping brush, stood with the headmaster at the entrance to the school.

'Look, can you see, Mr Gaunt? It's there again. That's the third morning it's been there.'

They were examining a blue estate car, which was parked on a small square of land just off the road.

'Yes, I can see,' said the headmaster, shading his eyes from the sun to get a better look.

'I think you should telephone the police. It might be some unsavoury character watching the kiddies. I mean you read all these stories in the papers of abductions and—'

Mr Gaunt cut him short. 'But from what you have told me, the car pulls up when the children are in school and departs a moment later, so it's not that the driver is watching the children. It is very odd. I think I might go and have a word with the man in the car and see what he wants.'

'You want to be careful, headmaster,' warned the caretaker. 'He might be casing the joint.'

Mr Gaunt laughed. 'I think you've been watching too many American films, Mr Leadbeater. Why, in heaven's name, should anyone be casing this joint? This is a school, not some gangsters' hang-out.'

'It might be a school inspector incognito or an undercover policeman.'

'Well, I shall go and see what he wants,' said Mr Gaunt.

'I'll come with you,' said the caretaker, 'and I'll take my sweeping brush in case it gets nasty.'

Mr Gaunt laughed again. 'You have a very vivid imagination, Mr Leadbeater,' he told him. 'Come along, we'll see what the chap wants.'

As the headmaster and caretaker approached the vehicle, the driver made no attempt to start the car and move off, but instead wound down the window. He was a smartly dressed man approaching middle age, clean-shaven and with short, neatly parted hair. A small, hunched figure sat on the back seat.

'May I be of help?' asked the headmaster. 'I'm Mr Gaunt, head teacher at the school.'

'I don't know if you can,' replied the man.

'You have been observed outside the school on a couple of mornings and we wondered why. You will, I am sure, understand our concern.'

'Yes, yes, of course. It's silly of me. I should explain.'

'I would be interested to know,' Mr Gaunt told him.

'Look, this is difficult,' said the man. 'Let me get out of the car and tell you why I am here.'

Mr Leadbeater clutched the sweeping brush like a weapon as the driver climbed from the vehicle.

'My name is John Baxter,' said the man. 'The little girl on the back seat is my daughter, Geraldine. I would like her to come to this school.'

'Why don't we go inside and discuss it there, rather than at the roadside?' suggested Mr Gaunt.

'I'd rather not leave Geraldine by herself,' the man said. He glanced back at his daughter. 'I can't persuade her to get out of the car. She's . . . well . . . she's extremely shy and frightened.'

'How old is she?' asked Mr Gaunt.

'She's eight but small for her age,' said the girl's father. 'We moved here from Nottingham a couple of weeks ago. My wife and I have just split up which, of course, has had an adverse effect on Geraldine. She attended Skillington School for a few days but didn't like it and has been at home since. I start my new job next week so have to get her settled in a school, but she just won't go.' He lowered his voice. 'She has a disability, you see, a speech impediment that makes her stutter. She has had to put up with a lot of name-calling, mimicking and bullying at Skillington. Children can be very cruel.'

'Did you speak to the head teacher at Skillington about it?' asked Mr Gaunt.

'Yes, I did, but I can't say that he was very helpful, just said that children have to cope with the rough and tumble of school life and she should ignore what the other children say and it will stop.'

'That is not true,' said Mr Gaunt. Bullying was a subject about which he felt very strongly. It was unusual for him to question what another head teacher had said, but he felt he needed to say it. 'Bullying should never be ignored or tolerated. In no way is it acceptable in a school, or anywhere else for that matter. It is spiteful and cruel and should be tackled head on.'

Mr Leadbeater nodded in agreement and lowered his sweeping brush.

'I'm pleased to hear you say that,' said Mr Baxter, 'but it has had such an adverse effect on my daughter that my efforts to get her to come into the school have come to nothing. I thought a different, more supportive environment might be better for her. I heard from my new employer that Risingdale might suit her. He spoke very highly of the education here and of you as the headmaster.' He sighed. 'Unfortunately, I cannot get my daughter to get out of the car.'

Mr Gaunt turned to the caretaker. 'Mr Leadbeater,' he said, 'will you take Mr Baxter into school. Please ask your wife to put him in my study and make him a cup of tea. I shall be in directly. I need to speak to Geraldine.'

The father looked worried. 'I really don't know about that,' said the parent. 'As I said she's extremely shy and—'

'Don't worry, I don't bite,' he was told. 'I just need to have a word with her.'

When the girl's father and the caretaker had gone, Mr Gaunt climbed into the front passenger seat of the car. The little girl observed him with wide, unblinking eyes. She resembled a startled rabbit caught in a headlight's glare.

Mr Gaunt didn't say anything for a moment. He felt the child's eyes upon him. 'I do so love this view,' he said at last. 'We have the finest scenery of any school in the county.' The child listened but remained tight-lipped. 'I'm the headmaster of this school, by the way. My name is Mr Gaunt.' His voice was low and gentle. 'I've been here for many years. The children are well behaved and the teachers the best in Yorkshire. This is a very happy school and I think, if you were to give it a chance, you would be happy here too.' There was another silence. 'Your father has told me you were bullied at your last school.' The girl nodded. 'One thing I don't allow in this school is bullying. It is horrible to be bullied. I was picked on at school and know how it feels. It wasn't that I was hit, it was what was said about me and to me. You see, my parents couldn't afford the expensive uniform and the other children laughed at what I wore and at the old satchel that I had. They also mocked me because I was on free school meals. I was told by my teacher to ignore what other children said, but I couldn't. I'm sure you have heard the old rhyme that "Sticks and stones may break my bones but names will never hurt me".' He saw the little girl in the mirror above his head. She was nodding. 'I think that is a very silly rhyme, don't you? Sticks and stones may break your bones but name-calling can hurt a lot more. Sometimes, it can break your heart.'

'It c–c–can,' came a whispered voice from the back seat.

'Now, if you can trust me, Geraldine, and be a brave girl and come in with me, I shall make sure that you will not be bullied. I promise you that. If anyone says anything cruel, you can come straight down to the school office and tell my secretary, Mrs Leadbeater, and I will deal with it. Do you understand me?'

The child nodded.

'I mean what I say,' said Mr Gaunt. 'I shall make sure that nobody bullies you. Just give us a chance, that's all I ask.'

'You're l–l–like my grandpa,' she said quietly, giving a small smile.

'And do you like your grandpa?' she was asked.

She nodded. 'He's n–nice and he's k–kind. I l–love him.'

'Well, I hope that you will find that I am nice and kind. So, shall we go into school, then?'

They found her father in Mr Gaunt's study, sitting on the hard wooden chair before the huge oak desk.

The child ran to her father and gave him a hug.

'Now then, poppet,' he said, smiling. 'Do you think you might like it here?' She nodded.

'Your daughter tells me I remind her of her grandpa,' said Mr Gaunt. 'I hope he's not a very old man.'

'Not that old,' Mr Baxter told him, laughing. He put his arm around his daughter. 'I have a feeling you will be happy here and that Mr Gaunt will make sure there is no bullying.'

'Why don't you stay with us for the day, Geraldine,' said the headmaster, 'and see how you like it? Will you do that?'

She nodded.

'That's settled, then,' said Mr Gaunt. 'If you would like to follow me, I'll introduce you to Miss Tranter. If you come here, and I really hope that you will, you will be in her class.'

*

Later that week in the staffroom, Joyce was telling her colleagues about the new girl.

'She's a timid thing, like a little mouse, and never opened her mouth for two days. She is obviously very bright judging from her writing, which is neat and accurate. I'm sure that her reading will be as good. When she did finally speak to me in a little whisper, I heard for myself that she has a pronounced stutter. Mr Gaunt had already told me she had a speech impediment and is very shy and apprehensive and that she was unhappy at her last school where she was bullied. I don't intend to pressure her to talk. Of course, my training in speech and drama will come in handy in helping her deal with her stammer. I have asked the speech therapist to call in with her advice. I am sure that when Geraldine realises that no one will make fun of her, she will open up.'

'I hope so,' said Mr Cadwallader. 'Children can be very unkind. How are the other children in your class treating this girl?'

'Very well,' replied Joyce. 'They wouldn't dare say anything hurtful because they know how I would react and then, of course, there's her minder.'

'Her minder,' echoed Mr Cadwallader.

'I considered which of the older children would best look after her at break times and make sure she wasn't picked on or made fun of and I thought of—'

'Vicky Gosling,' announced her two colleagues in unison.

'I spoke to Vicky and she was delighted to be given the responsibility.' Joyce smiled. 'She told me that if anyone picks on Geraldine, then she would "punch their lights out". Not something, of course, that I would sanction.'

*

Over the next couple of weeks, the new pupil began to come out of her shell and gained enough self-assurance to take part in the lessons. The children made no mention of her stutter and the teacher's warm and receptive manner allayed the anxieties of the child. Geraldine had agreed to sit with Joyce one lunchtime a week to be given help in coping with her stammer. The speech therapist called into the school to help and advise.

One morning, on her way into school, Joyce found Geraldine's father waiting for her at the gate. He was carrying a bouquet of bright yellow roses.

'Miss Tranter?' he asked.

'Yes.'

'I'm John Baxter, Geraldine's father,' he said. He held up the flowers. 'These are for you. I wanted to tell you what a difference you have made to my daughter's life. She loves it here at Risingdale and she loves being in your class. You are a remarkable teacher, Miss Tranter. I cannot thank you enough.'

Joyce was taken aback and for a moment was lost for words. 'It's a pleasure,' she said at last. She took the roses, breathed in the flowers' fragrance, and favoured him with a brilliant smile. 'This is most kind of you.'

Walking into school, Joyce thought about the words of the parent – that she was a remarkable teacher, that his daughter loved being in her class, that she had made such a difference in the girl's life. To hear such praise made her more determined than ever that she would not bow to Julian's pressure for her to give up teaching.

*

It had been an unusually busy Thursday morning at the general store and post office in Barton-in-the-Dale. The proprietor, Mrs Sloughthwaite, the very eyes and ears of the village and surrounding area, had had a constant stream of customers. A group of elderly ramblers, attired in lurid blue anoraks, waterproof trousers, heavy boots and knitted hats resembling tea cosies, all but cleaned her out of boiled sweets, mint cake and bottled water. The two zealous evangelists, whom Mrs Sloughthwaite referred to later as 'Jovial Witnesses', made a hasty retreat after being subjected to the shopkeeper's unrelenting inquisition.

Major Neville-Gravitas appeared for his panatellas and tried in vain to make a quick exit before he could be interrogated. Over the years he had endeavoured to brush off unwanted enquiries from Mrs Sloughthwaite but, along with the efforts of all the customers who ventured into her store, he had achieved little success. He had just reached the door that morning when the shopkeeper shouted after him.

'I was reading in the local paper that that pal of yours has fallen off of his perch,' she said.

The major turned. 'I don't follow your drift, Mrs Sloughthwaite,' he replied, staring at her blankly.

'It says here in the *Clayton Gazette* that that fat councillor friend of yours is dead.'

'Ah yes, County Councillor Smout. Very sad.'

'That's a mute point,' she observed, sniffing. 'I don't reckon he'll be greatly missed. He was a puffed-up individual from what I've heard, and it was him who tried to close the village school here in Barton and was caught out fiddling his travelling expenses.'

'That was malicious gossip,' the major told her, returning to the counter, 'and I would thank you not to repeat it. Councillor Smout was a dedicated public servant, and he was cleared of any financial impropriety. He produced all the receipts for the journeys he took. Indeed, when he was being investigated, he had the chits.'

'Yes, I bet he had,' said Mrs Sloughthwaite, with exaggerated emphasis. 'And what about his philanderising? I was told he was playing away from home with his fancy woman, taking her on all his trips, at taxpayers' expense, no doubt.'

'That was his personal assistant.'

'Well, if that's what he liked to call her.'

'And it is mere supposition that there was anything untoward,' answered the major.

'Everybody knew about his carryings-on and his drinking,' persevered Mrs Sloughthwaite. 'Mrs Pocock, who was a governor at the village school with him, said he always reeked of whisky. She said his breath could strip the paint off of the walls. They say that he put so much of it away, the fire wouldn't go out at the crematorium with all that alcohol in his blood.'

'You seem to be extremely well informed,' remarked the major.

The shopkeeper folded her dimpled arms under her bosom.

'I like to keep abreast of things,' she informed him. 'Mrs Sidcup, who does a bit of cleaning in the funeral directors', told me they had a job getting him into the coffin he was so big, and they had to hire more pall-bearers to carry it.'

'I must go,' the major told her, heading again for the door. He did not wish to prolong the disagreeable conversation.

He was not, however, escaping so easily. When it came to gleaning information, Mrs Sloughthwaite had the tenacity of invasive ivy.

'Mind you, I had to smile when I read the headline in the *Clayton Gazette*,' she chuckled. The major hovered indecisively in the doorway before turning back.

'What?' he asked.

Mrs Sloughthwaite held up a copy of the paper and pointed to the front page. A comma had been misplaced in the heading with an unfortunate consequence. What should have been written – 'County Councillor Cyril Smout dead, loss to Clayton' instead read – 'County Councillor Cyril Smout, dead loss to Clayton'.

'Perhaps the *Clayton Gazette* got it right for once,' she re-marked wryly.

Later that morning Mrs Pocock, a regular customer, made her weekly visit to share the latest gossip. She was invariably the bearer of bad news and she enjoyed imparting it. On her visits to the shop she enjoyed relating her disappointments and misfortunes and hearing of other people's tribulations. A bony, colourless woman with eyes as leaden as the ocean on a dull day and grey plaited hair circled around her head like a coil of old rope, she wore the melancholy expression habitual to those who felt themselves badly done to in life.

'Oh, hello, love.' Mrs Sloughthwaite greeted her with a smile.

'Good morning,' replied Mrs Pocock, frowning. Her words were clipped and tight.

'Do you know I've not sat down since I got up,' the shop-keeper told her. 'It's been like Piccalilli Circus in here this morning. I've not even had time to get a bite to eat. I'm rav-ished.'

'Famished,' muttered the customer, shaking her head.

'What?'

'Oh, nothing.'

'Major double-barrelled has just been in, sticking up for that councillor pal of his who collapsed on the golf course.'

Mrs Pocock pulled a face. 'Well, I can't say that I'm sorry Cyril Smout has gone. He was full of his own importance and no better than he should be. If it wasn't for my efforts when I was a governor, he would have got his way and closed the village school. And precious little thanks I got. After saving the school, they kicked me off the governors.'

'Yes, you told me,' said Mrs Sloughthwaite under her breath.

There followed a litany of grumbles from the customer: the unreliable bus service, noisy neighbours, unruly teenagers, rude shop assistants, litter on the streets, graffiti in the bus shelter. 'I've been into town to pay my rates, which, I might add, have gone up again,' she grumbled. 'I was coming back on the Clayton bus and this ignorant man on the seat behind mine, leaned forward and pushed his newspaper right in my hair. I turned around and said, "Do you mind? I don't like your paper in my hair." And do you know what he replied? He looks me in the eyes and says, "And I don't like your hair in my paper." Where has common courtesy gone, I ask you?'

Mrs Sloughthwaite changed the subject. 'Of course, you've heard about poor Mrs Fish's narrow escape in the church.'

'Oh yes, I met her in the village,' scoffed the customer. 'She does tend to exaggerate. From what I gather it was just a bit of plaster that fell from the ceiling and she wasn't even in the building at the time. To hear her, you'd think the whole of the church roof collapsed on top of her.'

'Mrs Fish is not enarmoured with the new vicar,' said the shop-keeper. She liked to feed her customers rationed titbits of gossip and was interested in their reaction, which would be passed on to other patrons of her shop. 'He seems to have rubbed a lot of people up the wrong way and upset the apple tart.'

'Bit of a cold fish is Mr Cherry,' ventured Mrs Pocock, sniffing self-righteously. 'He's certainly a change from the last vicar.'

'Yes, it was a pity when Reverend Underwood got elevated,' replied Mrs Sloughthwaite.

'I suppose it's difficult to get vicars these days,' observed the customer. 'I think they were scraping the barrel with Mr Cherry.'

'Well, you know what they say,' said Mrs Sloughthwaite, '"If you can't catch a peacock, then you'll have to settle for a wet hen".'

Mrs Pocock arched an eyebrow. She changed the subject.

The doorbell rattled on its spring and Mr Cherry, the new incumbent of St Christopher's, entered, there to deliver copies of the parish magazine. Mrs Pocock made a speedy exit, not wishing to get into conversation with the clergyman, who she thought might prevail upon her to buy a copy of the publication.

'Well, well,' said Mrs Sloughthwaite, 'speak of the devil.'

'I beg your pardon?' asked the cleric, rather startled.

'We were just talking about you.'

'Oh, I see.'

Mr Cherry was a lean, lanky individual of indeterminate age with unusually pale skin and long shaggy hair. The man's owlish eyes were magnified behind round wire-rimmed spectacles.

'I can't stay,' he said, keen to depart before the grilling. 'I just wanted to deliver the parish magazines.'

Mrs Sloughthwaite, displaying her honed skills at extracting information, managed to delay the cleric.

'I heard that poor Mrs Fish was nearly killed,' she said, with something approaching relish. She leaned over the counter and rested her substantial bosom and her dimpled arms on the top.

'I'm sorry?'

'When the roof collapsed.'

'No, no, she was quite unharmed,' replied the clergyman hurriedly.

'She was in here yesterday in a highly traumatical state of mind,' the shopkeeper carried on, 'and she said the church roof fell down on the very spot where she'd been sat sitting at her organ a few minutes beforehand and where the choir had been stood standing. They could have all been buried alive in the rubble.'

'Not the entire roof gave way,' explained Mr Cherry, in a high, querulous voice. 'It was merely a small portion in the Lady Chapel. Mrs Fish, as indeed all the members of the choir, emerged completely unscathed.'

'She told me the choir had just started practising the hymns "The Word of God Come Down in Earth" and "Lo, he comes with clouds descending" when all the ceiling started coming down to earth in descending clouds of plaster. I mean, it could have been catastrophical if they'd been beneath the roof when it collapsed.' There was a heave of her bosom. 'It's a wonder Mrs Fish got out in time, what with her bad hip and her poor eyesight. And she had her bunions to content with as well. Course, she's not been right since she slipped on an aubergine in the supermarket. She had a lucky escape.'

'Indeed,' agreed the cleric. 'They had a—'

'And from what I've heard your organ has bit the dust.'

'I beg your pardon?'

'The church organ. It's out of action, isn't it?'

'Yes, it is in need of some attention.' He gave a small, constrained smile.

'It's a blessing everyone got out alive,' said the shopkeeper.

'They had a quite miraculous escape,' said the cleric. 'God is very mindful to those of His own. I am hoping that the villagers will rally around and raise the money for the ceiling repairs.'

'You should get that off of the insurance, surely,' said Mrs Sloughthwaite. She tilted her head to one side.

'Unfortunately not,' the vicar told her. He shook his head slowly and heavily. 'Sadly, the insurance company has refused to pay out. It's evidently classed as "an Act of God".'

It did not seem to Mrs Sloughthwaite that God had been all that mindful of His own in allowing His church roof to collapse, nearly burying His organist and the choir. She recalled for a moment the last service she had attended at St Christopher's. Mrs Fish's rendition of the hymn, 'Onward Christian Soldiers' had been painfully laboured, and the choir's singing had been strident and discordant. 'Sounding like a colony of bats stapled to a wall,' she had commented at the time. Perhaps the Almighty had a sense of humour, she thought.

'God moves in a mystifying way,' reflected the shopkeeper.

'"God moves in a mysterious way",' corrected the vicar, '"His wonders to perform".'

'Well, He certainly moved in a mysterious way letting the roof collapse. It's a wonder nobody was hurt,' remarked Mrs Sloughthwaite.

'Indeed,' agreed the cleric, wearying of the conversation. 'I think you have already mentioned that.'

Before she could tackle Mr Cherry about her loss of business in selling confetti, the door of the shop opened to the tinkling of the bell, and a small, stout woman with a broad face and darting eyes entered. Mrs Sloughthwaite recognised the housekeeper of Marston Towers, having had a prolonged and most enlightening conversation with her when she had called in the shop some weeks before to place a card in the window advertising for a part-time cleaner for the big house. She rose from the counter, her face breaking into a big smile. This was the sort of customer the shopkeeper liked, for the woman had been most forthcoming with a deal of interesting information and juicy gossip about Risingdale.

'Well, I must get on, Mr Cherry,' said Mrs Sloughthwaite, as though he was wilfully detaining her. 'As you can see, I have another customer.'

The vicar departed.

'Hello, love,' the shopkeeper greeted her new customer cheerfully. Here was another woman who was incurably inquisitive and enjoyed a good gossip. 'It's nice to see you again. It's been quite a while since you last popped in. Have you had any luck in getting that part-time cleaner?'

'None at all,' answered Mrs Gosling. 'In fact, I've called in to ask you to take the card out of the shop window. Nobody seems interested. Well, I did have one applicant, but she was unsatisfactory. Sour-faced woman she was, who stank of cigarettes and mothballs. She started to tell me what she would and wouldn't do. Said she hated marble floors because they were the devil's own job to clean and bleach brought her out in a rash. I wish she'd have told me all this before she came for the job and not wasted my time.'

'"If wishes were horses, beggars would ride",' commented the shopkeeper, always equipped with an appropriate proverb or aphorism.

'So, I didn't appoint anybody,' stated Mrs Gosling. 'Nobody else was interested.'

'I recall saying to young Mr Dwyer when he called in to ask if I'd put a card in the window for a cleaner at the school,' said Mrs Sloughthwaite, 'that he'd be lucky to get anyone. I told him Risingdale is too insulated, up there at the top of the Dale.'

'They will certainly be lucky to get anybody to clean up at the school,' Mrs Gosling told her. 'I had a gruelling time when I worked up there. The teachers, apart from Mr Dwyer, made more mess than the kiddies and the caretaker Mr Leadbeater – "Leadswinger" would be a name that suited him better – never bestirred himself. If there was work in bed he would lie on the floor. It was left to yours truly to get the place ship-shape. Now I am the housekeeper at Marston Towers, I don't have half the work to do.'

'And without a cleaner and such a big place, as well,' added the shopkeeper sympathetically.

'Well, that's not strictly true,' the customer admitted. 'Mrs Mossup, the landlady at the village inn, put me onto this firm called "Spick and Span" in Ruston. It's a professional domestic cleaning service and two young women come out to Marston Towers twice a week and give the place a good going-over. Of course, I have to watch them like a hawk to make sure they don't miss anything. I told them to put away their fancy feather dusters and air freshener and start scrubbing.'

'"An old broom knows all the dirty corners",' remarked the shopkeeper.

'You're not wrong there,' conceded the housekeeper. 'There's not much that I miss.'

'Is that Mrs Mossup the woman whose daughter is having the baby?' asked the shopkeeper.

'The very same,' replied Mrs Gosling.

'And wasn't the son of your employer the ne'er-do-well who put that young woman in the family way and then went and got himself killed in the car crash? James was his name, wasn't it?'

'You have a very good memory,' remarked the customer.

It was the case that the shopkeeper was not only adept at extracting information from her customers, but she boasted the most amazingly retentive memory and, when it came to gossip, a gift for remembering the finest details.

'Miss Pratt, my teacher, thought I might have a photogenic memory,' Mrs Sloughthwaite disclosed.

It's a pity she couldn't remember the correct words, thought Mrs Gosling.

'So has the young woman had the baby yet?' asked the shopkeeper.

'Oh yes. Leanne – that's Mrs Mossup's daughter – has had a little boy,' continued Mrs Gosling. 'To be truthful, it wasn't all that little. It was a fair size by all accounts, over eight and a half pounds. Mind you the mother's a big lass. It started coming unexpectedly and Mr Dwyer had to rush her to the hospital. He only just got there in time. She very nearly had it in the back of his car.'

'Mrs Fish's granddaughter's child – another kiddie that was born out of wedlock, like that Leanne's baby – came early,' confided Mrs Sloughthwaite. 'Poor little mite, only weighed as much as two bags of sugar. Funny-looking little baby she is, but to hear her grandmother speak she's the loveliest child in the world.'

'Well, as they say,' remarked Mrs Gosling, 'no mother thinks her own child is ugly. To a mother, her baby is beautiful.'

'That's very true,' agreed the shopkeeper. '"Both the raven and the ape think their own young the fairest",' she added, with another few words of wisdom. 'The baby was put in a propagator in extensive care for two weeks,' she carried on. 'They've called the baby Etta. Fancy going through life with a name like Etta Fish. Parents call children all sorts of names these days. In my experience the more educated the mother and father, the dafter the name of their child. I read the births, marriages and deaths in the *Clayton Gazette,* and you would not believe what some parents call their children: Lance Corporal, Honour Commode, Lee King, Anne Teake. It's not fair being labelled with a name like that, for parents to condemn their children to a life sentence.'

'Leanne's gone for a family name,' Mrs Gosling disclosed. 'The baby's called Marcus after Sir Hedley's great-grandfather, with Hedley as a middle name. As my son said to me, "Having a name like that will take some living up to." I must admit Marcus Hedley Mossup is a bit of a mouthful.'

'We had a dog called Marcus,' said Mrs Sloughthwaite. 'Vicious little creature it was. Had to be put down in the end.'

'They had the christening last Sunday in Risingdale church. The place was packed,' continued Mrs Gosling. 'There wasn't a pew to be had. It seemed that the whole of the village turned out. There was a small, select reception at Marston Towers after the service with champagne and canapés.'

'With what?'

'They're sort of small squares of dried bread with bits of meat and fish on the top,' she was told. 'It's what all the sophisticated people eat.'

'Bits of dried bread don't sound to be my cup of tea,' said the shopkeeper.

Mrs Gosling gave a self-satisfied smile. 'It was left to me to organise everything and it went off very well, even if I do say so myself. Sir Hedley was most complimentary.'

'I do like christenings,' said Mrs Sloughthwaite. 'They always bring a tear to my eye. There's nothing quite as happy and heart-warming. At Mrs Fish's granddaughter's christening, the baby was as good as gold and gurgled all the way through.'

'Well, Leanne's baby didn't smile and gurgle all the way through, I can tell you that,' said Mrs Gosling. 'The little scamp put up a real fight for one so small, wriggling and kicking and screaming blue murder when the vicar took him from his mother. There was no way he was going to get dunked in freezing cold water. Leanne was so embarrassed, but Mr Pendlebury, the vicar, told her not to worry and that the child was destined for great things. He told her that the wildest colts make the best horses. Then, when he poured the water over the baby's head, it gave a deafening scream and gave Mr Pendlebury a hefty kick.'

'At Mrs Fish's granddaughter's christening the vicar here in Barton asked the father if he was fully prepared,' the shopkeeper told her. 'He's a nice enough lad is the dad but Mervyn's a bit limp under the cap as they say in Yorkshire. "Oh yes," he says, "we've plenty of food for the reception back at the house." "I mean are you fully prepared spiritually?" asked the vicar. "Oh yes," pipes up Mervyn, "we've a good selection of whisky and gin".'

Mrs Sloughthwaite broke off suddenly when another customer – a tall, frail-looking woman with a pale face as wrinkled as a raisin and a tragic expression – walked through the door. She raised her heavy frame from the counter and gave a broad smile.

'I was just talking about you.' She turned to Mrs Gosling. 'This is Mrs Fish, the woman I was telling you about. She used to play the organ at St Christopher's, but she's deserted the Anglicans for the Primitive Methodists.'

'I have,' agreed the customer, a pained expression on her face.

'She fallen out with the new vicar,' the shopkeeper carried on. 'He's criticised her playing. Said she was too slow and legarthic and that she needed to put in a bit of umph and get-up-and-go into her playing. I said if he's not happy with the way she plays the organ, then she should get-up-and-go to the Primitive Methodists and that's what she did.'

'I said to Mr Cherry—' began the customer, but she was cut off.

'Mind you, there's no organ to play now after what happened.'

'What happened?' asked Mrs Gosling. Her interest was immediately aroused.

'Well, I'd just finished playing the organ—' began Mrs Fish.

'And the church roof fell in right on the very spot where Mrs Fish had been sat sitting,' Mrs Sloughthwaite finished the sentence. 'She could have been incarcerated under the rubble.'

'It was a shock,' sighed Mrs Fish, managing to squeeze in a word, 'but it wasn't all that bad.'

'It might be a good time to give up playing in the church, Mrs Fish,' the shopkeeper told her, raising her voice a fraction like someone talking to an elderly person who was hard of hearing. 'I mean, you are getting a bit long in the tooth and what with your bad hip, poor eyesight and bunions, it must be a real effort.'

The old lady's mouth twitched then tightened. 'I'll have you know I'm not past it yet,' she retorted. 'There's still some snap left in my knicker elastic.'

On this rare occasion, Mrs Sloughthwaite and Mrs Gosling were both lost for words.

13

Sir Hedley found Mrs Gosling in the kitchen busy at the sink, scrubbing the draining board with a vengeance. She was sporting a pair of bright yellow rubber gloves and a frilly, flowered apron.

'Good morning, Mrs Gosling,' he said, coming up behind her.

'Oh, Sir Hedley!' she cried, jumping, and spinning around. 'You gave me quite a start. I didn't see you come in.'

'I'm sorry I startled you,' he said. 'I must say that I am surprised to see you bothering to clean the kitchen. I thought that the people we hired to do all this housework are due to come out here tomorrow.'

'They are,' replied the housekeeper, 'but I like to make sure the place is clean, tidy and ship-shape before they arrive.'

'I can't quite see the logic in that,' he admitted. 'I've employed them to save you having to do it.'

'I do it, Sir Hedley,' she told him, 'because I don't want them finding the place in a state. I have always been one to take pride in my work. It would reflect badly upon me if the house was a mess.'

The baronet smiled. 'I see,' he said, resigned to the fact that it would be fruitless to try and persuade his domestically obsessive housekeeper to step back and let "Spick and Span" deal with the cleaning. 'Well, if you could leave that for a moment, I need to have a word with you.'

'I can imagine what it is about,' she said, removing the rubber gloves and hurriedly wiping her hands down the apron. Her face could freeze soup in pans.

'Now, Mrs Gosling,' said the baronet, chuckling. 'I never took you for a psychic.'

'I beg your pardon?'

'That you are able to read minds.' He settled at the kitchen table.

'I'm guessing that Lady Maladroit will be coming back,' said the housekeeper. 'Well, I have to tell you, Sir Hedley, that if she is, then I don't intend to stay a moment longer. I am still very upset at what was said and—'

He held up a hand. 'Whoah!' he broke in. 'That is not why I wish to speak to you. Lady Maladroit will not be returning.'

Mrs Gosling gave a smothered, 'Oh.'

'It is something entirely different,' Sir Hedley told her. 'Now, why don't you sit down and I shall explain.'

'I was just about to make a cup of tea,' she told him, regaining her demeanour. 'Could you enjoy one?'

'Do you know, I think I could,' he told her. 'You make a very acceptable cup of tea. That was one of the things I missed when you left.'

'You mean, when I was sacked by Lady Maladroit,' came the quick reply.

'Yes. That was unfortunate and you are quite correct in feeling aggrieved, but now you are back, and I am very pleased that you are and, as I said, my wife will not be coming back to Marston Towers.'

She smiled at the compliment and tilted her head, her face pink with pleasure. 'The secret to making a good cup of tea is to use an earthenware teapot,' she told him. 'If you use a china teapot, it's likely to crack when you pour boiling water into it. A metal one can be used but I don't think the tea tastes quite the same. You rinse out the pot with boiling water, then pop in three large teaspoons of proper Yorkshire tea. I never use tea bags. You pour in the hot water and let it mash for two minutes. I'll put the kettle on.'

'Well, if I have to make my own tea, Mrs Gosling,' he told her. 'I shall know exactly what you do. Now, I wanted to—'

'You don't leave it too long, otherwise it'll stew,' she continued, 'and always put the milk in the cup first before pouring the tea. Semi-skimmed is the best to bring out the taste.'

'I shall remember that,' he told her, managing to squeeze in a word. 'Now, to business. There are just a couple of things I wanted to speak to you about. Firstly, I have young Dean Croft coming to see me at eleven o'clock this morning. He sounded rather down on the telephone and said he had something on his mind. I hope nothing is wrong.'

'I'm not at all surprised he's feeling down, having a father like the one he's lumbered with,' said the housekeeper. 'They say that children can bring with them innumerable cares – well, so can parents like Toby Croft. That poor lad of his was tret like a slave when he worked up at the farm. It's a wonder he's turned out as well as he has.'

'Actually, I find old Mr Croft quite a comical character,' replied the baronet.

'Comical!' exclaimed Mrs Gosling. 'It's not a word I would use to describe Toby Croft. He's a miserable, lazy, penny-pinching, bad-tempered old man and as devious as the devil in brown brogues. He was the same when he was a boy. I was in the same class as him at school and nobody liked him. Sneaky he was, telling tales, cheeking the teachers and stealing sweets off the other children. If I see him in the village, I don't give him the time of day. I blank him.'

'You don't mince your words, Mrs Gosling,' said the baronet, smiling again.

'I say it as it is, Sir Hedley,' she informed him. 'I'm a no-nonsense sort of person and if somebody rubs me up the wrong way, I let them know. If I have something on my mind, I get it off my chest.'

'Which I have learnt is a characteristic of Yorkshire folk,' observed the baronet. 'They are not a race to hide their feelings. I've often heard it said that if you wish to know your defects, you only have to ask a person from Yorkshire and your faults will be spelled out pretty quickly.'

'I always think it's best to be straight with people, Sir Hedley,' she answered, 'and not say flattering things to their faces and then backbite when they are out of earshot. There are some folk who will look you in the face and stab you in the back. I've always been a one to speak my mind and then people know what's what. I was forever telling the teachers up at the school when I was assistant caretaker there, about their messy classrooms, not that it made much of a difference. There's the kettle. I'll make the tea.'

Sir Hedley thought of his great-grandfather and wondered what he would have made of Mrs Gosling. Sir Marcus Maladroit lived in a different world where servants were unnoticed, obedient, deferential and not expected to express any opinions. They were required to be silent presences, to serve their betters willingly, gratefully, only speaking to the master or mistress when they were spoken to. Sir Marcus would not have tolerated such presumptuousness from a servant.

'When Dean arrives, could you show him into my study, please, Mrs Gosling?' said Sir Hedley, pushing the thoughts from his mind.

'He's been a changed young man since he left the farm and came to work for you here at Marston Towers,' said the housekeeper, pouring hot water into the teapot, swirling it around before tipping it into the sink. 'Mind you, that might have had a bit to do with Leanne, who seems to have taken quite a shine to him.' She spooned in the tea leaves and added the hot water.

'Really?'

'Oh yes, they're walking out, and they make a nice couple. Course, he's been keen on her for as long as I can remember.'

'Dean is an amenable and hard-working employee,' said the baronet. 'Mr Greenwood speaks very highly of him. I hope he has not got into any trouble. Anyway, I shall soon find out what the matter is. Now, the second thing I wish to tell you about is that I shall be away when the school breaks up for half term.' He paused for breath and gave a slight cough. 'I shall be spending a few days in Scarborough with Mrs Lister and Charlie. You might like to take this opportunity of taking a break yourself.'

He imagined that, at the very least, the disclosure would surprise her, but it had no discernible effect. 'No, no, Sir Hedley, I've much to do in the house. I have the silver and brasses to polish and the china to clean and with you out of the way, I can fettle your study. I'm just thankful I don't have all them stuffed creatures to dust. Nasty, dusty things they were. I gather the museum people took them?'

'Yes, they were pleased to take them off my hands.' The baronet thought for a moment. There was a meaningful silence as he gazed into the depths of the empty teacup which had been placed before him, as if he had noticed something at the bottom. 'I've decided that I am going to make my relationship with Mrs Lister common knowledge,' he told the housekeeper. 'I guess it will give rise to some disapproval in the village so soon after my wife's death, but I don't wish to keep things hidden any longer.'

'And why should you?' asked Mrs Gosling. She added milk to the cups and began pouring the tea. The liquid was a deep chestnut brown. 'What you do is nobody else's business but your own. As I have said, I always think it is best to be straight with people, then they know what's what. Life's too short, Sir Hedley. You have to seize an opportunity when it is offered and get a bit of pleasure when you can. Mrs Lister is a nice woman and Charlie is a grand little lad. You all deserve to have some happiness. Now, drink your tea before it gets cold.'

Dean Croft arrived promptly at eleven o'clock and was shown by Mrs Gosling into the study. He had made a real effort with his appearance and was dressed in a smart oatmeal jacket, white shirt and tie and clutched a tweed cap. He licked his lower lip. His mouth was dry.

Sir Hedley stood beneath a portrait in oils of an ancestor.

'Ah, Dean,' said the baronet. 'Do come along in.'

'Good mornin', Sir 'Edley,' replied his visitor, twisting the cap nervously. He stood awkwardly before his employer and scanned the room, his eyes coming to rest upon the oil painting on the wall above Sir Hedley. The picture showed a daunting, self-important-looking man in military uniform, who stared out of the frame in solemn disapproval. He bore a remarkable resemblance to the man standing beneath the painting: a portly, red-cheeked individual with an intimidating moustache. Dean took a deep breath. 'I 'ope that I'm not disturbin' yer, sir?' He was almost stammering.

'Not at all. It's such a beautifully bright and sunny day that I thought we might take a turn outside and get a breath of fresh air. It is rather stuffy in here.'

'Aye, that'd be fine,' replied Dean running his hand through his hair in an agitated manner.

He followed Sir Hedley along the white gravel path between closely clipped box hedges. The lawns were rich with the scent of freshly mown grass, the hedges carefully pruned. Shrubberies and trees were coming into their full summer thickness. The walled garden which they entered through an archway was split into four quarters separated by narrow paths. The air was infused with the scent of honeysuckle. Pink and yellow roses were trained up a trellis. In the centre of the area was an ornamental pond, the surface of which was covered in

the leaves of large lilies. In the carefully tended borders was
an abundance of flowers; hibiscus, bougainvillea, campanula
and helianthus, all coming into bloom. Great tangled boughs
of wisteria hung from a wall. They sat on an ornate cast-iron
bench overlooking the pond.

'We used to have some koi carp,' reflected Sir Hedley.
'Sadly, a hungry heron cleared the lot. They are lovely-look-
ing birds, amazing in flight, but my goodness they are greedy.
The hawks are the same – beautiful birds but a damned nuisance. A soaring falcon is a sight to see, but we could well
do without them. They take so many of the game birds. Of
course, we can't go shooting or trapping them. You know that
don't you?'

'Yes, Sir 'Edley.' Dean wanted to get to the reason for his
visit but was nervous of broaching the matter so merely nodded and said nothing.

'So how is the re-stocking of the game birds progressing?'
asked the baronet.

'Champion, sir,' he replied.

'That's good to know,' said Sir Hedley. 'I've got quite a large
party coming up from London for the shoot later this year so
you and Mr Greenwood will be kept pretty busy after August.
I imagine we will need to take on more people.'

Dean cleared his throat and gently chewed his lower lip. 'I
don't think I'll be here then, Sir 'Edley,' he said. His face was
pained.

'You're thinking of leaving?'

'That's what I wanted to see yer about.'

'I thought you were happy here?'

'I am, Sir 'Edley,' answered Dean. 'I'm dead 'appy. I love
t'job an' like workin' wi' Mester Greenwood. 'E's tret me well.
I'm reight grateful that yer gev me t'chance, but . . .'

'Then why on earth do you wish to leave?' asked Sir Hedley, brushing off the rest of the sentence.

'I need to get back to mi dad's farm,' replied the young man. 'It's goin' under. Everyone in Risingdale knows t'place is goin' to rack an' ruin. Mester Fairborn, whose farm's near mi dad's, collared me in t'village an' telled me Croft Farm is in a reight state. I called in last week to see mi mam an' she's at her wits' end. There were no sign o' mi dad.'

No doubt at the King's Head, thought Sir Hedley.

'Anyroad,' Dean continued, 'things at t'farm 'ave gone from bad to worse. Gates were oppen, walls were down, weeds everyweer, roof were leakin' an' beeasts not fed.'

'I see,' muttered Sir Hedley, brushing a hand over his bristly moustache. 'A sorry state of affairs.'

'I need to gu back an' sooart things out,' said Dean. 'If I don't then t'place will gu under.'

'I have to say that your father has largely brought this on himself,' said the baronet. 'He is a man of masterly inactivity at the best of times. He has the wherewithal to employ some people to help him around the farm. I cannot understand why he doesn't get some help.'

The boy gave a hollow laugh. 'Nob'dy will work for 'im, Sir 'Edley. 'E's so miserable an' bad-tempered an' tight as a duck's backside wi' 'is brass. Anyroad, I've thought things over. I don't want to gu back, but I feel I 'ave to. T'farm's been in t'family fer generations an' I can't see it gu to t'wall. Way I see it, I 'ave a duty to try an' keep things goin'. I feel I owe it to 'im.'

'I am of the opinion that you owe your father little,' observed Sir Hedley. 'I gather he didn't treat you all that well when you worked for him.'

'No, it's true enough that 'e din't tret me reight. 'E found fault wi' owt I did an' 'e never hexerted 'issen very much, but 'e is mi father after all an' I 'ave a duty as 'is son to gu an' 'elp.'

'You are being very magnanimous,' Sir Hedley informed him. 'I think it is commendable that you are prepared to give

up a job you like and are good at to help him. There are few
sons who would be as selfless.' He thought for a moment. 'I
am loath to tell you what to do, for in my experience nothing
is so liberally given as advice and it is seldom welcomed by
those who hear it, but I will say this. Your father must understand that if you do return to sort out the mess in which he
has landed himself, then he needs to change his attitude and
treat you fairly and value what you do. I think you need to
spell that out to him.'

Dean shook his head. 'There's abaat as much chance of 'im
changin' as weavin' a rope out o' sand or teachin' a crab to
walk straight,' he said.

'Nevertheless, I think you should make it clear to him.'

'I suppose I could try.'

'Well, I wish you luck,' the baronet told him, getting to his
feet. 'I am sorry to lose you. I shall keep the job open for a
few weeks and if things do not work out for you back at the
farm, then you may return. And there is no hurry to vacate
the cottage.'

'That's reight decent of yer, sir,' said Dean humbly.

A heron appeared above the trees, its wide wings beating
back and forth slowly and rhythmically as it sailed across the
sky, its long legs trailing behind.

'There's the rascal that ate my koi carp,' cried Sir Hedley,
shaking his fist in the air.

He walked with his visitor back to the house.

'I hear that you and Leanne are seeing something of each
other,' remarked the baronet.

Dean's face coloured up. 'Well . . . er . . . we 'ave been goin'
out a few times.'

'Well, good luck to you both,' he was told. 'She's a nice
young woman.'

The young man's face broke into a wide smile. 'Thank you,
sir,' he said.

When Dean had gone, Sir Hedley returned to his study. He sat at his desk, lit a cigar, and thought about what his house-keeper had said earlier that day. 'I say it as it is, Sir Hedley,' she had informed him. 'I always think it's best to be straight with people. I've always been a one to speak my mind and then people know what's what.'

'Wise words,' he said out loud before drawing on his cigar and blowing out a cloud of smoke.

*

That evening, Sir Hedley arrived at the King's Head a lit-tle after eight o'clock. The place was crowded and noisy. As he edged his way through the throng, the farmers, with their ruddy faces and great red hands, ceased commiserating about the price of cattle feed and the recent sheep auction and im-mediately fell silent. The commanding entrance of the squire secured their attention. It was not a usual occurrence for Sir Hedley to visit the inn. Many of the locals nodded, others wished him a 'Good evening'; all watched curiously as he ap-proached the counter.

'I'm sorry, sir,' the young barman told him, 'if you are here to see the landlady, I'm afraid she's out. She's visiting her daughter in the village this evening.'

'No, it was not Mrs Mossup whom I wished to see,' replied Sir Hedley. He turned to the morose-looking old farmer who slouched on a stool by himself at the end of the bar. 'This is the person I need to talk to.'

The old farmer screwed up his face. 'With me?' he asked.

'Yes, indeed, Mr Croft, with you.' Sir Hedley fixed him with a shrewd glance.

Toby considered his empty glass meaningfully. The hint was ignored.

'So, what is it abaat, squire?' he asked.

'Perhaps we might sit outside where we won't be disturbed,' it was suggested.

'Aye, if tha likes.'

To the front of the inn was a handful of tables with wrought-iron legs and straight-backed wooden chairs. It was a mild evening and there was a group of people enjoying the late sunshine. Sir Hedley and the farmer sat away from the other customers.

'Now then, squire, what can I do fer thee?' asked Toby.

'Your son came to see me this morning,' he was told.

'Oh aye.'

'He tells me he is going to leave my employment.'

The old farmer gave a sneaky smile. There was a gleam of inward satisfaction in his eyes. 'Aye well, I din't think it'd be long afore tha got t'measure of 'im. I knew 'e'd never tek to gamekeepin', I telled 'im so missen an' sed 'e'd soon come runnin' back to me wi' 'is tail between 'is legs when it din't work out. T'lad should—'

'That is where you are wrong, Mr Croft,' interrupted Sir Hedley. 'In fact, it has worked out very well, very well indeed. I have been more than pleased with Dean's work. He is a punctual, reliable, and hard-working member of my staff and I am very sorry to see him go. I can't say that I agree with the decision that he has made, but it is a principled decision and I admire him for it.'

'So why is 'e leaving if it—'

'Let me finish,' interrupted the baronet again. 'He is minded to return to your farm to help you out of the hole in which you have landed yourself.'

'What 'ole?' demanded Toby, his face flushed with resentment. 'I don't know owt abaat any 'ole.'

'It is common knowledge that your farm is going under, Mr Croft,' Sir Hedley told him bluntly.

'I don't know what tha's 'eard, but—'

'Let me finish,' said Sir Hedley. 'You know as well as any-one that it is only a matter of time before you will not be able to carry on and your land, house and outbuildings will have to be sold. Without your son's help, you haven't a chance of keeping your farm running.'

'I'm managing,' came the lame reply. He realised that what was being said was the truth. Since his son had left, he had not been able to manage and had let things go. The farm was deteriorating fast.

'Of course you are not managing. If you believe that then you are fooling yourself. Your farm is declining. Everyone can see that. Are you unaware of the strikingly obvious?'

'I'll admit it's not been too good lately,' Toby conceded.

'You need your son's help,' said Sir Hedley, spelling out each word like a parent talking to an inattentive child. He leaned closer so as not to be overheard. 'I will say this: if you reject his offer, then Dean will get his job back with me and you will end up without your farm. I am telling you this be-cause I like and admire your son. It would be in my interest if your farm did come up for sale. It could end up as part of the Maladroit estate.' His words were more like a warning than a statement.

This observation made the old farmer think. This was no idle speculation, for over the years Sir Hedley had acquired several of the failing farms around Risingdale, one being that of Richard Greenwood. Only recently Northfield Farm had been purchased and was now part of the Maladroit estate. The last thing he wanted was his farm to fall into the squire's hands. He weighed the matter.

Sir Hedley paused, expecting Toby to say something. When the farmer remained tight-lipped, he leaned closer across the table. 'Well?' he asked.

'If t'lad 'as a mind to come back, I won't turn 'im away,' said Toby.

'And if he does return, be under no illusion,' forewarned Sir Hedley, 'that if you don't treat him fairly, pay him a decent wage and involve him fully in the running of the farm, then his stay with you will be short-lived and he will be back working at Marston Towers as one of my gamekeepers. I have kept his job open for the time being in case he wishes to come back. I have told him that he may stay in the tied cottage until things are hopefully settled.'

Toby was disposed to telling the squire that he was in no position to start laying down the law. After all, this wasn't the Middle Ages when the Lord of the Manor ruled the roost. However, he had heard the threat in Sir Hedley's voice, and he held his tongue, for he was shrewd enough to know that it would be unwise to cross someone so influential as the baronet.

'Aye, I suppose so,' he grumbled.

'You are truly fortunate to have a son like yours,' said Sir Hedley, getting to his feet. 'Very fortunate.' He thought for a moment of his own son and wished that James had had the same feeling of familial duty as Dean Croft.

*

When Sir Hedley arrived back at Marston Towers later that evening, he found a message from Mrs Gosling on the table in the entrance hall. It had 'URGENT' written in bold letters at the top of the paper. The housekeeper informed him that Mrs Lister had telephoned to tell him that Charlie had been taken to Clayton Royal Infirmary. Their son had been in an accident coming back from school that afternoon, knocked down by car. Sir Hedley gripped the end of the table to steady himself, his other hand clamped hard to his chest to quell the hammering of his heart.

'Dear God,' he muttered, 'let him be all right.'

Then he hurried from the house.

He found Charlie's mother and Mrs Gosling at the end of a long creamy-yellow-walled corridor in the hospital. It smelled of disinfectant. The two women were sitting in unhappy silence on a pair of orange plastic chairs outside Ward 13. Mrs Lister was bent over and dejected like a broken puppet, with Mrs Gosling's arm around her shoulder. When she heard footsteps, she looked up and saw Sir Hedley striding with a purposeful step down the corridor to meet her, his face a picture of misery. Her face was drained of colour. She jumped up from her seat and rushed into his arms, burying her head in his shoulder with loud racking sobs. His arms went around her, and he held her close. They remained holding tight to each other, a motionless tableau. Then Sir Hedley drew away at last, lifted her face and wiped away her tears.

'There, there,' he said soothingly. 'Come and sit down and tell me what has happened.'

'Oh, Hedley,' was all she managed to say.

They went to sit next to Mrs Gosling. The housekeeper's face was pale and drawn. 'Charlie was coming home from school,' she said, 'and he ran into the road. A car knocked him down. The driver called for an ambulance. Then the police telephoned Mrs Lister to say what had happened. We tried to get in touch with you but—'

'Charlie has always been a one for doing that,' sniffed Mrs Lister, her eyes full of tears. She gripped Sir Hedley's hand. 'I'm forever telling him to be careful on the roads, but his mind is elsewhere sometimes and . . .' she trailed off and began crying again.

'How is he?' asked Sir Hedley softly. He tugged nervously at his moustache, dreading to hear the answer.

'They don't know,' Mrs Lister answered, dabbing her eyes and fighting off the tears. 'He's in intensive care. He was unconscious when they brought him in. They would only let me

see him for a minute. He had a cut on his head and bruising
on his face. He looked dreadful. They don't know if he's broken
any bones.' Her cheeks were wet with tears. 'I telephoned
Marston Towers to tell you, but Mrs Gosling said you were
out and she didn't know where you were.'

'I had some business to attend to in town,' he told her, 'and
then a meeting later on.' He tried to control his emotions, but
his voice betrayed the extent of his concern.

'I phoned my Clive and he drove us both to the hospital,'
Mrs Gosling explained.

'Thank you,' Sir Hedley told his housekeeper. 'It was good
of your son to do that.' He sat up. 'Perhaps I should go and see
how Charlie is,' he murmured.

'The nurse said to wait,' Mrs Lister told him. 'The doctor is
with Charlie now.' She raised her hand, which was trembling,
and pushed back a strand of hair. 'I don't think they can tell
you any more than what they have told me.' She then began to
cry again. 'Oh, Hedley, I hope he's going to be all right.'

'I'm sure he will be,' he said weakly and without conviction.
She heard the tremor in his voice and knew that he was close
to tears. He drew in a deep breath and turned to his housekeeper. 'You have been very good, Mrs Gosling, but now it
is getting late. There is nothing else you can do. I think you
should go home. It might be some time before we hear any
news.' He stood. 'I'll arrange for a taxi.'

'Oh, don't bother with that, Sir Hedley,' she said, heaving
herself up. 'I'll get my Clive to come and collect me. There's
a call box in reception. I'll give him a ring, but I'm more than
happy to stay.'

'No, no, you go. I guess there will be a long wait for Mrs
Lister and myself.'

'Are you sure?' she asked, her voice full of tenderness and
concern.

'Yes, I'm sure.'

'Would you like me to get you both a cup of tea before I go?' she asked. 'There's a machine at the end of the corridor.' A cup of tea seemed to her to be the cure for all potential disasters.

'No, thank you.'

'I'm sure that Charlie will be all right,' she said, resting a hand on his arm. 'He's a tough little boy. You will get in touch if there is any news?'

'Yes, of course. Now, you get off home.'

'Thank you for all you have done, Mrs Gosling,' said Mrs Lister.

When the housekeeper had gone, Sir Hedley sat down again, reached for Mrs Lister's hand and squeezed it. After what seemed an age a young female doctor approached.

'Mrs Lister, I am Dr McNeill, and I am looking after your son. The specialist will be in tomorrow to examine him and then we will get a clearer idea of his injuries. We are doing some tests at present and then later he will be going for some X-rays.' She had a solicitous and kindly manner.

'How is he?' Sir Hedley asked, swallowing hard.

'This is a good friend,' Mrs Lister told the doctor.

'He's still unconscious, but this sometimes happens after a concussion.'

'Will he be all right?' asked Mrs Lister. She swallowed nervously.

'It is rather too early to say at this stage.'

Sir Hedley thought he detected something dark and troubling in the doctor's eyes.

'But you are hopeful?' asked Sir Hedley.

The physician paused before answering. How many times had she heard some worried relative ask that about a loved one and how many times had she wished she could have reassured them that, of course, everything will be all right? In this case she was not optimistic.

'Could we go somewhere a little more private?' she asked.

Sir Hedley and Mrs Lister were shown into a small room off the corridor. Unlike the other parts in the hospital with their plain, pale walls and antiseptic smell, this area had a cosy appearance with rose-coloured curtains, a small sofa and two matching armchairs. On a wall were three vividly painted seascapes below a large and noisily ticking clock and on the windowsill a vase of large, bright flowers made the room look cheerful and welcoming. A selection of magazines and leaflets, the latter warning of the dangers of smoking and drinking and giving advice on healthy eating, covered the top of a coffee table.

Sir Hedley and Mrs Lister sat close together on the sofa, clutching each other's hands. Dr McNeill took a seat opposite. She drew a small breath before speaking.

'There is no easy way to say this,' she told them quietly. 'Charlie has had a very nasty bang to his head. He's suffered a severe concussion and he's in a serious condition. When the specialist examines him tomorrow we will find out more about—'

'Are you saying that there is a chance he might not recover, doctor?' interrupted Sir Hedley.

'I really can't say,' she told him. 'I'm saying that the next twenty-four hours will be critical.'

Mrs Lister began to sob.

'I have known patients make a full recovery,' the doctor reassured her.

'And others?'

'Let us try and be optimistic,' said the doctor. 'Charlie is young and healthy and we should be hopeful.' But she did not sound all that positive.

*

The following day as Mrs Lister phoned the school to tell Mr Gaunt what had happened to Charlie, Dean visited his father.

He was feeling apprehensive about the reception that he would receive. When he arrived at the farm, the air of neglect was evident. Hedges were overgrown; water troughs had a cover of thick green slime; rough, spiky grass, dandelions and ragwort sprouted through the broken paving slabs; and in the farmyard, mud and great splats of slurry had been churned up by hooves. A few long-legged chickens scratched in the dust. A horse viewed him mournfully from a field. Bits and pieces of old rusting farm machinery were covered in weeds. Dean saw his father, a stooped, shambling figure, coming along a track, whacking a cow's haunches with a thin switch to keep the beast on course. His was a hard face, rigid in its expression, a face not naturally given to smiling. Dean felt a stab of pity for him. The old man had aged and looked miserable and aggrieved as he came to a field which was riddled with rabbit warrens and molehills. He took a final draw on the cigarette, which had been screwed in the corner of his mouth, threw it down and, cursing angrily, herded the animal through the gate.

Dean walked down the track to meet him.

'Ey up,' he said hesitantly.

His father regarded him with milky, tired eyes. 'It's thee, then,' he mumbled. His face was blank.

''Ow's it goin'?'

''Ow's it goin',' he repeated, gruffly. 'See fer thissen,' replied the old man sourly. His brow was tense and the corners of his mouth twitched.

As his son came closer Dean detected the mingled smell of sweat, cigarettes and wood smoke.

'It dun't look too good,' he said.

His father gave a dismissive grunt. He raised his hand to his head and scratched his scalp.

High in the sky a hawk rode the air currents, sweeping in wide circles above the trees.

'I'm thinkin' o' comin' back,' Dean told him.

'Oh aye.' His father dropped his head and stared at his feet. He couldn't face his son's eyes.

'That's if tha wants me to.'

'Gamekeepin' dun't suit thee, then?' said Toby, still looking down. He knew, from what Sir Hedley had told him, that the job had suited his son very well, but he did not let on.

'Summat like that,' replied Dean. 'Tha din't answer mi question. Does tha want me to come back, or what?' He needed to hear his father say it.

'If tha's a mind to,' chuntered Toby. His voice, which Dean remembered as hard and defiant, now sounded flat and toneless.

'If I do come back, there'll 'ave to be a few changes,' his son told him.

'Oh, aye?'

'It waint be t'same as when I worked 'ere afore. There'll be no more shoutin' an' grumblin' an' criticisin' what I do an' thas'll 'ave to pay me a decent wage. An' we can't manage t'farm on us own. We'll have to 'ire some 'elp which'll mean tha sheddin' out some o' thy brass.'

Toby thought for a moment. He looked up and gave a wry smile. 'By the 'eck, tha's gorralot to say fer thissen, I'll say that fer thee. Tha's changed since tha's been workin' up at t'big 'ouse.'

'Tha's reight, I 'ave changed, Dad, an' I'm not prepared to purrup wi' thee carpin' an' complainin'. If tha wants me to come back, I will, but only on my terms.' He waited for a response, but Toby remained silent. 'Is that clear?' He spoke with a steely resolve.

His father looked down at his feet again and nodded grudgingly. He thought for a moment on what he had heard. Then he stared up at his son. His face had the expression of grim forbearance like a condemned man being dragged off to his execution. It displayed a mixture of defensiveness and defeat. 'Aye, I suppose so,' he muttered.

14

At Friday morning break, Joyce joined Tom in the playground. It was a bright, sunny morning in late May and they walked around enjoying the fine weather.

'So, Charlie's still in hospital, is he?' asked Joyce.

'Yes.'

'How is he?'

'Not too good, I'm afraid,' Tom told her. 'He is still unconscious and, from what his mother told Mr Gaunt, there's been no improvement in his condition. I can't imagine how she must be feeling.' He was careful not to mention the boy's father, unaware that Joyce knew of Charlie's paternity. She had discovered the secret when by chance she had been with Julian at the same hotel in Scarborough one weekend as Sir Hedley, who was there with Mrs Lister and her son. Like Tom, she had kept the discovery to herself.

'It sounds as if it's touch and go,' she said.

'I guess so. I thought of ringing Mrs Lister to see if there had been any change, but she has got enough on her plate at the moment. I'll give her a call later today.'

'Well, I do hope Charlie will be all right.'

'I know one shouldn't get emotionally involved in the lives of our pupils,' said Tom, 'but this news has really knocked me for six. Charlie is such a nice lad and has everything going for him. It's so sad.'

'It is,' agreed Joyce.

'You know I nearly knocked him over when I came for the interview here,' Tom told her. 'He ran right out in front of my car.' The teacher was quiet for a time. 'I think I will get someone from the police to speak to the children about road safety. Anyway, what are you doing missing your break? It's my turn for yard duty.'

'The vicar has arrived,' Joyce told her colleague, 'so I've escaped. He's a lovely man, is Mr Pendlebury, but my goodness he can talk. Once he gets started there's no stopping him. I left him with Bertha, who has much more patience than I.'

'I thought Mr Pendlebury spoke very well at the christening,' remarked Tom, 'although I did think his homily went on a little too long.'

'A little too long!' she echoed. 'It was over an hour.'

'I guess living alone he gets lonely and just wants someone to talk to.'

'Or to talk at,' said Joyce rather unkindly.

'So, how are things at home?' Tom asked.

'Greatly improved,' Joyce replied, looking smug. 'Julian has now got the measure of his nephew. Evidently Stanley has been interfering at the auction house, treading on toes and being a general nuisance. He has got up the noses of all the staff. Julian had it out with him and told him not to meddle and to leave the running of the business to Mr Cavill, the General Manager. There is quite an atmosphere in the house when they're together, so I shouldn't wonder if Stanley is asked to move out sooner or later, which would certainly suit me. I shall be glad to get away at half term. Julian and I are spending a few days in Stratford-upon-Avon during the break. We're booked into a plush five-star hotel and going to see a production at the Royal Shakespeare Theatre. Julian isn't that keen but he knows my love of drama.'

Tom thought back to when Joyce had told him that things at home were not going all that well and that the appearance of Stanley had cast a shadow over her relationship with her husband. That morning it was 'My husband this' and 'My husband that'.

'So, are you going anywhere nice over the half-term holiday?' Joyce asked.

It was Tom's turn to look smug. 'Janette and I are going to Paris.'

'Going to Paris?' cried Joyce.

'I've booked a hotel just off the Champs-Élysées – Le Bon Accord – for three nights. We'll drink chilled white wine in a swanky restaurant, have a coffee at a pavement café by the side of the Seine and visit Notre-Dame and Sacré-Coeur and have an evening at the opera.'

'Well, you're a dark horse and no mistake,' she said. 'So, is this relationship serious?'

'Yes, I think it's pretty serious.'

'Well, look at you! You're in love.'

'I suppose so,' he said softly, looking embarrassed. 'I suppose I am.'

'Now come along, spare no detail. Tell me all about you and Janette.'

Before Tom could answer, two infant boys approached.

'Miss, miss, will tha come ovver an' tell Vicky Gosling,' asked the first child, before wiping his nose on the back of his hand.

Joyce sighed. 'Tell her what, Andrew?' asked the teacher.

'Tell 'er to gerrer mitts off of our football,' replied the child. 'She's allus nickin' it an' wangin' it ovver t'wall.'

'An' when we telled 'er to gi o'er an' pack it in an' stop laiking abaat,' added his small companion, 'she telled us to shut us cake-oils or she'd bray us.'

Joyce looked at Tom. 'Words fail me,' she said.

*

In the staffroom the vicar, a plump, cheerful, rosy-faced individual wearing a dusty cassock and a clerical collar, was holding forth. Mr Pendlebury was a man who enjoyed speaking at length. He was one of those preachers who, on coming to the end of what they have to say, find it impossible to stop. However, his kindly disposition amply compensated for his shortcomings in the pulpit. His captive audience that morning, Mrs Golightly, smiled indulgently as he rattled on.

'As I walked up from the vicarage this morning,' said Mr Pendlebury, in his pulpit voice, 'I paused to look at the wide and silent landscape before me. The view up here never ceases to fill me with awe. Yorkshire is not called "God's own country" for nothing. The words of the poet Thomas Campbell, who lived nearly two hundred years ago, came to mind:

"Tis distance lends enchantment to the view,
And robes the mountain in its azure hue."

'Of course, he was not a great poet although his lyrical verse, "The Pleasures of Hope" was well received at the time. I guess he did not endear himself to his female readers.' He chuckled. 'He was reputed to have written:

"The minds of women are so small,
That some believe they've none at all".'

It's a good thing that Joyce is not in the staffroom to hear the poet's bon mot, thought Mrs Golightly for, had she heard this remark, her colleague would not have chuckled and the clergyman would have got a flea in his ear. An attitude like that was no laughing matter. She recalled the occasion when Joyce had crossed swords with Mr Pendlebury over the issue of the ordination of female priests in the Church of England. When he had asserted that, in his considered opinion, it was not really proper to admit women to holy orders, Joyce had given him the benefit of her views, which were very much in collision with his own.

'Poor Thomas Campbell,' sighed the vicar. 'His wife died, one son died in infancy and the other went insane.'

'You are here to talk to Mr Cadwallader's class, I take it?' Mrs Golightly asked, before the vicar could start speaking again.

'Indeed, I am.'

'I hope Miss Tranter's class don't disturb you. The children are practising this morning for the choral speaking competition for the Clayton and District Festival of Speech and Drama in July. It might be a little noisy.'

'Oh, I shall not worry my head about that,' said the vicar. 'I think it an excellent training to teach young people to speak clearly, confidently and with enthusiasm and choral speaking is a perfect vehicle to encourage this. Children should learn to use this wonderful language of ours effectively. When I was at theological college, my tutor, Dr Augustus Prendergast, a very erudite and accomplished author and orator – he wrote the seminal work *Flashes from the Pulpit* – gave some valuable advice on delivering a sermon and told us that speaking in public demands skill, application and practice.' Perhaps the Reverend Doctor Prendergast should have said something about the importance of brevity and intelligibility, thought Mrs Golightly, for Mr Pendlebury's sermons were legendary in their length and scholarship and for him sharing with his congregation his considerable historical and biblical knowledge.

'So, what piece are the young people to perform?' asked the cleric.

'It's an extract from "Hiawatha",' he was told. 'It's a famous narrative poem and Joyce thinks it will give the children ample opportunity to use their voices to good effect. Miss Tranter trained in speech and drama before she became a teacher, you know.'

'Yes, I heard that she had trod the boards,' said the vicar. 'It is said that the teacher must have something of the actor within him . . . or her.'

'That's very true,' agreed Mrs Golightly. 'There is a deal of performance in teaching. Perhaps you might like to hear the children's recitation next time you are in school. I am sure Joyce and the children would welcome having an audience.'

'That would be splendid,' replied Mr Pendlebury. 'I should like that very much. "Hiawatha" was a favourite poem of mine when I was at school. I can still recall the opening verses: "On the shores of Gitche Gumee/Of the shining Big-Sea-Water".'

'What is the theme of your lesson with Mr Cadwallader's class?' Mrs Golightly enquired quickly before the vicar could give her the benefit of any more of the poem. She immediately regretted asking, for once started, Mr Pendlebury was not a man to be put off his stride.

'It's about saints, those special people who set us a good example in kindness, compassion and self-sacrifice,' the vicar droned on, adopting the tone of one of his sermons. 'I am going to tell the children about St Robert of Knaresborough who lived in a cave by the River Nidd and about some of the lesser-known saints like Polycarp and Sextus. Fascinating lives they led. Then there's St Drogo, the patron saint of sheep and unattractive people, and St Jude, the patron saint of hopeless cases. I was telling Mr Dwyer, in one of my earlier visits to the school, about St Alkelda, the Saxon princess and revered nun who was garrotted by the Vikings. There's a church dedicated to her at Giggleswick. Then there's the legend of St Oswine of Deira, a greatly venerated Yorkshire saint in the Anglican Communion who was hacked to death at Gilling.'

'These saints seemed to have had singularly unfortunate lives,' remarked Mrs Golightly, giving a small shiver.

'Yes, indeed many saints suffered terribly for their faith,' said Mr Pendlebury, giving a priestly nod. 'Now, speaking of "Hiawatha", did you know that he was the leader of the Mohawk people?'

'No, I wasn't aware of that.'

'Sadly, his wife and daughters were slaughtered by an enemy tribe.'

'Oh dear,' sighed the teacher, hiding behind a sad smile.

'Did you also know,' carried on the vicar, 'that a member of his tribe was a native American saint?'

'No, I can't say that I was aware of that either,' replied Mrs Golightly, easing back her sleeve surreptitiously to check the time on her wristwatch.

'Well, there was. Her name was St Kateri Tekakwitha, known as "the Lily of the Mohawks". She is the patroness of ecology and the environment – a great inspiration in her selfless devotion.'

'I hope she had a happier life than the other saints you mentioned,' remarked the teacher.

'Unfortunately not,' said the vicar, shaking his head again. 'At the age of four she was terribly disfigured and left half blind with smallpox.'

'Oh dear,' muttered Mrs Golightly. She had arrived that morning in such a cheerful frame of mind. She now felt thoroughly depressed.

The vicar carried on unrelentingly. 'A remarkable woman was St Kateri Tekakwitha. Unfortunately, she died at the age of twenty-four.'

Saved by the bell, said Mrs Golightly to herself, when she heard the strident ringing which denoted the start of lessons.

'Well, there's the end of morning break,' she said, getting up from her chair. 'I look forward to hearing more about St . . .'

'Tekakwitha,' prompted the vicar.

'Another time,' she said. 'Do call in and hear the children performing "Hiawatha". I am sure Miss Tranter will be happy to see you.'

*

At lunchtime Mr Gaunt came into the staffroom. He was in a particularly good mood. He had spent a most pleasant evening in Moira's company. She had invited him around to her small flat for dinner and they talked and talked into the early hours with hardly a mention of school or animals.

'I thought you might be interested in these,' he told the teachers, as he sat down at the table. 'Mrs Leadbeater has been on at me for some time to clear out the cupboards in my study, but I've never got around to it. Since I shall be leaving at the end of term, I have made a start and come across these old school logbooks and inspection reports. They make fascinating reading.' He opened the first book and ran a finger down a page. 'This is after a visit from the school inspector in 1881. I imagine school inspection then was still in its infancy. It seems the chief function of HM Inspector at that time was to assess the amount the Treasury should pay schools. Some inspectors did not seem to be overly concerned with curriculum matters. This inspector, however, a Mr Moulton-Brown, did comment on the subjects taught. He sounds a bit of a tartar.' The headmaster read:

"The condition of the school is far from satisfactory. The singing, which is the main object of interest, is even worse than at last year's inspection; the children's musical capacity is on a level with their behaviour, which is deplorable. Of the teachers, several should consider retiring from the classroom for their general appearance, subject knowledge and class control are lamentable."'

'My goodness,' said Mr Cadwallader, 'Old Mouldy-Brown doesn't mince his words, does he?'

'He also has much to say about the headmaster,' continued Mr Gaunt:

"'The management of the school is entirely unsatisfactory. The headmaster is lazy and inept and is neither intended by nature nor fitted by art for the situation in which he is placed".'

Mr Gaunt wiped away a film of dust from another volume and opened the cover. 'This school inspector, a Mr Harcourt, was clearly not taken with the inhabitants of Risingdale when he visited the school in 1890. Here he writes:

"When I was in Yorkshire, I regret to say that I was not favourably impressed by the manner of the people. They appeared to me to be a bluff and unfriendly class of person. If at any time in the course of a walk I applied to anyone for information, I inevitably received a brusque reply of 'off-comed-un', which I believe means 'outsider', coupled with a choice expression I should be very sorry to repeat".'

'Sounds like an ancestor of Toby Croft,' remarked Tom.

'Later,' said Mr Gaunt, 'it says the school inspector told the class of older children that on his way to the school, he had come across an old, run-down, empty building all shut up where nobody lived and nobody went any more. He asked a boy if he could tell him what sort of house this was and the child replied, "The House of God".'

'Does he say anything about the infants?' asked Mrs Golightly.

'Let me see,' said the headmaster, flicking over a page. 'Ah yes, here we are. He seems more impressed with the small children. Listen to this:

"A little experience has taught me that infants should be left in the hands of their teachers, and that the inspectors should look on".'

'Well, I'll not argue with that,' said Mrs Golightly.

'He describes the infant teacher here,' continued Mr Gaunt, 'as "getting rather middle-aged for the little ones; always motherly, but not always fresh and gamesome".'

'He could be describing you, Bertha,' said Mr Cadwallader mischievously.

*

Mrs Golightly would be the first to admit that she had something of a motherly air about her, that she was undeniably middle-aged and 'not always fresh and gamesome' but she loved the children and was deeply committed and hard working. She thought of herself as a teacher-mother, that she must provide for the young child in her care the feeling of love and safety that the child has with a mother, and the same surety of sympathy and understanding. She knew that she was rather set in her ways and that her methods could be regarded by some modern educationalists as too out-dated. Many of the developments and innovations in early childhood education had passed her by, for she was disinclined to abandon the tried and tested methods that had proved so successful over the years. She was understandably nervous when a senior HMI, Miss Tudor-Williams, came to inspect her teaching, but the report that followed was praiseworthy, judging the teacher's relationship with the children, the quality of the environment and the broad and balanced programme of study to be excellent. The standards achieved by the children were rated as more than satisfactory.

'I was so worried at what she would say,' Mrs Golightly had told her colleagues after the inspector had left. 'I imagined she would criticise my reading scheme as being dated, the teaching of phonics as old-fashioned and the way I taught the children their tables inappropriate, but she seemed satisfied and said my methods, albeit traditional, were bearing fruit. Everything went so well.'

Towards the start of each day Mrs Golightly would select several of the children to sit and read to her and talk about what they had read. The reading corner was an attractive area of the classroom with a small multicoloured carpet, several large, coloured cushions, a Wendy house, dressing-up box and a collection of bright glossy-backed picture books. By the end of each week Mrs Golightly had heard every child read to her and a record was made of their attainment and progress. Any child who struggled with the words, she would spend a lunch-time giving extra help and, as she termed it, 'bring them up to scratch'. She would also write to the child's parents asking them to spend some time listening to their son or daughter read to them for half an hour every night. 'Reading is the fundamental tool of all learning,' she stated in the letter, 'and we must work together to help your child become a proficient reader.' She went on to write that 'reading should be a pleasant activity and not regarded as a chore.' Mrs Golightly was justifiably proud that no child moved into the juniors unable to read.

That Monday morning, the first child to bring her book to the teacher was a pretty girl, with an abundance of fiery curls, a dimpled smile, great wide eyes, and round rosy red cheeks as plump as apples. Mrs Golightly had been at school with the girl's grandmother and taught the child's mother, so she knew the family well. Little Marigold, the best reader in the class, was a child who exuded confidence. The teacher was intrigued by her pupil's responses to questions and amused by her sharp observations on life. Marigold had left the reading scheme well behind and was now what was termed a 'free reader', able to select the books she wished to read.

'What is your book called, dear?' asked the teacher.

'*Hubert Saves the Day*,' the child told her. 'It's about an old carthorse that everybody laughs at because he's so old and slow.' She studied the teacher momentarily before adding, 'It's not nice to laugh at animals and people just because they are old and slow, is it, Mrs Golightly?'

'No, dear, it is not,' agreed the teacher.

'I mean they can't help being old and slow, can they?'

'No, they can't.'

'And one day everyone will end up old and slow, won't they, Mrs Golightly?'

'Yes, indeed they will,' agreed the teacher, suddenly feeling her age. 'So, what happens in the story?'

'In the end,' chattered on the child, 'Hubert becomes a hero when he saves the other horses from a fire in the stables.'

'And did you enjoy the story?'

'Oh yes, it was really exciting.'

'Of course, you have a horse yourself, don't you, Marigold?' said the teacher.

'Actually, she's a Connemara pony, not a horse, Mrs Go-lightly,' said the girl primly. 'She's called Spangle and she's grey and fourteen hands high and she's having a foal soon.' The child thought for a moment. 'You know, miss, I wish people could do what Spangle does. It would save a lot of messing about.'

'And what is that, dear?' asked the teacher.

'Walk and wee at the same time,' answered the child.

Over the years Mrs Golightly had become quite accustomed to precocious young children like Marigold. She had been tickled by their humour, impressed by their manifest confidence, intrigued by their responses to her questions and amused by their sharp observations on life. Young children, she found, were not judgemental and, unlike some adults, there was never a patronising smirk or a cynical twist of the mouth. For little ones everything in the world was new and exciting and colourful.

Having rattled through the book, Marigold was told what an excellent reader she was.

'Yes, I know that, miss,' she said in a matter-of-fact voice. 'And you're a very good listener, not like my grannie. She sometimes used to fall asleep when I was reading. I didn't say anything because, as my mummy says, it's because she's getting on and is a bit old and slow at her age.'

'Well, do give my best wishes to your grandmother, Marigold,' said Mrs Golightly, managing a small smile. 'I think I told you that I was at school with your grannie and we were the best of friends.'

'Oh, she's very poorly in hospital at the moment, miss,' the child replied, 'and my mummy says she might never come out.'

'Oh dear,' sympathised the teacher.

'Of course, it is to be expected at her age, isn't it?' remarked the little girl, speaking like someone well beyond her years.

'Yes,' murmured the teacher. 'I suppose it is.'

The next reader, a sturdily built little boy with a healthy complexion, a dusty freckled face and black curls, was willing and good-natured and, like his brother George in Mr Dwyer's class, he invariably had a smile on his round face. Gareth was not the most self-assured reader, but he tried his best and read the words in his book clearly and loudly with his finger under each word. His reader was one in a series in the 'Merrytime Reading Scheme' and called *Down on Farmer Foster's Farm*. The cover of his reader depicted a round, red-faced farmer on his bright red tractor surrounded by happy-looking farmyard animals.

'Off you go, then, Gareth,' instructed the teacher, patting him on the hand, 'and don't worry if you struggle over any of the words. I'll be here to help you.'

The boy took a deep breath and began reading:

"'Percy Pig is a lazy pig,
A lazy pig is Percy.
In rain or shine,
He spends his time,
Sleeping all day long.

Percy Pig is a lazy pig,
A lazy pig is Percy.
He likes to lay
All through the day,
Sleeping in the sun.'"

'You read that very well, Gareth,' said Mrs Golightly when he had finished.

'Aye, I try, miss,' he replied philosophically.

'Well, I am very pleased with you.'

The boy's face cracked into a grin. 'Are you, miss?'

'Yes, I am,' she replied. 'Your reading is coming along a treat.'

'I do like learnin' to read,' Gareth told her. 'One day I want to be a "free reader" an' read a book all on mi very own. I like to read abaat all t'animals on Farmer Foster's farm. Mi favourites are Sally, t'sheepdog, Gordon, t'grumpy goat an' Basil, t'bashful bull. I'm not keen on t'pictures, though.'

'And why is that?' asked the teacher.

The boy sucked in his bottom lip. 'Well, tek Percy t'pig for a start. 'E's not like any pig what I've seen. All t'pictures in t'books allus 'ave pink pigs wi'out any bristles an' wi' curly tails. Most o' pigs on our farm an' them what's on mi Uncle Wesley's farm aren't like that at all. They're full o' bristles an' none of 'em are pink. There's yer Yorkshire large white, an' yer Saddlebacks, they're black and white.'

'You certainly know your pigs, Gareth,' said the teacher.

'Aye, there's not much I don't know abaat pigs, miss,' he replied. 'Pigs are cleverer than dogs, tha knaas, an' they're not greedy like what some people say an' they don't sweat much either. They're clean an all an' neat an' allus shi—' He stopped himself. 'An' allus gu to t'toilet away from where they feed.'

Mrs Golightly chuckled. How she loved her job. Young children are so wonderfully forthcoming and open, she thought. It's a pity that most adults lack such unworldliness and honesty.

*

At afternoon break, the teachers were discussing what they would be doing over the half-term break the following week.

'I'm spending a few days with my friends Cheryl and Peter,' said Mrs Golightly. 'They live in a charming cottage near Whitby with wonderful sea views. I'm so looking forward to the walks on the beach, the fresh sea air and the sunshine and having fish and chips sitting on the harbour wall.'

'I'm not doing anything special,' Mr Cadwallader told his colleagues. 'I might do a bit of decorating if the mood takes me.'

'Tom's taking Janette to Paris,' revealed Joyce, with a cheeky glint in her eyes. 'Aren't you, Tom?'

'Yes, I am,' he replied.

'Oh, that's nice,' said Mrs Golightly.

'I'm guessing that you and the delectable Miss Fairborn are something of an item, then?' enquired Cadwallader.

Tom blushed. 'Yes, I suppose you could say that.'

'I think you make a lovely couple,' said Mrs Golightly. 'It's about time you found a nice young woman, Tom, and settled down.'

'He's not getting married, Bertha,' said Joyce. 'Give him a chance.'

'Course, marrying a bank manager has distinct advantages,' stated Mr Cadwallader. 'He'll have no problem getting an interest-free loan for one thing, and of course, her father is not short of a bob or two.'

'He's not marrying her for her money,' came in Mrs Golightly.

'Who has said anything about marriage?' asked Tom. 'We are just going away for a few days.' Of course, he had the idea of marriage on his mind and thought Paris would be the perfect place to propose. Not wishing to be the centre of the discussion any longer, he changed the subject. 'Joyce tells me she is off to Stratford-upon-Avon,' he said.

'Oh, that's nice,' said Mrs Golightly, repeating herself.

'Julian's booked a luxury hotel by the river and a meal at the Black Swan,' Joyce told her colleagues. 'Then we are going to see a production of *Richard III* at the theatre.'

'You really know how to have fun,' remarked Mr Cadwallader sardonically. 'I can't imagine anything more depressing that seeing some bloody tyrant with a big hunched back murdering his way through a play for two hours. Mind you, not many in the audience will understand a word. The theatre will be full of all these American tourists who think it's the done thing to see a bit of Shakespeare at Stratford while they're in England.'

'It's not the sort of play I would wish to see,' said Mrs Golightly. She suddenly thought of the disfigured and half-blind Mohawk saint the vicar had mentioned earlier. 'Why is it, Joyce, that the really horrible characters in Shakespeare are evil-looking, disabled or illegitimate? In my experience, I have often found handsome people can be the worst in terms of personality and behaviour and I have noticed that those who are unfortunate-looking turn out to be the nicest.'

'You are mistaken, Bertha,' said Joyce. 'Most of the villains in Shakespeare are not evil-looking. There is nothing physically repellent about Macbeth or Iago or Brutus or Claudius for example – quite the reverse, in fact.'

'I went with my husband to see a Shakespeare play once,' said Mrs Golightly. 'It was *Hamlet,* and it was spoilt by this irritating couple sitting behind us who talked and rustled sweet papers all through the performance. The woman kept on asking the man what was going on. I had never seen my Norman get so angry. He turned around and said to the couple, "I wonder if you might speak a little louder, I'm afraid I can't quite hear what you are saying very clearly because those inconsiderate people on the stage are making such a dreadful racket." That shut them up until the end of the play, when the theatre went quiet and everyone on stage seemed to be wounded and bleeding and dying or dead. When it came to the last really dramatic speech, the woman behind said to the man, "I hope you remembered to turn the casserole off before we came out." Norman and I did laugh about it later.' She sighed. 'I do miss him so.' Her voice took on a wistful sadness. Her husband had been killed in a road accident on his way home from work a month after they had been married.

Joyce felt a stab of pity for her friend. It is heart-rending, she thought, for a wife to lose a husband so shortly after they are married. She quickly tried to lighten the atmosphere. 'Well, I for one shall really enjoy *Richard III*,' she said cheerfully. 'It's a wonderful play. Last time I saw it was years ago when I was studying in London and my friend Lynda and I went to the National Theatre. We had seats in the middle of the front row. I felt the hairs on the back of my neck rise up when the actor playing the lead came on stage. He was chilling. I could almost hear my heart beating. He walked to the front, fixed me with the most frightening stare and gave a twisted smile that put the fear of God in me. "Now is the winter of our discontent," he boasted, "made glorious summer by this sun of York." I dug my nails in the arms of my seat, held my breath, and then let out a sort of strangled cry. I was so frightened. Lynda leaned over and whispered in my ear, trying to stop herself laughing, "Don't worry, Joyce, it's only pretend, you know".'

'Actually, Richard III was not that bad a king,' said Tom. 'As Governor of the North he was well regarded and had a reputation for hard work and fairness. He spent a lot of time at Middleham Castle. Shakespeare was writing for a Tudor, the granddaughter of Henry VII, so it was politically convenient for him to make Richard out as a villain and furthermore he was not a hunchback—'

'Tom, could I stop you there,' declared Joyce. 'This is getting to sound like one of Mr Pendlebury's endless sermons.'

'I just thought you might be interested,' he replied.

'You know the part of that famous speech you were just quoting, Joyce,' said Mr Cadwallader.

'You mean: "Now is the winter of our discontent made glorious summer by this sun of York"?' she asked.

'Yes, that's the one. Well, I was driving through Clayton last December past a shop that sold outdoor clothes and camping equipment. I guess the owner must have been a bit of a Shakespeare buff. He had put a big sign in the window which said: "Now it is winter, it's our discount tents." I thought it very droll.'

15

'That was such a silly thing to do,' scolded Mrs Lister. Her tender voice and relieved smile belied the reprimand. She was sitting at the bedside holding her son's hand. Sir Hedley sat opposite with a gentle expression on his face.

'I know,' replied Charlie sheepishly. He was propped up on the pillows in the hospital ward looking bright-eyed and happy, despite his heavily bruised and swollen face and the livid, carefully stitched cut on his forehead.

'Whatever made you run out into the road?' asked his mother, taking in her son's pallor and the bruising on his face.

'I didn't want to see it get squashed.'

She was puzzled. 'See what get squashed?'

'The hedgehog.'

'The hedgehog,' she repeated.

'It was in the middle of the road all curled up and I thought if I was quick I could put it on the verge but then I was hit and I don't remember anything after that until I woke up in hospital.'

'Oh, Charlie,' sighed his mother, shaking her head, 'whatever am I going to do with you?' She brushed a lick of hair from his face and looked at him lovingly.

'I suppose the hedgehog got squashed,' pondered the boy.

'Never mind the hedgehog,' said Mrs Lister. 'It could have been you that got squashed. Your father and I were out of our minds with worry.'

Sir Hedley, who had remained silent and amused listening to the exchange, nodded. 'We were,' he said.

Charlie looked at his father. 'I suppose I'm going to be punished,' he said, wide-eyed.

'Oh yes, indeed,' replied Sir Hedley, with mock seriousness.

'Is it bread and water for a week,' his son quipped lightly, 'or thrown in the cellar at Marston Towers? Or is it being beaten within an inch of my life with a big stick?'

'Now that sounds a good idea,' teased his father.

'But you won't hit me,' said Charlie. 'I know you won't.'

'And what makes you think that?'

'Because when I was growing up and asked about you, Mum said you were kind and clever and people who knew you liked you.'

'Did she?' Sir Hedley exchanged a glance with the boy's mother. 'Well,' he said, 'it looks like the big stick is out of the question then. But you know, Charlie, what your mother said is right, it was a silly thing to do, so let us not have a recurrence. You might not be so lucky if you run into the road again.' He ruffled the boy's hair.

'Ow!' cried Charlie, grimacing at the pain. 'I have a contusion up there.'

'I'm sorry,' said his father, 'I wasn't thinking.'

'And what's with this contusion?' asked Mrs Lister. 'The words you come out with.'

'It's something the doctor said,' replied her son. 'It's really a bump on the head.'

'Well, let us have no more contusions,' said Sir Hedley.

'I'll be careful,' promised Charlie. 'Can I ask you something?'

'Of course.'

'Before I go up to the grammar school next September, can I change my name?'

'I rather like Charlie, myself,' said his father. 'So, you want to be called Charles from now on, do you?'

'No, the other name. I would like to be called Charlie Mal-adroit when I start at secondary school. I'd like to have the same name as you. I mean, you *are* my father. Could I?'

'Nothing would make me happier,' replied Sir Hedley, 'but I think you should ask your mother.'

'Can I, Mum?' asked Charlie.

'Of course you can,' she replied.

A flash of pure pleasure lit up the boy's face.

'I'm proud of you, Charlie,' said the boy's father. 'Do you have any idea how proud I am of you?'

Charlie's mouth trembled and eyes filled with tears, which appeared strange because he was smiling so vigorously.

Dr McNeill arrived. She examined the chart at the bottom of the bed. 'Now, young Charlie,' she said, 'let me see how you are getting on.' She looked at him and frowned. 'My good-ness, you look like you have been in the wars. You were lucky not to have broken any bones.' She took his pulse, shone a small torch in his eyes and inspected the cut on his forehead. 'How are you feeling?'

'Pretty good,' he replied.

'Well, I'm pleased to hear it.' She wagged a finger and grinned. 'No more running into roads.'

'No, doctor.'

'Well, I think you can go home,' she said.

*

When Tom had bought Roselea Cottage, the former home of Mrs Golightly, he realised he would have his work cut out.

One of his first jobs after he moved in was to tackle the garden. As he had inspected the rutted, tussocky lawn with its bare patches and molehills, considering where to make a start, Toby Croft, a cigarette clamped between his lips, had appeared at the gate.

'Tha wants to go steady choppin' back them roses,' he had told Tom. 'They want dead 'eadin' at this time o' year not cuttin' back. Back-endish is not best time to do that. Tha wants to wait till spring to prune 'em. I'll send our Dean down to lop off a few of them branches on yon oak tree an' cut yer 'edges back.'

Dean, his son, a fair, thick-set young man with a weathered face and tight, wiry hair, had arrived the next day. He was dressed in a loose-fitting grey jumper with holes at the elbows, baggy shorts, and military-style boots. His legs were wind-burned to the colour of copper. The young farmer had said little, but he had worked tirelessly all day. The trees with their long, overhanging branches were cut back, clumps of wind-bent thorn and hazel were pruned, the high hedges and towering laurels were trimmed, the dead flowers cut down and the borders, which were clogged with tangled grass and matted weeds, dug over.

When Toby had returned the next day to view his son's handiwork and offer more unsolicited advice, Tom had told him how pleased he was with the work.

'It's coming along very nicely,' he had said. 'Your Dean has done a grand job. He's a really good worker.'

'Aye, well, I'm glad 'e's good for summat,' the farmer had replied grudgingly. 'Thing abaat that lad o' mine is 'e's strong in t'arm an' weak in t''ead.'

Now, months later, the garden was transformed, with neat hedges, trimmed lilac bushes, a velvety, weed-free lawn and a profusion of bright pink and vibrant yellow flowers in the borders. On Saturday after coming back from his early morning run, Tom sat on the bench in the garden, leaned back, breathed in the fresh air and surveyed the stunning pastoral beauty before him: the rolling emerald fields, the bone-white limestone outcrops gleaming in the sunlight, the dark and distant fells, the scattering of grey farmhouses and hillside barns

and the endless dry-stone walls. A blanket of calm seemed
to cover the whole scene. There was a sense of timelessness,
unique to the quiet spaces in the world, as if the noise of hu-
mankind had been swallowed up.

His reverie was disturbed.

'I say,' came a surprisingly high-pitched voice. 'I'm awfully
sorry for disturbing you, but would you be so obliging as to
point me in the right direction? I'm afraid I have gone completely astray.'

'I'm sorry,' said Tom. 'I didn't quite catch that.'

'I'm lost.'

The speaker, standing at the gate, was a lean individual
with a pale, chinless face, large aristocratic nose and the bright
brown eyes of a fox. His blond hair was scraped back across
his scalp and into a ponytail. Tom got up and joined him. The
young man was dressed inappropriately for the time of year
in a bright tweed hacking jacket, green woollen stockings and
matching plus-fours. He sported a pair of substantial walking
boots. A rucksack clung to his back like a barnacle and he
carried a shepherd's crook with a polished beech shaft and
curved horn handle.

'So, you're lost?' Tom said.

''Fraid so. I'm in search of Marston Castle,' said the hiker
in an upmarket accent, 'but I appear to have taken the wrong
turning.'

'Well, I'm afraid you are heading in the wrong direction,'
Tom told him.

'Oh bother. I must have misread my map.'

'You need to go back into the village,' Tom explained, 'keep
walking past the King's Head inn, the duck pond, and a row
of terraced cottages until you arrive at St Mary's Church.
Just beyond the church is the path you need to take. Follow
it for a couple of miles and you will then arrive at Marston
Castle.'

'Thank you so much,' said the young man, pumping Tom's hand vigorously. 'You have been frightfully helpful.'

'I take it you are interested in castles,' said Tom.

'I'm researching the fortifications of Yorkshire for a book I am in the process of writing,' he replied. 'Marston Castle is not that well known but, in its day, it was an important fortress. I'm hoping that it's more than just a pile of old stones.'

'I think you'll find it's much more than that,' answered Tom. He recalled the time when he had first come across the stronghold on one of his Saturday morning runs. He had breasted the hill, stopped to get his breath and then he had stood stock-still and stared in amazement. Before him had risen the imposing ruin of a grand castle, a great rectangular space, enclosed by huge corner towers and half-destroyed walls. 'It's in not that bad a state considering it's twelfth century,' continued Tom. 'It was built by a Norman nobleman, Sir Guilbert D'Arbour who came over with William the Conqueror. You will find his descendant's tomb in the village church.'

'I say, you know quite a deal about Marston Castle,' he said, sounding impressed. 'You are not a historian by any chance?'

'I'm a teacher at the village school,' Tom told him, 'and my class has done a history project about it. If you're wanting to meet someone who knows far more than I about Marston Castle, then I can put you in touch with the very person to whom you need to speak.'

The man's face broke into a brilliant and grateful-looking smile.

'Tip top! That would be super,' he said, his voice shot with excitement.

'Dr Merryweather is the curator of the Clayton Museum,' Tom told him, 'and was in charge of an excavation at the castle and knows more about the building than anyone. I have a contact number and can get in touch if you like and fix up a meeting.'

'That's awfully decent of you.'

'If you hang on a minute, I'll make the call.'

Tom went into the cottage and returned moments later to find the man comfortably settled on the garden bench, legs stretched out in front of him and eyes closed. His thin face was lifted to the sun.

'It's all fixed,' he said. 'Dr Merryweather would be happy to meet you at the King's Head around twelve o'clock. If you like, I could come down and introduce you.'

'Thanks awfully,' he enthused. 'That would be super. I've got time to have a look at the castle before we meet. My name is Ben, by the way.'

'I'm Tom Dwyer. I'm pleased to meet you.'

The young man shook Tom's hand again and then strode off down the track, whistling to himself.

*

Tom arrived at the King's Head just before noon. The place was empty save for two hikers and an elderly couple. Mrs Mossup bustled down the varnished wooden bar to greet him as he approached.

'Hello, Tom,' she said. 'I don't often see you in here on a Saturday lunchtime.'

'I'm meeting a couple of people,' he explained. 'I say, Doris, it's very quiet in here today.'

'There's a big auction at the Clayton Auction Mart,' the landlady told him. 'That's where everybody is. Is it a pint?'

'Just a half, please.'

She turned to the young barman. 'Get Mr Dwyer half a pint, please, will you, Wayne? He'll have this on the house.'

'Thank you, Doris,' said Tom, 'that's very kind of you. So, how are Leanne and the baby?'

'They're both doing fine. I cannot tell you how grateful we are to you, getting her to the hospital in time. I had visions of her having the baby in the back of your car.'

'So did I,' replied Tom, remembering the fraught journey to Clayton Royal Infirmary.

'She's a very lucky girl, is Leanne,' Mrs Mossup carried on, 'having her own little cottage on Rattan Row courtesy of Sir Hedley and all her bills paid for as well. She's certainly fallen on her feet.'

'And is she still seeing Dean?'

'Oh yes, they're getting on like a house on fire. He treats her very well and he is wonderful with the baby. Anyone would think that the child was his. He's a changed young man since he has worked up at the big house. He's now gone back to run his father's farm and is making a real success of it, from what I've heard. Turned the tables on the old skinflint, he has. Toby Croft used to order him about and the poor lad got precious little thanks. Now Dean's managing things.'

Tom's drink arrived. He took a gulp.

As if on cue, the young man they were discussing walked in. He was dressed in a smart linen suit, pale blue shirt and colourful tie. Tom recalled the tongue-tied young farmer who had come to sort out his garden, dressed in the old grey jumper, baggy shorts and big boots. The landlady was right, he was a changed man.

'Hello, Dean,' said Tom.

'Nah then, Mester Dwyer,' said the young man, ''Ow tha doin'?'

'I'm fine, thank you. How about you?'

'I'm champion,' he replied.

'Will you join me for a drink?'

'No thanks. I'm not stoppin'.'

'I hear you are quite a hit with Leanne's baby,' said Tom.

Dean's face lit up. 'Oh aye, Bobby's a grand little 'un.'

'Bobby?' said Tom, baffled. 'I thought the baby is called Marcus.'

'Oh aye, 'e is, but I calls 'im Bobby 'cos I were allus tellin' folk e's a real bobby-dazzler an' t'name sort o' stuck.'

'Dean's come to collect me to take me down to babysit while he and Leanne go out for lunch,' said Mrs Mossup. Her round face took on a smug expression. 'They're going to Middleton Manor. Now there's posh.'

'I've left mi dad 'oldin' t'fort up at t'farm,' Dean told Tom, 'an' 'e's not that chuffed. T'vet's due there this afternoon to do a cleansin'.'

Tom looked puzzled.

'Removal of a cow's afterbirth,' Dean explained. 'Not a pretty sight.'

'I see.'

'Mi dad's not dead keen on Miss Macdonald. 'E thinks all vets are parasites with their fancy fees and that being a vet is not a woman's work, but I tell thee, Mester Dwyer, she knows what she's abaat. At lambin' time one o' yows gorra single lamb jammed tight an' we couldn't shift it. By, it were a big un. Mi dad an' me 'ave big 'ands, tha sees, an' there weren't enough room inside fer us to get an 'old on it. We fetched Mester Fairborn. There's nowt much 'e dun't know abaat sheep. Anyroad, 'e's gorr 'ands like shovels an' 'e couldn't shift it either, so we sent fer t'vet. Miss Macdonald, wi' 'er small 'ands, gorrit out in no time. Aye, she knows 'er stuff an' in't afraid o' gerrin 'er 'ands mucky. Come on then, Doris, let's get movin'. Leanne'll be wonderin' where we've got to.'

Soon after Mrs Mossup's and Dean's departure, Ben arrived. He joined Tom at the bar.

'Hi,' he said. 'Any sign of Doc Merryweather?'

'Not yet,' replied Tom. 'May I get you a drink?'

'Thanks, that would be super. A dry white wine would be just the ticket.'

Tom ordered the drink.

'So how did you like Marston Castle?' he asked.

'Oh, it's mind-blowing,' replied Ben, his eyes bright with enthusiasm. 'It was originally a timber and earth motte-and-bailey stronghold. An outer curtain wall was added with three towers. The south-west angle of one tower is in a good state of preservation. Of course, it's seen quite a bit of action over the years but—'

'May I stop you, Ben?' said Tom when he saw the attractive young woman with long blond hair come into the inn. She waved and came over to the bar.

'May I introduce Dr Sandra Merryweather,' he said.

'Oh gosh, you're a woman!' cried Ben. 'I thought you would be a man.'

'I'm sorry to disappoint you,' she said, smiling. She faced him with a cool but bemused stare, running her eyes critically over his face as an employer might examine an applicant for a post. He was unusual-looking, she thought, but there was something attractive about this long, thin, sinuous man with a pale narrow face and intense brown eyes with their small sandy eyelashes.

'I do apologise,' he said, clapping his hand to his forehead. 'I must sound a real chump. Foot in mouth. Let me start again.' He took her hand in his and shook it enthusiastically. 'I am really pleased to meet you, Dr Merryweather. Thank you awfully for agreeing to see me. I'm Ben Beauchamp.'

Dr Merryweather's eyes lit up.

'You're not *the* Benedict Beauchamp, the writer and historian, are you?' Tom detected a catch of excitement in her voice.

'The very same,' he replied.

'I've read your books. They're amazing.'

'Well, thank you so much.'

'I can't believe I'm meeting you,' she said. 'Your study *Medieval Castles of the South of England* is a classic.' A blush rose to her throat.

'That's very kind of you to say so, Dr Merryweather.'

'Sandra, please,' she said, resting a hand on his arm.

'Look, why don't you both find a table,' said Tom, 'and I'll bring your drink over, Sandra.'

'Just an orange juice for me, please,' she said.

When Tom joined the two historians, they were in animated conversation.

'Interestingly enough, Conisbrough Castle has the cylindrical and polygonal donjons popular in France at the time,' Ben was relating. Sandra watched him intently, like a cat watching a fish tank. 'It survived pretty well intact unlike its neighbour at Tickhill, which was knocked about a bit at the time of the English Civil War. Now as regards Marston Castle . . .'

Tom might have been invisible, for the two historians were so absorbed. He placed the orange juice down on the table.

'Well, I'll leave you to it,' he told them. 'I can see you have much to talk about.'

They were so engrossed in conversation that they didn't hear him.

Tom smiled and watched the two of them with a kind of half-amused detachment. He recalled the landlady's remark about Dean and her daughter – that they were getting on like a house on fire. Here was another couple, he thought, who were doing the same. Having paid for the drinks, he left.

It came as no surprise to him when, a few months later, Tom read the announcement in the paper:

Mr and Mrs Anthony Merryweather of Malton, North Yorkshire are pleased to announce the engagement of their daughter Dr Sandra Mary Merryweather and Dr Benedict Beauchamp, elder son of Professor and Mrs Simon Beauchamp of St Neots, Cambridgeshire.

*

Mr Gaunt had been delighted when Moira Macdonald accepted his invitation to join him for a meal. He had anticipat-

ed a quiet, intimate evening at Le Bon Viveur, the most exclusive restaurant in Clayton, where he could perhaps rekindle
the relationship with her he had enjoyed years before.

'I am so looking forward to this evening, Gerald,' Moira
said when she spoke to him over the phone. 'What time will
you be collecting me?'

'I have arranged to pick you up in the taxi at seven o'clock,'
he told her.

At the restaurant they were shown to a corner table that was
draped in a stiff white linen cloth and set out with bone-china
plates, crystal glasses, starched napkins, and heavy silver cutlery. In the centre was a slender vase containing one red rose.

'Are you all right, Gerald?' Moira asked, when they had sat
down. 'You've not said above a couple of sentences since we
got in the taxi.'

'I don't wish to burden you with my worries, my dear,' he
replied.

'A trouble shared,' she began.

'I think it's withdrawal symptoms, Moira,' he told her. 'Risingdale School has been my life. I shall miss it so much. It will
be a big wrench to leave. I wonder if I have done the right
thing in handing in my resignation.'

'I'm sure that you have,' she reassured him.

'I just hope that my successor treats the staff well,' he said.
'Some people would regard them as a rather motley crew, I
guess, but they are good-hearted, dedicated and hard working. I shall miss them.'

'You could always call in and see them from time to time?'

'No, no, I don't think the new head teacher would welcome
that.'

'Now, changing the subject,' she said, 'I have a surprise for
you that I hope will cheer you up. It is my present on your
retirement.'

'Cufflinks.'

'No.'

'A tie?'

'Let me finish,' she said, laughing. 'Over the half term, we are going on a short weekend break.'

'A weekend break,' he repeated. He smiled. There was no shilly-shallying with Moira. That was one of the things he liked about her, that direct and confident way of doing things. He recalled the occasion at the NFU farming charity dinner when she had taken the bull by the horns by asking him out.

'It's a nice idea, but I don't think I can,' replied Mr Gaunt. 'I have the animals on the farm to see to and—'

'Gerald, it has all been sorted,' she cut him off. 'I spoke to Clive Gosling a couple of weeks ago when I visited his farm to look at a sick heifer, and he has agreed to look after the animals while we are away.'

'Oh, I see.'

'So it is all settled.'

'Might I ask where you are taking me or is it a surprise?'

'Edinburgh,' she replied.

'Edinburgh!' he exclaimed.

Diners at a nearby table looked over, hearing his raised voice.

'A break will do us both good. We are to stay at a small hotel off the Royal Mile. You will forget about school and I will forget about sick animals.'

Before Mr Gaunt could respond, the restaurant owner, a lean olive-skinned individual with glossy boot-black hair scraped back on his scalp and large blue-grey eyes, scurried over. He beamed to display a set of unnaturally brilliant white, even teeth and gave a slight bow.

'Madame Macdonald,' he said effusively, 'it is so good to see you.' He took her hand and kissed it. 'You saved my Pippin's life.'

'Mr Le Fèvre brought his dog to the surgery,' Moira explained to Gerald. 'Pippin had a serious infection, but he has made a good recovery.' She smiled at the restaurant owner. 'And how is the little fellow now?'

Mr Le Fèvre smiled from ear to ear. 'He jumps for joy.'

Moira pictured the squat little pug, which wheezed and panted; his flat face looked as if he had walked into a door. She found it hard to picture the waddling animal jumping for joy.

'And this evening,' said Mr Le Fèvre, 'there will be no charge for the wine.'

'That's very kind of you,' she told him, 'but that is really not necessary.'

'No, no!' he cried, wagging a finger. 'I insist. It is my pleasure and the least I can do after what you have done.' He placed two red leather-bound menus before them. '*Bon appetit*,' he said, flashing his set of sparkling teeth before striding off.

'I have an idea,' said Mr Gaunt, 'that Monsieur Le Fèvre is about as French as I am. Have you noticed how a touch of Yorkshire creeps into his accent now and again?'

'Now, Gerald,' said Moira, ignoring his observation and keen to tell him about their trip to Scotland, 'the hotel is booked – two single rooms – and the train tickets, so there is nothing you have to do.'

'Well . . .' he started to say.

'Excuse me.'

The speaker, a small, stout woman with permed tinted hair the colour of purple broccoli and the staring eyes of a deep-sea fish, leaned over from the next table. She was bedecked in an assortment of heavy gold jewellery. Her companion was a thin, morose-looking man – all chin and nose. 'I couldn't help but overhear your conversation with the proprietor,' she said. 'You are a vet, I believe?'

'That's right,' replied Moira.

'I hope you don't mind me having a quiet word,' said the woman.

'Well, as a matter of fact . . .' started Gerald, intending to tell the woman they were here for a quiet meal and would not appreciate the interruption.

Moira cut in. 'What can I do for you?' she asked the woman.

'It's Rufus, my macaw. He's not himself. He's off his food and won't sit still on his perch. Do you think he's pining for a mate?'

Mr Gaunt sighed elaborately.

'Perhaps if you would like to bring him into my surgery, I can take a look,' replied Moira.

'Oh, I couldn't do that. I never take him out.' She lowered her voice. 'You see, he's a bit of an embarrassment.'

'In what way?' asked Moira.

'The old gentleman – he was a neighbour of ours who asked us to take Rufus – was going into a care home and they wouldn't let him take his macaw with him.'

'More's the pity,' mumbled her companion.

'He taught the bird a few, how can I put this, choice words,' said the woman. 'Not Sunday school words, if you get my meaning. If anyone comes near Rufus, he tells them to . . . well, to go away, but not in those terms. I have tried to teach him more suitable greetings but without any success. Last week the gas engineer, who came to fix the boiler, thought it was my husband speaking and not Rufus. He was told to—'

'To "F-off",' barked her husband.

'Albert!' snapped the woman. 'There's really no need for that.'

'Well, he did,' grumbled the man, 'and the chap who came to fix the boiler did just that, he cleared off and now we have no hot water.' He leaned over to Mr Gaunt. 'And I'll tell you this, if it was up to me, I'd ring the bloody parrot's neck. I mean, it's not the sort of thing you want to hear in the morning, coming down for your breakfast and the first thing you hear is that squawking creature telling you to "F-off!"'

'So, I was wondering,' said the woman to Moira, 'if you could do a home visit?'

'Not for pets and small animals, I can't,' she was told.

'But you do visit the farms?'

'It's rather difficult for a farmer to bring a flock of sheep or a herd of cows into the surgery,' Gerald told her irritably.

'I think he might be stressed,' continued the woman, ignoring the observation.

'I'm bloody stressed, never mind the bloody parrot,' announced her husband under his breath.

'Albert!' cried the woman. 'Will you stop swearing. You can hardly blame Rufus for using such language when you use it yourself.'

'Look—' began Mr Gaunt.

'You might be better consulting an avian veterinarian,' suggested Moira. 'I'm afraid I'm not that knowledgeable about bird diseases.'

Mr Gaunt closed his eyes and breathed in deeply, then gave another audible sigh. The last thing he wanted was a blow-by-blow account of some parrot's disease.

'Look—' he began again.

The waiter arrived.

'Are you ready to order, sir?' he asked.

'In one moment,' replied Gerald, consulting the menu.

'The chef's specialities this evening, sir,' the waiter told him, 'are for starters Mousse de Saumon canapés followed by Cuisse de Pintade aux Girolles, Écrasée de Pommes de Terre.'

'Which are?

'Smoked salmon mousse and the leg of a guinea hen prepared with wild chanterelle mushrooms and served with hand-mashed potatoes.'

'That sounds just the ticket,' said Gerald. 'I'll have that.'

'And the same for me,' said Moira.

The woman on the next table leaned over again, patted Moira on the arm and informed her, 'Poor Rufus, he's in such a sorry state. His feathers are falling out, he's started regurgitating his food and has had the most dreadful diarrhoea.'

*

On most Sunday mornings Gerald and Moira went for a long walk in the countryside surrounding Risingdale. On one outing, some weeks after their meal at Le Bon Viveur, the subject of the parrot came up.

'You remember the woman whom we met, the woman with the macaw?' she asked.

A look of distaste passed across Gerald's features. 'Yes,' he replied. 'She very nearly spoilt the evening with that repellent account of her wretched parrot's ailments. It quite put me off my dinner.'

'Well, she brought Rufus into the surgery.' Gerald gave a dismissive grunt. 'She stayed in her car until the waiting room had emptied before bringing in her macaw, not wishing the owners of the other pets to hear the bird's expletives. I must admit our feathered friend had quite a wide vocabulary.' Gerald rolled his eyes towards the sky and remained silent. 'Don't you wish to know the outcome?' she asked.

'If I must.'

'I cured it.' There was an air of triumph in her voice.

'Did you?'

'I called a colleague from college, someone who is an expert on bird diseases, and he told me what to do. The owner of the macaw was delighted and rang to tell me the bird was now fighting fit and as talkative as ever. The parrot's recovery of course did not suit her husband. I gather he imagined that the bird's days were numbered.'

'I can sympathise with the chap,' said Gerald.

'Anyway, he gave his wife an ultimatum that the macaw had to go, or he would.'

'So, what chump took the foul-mouthed parrot off their hands?' asked Gerald.

'Oh, his wife has still got the macaw. Her husband took the bird at its word when it told him to . . . well, you know what.'

'So, Albert has—?'

'Yes,' interrupted Moira, 'he left.'

16

On the last evening they spent in Paris, the young couple sat at a table in the fashionable (and expensive) Maison Blanche restaurant on the Avenue Montaigne, with the great city glittering and glamorous stretched out before them. After the meal, Tom watched the woman he loved for a moment with a sort of ache. He was the most fortunate of men, he thought, to be loved by this beautiful, sensuous, clever, good-natured woman. Janette's green eyes had been animated in the candlelight, which had caught her hair, making it shine like burnished gold. Her chest rose and fell with each breath. He reached across the table and took her hand in his. His heart was hammering so hard in his chest, it felt painful. She noticed how his hands were shaking slightly. Tom then swallowed hard, told her how much he loved her and asked her to be his wife. 'Yes, yes, yes!' she cried without a second's hesitation. He slipped a ring on her finger, a white-gold band, the single diamond flanked by two shining emeralds which matched the colour of her eyes.

The following evening when they were back home, Tom visited the Fairborn farm to ask Janette's father for his permission to marry his daughter. 'Dad's a bit conventional and over-protective,' she had told her new fiancé, 'so you will have to ask his permission. I know it's a bit behind the times but he's old-fashioned.' She had seen the expression on Tom's face. 'Don't look so worried, he's a pussycat.'

In the sitting room, seated on the sofa next to Janette, Tom regarded Mr Fairborn with a high degree of nervousness. He felt his heart beat faster and pressed his feet into the carpet to stop his legs from shaking. Janette's father stood by the elaborately carved mantelpiece, presenting an intimidating figure. A tall, stocky man with a rugged face the colour of an over-ripe russet apple, he had piercing brown eyes and hands the size of spades. 'Pussycat' was not a word which readily came to mind, a ferocious lion more like. Tom had rehearsed in his head what he would say. He tried to appear interested as the man rattled on, but his heart thumped in his chest.

'I've never been to France,' Mr Fairborn held forth, 'and to be frank, I've no desire to go there or any other foreign place for that matter. There is everything anyone would want here in Yorkshire. I cannot understand why folk feel the need to go abroad.'

Not a good start, thought Tom.

'Yorkshire's got everything you would want,' Janette's father talked on. 'It's got the scenery, the history, the food, and, more importantly, the people. But I will tell you this, French farmers have got it easy compared to us. They get more help from their government than we do from ours. They get all these subsidies and handouts and if they don't get what they want, they pile loads of manure on the streets and block the traffic.'

'Dad,' Janette remonstrated, 'do you have to talk about manure?'

'I'm just saying,' he said, 'that the French farmers get a better deal than us.'

Things then went quiet for a moment. Janette nudged Tom. 'Ask him,' she whispered in his ear.

'Course, some of the best cattle are French,' Mr Fairborn continued, warming to his theme. 'Limousin, Aubrac, Normandie – they are all good beef stock. I once saw this Charolais bull at the Clayton Agricultural Show. By, he was an impressive bugger, pardon my French, nearly two ton in weight and seven foot high.'

'Look,' Janette said impatiently, 'I'm going to leave you two alone for a minute.' She gave Tom a knowing look before going out of the room. The door was left ajar so that she could wait outside and eavesdrop.

'Oh yes, the French farmers have it made,' Mr Fairborn said.

Tom stood up and took a breath. His prepared speech had gone from his head. He searched for the words to use.

'Did you know that France has more cattle than any other country in Europe?' Janette's father asked.

'Mr Fairborn,' Tom said. He had taken another deep breath to control his racing heart. 'I need to speak to you.'

'Oh yes?'

'Yes, I do.'

'What about?'

'The thing is, I . . . the thing is . . .'

'Spit it out.'

'The thing is, I love your daughter,' he blurted out.

'Do you indeed?'

'And I would like to marry her.'

'Would you now?'

'Yes. I would like to ask for your daughter's hand in marriage.'

The farmer sucked in his bottom lip and nodded sagaciously.

'Well now,' Mr Fairborn said, 'you want to marry my Janette, do you?'

'Yes, I do.'

'She's very precious to me.'

'And to me,' Tom told him quickly. 'I love her.'

'I shall have to give it some serious consideration,' Janette's father told him.

'Pardon?' Tom had assumed that asking the father's permission was merely a formality. He had clearly misjudged the situation.

'It's a big decision,' Mr Fairborn said. 'I mean, getting wed is an important step in anyone's life. I'm sure you've heard it said, "Marry in haste, repent at leisure." You've not known her all that long.'

'Long enough to know I want to marry her.'

'Marriage is a big step,' Mr Fairborn pronounced.

Janette had heard enough and rushed into the room. She wrapped her arms around her father. 'Oh, Dad,' she cried, 'stop being such a tease. Say "Yes" this minute.'

'I hope you know what you'll be taking on, Tom, if you marry this lass of mine,' her father said. 'She'll be wearing the trousers before long if you're not careful.'

'Dad,' Janette cried, 'say "Yes".'

Mr Fairborn's face broke into a great smile. He kissed his daughter's cheek. 'Go on then,' he said. 'Yes.' Then he shook Tom's hand heartily. 'Look after her, Tom.'

'I will.'

'And did you know,' he said, 'there's over fifteen million cows in France. Now there's a thing.'

*

Meanwhile, Sir Hedley and Mrs Lister, having returned earlier that day from Scarborough, were being served tea by the housekeeper in the drawing room at Marston Towers. They sat together on the sofa. Charlie was in the library looking at the books. The bruises on his face were fading, the cut on his head was healing well and he had the colour back in his cheeks. The break at the seaside had been a tonic.

On a tray was a large and ornate silver teapot with a long spout and ebony handle. Mrs Gosling had decided that the earthenware teapot she regularly used was inappropriate for the drawing room and for serving guests. Also on the tray were a silver strainer, two delicate bone-china cups, saucers and plates edged in gold, an antique creamer, tongs for the sugar cubes, doilies and a large block of fruit cake.

There was an awkward silence in the room, broken only by the striking of the longcase clock in the hall and the sound of the tea being poured into the cups. Mrs Gosling sensed the edgy atmosphere and had an idea what was the reason. She passed around the teacups. Mrs Lister sipped her tea and appeared a little uncomfortable. Sir Hedley looked uncharacteristically serious and solemn. He stared down at his cup in his hand, needing a pause before he could broach what he wanted to say.

'A piece of cake, Mrs Lister?' asked Mrs Gosling.

'No, thank you. It looks delicious but I couldn't manage it. I don't want to spoil my dinner. I'm sure the cake won't last long if Charlie sees it.' She gave a small nervous laugh.

The housekeeper tried to sound cheerful, but she knew something was not right. She brushed her hands awkwardly down her apron.

'He appears to have made a good recovery,' she said.

'I'm sorry?'

'Young Charlie,' said the housekeeper. 'He seems to have got over his accident. It must have been a nightmare for you both.'

'It was,' agreed Mrs Lister. 'It was good of you to come to the hospital with me, Mrs Gosling. Do thank your son for all his help.'

'I remember my Clive getting knocked down by an ice-cream van in Skegness. Thank God, like Charlie, he wasn't hurt above a few cuts and bruises. When they got him in the ambulance, he asked what happed to his ice cream.'

Mrs Lister gave another small smile.

'Piece of cake, Sir Hedley?' asked the housekeeper.

'Just a sliver,' he replied.

'I'm glad the weather stayed fine for you in Scarborough,' said Mrs Gosling, 'and that you had a nice time. I'm sure young Charlie enjoyed the visit.'

'Oh, yes,' said Mrs Lister, without elaborating.

'Well, if that's all, Sir Hedley,' she said, 'I'll see how the dinner is getting on. I've made your favourite – roast pheasant with onion gravy with rhubarb crumble to follow. Will you and Charlie be staying, Mrs Lister?'

'Mrs Gosling,' said the baronet, placing down his cup and plate on a small occasional table, 'would you sit down for a moment, please? I have something to say to you.'

'Sit down, Sir Hedley?' she said in a rather shaky voice.

'Yes please, if you would be so kind.'

Mrs Gosling smoothed her hands down her apron again and then took a seat in an elegant blue covered chair. She perched stiffly upright on the edge.

'There is something I wish to discuss with you,' said the baronet after a moment's consideration.

'Oh yes?' said the housekeeper. She felt butterflies in her stomach.

'You might have guessed what about.'

Mrs Gosling nodded. 'I think so,' she muttered.

'There are to be a number of changes in the house from now on,' Sir Hedley told her.

The housekeeper felt her chest tighten. She shifted uneasily in her seat and gazed at him with a troubled expression. He is going to fire me, she thought. That vase was a priceless heirloom, probably worth a small fortune. How could I have been so clumsy?

'It was an accident, Sir Hedley,' she blurted out before he could continue. 'It just fell out of my hands.'

'I'm sorry?' he asked, looking perplexed.

'The fancy white porcelain vase with poppies painted round the side. It was on the landing,' stammered Mrs Gosling. 'I was giving it a bit of a dust. I picked it up and it just slipped out of my hand. I am usually so careful with things. I'm ever so sorry, Sir Hedley. I'll pay for the damage. You can take it out of my wages. I hope it wasn't valuable like the Rocking-ham vase in the drawing room.'

The baronet's face broke into a great smile. Then he let out a crack of laughter.

'I'm sorry, Sir Hedley,' said the housekeeper, 'I can't see as how it's all that funny.'

'Oh, but it is,' he replied. 'My dear Mrs Gosling, I do not wish to speak to you about some bit of china. I was not aware that it was broken and to be frank I could not care less. It is of no consequence. It was an ugly piece anyway and I never liked it. I wanted to speak to you about certain changes which are to take place here at Marston Towers.'

'Then, you're not going to sack me?'

'Good gracious, of course I'm not going to sack you. I could not manage without you. The place has never been so spot-less. And you were such a help when Charlie had his accident. You're indispensable.'

The housekeeper's face flushed with pleasure.

Sir Hedley turned to the woman who sat next to him. She had remained silent during this exchange. Then he took her hand in his. 'We want to tell you our news. While we were in Scarborough, Mrs Lister and I were married.'

'Married?' Mrs Gosling gave a little involuntary gasp.

'That is correct. It was a quiet affair at the register office. Christine wanted no fuss. Charlie was the best man. He has been sworn to secrecy for the present but, as you may im-agine, he is delighted.'

'So you are now Lady Maladroit,' said Mrs Gosling, look-ing at Sir Hedley's new wife.

'Yes, I suppose I am,' she replied.

'My goodness,' said the housekeeper. 'Well, I really don't know what to say.'

'My wife is a little worried about how people might react,' the baronet told his housekeeper. 'I am sure that there will

be a deal of talk and disapproval about my marrying so soon
after my first wife's death. We trust this will not cause *you* any
problem.'

Mrs Gosling sighed with relief. 'Lord above, Sir Hedley,
why should it cause me any problem?' she asked. She regarded the elegant, pale-complexioned woman with violet eyes and
curly black hair. How different she was from the last Lady of
the Manor, that gaunt woman with the long, pointed nose and
heavy hooded eyes and with an expression that could cut rock
in two. A smile enveloped Mrs Gosling's whole face. 'May I
offer you both my warmest congratulations. It's the best news
I've heard in a long time.'

'I do so hope you will stay on here as housekeeper,' said the
new Lady Maladroit, smiling with relief.

Mrs Gosling shuffled in her chair and she too smiled. 'I
should be delighted to stay and honoured to do so,' she said.

*

On the first day back after the half-term break, the teachers,
with the exception of Miss Tranter, were in the staffroom before school.

'I wonder where Joyce has got to,' said Mrs Golightly anxiously. She fingered the large rope of amber beads around her
neck, a purchase from Whitby where she had spent the half-
term holiday. 'She's always here by this time. You don't think
something has happened to her?'

'She's probably overslept,' remarked Mr Cadwallader casually, looking up from his newspaper. 'Probably overdid
things in Stratford. Stop worrying, Bertha.'

'Perhaps I ought to ask Mrs Leadbeater to give her a ring
and see if she is all right.'

'It might be a good idea,' said Tom. 'It's not like Joyce to be
late.'

'The children will be in school in five minutes,' stated Mrs Golightly. 'I think I *will* ask Mrs Leadbeater to ring her.'

The staffroom door opened and the headmaster came in. His face wore an expression of utter dismay.

'We were wondering where Joyce is, Mr Gaunt,' began Mrs Golightly. 'She's usually here by this time and—'

The headmaster held up a hand to stop her.

'One moment, Bertha. May I have your attention, please,' he said, looking down for a moment before continuing. 'I'm afraid Joyce will not be in school for the remainder of the week.'

'Is she ill?' asked Mr Cadwallader.

'Owen!' said Mr Gaunt rather tersely. 'Would you just listen to what I have to say? As I have said, Joyce will not be in school this week so I shall be taking her class for the time being.' He took a breath. 'She rang this morning to say that her husband had a heart attack last night.'

There was stunned silence.

The headmaster continued. 'Evidently, she and Julian arrived back from Stratford late in the evening after a long drive. Joyce's husband felt tired and went straight to bed but got up in the night with pains in his arms and chest. He was rushed to hospital, but he died in the ambulance.'

'My God!' exclaimed Mr Cadwallader.

'He died?' said Mrs Golightly.

'I'm afraid so,' Mr Gaunt told her, heaving a sigh.

'Poor Joyce,' muttered Tom.

'This is terrible news,' said Mrs Golightly. 'She must be distraught, poor thing. I must go and see her after school.'

'I'm sure she would welcome your support, Bertha, at this very difficult time,' said Mr Gaunt. 'I have arranged for some flowers to be sent and there will be a condolence card in my office tomorrow for you to sign. I will call in to see her later in the week.' He shook his head. 'Awful news. Joyce has only been married such a short time. It's so very sad.' He lowered his head and cleared his throat with a small cough. 'Well, that's the bell for the start of school. I think we should try and carry on as normal.'

Tom had arrived at school that morning exploding with excitement. He was eager to share with his colleagues his wonderful, extraordinary, unbelievable news and planned to tell them during the lunch hour. Now, he realised it was not the best time to let them know that he was engaged to Janette.

*

After school on the Monday, Mrs Golightly went to see her friend and colleague. Following her marriage, Joyce had moved into her husband's home – a large stone villa with a greasy grey slate roof, mullioned windows and thick dark ivy creeping up the walls. To the front were a sweeping gravel drive, a large lawned garden with a rockery, empty flower beds and glossy-leaved privet hedges. There were no bright flowers or blossoming bushes. It seemed a gloomy place. Above the doorway of the house the name Carlton Lodge and the date 1887 were carved.

The heavy black door was opened by a plump-faced, corpulent little man with a receding chin, stringy, plastered-down hair and staring, watery eyes.

'Look,' he said, sighing and shaking his head like a tetchy terrier, 'I wish you people would stop calling. I've told you before I don't believe in God, to me religion is just a ridiculous superstition and you have not the slightest chance in hell of converting me.'

'I'm here to see Joyce,' Mrs Golightly told him.

'Oh, I thought you were someone else.' His tone was less than apologetic. 'What can I do for you?'

'I'm a colleague of Joyce's,' he was told. 'I teach with her at the school.' When he didn't answer she added, 'I would like to see her.'

'Well, she is very upset at the moment. I don't think she is up to seeing anyone.'

'Yes, I imagine she is very upset,' replied Mrs Golightly tersely. 'Would you mind telling her that I am here?'

He sighed wearily. 'Very well.' Leaving Mrs Golightly on the doorstep, he disappeared into the house, returning a moment later. He stepped back. 'She will see you,' he said. 'First door on the right.'

'Thank you for coming, Bertha,' said Joyce, giving Mrs Golightly a hug. She was dressed in a plain black dress and wore no jewellery save for a small silver cross on a thin silver chain. Her unadorned face was drawn and tired and her eyes red-rimmed. 'Do sit down.' She noticed Julian's nephew, who was standing like a sentry at the door, watching. 'Could you make some tea, please, Stanley?' she asked. 'I'm sure my friend would enjoy a cup.'

'Yes, right,' he said, blowing out his cheeks like a peevish child. He left the room.

'Oh, Joyce,' said Mrs Golightly, sitting straight-backed on a heavy, dark wooden Windsor chair, 'I'm so deeply sorry for your loss. I know when you lose a loved one people often say, "I know how you feel", but, of course, most of them do not. I *do* know what you must be feeling. As you know, Norman died soon after we were married. Like you, we had such a short time together before he passed away. You imagine that you will spend the rest of your lives together, that your partner will be always with you like the weather, sharing your joys and your sorrows, and then they go.' She sighed. 'They say that time is a great healer, and that life does go on. I know it is a tired phrase but there is some truth in it. I have learnt to smile again at Owen's stories, listen with interest to Tom's plans for the future and hear about your amateur dramatics. And teaching the little ones has been such a comfort. I have learnt to get through those dark days, as you will, and gradually with time life will become bearable. I know that I could not have got through it without the support and friendship of you all at the school and it will be the same for you. There, I have spoken long enough. I'm getting all weepy now.'

'Thank you, Bertha,' said Joyce quietly. Her colleague was right; she had spoken long enough. It had struck her when her parents had died how people felt it necessary to relate experiences of their own loss. Her colleague meant well but her words offered little comfort. She hoped Bertha would not come out with the usual platitudes: 'It's a blessing that it was quick', 'At least he felt no pain', 'He's in a better place', 'It was meant to be', 'He'd had a good life' and the dreaded question, 'How are you feeling?'

'So, how are you feeling?' asked Mrs Golightly.

She sighed. 'Just about coping,' she said. 'I'm gradually coming to terms with things. It happened so unexpectedly. Julian and I had such a lovely time in Stratford. He has been stressed of late with one thing and another, but he seemed and felt so much better during the few days we had been away together. He would insist on driving home at night in all that wind and rain and—' She broke off and took out a small handkerchief from her sleeve and dabbed her eyes.

They talked for a little longer until Stanley appeared with a tray. He placed it on a side table and then lowered himself into a chair with a thump.

Seeing that he was making no effort to serve the tea, Mrs Golightly got to her feet. 'Shall I pour?' she suggested.

When the visitor had gone, Stanley, sitting opposite Joyce, stretched out his legs and gave an unctuous smile.

'I want you to know, Joyce,' he said condescendingly, with the air of one conferring a favour, 'that you need not bother your head about making any arrangements for Uncle Julian's funeral. I shall take charge and see to everything.'

Joyce stared at him for a while before speaking. 'Thank you for the offer, Stanley, but I have already organised things,' she said. 'I spoke to Mr Firkin, the funeral director, this morning and he will manage what needs to be done according to my wishes. He will book the crematorium and sort out any other details. I shall be speaking to some caterers tomorrow when I go into Clayton to register the death. There will be a reception here for Julian's friends and employees after the service.'

'I see,' he said. 'Well, at least you don't need to concern yourself about the auction house. I shall ensure that things carry on as usual. I am sure Uncle Julian would have wanted that. I will see to it—'

'I have already spoken to Mr Cavill,' interrupted Joyce, 'and he has had my instructions to continue as before. Everything is in hand.' Then she added pointedly, 'He will be in charge of the business.'

Stanley sniffed. 'It seems you have thought of everything,' he said, vexed.

'Yes, I think I have,' replied Joyce.

'And in so short a time,' he couldn't help adding, with a hint of sarcasm. 'I do admire your efficiency.'

'On Friday morning Mr Oglethorpe, Julian's solicitor, is coming here to speak to me about Julian's estate,' Joyce informed him. 'Since he tells me that you are named in the will, he has asked that you hear what he has to say.' Before Stanley could respond, Joyce stood. 'Well, I'm feeling rather tired, so I shall have a rest.' She swept out of the room, leaving a trace of expensive perfume.

When she had gone, Julian's nephew poured himself a large whisky and downed it in one great gulp. Feeling careless and confident, he slumped into the chair, stretched out his legs, rested his head on the back and smirked. When I take over the business, he said to himself, there will be more than a few changes.

*

Mr Oglethorpe, a tall middle-aged man of elegant bearing, had neatly parted hair greying at the temples, a thin face, high cheekbones and large dark eyes behind rimless gold spectacles. He wore a dark well-cut suit and an understated perfectly knotted blue striped tie.

'Do sit down, Mr Oglethorpe,' said Joyce, gesturing to a wing-backed armchair.

'Thank you,' he replied.

The solicitor sat and placed a folder on his knees. Stanley, in his badly fitting suit, shiny at the elbows, was ensconced in the most comfortable armchair with his legs out in front of him and his hands crossed over his chest like a bishop. He was chewing the inside of his cheek. Joyce sat on the sofa, her hands resting in her lap.

'First of all, Mrs Sampson,' said the solicitor, with a prac-tised expression of sorrow on his face, 'may I extend my deepest sympathy for your loss. Your husband was my friend as well as my client and he will be sadly missed.'

'Thank you,' replied Joyce. She was disinclined to tell him that she went by her maiden name of Miss Tranter.

Mr Oglethorpe took up the folder, opened it and examined the contents for a few moments. 'Your late husband specif-ically requested that his last will and testament should be read in the presence of his wife and nephew,' he said, looking at Joyce. 'The reading of a will these days is a rather unusual request, but I am obliged to follow the instructions set down here. If I may, I will summarise the contents and leave it with you to peruse the entire document at your leisure.' Joyce nod-ded. 'Please stop me if there is anything you wish to ask.' He cleared his throat. 'Your husband has made a number of be-quests and to each of his employees at Smith, Skerrit and Sampson he has left one thousand pounds in gratitude for their hard work, cheerful good humour and loyalty over the years they have worked for him. To Mr Cavill, the General

Manager, he has left the sum of five thousand pounds, with the hope that he will continue to remain with the firm.'

There will be little chance of that, thought Stanley. The General Manager would be the first to go and most of the other employees would follow. He sat up in his chair when his name was mentioned, and he leaned forward.

'To his nephew, Stanley Arthur Sampson,' resumed Mr Oglethorpe, 'he has left ten thousand pounds and the tantalus. I will read—'

'Excuse me,' Stanley rushed in impatiently, not giving the solicitor time to continue. He was now sitting bolt upright in his chair. 'Is that it?'

The solicitor removed his glasses and glanced up. There was a censorious expression on his thin face. 'I beg your pardon?'

'Is that all my Uncle Julian has left me?' he asked in the petulant tone of the aggrieved.

Mr Oglethorpe gave him an icy look. 'Yes,' he replied simply.

'But my understanding was that he intended to leave me—'

The solicitor cut him off. 'I will repeat that this will clearly states that you are to be left ten thousand pounds and the tantalus and nothing else. If I may continue.'

'And what the hell is a tantalus?' asked Stanley angrily.

'I believe it to be a small lockable item of furniture that contains two or more decanters,' he was told. He pointed to an Art Deco mahogany-and-gilt side table. 'I believe it is over there on the tabletop. Now, I should like to continue without further interjections.' He replaced his glasses, took a breath and regarded Joyce in a kindly avuncular way. His voice softened. 'I will read this next part of the will, if I may, Mrs Sampson.' He gave a small cough. 'I leave to Joyce, my dear wife, friend and helpmate, who has brought such love and sunshine into my life, the house and contents and the remainder of my estate and in addition the auction house of Smith, Skerrit and Sampson.'

Stanley was not able to contain himself. 'The auction house!' he exclaimed. 'He has left it to Joyce?'

'That is what I have just said,' the solicitor told him, peering over his rimless gold spectacles.

'I see,' muttered Stanley.

When the solicitor has been shown out, Joyce returned to the sitting room, where she found Stanley helping himself to a large whisky. When he turned to face her, she saw the flare of anger in his eyes.

'Well, there's a surprise,' he said bitterly. 'I was under the distinct impression that Uncle Julian wanted me to take over the family business.'

'Then you were under a misapprehension,' said Joyce coldly.

'I'm sure that was his intention.' He scowled and took a gulp of his drink, 'that is, until he got married. It was understood . . .' There was something in Joyce's face that made his words trail away.

'I think, Stanley, that it is time for you to leave,' she said calmly. Her eyes were fixed upon him. 'It would not be fitting now that Julian is dead for you to remain in the house.'

'You wish me to leave?' he asked, glaring at her, his brows lowered.

'Yes. I do,' stated Joyce.

'Well, haven't you done well for yourself?' he said indignantly. 'Not been married above a few weeks and now you have everything.'

'Not quite everything, Stanley,' Joyce replied. 'You were left the tantalus. When you go, don't forget to take it with you.' With that she left the room.

The following morning, the cuckoo had flown the nest.

17

Joyce returned to school the following Monday. Tom, who was always the first to arrive, was surprised to find her there before him, sitting at the desk in her classroom, looking thoughtful. She was modestly dressed in a dark blue cotton dress and sensible flat black shoes and there was no sign of the carefully applied make-up, the bright red lips and scarlet nails.

'Hello, Joyce,' Tom said, trying to sound cheerful. He came to sit next her.

He noticed her pale face and the dark circles around her eyes. She looked worn out by grief.

'Oh hello, Tom,' she replied, giving a half-smile.

'I was so sorry to hear about Julian's death,' he said.

'It was so sudden. We had such a lovely time in Stratford and had plans to—' She broke off and dabbed her eyes.

'There is not much one can say to make you feel any better at a time like this. I wish there were, truly. You know, of course, that your friends are here for you.'

'Yes, I know.' She reached out and touched his hand. 'Thank you.'

Tom took a deep, steadying breath and cast around for a change of subject. 'You're here early.'

'I couldn't bear to stay in that house a minute longer. It is so dark and depressing and full of all the heavy furniture and antiques. It's like living in a museum. I intend to sell it and move back into the apartment block where I used to live. I never liked living there and it's far too big for just one person.'

'I take it the nephew is no longer with you,' he said.

'No, thank goodness. He's gone, taking with him Julian's gold cufflinks and his wristwatch. I was given them at the hospital and I left them on the dresser. They have disappeared. I did not like Stanley, but I never put him down for a thief. Well, he can have them. I am just pleased he is now out of my life. He didn't get what he expected from Julian in the will and was angry and resentful. He thought he'd be inheriting the business, but Julian left it to me.'

Tom's dark eyes softened in sympathy. 'Well, it's good to have you back,' he told her.

She gave another small, half-hearted smile and rested a hand on his arm. 'I'm glad to be back. I don't know what I would do without my friends here at the school and in the theatre group.' Tears welled in the corners of her eyes. 'Everyone has been so kind.' She thought for a minute. 'I did love Julian, you know, in my own way. It wasn't anything passionate, a sort of mad love affair, a romance like that of Elizabeth Bennet and Mr Darcy or Romeo and Juliet, but I was very fond of him. A single woman is often not regarded for what she is or treated very sympathetically, particularly when she gets older. Before Julian I sometimes used to sit in my apartment on dark winter nights and think of the lonely life ahead of me. Then I met Julian and he rescued me from a solitary old age. He offered me kindness and care and security. I shall really miss him. I guess now it's back to the lonely life.' She shook her head. 'I'm sorry, I'm getting maudlin.' She brightened up. 'So how did you and Janette get along in Paris?'

'I've waited until you were back at school to tell you,' said Tom. 'I wanted you to be amongst the first to hear my good news. Owen and Bertha don't know yet, nor does Mr Gaunt.'

'Well, spill the beans.'

'I'm engaged. I asked Janette to marry me when we were in Paris and she has agreed. I'm the luckiest man in the world.'

'Oh, Tom,' said Joyce. 'I'm so happy for you. I always knew things would turn out like this. I think it's Janette who is the luckiest person in the world to have you for a husband. This news has really brightened up my day.' She leaned across the desk and kissed his cheek.

'Will you be our matron of honour?' he asked.

'Of course I will.'

'We've not thought about the wedding yet. It is early days, but Janette is keen to have the service in the village church and Mr Pendlebury to officiate. He'll be assisted by Father Daly of St Bede's.'

Joyce's mouth curled into a smile. 'It's likely to be a long wedding service,' she said. 'You know what the vicar's like when he gets started. I have asked him to conduct Julian's funeral next Saturday but told him to keep things short. I would like you and Mr Gaunt to recite a poem or do a reading, if you would.'

'Of course,' said Tom. 'I should be honoured.'

Mrs Leadbeater arrived at the classroom door, looking sheepish. Her husband stood behind her, grim-faced. It was unusual for the secretary and her husband to arrive at school so early.

'We are sorry to disturb you, Miss Tranter,' said Mrs Leadbeater, 'but Bob and I just wanted to say how very sorry we were to hear about your loss.'

'Thank you, Beryl,' replied Joyce.

'It's very difficult to know what to say at times like this, but we want you to know that we are thinking of you. That's all we wanted to say.'

'That's kind of you both. I do appreciate those kind words. They are a great comfort.' She was grateful that they didn't spout the usual platitudes about her husband 'going to a better place' or 'having had a good life'.

'Mr Gaunt telephoned this morning to say he will not be in school until this afternoon,' the school secretary told her.

'He's been summoned to the Education Office for something or other. He wanted me to let you know he is sorry not to be here himself to welcome you back, but you are in his thoughts.'

*

The atmosphere in the staffroom had been subdued during Joyce's absence. There had not been the usual banter; the teachers had been uncharacteristically quiet as they thought about their grieving colleague.

'It's so good to have you back, Joyce,' said Mrs Golightly before the start of school.

'It certainly is,' agreed Mr Cadwallader. 'We were so sorry to hear about you husband's death. It must have come as quite a shock.'

'Yes, it did,' responded Joyce, hearing the blindingly obvious.

'I know it's of little consolation,' he told her, leaning back in his chair, 'but at least it was quick, and he didn't suffer. He'd had a good life and now he's in a better place.' Joyce sighed inwardly. 'So, how are you feeling, Joyce?'

'Pleased to be back,' she answered, wanting to tell him to shut up with his banalities. She changed the topic. 'You have some good news, don't you, Tom?'

'I do,' he agreed.

'Do tell,' urged Mrs Golightly.

'I'm getting married,' he said, savouring the dramatic simplicity of the announcement.

Things immediately brightened up.

'It's wonderful news, isn't it?' Joyce said.

'Indeed it is,' agreed Mr Cadwallader, getting up to shake Tom's hand.

Mrs Golightly beamed. 'I'm so happy for you, Tom. Janette is a very lucky girl. You will make a wonderful husband and a brilliant father.'

'He's to become a father, is he?' exclaimed Mr Cadwallader.

'No, no,' said Tom hastily. 'Janette is not . . . I'm not . . . Becoming a father is a little premature. We're not married yet.'

'Oh, but you will have children, won't you?' said Mrs Golightly. 'One of the great regrets I have is that Norman and I never had a family. Children bring such joy and pleasure into one's life.'

'And they can also bring with them countless troubles and worries as well,' stated Mr Cadwallader, 'as Sir Hedley has found out to his cost.'

'Speaking of Sir Hedley,' said Mrs Golightly, 'I couldn't believe my ears when I heard he has married Mrs Lister, and so soon after his wife's death.'

'Sir Hedley's married Mrs Lister?" exclaimed Joyce.

'Oh, of course you won't have heard,' said Mrs Golightly. 'I was telling Tom and Owen about it when you were off school. Sir Hedley and Mrs Lister went off to Scarborough over half term and got married. I met Mrs Gosling in the village and was told the startling news. It's the talk of Risingdale.'

'Well, well,' muttered Joyce. 'Who would have thought it?'

'Evidently he's been having an affair with Mrs Lister for years and Charlie is his son,' she said. 'It's beyond belief. Fancy him having a mistress and nobody had any idea.' She was ignorant of the fact that both Tom and Joyce had been aware of the relationship.

'I'm certain young Charlie won't bring Sir Hedley any troubles and worries, Owen,' said Tom. 'He's a good-natured and endearing boy and a credit to his mother. It was a godsend that he came out of the accident with only a few cuts and bruises. It could have been a lot worse.'

'I won't disagree with you that he's a good lad,' said Mr Cadwallader, 'but I reckon he will receive a fair amount of stick from his classmates. There's no doubt in my mind that he will come in for some bullying.'

'No, I don't think he will,' Tom disagreed. 'The children have taken the news in their stride and so has he. He is a popular boy and one thing I have learnt since becoming a teacher is that children can be amazingly resilient. I've known Charlie long enough to predict that he will be able to deal with any remarks, if indeed there are any. The fact that Sir Hedley is his father will stop a lot of speculation and comment from those in the village as well.'

Joyce, who had been listening to this exchange with interest, smiled.

'You all know my views about Sir Hedley Maladroit,' she said. 'These titled landlords with their vast estates, thinking they are still Lords of the Manor, are outdated, but I don't blame him for finding some warmth and tenderness outside his loveless marriage. His wife was a dragon. As you know, my first marriage was a disaster like his, so I know how he must have felt.'

Mrs Golightly stole a glance at Tom, thinking that talk of disastrous marriages was not the most fitting observation a newly engaged young man should hear.

As she had sat in the gloomy sitting room the day after Julian's nephew had departed, Joyce for some reason thought about her first deeply unhappy marriage and how different it had been compared to her second. She had wished many times, when the unwelcome thoughts had invaded her head, to forget about the cruel and dominating ex-husband who had treated her badly and undermined her confidence. But she seemed unable to banish those thoughts. She could not seem to erase them from her mind. It was true that the bully forgets but the bullied never do. She wished she could take the duster she used to clean the blackboard in her classroom and wipe the memory away like the chalk marks. In that dismal sitting room she had felt so empty and alone. She had stared around her as if seeing the place for the first time: the dark oak dresser with the rack of blue Delft plates, the Georgian corner cupboard, the elaborately carved sideboard bearing Meissen and Spode plates and figurines, the overstuffed sofa and chairs with the dark velvet cushions and the gloomy oil paintings on the wall. The house was full of Julian's presence. She closed her eyes and immediately saw the image of her husband when she had first met him. He had come to her apartment to ask if she would consider returning the stolen necklace she had bought at his auction house. She had opened the door to find a distinguished-looking man with a head of carefully combed silver hair and the face of a Roman senator standing outside. He had been dressed in an expensive-looking woollen overcoat unbuttoned to reveal an equally expensive-looking charcoal-grey suit with narrow chalk stripes and matching waistcoat with gold chain and fob. He had sported a blue-and-white silk bow tie. She had noticed the impeccable cuffs and the heavy gold cufflinks. Thinking of that first meeting, tears had run down her cheeks.

The bell now went for the start of school. When Joyce emerged from the staffroom, she found a group of children waiting outside. At the front was a plain, stocky boy, brown skinned and brown haired. He held a huge bouquet of bright flowers.

'These are for you, Miss Tranter,' he said. 'We had a collection. We were very sorry to hear about your husband.'

Joyce tried to hold back her tears as she took the flowers from her pupil.

'Thank you, Mark,' she said, 'they are lovely.'

As the children headed off to their classroom, one child held back. He was small with grubby knees and the ever-present dewdrop on the tip of his nose. A front tooth was missing. He was carrying a wilting bunch of half-dead flowers, wrapped in a sheet of newspaper.

'I got these for you, miss,' he said. 'I picked 'em from t'gar-den in t'churchyard on mi way to t'school. There were plenty there, so they won't miss 'em.'

'That's a very kind thought, Nathan,' said the teacher, looking at the flowers that had probably been placed at a grave, 'but you know you shouldn't have taken them from the churchyard.'

The boy thrust the flowers into Joyce's hand and stuck out his jaw. He looked affronted. 'Well, you 'ad berrer 'ave 'em,' he told her, ''cos I'm not purrin 'em back.'

*

At lunchtime, Mr Cadwallader remained in his classroom thinking about the earlier conversation and Bertha's view about how children bring such joy and pleasure into a par-ent's life. He had never brought any joy or pleasure into his parents' lives; he was convinced of that. His was a poor sort of childhood in many ways. Growing up, the boy's father, a self-absorbed and forbidding man, and his aloof mother, dis-played little, if any affection for this dull and withdrawn child. It was almost as if they resented his presence. His father had not been a cruel man. He had never hit his son or shouted but he was for the most part distant and cold, despairing at the boy's lack of success at school and his failure on the sports field. Mr Cadwallader tried to recall an occasion when his father had laughed or even smiled. There had been none he could remember. He had a clear memory of a childhood punctuated by his parents' snappish demands: 'Sit up prop-erly, don't slouch'; 'Close the door, you were not born in a barn'; 'Tidy your room, it's like a pigsty'; 'Don't fiddle with your food'; 'For God's sake, stop mumbling.' Certain scenes from his childhood presented themselves to the teacher now. They were sharp, clear memories, coming like spectres of the past, but there were no bright moments amongst the darkness. He remembered the fretful time when he had taken home his school report and had stood, staring at the floor, in front of his father, who had shaken his head and mouthed, 'Pitiful, pitiful'; the occasion when he had overheard his mother on the telephone talking to someone and saying that her son was 'a strange boy' and that she sometimes thought it would be better to raise geese than children; the evening when his father had told the visiting vicar that his son, who had failed to get into the grammar school, was 'a sad disappointment'. If he had had better parents, he thought, he might have turned out differently – more confident, sociable, with the ability to charm the opposite sex. Someone like Tom Dwyer.

Once, Mr Cadwallader had opened up to Tom about his early life. 'My parents took little notice of me,' he had confided, 'the teachers certainly didn't. Girls I took out soon tired of me. I was inconsequential, boring, I suppose.'

He could envisage what sort of father Tom would make. He would be someone whom a child would not only love but also admire and respect for the person he was, a father he would want to grow up to resemble, patient and caring, a father who would take his children to the football match, the cinema, the zoo, the theatre, the museums, delighting in their company. They would have the richest of experiences. They would be loved and cherished. He would never say that they were 'sad disappointments'.

In the bright classroom with the sun streaming through the window, the teacher felt despondent.

Tom's appearance at the door brought him back to the present with a jerk.

'May I come in?' asked the teacher.

'By all means,' replied Mr Cadwallader, raising a small smile.

'I want to ask a favour.'

'Of course, what can I do for you?'

'Would you be my best man, Owen?' Tom asked him.

'What?'

'I would like you to be my best man when I get married.'

'Really?'

'Of course,' said Tom.

'I should have thought that one of your old pals from your footballing days would be more suitable.'

'Not at all. Who else would I choose but you? You're my closest friend.'

Mr Cadwallader was so taken aback by Tom's words that he felt sudden tears springing in his eyes.

'You want me to be your best man?' he asked.

'Of course. So, will you?'

'I should be honoured,' his colleague told him.

*

Mr Gaunt arrived back at school just before the start of classes. He had a quiet word with Joyce, repeating what he had said when he had visited her at her home the week before: that he was so sorry for her loss. Then he spoke to the staff.

'First of all, I just wanted to say it is good to have you back with us, Joyce. We appreciate how hard it has been for you at this very upsetting time. You know that your friends here at Risingdale School have been thinking about you and that we will be here to offer any support you might want.' Joyce nodded and mouthed a 'Thank you.' 'Now, I do have some interesting and surprising news to impart,' Mr Gaunt continued.

'Yes, Tom has already told us,' said Mrs Golightly, assuming the headmaster was aware of Tom's engagement and wanting to share the good news. 'We are all of us thrilled.'

The headmaster looked puzzled. 'Tom has already told you the news?' he asked.

'Only this morning,' said the teacher. 'He's been keeping it up his sleeve for some time.'

'Well, it couldn't be made common knowledge,' said Mr Gaunt. 'I was told specifically not to tell anyone until the news broke.'

'I'm sorry,' said Tom, equally puzzled. 'You knew all about it?'

'Of course I did.'

'Did Mr Fairborn tell you?'

'What has John Fairborn got to do with this?'

'I am just intrigued to know how you knew,' said Tom.

'Nobody knew,' the headmaster told him. 'It is not going into the *Clayton Gazette* until tomorrow morning.'

'It's going in the paper?' asked Tom.

'That's where I've been this morning to do an interview.'

'I think perhaps we are at cross purposes here,' suggested Mr Cadwallader. 'We are under the impression, Mr Gaunt, that the interesting and surprising news to which you are referring, is Tom's engagement to Miss Fairborn.'

'Engagement!' exclaimed the headmaster.

'That he is to be married,' said Mrs Golightly.

'I had no idea,' Mr Gaunt said. 'Many congratulations, Tom. Miss Fairborn is a delightful young woman. You make a lovely couple.'

'Don't keep us in suspense,' said Joyce to the headmaster. 'We are all keen to know your news.'

'Ah yes,' said Mr Gaunt, 'my piece of news. I have been awarded an OBE in the Queen's Birthday Honours.'

*

The funeral service for Julian Sampson took place on a bright morning. Clayton Crematorium was a plain grey block of a building with an equally plain interior of oatmeal-painted

walls devoid of any religious imagery, functional pine furniture and long windows containing just a hint of coloured
glass. The chapel was packed with the employees from the
auction house, representatives from the Clayton Rotary Club,
members of the Clayton and Ruston Amateur Players, Mr
Oglethorpe and all the staff from the school. Joyce was surprised and touched to see Sir Hedley and the new Lady Maladroit and Mrs Gosling attending. The one notable absence
was Stanley.

The coffin of polished oak with ornate brass handles rested
on a bier before a carpeted stage. A simple wreath had been
placed on the top. The cloying scent of lilies filled the air.

Joyce sat with Mrs Golightly on the front pew, her face a
mask, her eyes red-rimmed. Colours from the tinted windows
dappled her head and shoulders. At first, when she was told
that her husband had not survived the heart attack, she could
not take it in. The day afterwards had been a blur. It had been
a relief, in a way, to undertake concrete things: discussing the
funeral with Mr Pendlebury and Mr Firkin, choosing the coffin, the flowers, the music, the readings, organising the reception, speaking to Mr Cavill about the business and to the
solicitor. She had done all this with numb efficiency. It was
only now at the funeral that grief caught up with her and she
wept as she listened to the readings.

Mr Gaunt read a short passage:

'"When I am gone, cry for me a little.
Think of me sometimes but not too much.
Remember me now and again as I was in life,
At those moments pleasant to recall,
But not for too long.
Let me rest in peace
And I shall leave you in peace,
And while you live let your thoughts be with the living".'

Tom, the last speaker, recited 'The Irish Blessing':

"'May the road rise up to meet you,
And the wind be ever at your back.
May the sun shine warm upon your face,
And the rain fall soft upon your fields,
And until we meet again,
May God hold you in the hollow of his hand".'

Mr Pendlebury's homily was heartfelt and thankfully short.
He concluded the service by quoting from scripture:

"'Therefore, you too have grief now; but I will see you
again, and your heart will rejoice, and no one will take your
joy away from you".'

*

As the mourners made their way out of the chapel, the funeral
director approached Tom. Mr Firkin had a broad face with a
ruddy complexion and tufts of sandy hair that retreated from a
red dome of a head. His appearance and demeanour were not
what one might consider appropriate for one in his profession,
for he was a jolly, good-natured man with a broad smile and
a chuckle that had a way of making other people chuckle too.

'I thought you recited that poem very well, Mr Dwyer,'
he told Tom, patting him on the back. 'From my experience,
most folk would rather be in the coffin than having to stand
up and speak on occasions like this. They are frightened, you
see, of making an exhibition of themselves, that they will break
down crying and start the bereaved off. I thought Miss Tranter managed to hold herself together admirably. Her husband
was an auctioneer, I gather?'

'Yes, he was the owner of Smith, Skerrit and Sampson, the
big auction house in Clayton,' Tom informed him.

'Aye, so I've been told. He wasn't short of a bob or two then?'

'I guess so.'

'I should have thought that he'd have had something a bit more elaborate myself,' observed Mr Firkin, 'him being quite a distinguished public figure. I appreciate that a cremation is cleaner and tidier, but I prefer a burial myself. I laid to rest an auctioneer last year and it was a grand affair. It was Mr Frampton's internment. Lovely man he was, with a great sense of humour. He planned his own funeral from his hospital bed, what readings he wanted, all amusing, and the music that should be played, all of it cheerful and lively. He wanted it to be a celebration of his life rather than some miserable gathering. His choice of one hymn – "If I had a hammer" – I thought was most appropriate. He stipulated that those people who attended his funeral had to wear something colourful. Then there was a big bash at his house, and they all tucked in. It has always struck me how strange it is that grief can sharpen the appetite. Mr Frampton didn't want anything morbid. I like the idea of celebrating a person's life and giving them a good rousing send-off. I mean we all have to go, don't we? Funerals always remind people of their own mortality.' He said this in a misplaced cheerful voice. 'As they say, "every door opens except Death's door".'

'Very true,' agreed Tom, wishing to get away.

'Yes,' declared Mr Firkin almost chirpily, 'we are all grains of sand on the vast seashore of eternity. In the midst of life there's death. "Never send to know for whom the bell tolls; It tolls for thee".'

'Indeed,' said Tom. 'Well, I must be off.'

'Even when Mr Frampton went to meet his Maker, he made people smile,' the funeral director rattled on. 'He wrote his own epitaph and had it carved upon his tombstone with a little auctioneer's hammer fashioned next to it. "Francis

'Frankie' Frampton, auctioneer. Going, going, gone", it said. Now, I call that style.'

Tom thought of Joyce's husband. He had found Julian a rather serious and conventional sort of man, not one to have the hymn 'If I had a hammer' at his funeral service nor one to consider 'Frankie' Frampton's epitaph stylish and he would certainly not have countenanced something similar on his own tombstone – had he had one.

*

'He was not a one to drag his heels, was he?' remarked Mrs Sloughthwaite.

Mrs Gosling, the first customer of the day at the Barton Village Store, was relating the latest news from Risingdale. She was telling the shopkeeper of the recent marriage of Sir Hedley Maladroit.

'Of course, he'd known Mrs Lister for a long time. He'd been having a –' she thought of the best word to use – 'a close personal relationship with her for over eleven years.'

'You mean, she was his bit on the side?'

Mrs Gosling pulled a face. 'Well, yes, if you put it like that. I should prefer to say a loving friendship. Sir Hedley's marriage had been on the rocks for a long time. He got no affection at home. His wife made his life a misery. She was a nightmare. I can quite understand why he went elsewhere.'

'Well, you know what they say – "It takes two to tangle",' remarked Mrs Sloughthwaite. 'There's always two sides to every coin.'

'Yes, well, Sir Hedley's marriage was one-sided,' said Mrs Gosling, springing to her employer's defence.

'So, what's the new wife like then?'

'She's as different from the old one as chalk is to cheese, very easy to work for and with a nice nature.'

'That's as may be, Mrs Gosling,' answered the shopkeeper, 'but I don't approve of extra-maritime affairs. There's too much immortality in the world if you ask me. If you are married, then you should stay married, through thick and thin, the good times as well as the bad, not be playing fast and loose with another woman. It's no wonder that that son of his had an illegitimate child with the barmaid at the pub, with a father carrying on like that.' She shook her head. 'These aristocratical people should set a better example. It sounds like Sodom and Glochamorra up there at Risingdale, the way they carry on.'

'You're entitled to your opinion,' retorted Mrs Gosling, coming again to her employer's defence, 'but why put up with a loveless marriage? Life's too short.'

'Well, I can't say that my marriage was all beer and skittles,' Mrs Sloughthwaite admitted, 'but I put up with the rough as well as the smooth. Marriage isn't always rainbows and sunshine.'

Mrs Gosling, who liked and respected her employer and was fiercely loyal, changed to a safer subject. 'The other bit of news is that one of the teachers at the school, Miss Tranter, has lost her husband.'

'Lost him?' repeated Mrs Sloughthwaite. 'He's gone missing?'

'No, no, he's passed away. They came back from a visit to Stratford over half term and he had a heart attack and died on the way to the hospital. Course, he was a lot older than she was. Left her with a big house, a Mercedes car and the business. I reckon she'll give up teaching now she's so comfortably off.'

'It's a fact that we all have to succumb,' remarked Mrs Sloughthwaite, 'and go the way of all earth. It's a blessing that he had a quick exit. Mrs Pocock's husband met the same untimely end. She found him in the kitchen lying prostate on the floor. When she couldn't rouse him, she sent for the ambulance. The paraplegics gave him artificial resurrection but it did no good. He entered the sweet hereafter before they got him to the hospital. Course he was asking for it. I mean he drank like a fish, smoked like a chimney, was way overweight and the only exercise he had was walking to the pub and back.' She leaned on the counter. 'Anyway, there's nothing much happened here in Barton, except that Mrs Fish has now gone back to the Primitive Methodists. After the roof in the church fell in and nearly buried her alive, she felt she would be safer in the chapel. The minister is deaf, so I don't suppose he'll be too critical of her playing. I heard yesterday that Mr Cherry, the vicar, is off to do missionary work. I can't say he will be missed.'

'I couldn't bear the heat in Africa,' remarked Mrs Gosling, 'and having to convert all those heathens.'

'He's not going to Africa,' she was told, 'he's going to Lancashire to convert the heathens there.'

'I shall have to make tracks,' said Mrs Gosling. 'Sir Hedley and Lady Maladroit have a select reception this evening and I have to be on hand.' On reaching the door, she turned. 'Oh, I nearly forgot, there is another piece of news you might be interested in.' The shopkeeper's ears pricked up. 'Mr Dwyer, you remember he's the young teacher at the school – well, he's getting married.'

'Is he indeed,' said the shopkeeper.

Later that morning Mrs O'Connor called at the village shop. She could hardly contain her excitement as she burst through the door, keen to tell Mrs Sloughthwaite the wonderful news of her nephew's engagement.

'I can't wait to tell you,' she said in breathless anticipation at what her friend would say.

Mrs Sloughthwaite raised herself from the counter. 'So, your Tom is getting married then,' she said.

18

Over the next few weeks, life for the residents of Rising-dale settled into a contented and comfortable existence. Tom spent many an evening with Janette discussing the wedding, deciding on the bridesmaids, trying to agree on the guests they should invite, considering the various venues for the re-ception, who would make the cake, where they would go for their honeymoon – endless conversations which he began to weary of. In the end he was quite content to let Janette decide on most things, recalling, with a wry smile, her father's words that, 'She'll be wearing the trousers before long if you're not careful.' Mr Fairborn had suggested that the young couple should come and live on the farm with him after they were wed, but Janette, despite her father's badgering, told him she wished to start her newly married life with just Tom in his cottage.

'Of course, we shall have to give the inside of the cottage a thorough makeover,' she had told her fiancé. 'Some nice modern furniture, bright curtains and carpets and, of course, a new kitchen.'

'Yes, dear,' Tom had said.

Joyce had wasted no time in moving back into the apart-ment block where she had once lived. The contents of Julian's house had been put into auction. She kept the silver-framed photograph of their wedding day, the jewellery her husband had bought her, his gold Hunter watch and chain and the small burr walnut writing desk, but nothing else. The house was sold within a month and the Mercedes went back to the garage from which it had been purchased. She threw herself into producing plays, giving the occasional lecture in drama and theatre arts to students at St John's College and became a valued member of the Society of Teachers of Speech and Drama.

Mrs Golightly became Chairperson of the Flower Arranging Society and was elected President of the Clayton and District Women's Institute. When Mr Cadwallader had the temerity to observe that the WI was 'all jam and Jerusalem', she had given him a lecture on how canny, politically and environmentally aware the members were.

'Some of the early founders of the WI,' she told him, 'were in the forefront of fighting for women's emancipation and the promoting of family values. Edith Rigby, for example, set fire to Lord Leverhulme's holiday bungalow in protest of the treatment of women and threw a black pudding at Winston Churchill.'

Mr Cadwallader was asked to be the secretary of the local branch of the Royal British Legion and became active in raising money for the support of veterans.

Mr Gaunt planned his retirement, intending to develop his smallholding and spend a few weeks of the year cruising the oceans around the world with Moira, to see places they had always wanted to visit.

Mrs Mossup, with a great smile on her face, enjoyed watching Leanne (who had lost weight and made 'Weight Watcher of the Month' at the local branch) and Dean, perched on bar stools in the King's Head like lovebirds, holding hands and looking into each other's eyes. Her daughter had abandoned the tight skirts and loud jumpers, along with the loud laugh. The landlady had a vision of her daughter walking down the aisle at St Mary's on the arm of Sir Hedley.

As for Dean, he had transformed his father's farm, increased the livestock, won a blue ribbon at the Clayton Show

for his Swaledale tup and converted one of the barns into a
holiday cottage. Toby Croft, at first grumbling and complaining about the new arrangement, soon came to like his new life.
He had more time to spend in the King's Head and his son
made few demands on him in terms of work. He didn't seem
to mind that he had lost the authority that he once had. He
would continue to offer his advice about how the farm should
be run with suggestions on improvements, but Dean would
nod sagely and tell his father that he would 'think about them'.
Of course, he never gave them a moment's thought.

Sir Hedley, his new wife and child, attended to by the indomitable housekeeper, settled into a happy and relaxed life
at Marston Towers. People in the village, although gossiping
behind their backs, treated Sir Hedley and his new wife with
affability and deference. Charlie spent a deal of his time in the
library poring over the old tomes, going for long walks and
playing his guitar.

The children in Tom's class looked forward to the end of
term, the long summer holidays and starting their new life in
September at the secondary schools – some to the grammar,
others to the comprehensive.

Everything seemed to be harmonious, peaceful and undisturbed in the village at the top of the Dale – until a large dead
fly fell into the ointment.

Three weeks before the end of the summer term, Mr Gaunt
called in to the staffroom.

'I just wanted to let you know that the newly appointed
headmaster of the school will be coming in next Friday afternoon to look around and to meet you all,' he told the teachers
at morning break. 'Would one of you let Tom know, please?
He is on playground duty at the moment. My replacement
is a Mr Cuthbert Smart, and he is at present head teacher at
Skillington Primary School which, as you know, will be closing at the end of this term.'

'He's being redeployed here?' asked Mr Cadwallader.

'Yes,' replied Mr Gaunt.

'What is he like?' asked Joyce.

The headmaster had not been overly impressed with his successor after the brief telephone conversation he had had with Mr Smart. The speaker had sounded a rather humourless and strait-laced individual and Mr Gaunt had heard little that was positive about the man from those who knew him. He recalled the conversation he had had with Mr Baxter about the bullying his daughter had endured at Skillington and the fact that Mr Smart had not taken it seriously enough to tackle it. However, he felt it prudent not to share his reservations with the teachers. He just hoped that his successor's poor reputation was not well-deserved. Mr Gaunt was by nature an optimist and hoped that once the new headmaster had visited Risingdale, met the team of enthusiastic and committed staff and the well-behaved and interested children, and seen what a happy and successful school it was, he would appreciate how fortunate he was to have secured this new position. Hopefully, he would not wish to change things. Now, when asked about Mr Smart, he was cagey.

'Actually, I've not met him,' he told Joyce. 'I've just had a short conversation with him on the telephone.' He thought for a moment of what he would say next. 'Mr Smart has had a deal of experience as a teacher and as the head teacher at a village school very much like our own, so he will know the ropes. You will find out all about him when you meet him next Friday. He will be here at three o'clock before the end of the school day so will have a chance to see the children as well as yourselves.'

*

Toby Croft, a cigarette dangling from his lips, was in a good mood as he ambled along the country road. Ahead of him was a small flock of creamy sheep, moving unhurriedly behind a bright-eyed, black and white border collie. When his son had left the farm to work as assistant gamekeeper for Sir Hedley, Toby had been compelled to try and run things by himself. He had employed some casual workers but, unable to put up with his grumbling and griping, they had left in quick time. The farm, which had been going downhill, was now flourishing since his son had returned and taken over the running.

A car horn behind beeped. Toby ignored it and continued to saunter down the road. When there was a persistent honking, he stopped, removed the cigarette, gave a shrill whistle and shouted, 'Lie down!' The sheepdog turned, crouched low to the ground, head on its paws, and eyed the sheep, which came to a sudden halt. Toby then put the cigarette back between his lips, sucked on it and exhaled a cloud of smoke. Then, in no hurry, he approached a shiny black saloon car.

The driver wound down the car window and poked his head out. He was a thin-faced individual with an unusually sallow angular face, a pointed nose and small, black, appraising eyes. Jet-black brilliantined hair retreated from the pale dome of his head.

'Did tha want summat?' Toby asked, removing the cigarette. He gave a wheezing cough and spat on the ground.

'Are you in charge of these animals?' the man replied pugnaciously.

'What animals would them be?'

The driver gave a heavy sigh. What other animals did the yokel think he was talking about, he thought. 'The sheep,' he said impatiently. 'Are you in charge of them?'

'No,' countered Toby. His face was expressionless. He replaced the cigarette, sucked on it and blew out a puff of smoke. The driver wafted it away with a hand.

'Well who is?' he demanded.

Toby plucked the cigarette from his mouth and nodded in the direction of the sheep. ''Er at t'front.'

The driver thrust his head out of the car window further and peered ahead.

'I can't see anyone,' he said tersely.

'Mi sheepdog. She's in charge,' he was told.

'Well, will you instruct your dog to get these animals off the road?'

Toby took exception to this bossy self-important man. Below his brow his eyes narrowed into slits. 'An' 'ow's she's gunna do that?' he asked. 'They're sheep, not bloody kangaroos.' He replaced the cigarette, took a final pull on it, then dropped it on the grass and ground it underfoot.

'What are you talking about?' The man's voice increased in pitch and agitation.

'I cud be mistaken, but I 'ave it on very gud hauthority, that sheep can't leap over a four-foot dry-stone wall.'

'Oh, for goodness' sake,' said the driver, with a heavy sigh. 'I have an important appointment this afternoon and I am late for it already, having been stuck behind two caravans and a tractor.'

'Can't 'elp that.'

'Look there's a gate ahead. Move the sheep into that field,' he instructed.

'Can't do that.'

'Why can't you do that?'

''Cos it's not my field.'

'I'm sure the farmer won't mind.'

'You know Mester Fairborn then, do ya?' asked Toby.

'What the devil has that got to do with anything?' barked the man. His eyes flashed.

'It's 'is field an' 'e waint want 'is sheep gerrin mixed up wi' mine an' fer that matter, I don't want mine gerrin mixed up wi' 'is. It'll tek an age to sooart 'em out. Thas'll 'ave to 'ang on 'til I get to my field.'

'And where is that?'

'Not that far.'

'And how long is that likely to take?' asked the driver angrily.

'It'll tek as long as it teks,' he was informed.

'You are being most unreasonable!' exclaimed the driver. 'You should show more consideration.'

'Don't thee thou me, thee thou thissen and see how thee likes it,' snapped Toby.

The driver had not the first idea what the man was talking about, but he persisted in berating the old farmer.

'People like you shouldn't be taking animals along a public thoroughfare and holding up traffic,' he rebuked Toby.

'An' people like thee should get back to t'town weer tha belongs instead o' 'arassin' them what lives an' works 'ere. Anyroad up, I can't stand 'ere arguing t'toss wi' thee, I've got mi sheep to see to.' Before the man could respond, Toby whistled and the sheepdog set off again, followed at a snail's pace by the old farmer and his flock of sheep.

It wasn't long before they arrived opposite the entrance to the gate leading into Toby's field. The collie steered the sheep off the road. The car raced past, its tyres screeching on the tarmac, and disappeared in a crash of gears and a cloud of exhaust smoke. Toby leaned on the gate, lit another cigarette, drew on it, and blew out a cloud of smoke. He observed a rook, jet black and shiny, as it pecked methodically at the remains of a roadkill, then he bent down and gave the dog, which sat panting at his feet, a pat on the head.

'Mebbe I should 'ave telled that bloke abaat that bad bend up ahead,' he said.

*

Mr Gaunt saw the shiny black saloon car pull up before the school on a small square of land just off the road. He glanced at his watch. It was four o'clock. He watched from the window of his study to see a thin individual with a pallid complexion and dressed in a pale grey suit, climb from the car and examine the wing. He saw him shake his head angrily. The visitor then approached the gate and stood and stared at the school like a tourist studying an historic building. His was a hard face, rigid in its expression, a face not naturally given to smiling. After a minute, he crossed the playground. Mr Gaunt hurried from his study to meet him.

'Good afternoon,' he said, emerging from the school and smiling broadly. 'I'm Gerald Gaunt, the headmaster here at Risingdale and you must be Cuthbert Smart, the lucky chap who will be taking over when I leave.' He held out a hand.

For a moment Mr Smart was rendered speechless by the appearance of the headmaster – the old, creased jacket with leather elbow patches, the baggy flannel trousers, loosely knotted tie, and frayed shirt. He did not set a particularly good example, dressed like some sort of vagrant, he thought.

He found his voice. 'Yes, that's right,' he replied. The smile was not returned. 'Good afternoon.' His handshake was clammy with a lifeless feel to it.

'Do, do come along inside,' said Mr Gaunt. 'Did you have a good journey?'

'No, I did not,' replied the man.

A moment later, Mr Smart was shown into the headmaster's study and he was even more appalled by the state of the room. Like its occupant it was shabby and untidy, with a cluttered desk and piles of papers and magazines stacked haphazardly.

'Do sit down,' said Mr Gaunt, gesturing to a hard spindle-backed chair which was before his desk. Mr Smart sat down. The chair creaked under his weight. 'I was rather expecting you earlier.' There was no hint of criticism in his tone of voice.

An irritated look clouded Mr Smart's face. 'I'm afraid I was delayed,' he replied in a plodding voice. 'My journey here was calamitous. I was stuck behind two caravans and a slow-moving tractor for several miles and then the road was blocked by a disagreeable farmer and a flock of sheep. Some people are so inconsiderate.'

'This is the country,' remarked Mr Gaunt, his smile fading. 'One has to expect tractors and caravans and sheep on the roads, particularly at this time of year.'

The man bristled but decided not to argue the point. 'Then I arrived at a very sharp bend and came off the road, hitting a wall and damaging the wing and the side of my car.'

'I'm sorry to hear that. I hope you're not hurt.'

'No, no, I'm fine,' he replied tonelessly.

'If you don't mind me saying, when you start here you might be off better with a four-wheel drive,' advised Mr Gaunt. 'By December we sometimes get thick snow and driving winds, then come the blizzards and treacherous black ice. It will be difficult in the car you have to get up the hill.'

'It is something worth considering,' replied Mr Smart, with a detached kind of indifference and thinking to himself that he had no intention of changing his car, which he had only recently purchased.

'Yes indeed,' Mr Gaunt carried on, leaning back in his chair. 'We have had some very heavy falls of snow up here at the top of the Dale. You may have noticed my alpenhorn in the corner. Some years, as I mentioned, we do get very inclement weather and I have to close the school. And that is when my alpenhorn comes in very handy. A few good blows on that echoes down the Dale and lets the villagers and those on the surrounding farms know that the school is closed and there will be no lessons that day. It warns parents that the school bus is not running and saves them trudging up with their children to find we are shut.'

'How interesting,' said Mr Smart, sounding not in the least bit interested.

'Oh, do forgive me. Here I am rambling on and I haven't offered you a drink yet. May I get you a cup of tea?'

'Thank you, no. I only drink herbal tea.'

'I see.' For a moment there was an awkward silence. 'Well, let me tell you something about Risingdale School.'

The future headmaster, a man of unshakeable self-belief, took a small black notebook and pencil out of his pocket and scribbled away as Mr Gaunt spoke. His first impressions of the school and the headmaster were most unfavourable.

'The school was built over a century ago,' Mr Gaunt told him, 'originally for the children of the estate workers employed by the current local squire's grandfather. It is set high up at the top of the Dale apart from the village and a good few miles from the nearest town of Clayton. We are blessed with one of the finest views of any school in the county. We have just over sixty pupils on roll and—'

'I am surprised that the school was not on the list for closure,' commented Mr Smart, 'with so few children. We have a similar number of pupils at Skillington but the powers that be have seen fit to close the school.'

'I am sure it was considered but to do so would involve a great deal of travelling for the children and our numbers have remained healthy. Indeed, next term there will be an increase in the intake. The children come largely from the surrounding farms and are biddable and well behaved and try their best. There are four teachers on the staff. Mrs Golightly, who is in charge of the infants, is an experienced and amiable woman, a tad traditional but none the worse for that. Miss Tranter is the teacher of the seven-and eight-year-olds. She was a former professional actress and is a competent and committed teacher. Mr Cadwallader takes the nine-year-olds. He came into teaching late, having spent some years in the British Army. He is a bit of a character is Owen, but a solid enough teacher and the children like him. Lastly is Mr Dwyer, new to the profession. He is a former professional footballer who had to give up his very promising career after some injuries. He is an exceptional teacher, enthusiastic, dedicated and hard working. He teaches the top juniors. It is a happy team.'

'Who are the governors?' asked Mr Smart.

'Do you know, we haven't had a governors' meeting for as long as I can remember,' Mr Gaunt told him, rubbing his chin. 'They let me get on with the job without undue interference, which suits me. The Chairman is Sir Hedley Maladroit, who is most supportive. Then there's the Reverend Michael Pendlebury, the Rector of Risingdale; Dr Entwhistle, the local GP; Mrs Sidebottom (pronounced Sitheebothome), the foundation governor; the Reverend Robert Cockburn (pronounced Coburn), the Methodist minister and Mrs Edna Midgley, who represents the parents.'

'It is unusual not to have regular governors' meetings,' observed Mr Smart, looking up from his notebook. 'As I recall, the directive from the Education Office requires schools to have meetings at least once a term.'

'Is that so? Well, in Risingdale there seems to be no need to have them,' replied Mr Gaunt. 'Like me, they are all busy people.'

'It is a requirement,' Mr Smart pointed out.

'Is that so?' said Mr Gaunt again. 'Well, we don't seem to require them here.'

The more Mr Smart saw and heard, the more dissatisfied he felt about the state of the school.

'What about pupil achievement?' he asked.

'Oh, we do pretty well,' he was told. 'With the arrival of Mr Dwyer, we have achieved remarkable success with the sports and last year won the football shield – quite an achievement for such a small school as ours. One of our pupils, a talented young artist – some of his pictures are on my wall – won the County Art Competition and another was awarded first prize in the County Poetry Competition. We also have had success in the Choral Speaking and our team won the Speech and Drama Festival silver trophy for the second year running.'

Mr Smart appeared anything but impressed. 'I was thinking more of academic achievement,' he said.

'Oh, I see. Well, we hold our own. There is a wide range of abilities in the school and the teachers try to ensure every child reaches his or her potential. Most of the children go on from here to the comprehensive at Clayton, which has a good reputation. Some of the pupils have gained places at the grammar school but I am not a believer in selective education so I don't usually enter the children for the eleven-plus examination unless a parent specifically wishes me to do so. This year, however, I was persuaded by Mr Dwyer to enter nine children from his class for the examination.'

'And how many passed?' he asked with pencil poised.

'All of them,' replied Mr Gaunt.

Mr Smart shifted uneasily in his chair. He had entered all the top juniors for the eleven-plus examination at Skillington and only two had passed.

'Shall we have a tour of the school?' suggested Mr Gaunt. 'I am afraid because of your late arrival you will not be able to meet any of the children or the staff, but I am sure you will be interested in looking into the classrooms.'

Mr Smart stood, adjusted his tie and straightened his jacket.

He slipped his notebook and pencil into a pocket. 'Yes. I should like that,' he replied.

The infant classroom was tidy and colourful, and it was obvious the teacher had made a real effort to provide a stimulating environment for the children. There were plastic-topped tables and little melamine chairs, some large, coloured cushions, and a small, carpeted area. In one corner was a Wendy house and a modest collection of picture books. Along one wall children's colourful artwork had been mounted: round figures with smiling faces, huge eyes, and stick-like fingers. On another wall were glossy posters of animals and birds with their names neatly printed below, illustrated exercises in number, calendars, clock faces and lists of key words. A large table had painting materials, coloured crayons, a sand tray, and large boxes containing a variety of building blocks and educational toys.

Mr Smart made no mention of the inspiring environment but, picking up a reading book, remarked, 'This is a very dated scheme. I am surprised it is still in use. There are so many more appropriate materials available these days, schemes that reflect contemporary society.'

Mr Gaunt was getting increasingly annoyed by the man's behaviour. There seemed to be no warmth in his manner and not a positive judgement about the school, no enthusiasm at starting as the new headmaster in a few weeks' time.

'The proof of the pudding is in the eating, Mr Smart,' he replied, sounding reproving. 'No child leaves Mrs Golightly's class unable to read. Furthermore, the children love books and reading.'

In Mr Cadwallader's classroom, Mr Smart ran a long finger along the bookshelf.

'It's rather dusty in here,' he observed distractedly.

'Yes, I am aware of that. We are without a cleaner at present,' Mr Gaunt said, failing to conceal his irritation. 'It's been difficult to find someone prepared to travel so far up the Dale.'

They arrived at Tom's classroom. It was tidy and bright with children's paintings, poems, posters, and collages decorating the walls. There was a small reading corner, a shelf stocked with glossy-backed books, a set of dictionaries and a table displaying shells, coloured stones, and fossils. In the corner was a computer. On the high windowsill was a small selection of stuffed birds: a fierce-looking kestrel grasping a mouse in its talons, a wide-eyed owl, a sharp-beaked raven, and a magpie. There was a beady-eyed badger with a long, sad face, a mole, and a rabbit. Instead of the modern tables and chairs usually found in most primary schools, the room was furnished with antiquated, straight-backed wooden chairs and highly polished wooden desks with lids and holes for inkwells. The ceiling was a pale blue colour and the beams with curved wooden supports that stretched across it were painted navy blue. There was a Victorian fireplace, its mantel of dark slate; the heavy black iron grate was filled with dried flowers in various shades.

'Why are there no tables in here?' asked Mr Smart. He sounded like a schoolteacher addressing a child. 'Surely these desks are most unsuitable in this day and age?'

'I did suggest to Mr Dwyer that they be replaced,' Mr Gaunt explained, his tone of voice now less genial. 'He wanted the desks to stay. I have no problem with that. There's little storage space in here and the desks have somewhere for the children to keep their books.'

'Is this the only computer in the school?' Mr Gaunt was asked.

'Yes.'

'If I remember rightly there was funding available for schools to have several. I recall a communication from the Education Department informing head teachers of this.' Mr Smart smiled thinly.

'So I believe,' responded Mr Gaunt. He felt a pang of foreboding. This martinet would destroy everything that was good about Risingdale School.

Mr Smart did not pursue the matter but stared instead at the stuffed animals and birds on the windowsill. There was a grim expression on his hard face. 'Wasn't there a directive from the Education Department prohibiting stuffed animals in schools?'

'Yes, I recall something of the sort, but we get a great many directives, most of which I consign to the wastepaper basket.'

Mr Smart raise an eyebrow. 'Really?'

'Education, in my opinion, is not about process and paper-work, it is about teaching. It is the deeply committed and enthusiastic teacher who makes the difference, not directives. I am sure we can agree on that.'

Mr Gaunt was now heartily sick and tired of the man's off-hand, censorious manner. The sooner he left the school the better, he thought. 'I'm sure you have seen quite enough,' he said, heading for the classroom door.

'There are one or two other questions I would like to ask,' said Mr Smart.

'I am sure the Education Department will furnish you with anything else you need to know,' Mr Gaunt replied. 'Now I have to make tracks. I have a smallholding and have animals to feed.'

Driving home, Mr Gaunt was seething. He was rarely in a bad temper, but his successor had made him so angry. The man, who had made it clear he was dissatisfied with everything he had seen, would undoubtedly undo all the good in Ris-ingdale School and alienate the staff. He thought of what he might say to the teachers. They would surely ask him about the man who would be taking over. He wished at that moment that he had not resigned.

Mr Smart too was in a bad mood as he drove back to Skil-lington. The school was moribund – a shabby and untidy headmaster's room, dust everywhere, an out-of-date reading scheme, stuffed animals, ancient desks, just the one computer and a defunct governing body. Then he thought of Mr Gaunt, unkempt and disorganised, a man so laid-back and casual with his cluttered office and ridiculous alpenhorn. Things, he determined, would have to change.

When he approached the bottom of the steep hill where he had had the accident, he stopped and banged his hands hard on the steering wheel.

'This is too much!' he snarled.

The road was blocked by a herd of heavy-uddered black and white cows, jostling and pushing at each other, lowing in complaint and leaving behind great splashes of manure. To the side was the grizzled old farmer whom the driver had argued with earlier. He was sauntering along, a cigarette dangling from his lips, whacking the animals' haunches with a thin switch to keep them on course.

19

Monday morning found three of the teachers in the staffroom before school.

'Mr Gaunt was dressed up like a dog's dinner this morning,' remarked Mrs Golightly, cradling a mug of tea. 'The last time he turned up so smart we had a visit from the school inspector. You don't think Miss Tudor-Williams will be coming back, do you?'

'Well, something's got him all jittery,' remarked Mr Cadwallader, before reaching into the biscuit barrel. 'He was certainly in a funny mood. I said "Good morning" to him, and he walked straight past me as if I wasn't there. He was in a world of his own.'

'I reckon he's thinking about leaving,' said Mrs Golightly. 'It'll be preying on his mind. He'll miss being the headmaster here, and that's for sure. He's given his life to this school. It'll be a big wrench for him giving it all up and strange for us not having him around. I shall really miss him.'

'We all will, Bertha,' said Joyce.

'He's in a class of his own, is Mr Gaunt,' added her colleague, chomping on a biscuit. 'He'll be a hard act to follow.'

'Of course, he should never have resigned in the first place,' said Mrs Golightly. 'He should have stayed until he was sixty-five. I shall find it difficult getting used to a new headmaster who will probably want to make changes. I like things to stay the same.'

'Don't we all, Bertha,' agreed Mr Cadwallader, spilling biscuit crumbs down his jacket. 'It was a waste of time all of us having stayed after school for half an hour on Friday afternoon to meet this new chap and he never turned up. I hope he's a bit more reliable when he takes over.'

Mr Gaunt entered the staffroom with Tom. He was immaculately dressed in highly polished shoes, crisp white shirt, sober grey suit, and college tie. Usually when he met the teachers before school, the headmaster was good-humoured and chatty. That morning he was glum.

'Ah, now we are all present,' he said, 'there are a couple of things I wish to say. I have asked Mr Leadbeater to keep an eye on the children in the playground for the time being. Firstly, I shall be out of school this morning. I have a meeting at the Education Office with the Director of Education. Hence the suit and tie. I am told it is a small reception to thank me for my time working in the education service and for them to make a presentation. A nice gesture but quite uncalled for, and not the sort of thing I particularly welcome, but I have to show willing.' He gave a faint smile.

'That's nice,' said Mrs Golightly. 'I'm pleased that they are showing their appreciation, Mr Gaunt, after all your years of service.'

'Secondly, I wanted to explain why Mr Smart was unable to meet you all on Friday last. I am afraid he had an accident on his way here. He came off the road at that bad bend by the Fairborn farm. Fortunately, he wasn't hurt but it delayed his journey. We had a tour of the school and –' he paused for a moment – 'I am sure, he is looking forward to meeting you all in due course.' Mr Gaunt imagined, with a sinking heart, what the encounter with the staff would be like. The teachers, he could foresee, would find the man insufferable. 'Mr Smart telephoned me this morning and has expressed a wish to visit the school again, earlier in the day this time, to see you and meet the children,' he continued. 'This is something I will arrange later this week.' He turned to leave.

Joyce was the first to put her thoughts into words. 'What's he like?' she asked bluntly.

Mr Gaunt hesitated; he wondered if he should tell her his honest opinion of Mr Smart but then he thought that it would be better to be circumspect. Let the teachers make up their own minds when they meet him. 'What is he like?' he repeated under his breath, thinking how best he might respond. He certainly was not going to give the man a glowing reference. 'Cuthbert Smart is er . . . he's an interesting man with er . . . a deal of experience.'

Joyce and Mr Cadwallader held each other's stare for a moment.

'But what did you make of him, Mr Gaunt?' pressed Joyce.

'Do you think he will fit in?' asked Mr Cadwallader.

'Is he nice?' questioned Mrs Golightly.

'I er . . . didn't get to know him well enough to describe him as nice,' volunteered the headmaster evasively. He felt it would be counter-productive to tell the staff what he really thought about his successor, that he was a stiff-necked, condescending and humourless individual who would spread despondency, not a person after his own heart. 'Mr Smart is a serious, straight-talking sort of man who told me he has some ideas for a few changes.' Mrs Golightly and Joyce exchanged meaningful glances. Mr Gaunt considered adding that he felt sure his replacement would soon settle in, but he had strong reservations on that score. He couldn't think of anything more to say.

'Did he comment on what he had seen?' asked Mr Cadwallader.

'And did he say anything about the changes that he has in mind?' added Mrs Golightly before Mr Gaunt could respond.

'And will he be doing any teaching?' asked Joyce.

'My goodness, all these questions,' said the headmaster, feeling uncomfortable. 'Mr Smart seemed interested in what he saw but he stopped short of discussing what changes he might wish to make. He didn't mention doing any teaching. I am sure he will be able to answer your many queries when you meet him.' He glanced at his watch. 'Now, I really must make tracks. I'm expected at County Hall.' Then he left the room before he had to face any more difficult questions.

'Well, Mr Gaunt wasn't very forthcoming,' observed Joyce. 'He was most evasive.'

'This Cuthbert Smart sounds like a bit of a cold fish to me,' observed Mrs Golightly, taking the lead from her colleague.

'I don't like the sound of him at all,' said Mr Cadwallader. 'To describe someone as "interesting" could mean anything – "attention-grabbing", "provocative", "out of the ordinary", "odd".'

'Or exciting and inspiring,' said Tom, trying to put a positive slant on what the headmaster had told them and reassure his colleagues.

'Oh, for goodness' sake, Tom,' huffed Joyce. 'Were you listening to what Mr Gaunt said? Did the man sound exciting and inspiring? I think not.'

'Let us not judge the man before we have even met him,' he answered her. 'I'm sure Mr Smart is a decent enough sort of man.'

As he said this, however, he had the uneasy feeling that the new headmaster might prove to be the very opposite.

*

Mr Gaunt arrived at County Hall later that day for his appointment with the Director of Education. He paused at the great black wrought-iron gates beyond which a neat, gravelled drive curved through formal gardens to an imposing grey stone edifice with its flight of stone steps and imposing pillars. He thought for a moment. He was not in the mood for a celebration. Mr Smart and the future of Risingdale School had been on his mind since the demoralising encounter on the Friday last. He would be poor company and hoped this meeting would be a simple and relaxed affair and over soon.

After a while he entered the building and walked down the long echoing oak-panelled corridor. The interior of County Hall was cool and dark and reflected his gloomy mood. He made his way up the wide curving staircase and followed a sign directing him to the office of the Director of Education. At the reception desk he gave the secretary his name and said that he had an appointment.

'Oh yes, Mr Gaunt,' said the young woman affably, 'you are expected.'

He was shown directly into the inner office. A stout, rosy-faced woman with pale appraising eyes and thinning grey hair tied back tightly on her scalp, rose from her desk to greet him.

'It's such a pleasure to see you again, Mr Gaunt,' said Ms Tricklebank, warmly shaking his hand and smiling widely. 'If you would like to follow me, our small get-together is taking place in the Mayor's Parlour. Everyone is so looking forward to seeing you.'

The 'small get-together' was anything but. The room was packed with a crowd of noisy people which, on catching sight of the honoured guest, broke into spontaneous applause.

The Mayor's Parlour, with its high ceiling and intricately plastered gallery, was an elegant and richly furnished chamber dominated by a solid mahogany partners' desk with a tooled red leather writing inset. Various awards were displayed on the Carrara marble mantel above which was a huge portrait in oils of Queen Victoria in her imperial robes and crown. She stared down imperiously from her gilded frame. Along a wall were a set of gilt, ornately backed chairs and two matching marble-topped console tables. There were several green leather-bound armchairs and a chesterfield sofa. A glass-fronted cabinet contained a collection of the town's silver.

The Mayor, a handsome woman approaching middle age, came to greet him. She was accompanied by a remarkably thin young man who sported a shock of frizzy ginger hair.

'Good morning, Mr Gaunt,' she said, shaking his hand. 'I am pleased to meet you. I have heard so much about you.'

'All good, I hope?'

'Indeed, everyone speaks most highly of you. Let me introduce you to Councillor Wayne Cooper, who has recently been appointed as Chairman of the Education Committee.'

'We do know each other,' the councillor told her. 'I am pleased to meet you again, Mr Gaunt,' said the man. He shook his hand. 'I well recall when you came to speak to the Education Sub-Committee earlier this year when we were considering the future of the small schools in the county.' He turned to the Mayor. 'Mr Gaunt was asked to address us as part of our consultation exercise,' he explained, 'and gave the elected members an extremely good insight into the work and life in a small rural primary school. It was a most convincing argument.'

'And you were most supportive, I remember,' said Mr Gaunt.

'I was impressed with what you had to say. Indeed, your presentation went a long way in convincing the members that some of the small rural primary schools should be preserved.'

At the Sub-Committee meeting Mr Gaunt had described Risingdale, a school staffed by dedicated, fully qualified teachers who, like he, had chosen to work in this sphere of education there rather than in a big city school, because they were passionate believers in the type of learning the small school could provide. He had told the councillors about the children, who were drawn from largely farming backgrounds;

they were well behaved and worked hard and achieved a good standard of work.

'All our children,' he had gone on to say, 'have a deep knowledge of the environment, not only relating to farming but also about the flora and fauna that flourish in the area. They have a sound knowledge of the history and the geography of the region and beyond.' He had concluded. 'To my mind, education is about developing healthy, happy, well-behaved children who are caring and truthful, who love to learn and achieve excellent academic standards.'

'I do have to admit,' Councillor Cooper told him now, 'that I did have a little inside knowledge about Risingdale School before you spoke to us.'

'Really?'

'My cousin's son is a pupil there. Edward is in Mr Cadwallader's class.'

Mr Gaunt pictured the thin boy with the same frizzy ginger hair.

'Ah yes, young Eddie,' he said.

'And I believe you taught Lloyd Cooper, another cousin of mine.'

'Lloyd Cooper,' repeated Mr Gaunt, nodding. 'Yes, yes, I do remember him.'

'You met Lloyd when you last visited County Hall,' said the councillor. 'He told me you and he had a most interesting conversation.'

'We did indeed. He was telling me he is the head gardener here.'

On his way to speak to the Education Sub-Committee, Mr Gaunt had come across a young man in a blue overall and large boots, pushing a barrow-load of hedge clippings and dead flowers before him. He had stopped and observed the headmaster.

'You don't recognise me, do you?' the man had asked.

Mr Gaunt had screwed up his eyes and examined the speaker's face. 'I'm afraid not,' he had replied.

'I've grown a bit since you last saw me. You used to teach me. I'm Lloyd Cooper.'

'Lloyd Cooper,' the headmaster had repeated. He had then recalled the shy, nervy, underconfident child who found schoolwork hard. His reading had been poor, and he had struggled with his writing, but he had a sunny disposition and was helpful and well behaved.

'I loved Risingdale School,' the young man had told him. 'It was like being in a big family. Everybody knew everybody else and we all got along.'

'Lloyd had many happy memories of his time at Risingdale School,' Councillor Cooper continued now. 'He would be the first to admit that he wasn't a high-flyer but with your encouragement and that of his teachers he has made something of his life. He has a great respect and admiration for you. He said you always had the children's interests at heart.'

'That is most kind of him to say so,' Mr Gaunt replied. There was a lump in his throat. I hope that my successor will generate great respect and admiration, he thought, and have the children's interest at heart. But he rather doubted it.

Having been introduced to one after another of the guests, all of whom told him how well he was regarded and how much he would be missed, he was presented with an inscribed silver tankard and a certificate detailing his long service in education.

Listening to such commendation, Mr Gaunt decided that he would take this opportunity of sharing with Ms Tricklebank his views on education and his reservations about Mr Smart. He had not been asked by the Director of Education to be involved in the appointment of his successor or give his opinion of the prospective headmaster of Risingdale School and she might deem it inappropriate for him to comment, that it was not his place to meddle in the appointment, but he felt duty bound to tell her about his misgivings.

The Director of Education smiled again warmly as he approached her.

'I am sure you will have gathered how highly you are regarded, Mr Gaunt,' he said.

'Yes, I was greatly moved.'

'To be frank I thought you might have stayed on a few more years. It was quite a surprise when I heard that you have decided to retire early.'

'May I be frank with you, Ms Tricklebank?' he asked.

'Oh dear, this sounds a bit ominous,' she said.

'I have decided to finish because I feel like a square peg in a round hole,' he told her. 'As I mentioned to my Chairman of Governors, I have been finding it increasingly difficult of late to accept the many vagaries in education and all the regulations, paperwork, pressures and directives. Schools to my mind are changing, and not always for the better. I do not fit in any more. You may consider that I am speaking out of turn here but I consider I have to say it before I leave the school. I feel I need to get things off my chest.'

'Please do,' replied Ms Tricklebank, not looking forward to what she was about to hear. She could tell by Mr Gaunt's tone of voice that there were going to be a few home truths.

'There seems to be such a climate of over-prescription these days in education,' he told her, 'an insensitivity to local needs and realities. For me, the pace of change is too fast and there are many ill-considered regulations and inconsequential initiatives, which take us away from the real purpose of education. Never has grandma been told so often or in such a detailed manner how to suck eggs.'

'I'm sorry you feel like that,' she said. 'The fact is, education has to move with the times.'

'Well, I cannot move with them,' Mr Gaunt told her. 'That is why I have decided to leave. My successor, who has visited the school, seems intent on making many changes at Risingdale when he takes over in September. Having heard what he has to say, I am not at all convinced he will be successful in gaining the teachers' confidence and respect and maintaining the quality of the education provided.'

Ms Tricklebank sighed inwardly. She did not wish to pursue the matter. She was not inclined to discuss another head teacher with him. It would be unprofessional. Mr Gaunt was, without doubt, a dedicated and well-liked headmaster, but he lived in the past. Things in education were changing. It was perhaps time for him to retire. 'Thank you for your honesty, Mr Gaunt,' she said. 'I can assure you we in the Education Department will keep an eye on things at Risingdale when the new headmaster takes over. Now, I am sure you will wish to meet some of the other guests.'

It was in the corridor, as he made his way out, that Mr Gaunt chanced upon his least favourite education officer. Mr Nettles was a tubby, pasty-faced man with thick blond hair sticking up from his head like tufts of dry grass. He wore small steel-rimmed spectacles and a permanent frown. The education officer was blessed with the ability to seem extremely busy whilst avoiding work of any kind.

'I'm glad I've caught you,' he said, having appeared out of a side door. He was carrying a box file under his arm and held a thick bundle of papers. He was a man who always gave a convincing impression of being diligent and hard-pressed. 'I just wanted to wish you well on your retirement. It goes without saying that you will be greatly missed.'

If it goes without saying, thought Mr Gaunt, then why say it?

'You think so?' he replied.

'I beg your pardon?'

'That I will be greatly missed.'

'Unquestionably.'

'I hardly think you will miss me very much, Mr Nettles.'

'It is true that we have had our differences,' said the education officer, 'but I have always respected you and admired your dedication.'

'I see that you have recovered from your accident,' said Mr Gaunt.

Having sent around schools another of his directives concerning the dangers of snow and ice, Mr Nettles had slipped on an icy patch of ground outside County Hall, fallen down the steps and succeeded in breaking both his wrists.

'Oh, my wrists are fine.' He gave a tight little smile. 'They do tend to ache a little at times and I have had to forsake my Morris dancing for the present, but the twinges are to be expected.'

'And I see that it hasn't stopped you from writing your various directives,' commented Mr Gaunt sardonically, motioning to the papers in Mr Nettles' arms.

The sarcasm was lost on the education officer. 'No, no, I'm still as busy as ever.' He looked diffident. 'Have you had the opportunity of meeting your successor yet?' he asked. 'Mr Smart did mention to me that he was intending to visit Risingdale.'

'He has been to look around the school and arranged another visit,' Mr Gaunt told him.

'He's a very capable man, is Cuthbert Smart.'

'Is he?'

'Oh yes. He is a man with some interesting ideas and with a great deal of experience. At present he is the headmaster at Skillington School.'

'Yes, so I believe. That is the school that is to close, isn't it, the one where the numbers, unlike Risingdale, have been declining?'

'Yes, unfortunately, despite my efforts, it wasn't viable to keep Skillington open,' said Mr Nettles. 'Mr Smart has been there for most of his career and he will be very sorry to leave. He will be greatly missed.'

'Really?'

'However, he was telling me that he is very excited about starting at Risingdale.'

He didn't sound very excited to me, thought Mr Gaunt. He was about as excited as a block of petrified wood.

'He is looking forward to taking things further at the school,' Mr Gaunt was told.

'And what does "taking things further" mean?' he asked.

'Well, making the necessary changes,' explained Mr Nettles.

'And what are these necessary changes?'

The education officer shifted uncomfortably.

'Risingdale has to move with the times, Mr Gaunt,' he said condescendingly. 'I am sure there are a few changes Mr Smart would wish to make.'

'I am sure he thinks there are,' agreed the headmaster. 'I am not averse to change to suit our times and circumstances, but I believe that the great principles in education ought to remain the same.'

'Yes, yes, of course,' stuttered Mr Nettles.

'I would add,' continued Mr Gaunt, 'that I would caution Mr Smart to tread very carefully before making many changes at Risingdale. It is a happy and successful school. I am sure that you would agree that change for change sake is not a desirable undertaking.'

'Yes. Of course.'

'"Be not the first by whom the new is tried, nor yet the last to lay the old aside".'

'I beg your pardon?'

'The words of Alexander Pope,' Mr Gaunt told him. 'And wasn't it Dr Johnson who said that "all change is of itself an evil"? Wise words, don't you think?'

*

Mr Smart returned to Risingdale School early the following Monday morning to meet the teachers and the children. Mr Gaunt, with a hint of gritted teeth, saw the shiny black saloon car pull up outside. He tapped his fingers edgily on the desk and decided that he would not go out, as he had done previously, to greet his successor at the entrance to the school. By nature, he was a genial and gracious man but with his successor he could not find it in his heart to be anything other than formal and aloof. He was not looking forward to a second onerous encounter with this stiff-necked, humourless, and pompous man.

Mr Smart, stony-faced, stood before Mrs Leadbeater without speaking. When he had telephoned the school to make the appointment for his visit, he had been noticeably short and offhand with her. The secretary peered up and over her unfashionable horn-rimmed spectacles and waited for the visitor to smile, wish her a 'Good morning', introduce himself, and tell her what he wanted. Since this was unforthcoming, she spoke.

'May I help you?' she asked laconically.

'Yes,' he replied, 'be so good as to tell Mr Gaunt that I have arrived?'

'And you are?' she asked, knowing full well to whom she was speaking, for Mr Gaunt had acquainted her with the fact that his successor would be visiting that morning.

He bristled. 'I am the new headmaster,' he replied. 'I telephoned to say I would be coming to visit this morning.'

If he expected any change in the woman's demeanour, he was disappointed, for Mrs Leadbeater remained straight-faced and unimpressed. He could tell by her downturned mouth that she did not like what she saw. He certainly did not like what *he* saw. He thought of his secretary at Skillington, that fussy, amiable and deferential Mrs Bosomworthy. Perhaps he could arrange for her to be redeployed here and replace this hard-faced virago in the unfashionable glasses. He would give the Education Office a call when he was back at Skillington and have a word with Mr Nettles.

'If you wait,' she told him, 'I will tell the headmaster' (she chose the word deliberately) 'that you are here.' Since he never mentioned the word 'please', neither did she.

A moment later the visitor was shown into Mr Gaunt's study and, without being asked to sit down, placed himself on the hard, wooden chair in front of the desk.

'Good morning,' he said. The chair creaked beneath his weight.

'Good morning,' replied Mr Gaunt. There was no trace of the welcoming smile. 'I trust that this morning's journey was less eventful than the last.'

'Yes, although I find the narrow twisting roads a bind.' He exhaled a measured breath. 'I suppose I will have to get used to them.'

'Yes, I suppose you will.'

Mr Gaunt could have given the man the advice he had given Tom when he started at the school, to take it very slowly driving on the country lanes, for he would likely come across tractors pulling out of farm gates and lambs wandering across the road, but he realised that any advice he might give to Mr Smart would be ignored. He was therefore not inclined to provide him with such information nor was he going to offer him a cup of tea – herbal or otherwise. In fact, he did not wish to engage in any further conversation with the man. The sooner he was out of the school the better. A stubborn silence settled between them. Finally, he spoke.

'Would you like me to introduce you to the teachers and the pupils?' he asked.

'No, no, I can manage that myself,' he answered before adding, 'that is, if you have no objection.'

'Not at all. You know which classrooms are which. Everyone is expecting you.'

'Clearly the school secretary wasn't,' replied Mr Smart petulantly. 'I must say, I found her manner rather abrupt.'

Mr Gaunt could not resist responding.

'Really? Mrs Leadbeater is usually so friendly and hospitable.' Mr Smart opened his mouth to speak but Mr Gaunt carried on. 'Well, I am sure you are very keen to make a start,' he said, getting up from his chair to indicate the meeting was over.

Mr Smart rose to his feet, straightened his jacket, adjusted the crease in his trousers and left the room.

When the visitor had departed, Mr Gaunt rested his head in his hands and shook his head. 'What will the teachers make of the man?' he murmured.

The teacher of the infants welcomed the visitor with a broad smile on her face and wished him a cheerful, 'Good morning. Do come along in. I am Mrs Golightly, and you must be Mr Smart.'

'That's right.' He managed a thin smile and gazed around the room.

All classroom noise ceased and twenty pairs of solemn little eyes gazed at the visitor in the rather unnerving way of young children. Mr Smart had always felt uncomfortable in the presence of infants. They looked you in the eye and asked the bluntest questions. They could be noisy and unpredictable, easily moved to fits of giggles and just as easily moved to tears.

'Shall we all say a nice, "Good morning" to Mr Smart, children?' said the teacher.

The little ones chorused loudly, 'Good morning, Mr Smart, good morning, everybody.'

He didn't reply.

'On Monday mornings,' Mrs Golightly told the visitor, 'I take the opportunity of hearing some of the children read while the remainder is engaged in painting or other activities. You might like to take a wander around and have a word with them.'

'I'll watch, if I may,' he replied.

'Well, as you wish. If you would like to bring a chair over,' said the teacher, 'we'll go to the reading corner.'

'I beg your pardon?'

'That's where I hear the children read. It's more relaxed than hearing them at my desk.'

'I see.'

Mr Smart picked up a small, child-sized melamine chair and joined her. He sat down and his buttocks spread over the sides.

Mrs Golightly sat on a comfortable armchair. 'Come along then, Gareth,' she said to a chubby child with a freckled face and black curls, 'let us see how you've been getting on.' The little boy brought his reading book, the last in the 'Merrytime Reading Scheme', sat next to Mrs Golightly and opened the cover. He straightened the page with his hand and stared at the teacher. 'This gentleman is going to listen to how well you read,' said the teacher. 'Off you go then, nice and clearly.' Gareth read slowly and accurately about Gordon, the mischievous goat who ate the washing on the line in Mrs Foster's garden. Sometimes he stopped and giggled. He closed the book with a beam on his face.

'He's really naughty, Gordon, isn't he miss?' said the boy.

'Yes, he is,' replied the teacher. The story reminded the teacher of the occasion when Mr Pendlebury had held a special service to celebrate the Feast of Saint Francis of Assisi and had asked the children to bring along their pets for a blessing. One child had arrived at the church with a goat. The animal had taken a liking to Mrs Golightly's handbag, grabbed it with its long yellow teeth, and begun munching furiously.

'Well, your reading was wonderful. I am very pleased with you and I think you know what I've got in my bag, don't you?'

The boy's eyes brightened, he beamed and nodded, feeling a glow of pride.

The teacher reached into her bag and took out a silver badge, across which was written 'I am a Free Reader'. She pinned it on the child's cardigan. 'Congratulations, Gareth,' she said, 'you can now choose a book from the Reading Corner.'

Before Mrs Golightly could call out another pupil to read to her, Mr Smart leaned forward. The chair bent slightly under his weight. The altercation which followed went back and forth like a game of shuttlecock.

'Have you the scheme of work?' he asked.

'No,' she replied.

'All teachers are required to work to a scheme of work,' she was told. 'There was a directive from the Education Office.'

'Was there?'

'Yes.'

Mrs Golightly looked him in the eye. 'Mr Smart,' she said, 'I have done this job long enough not to require a scheme of work.'

'All teachers are required to have a scheme of work,' he told her.

'Well, I haven't got one.'

'So, when do you introduce the children to the disciplines of formal learning?'

'When they are ready.'

'I see.'

'And I do so without supressing the children's eagerness to explore and enjoy new experiences. In my view, a dislike for reading or an inability to handle number work arises when children are taught these skills before they are ready.'

'I see you are using an old reading scheme. Do you not think that it is out of date?' His tone was reproachful rather than enquiring.

'It serves its purpose,' she replied, stiffening at the perceived criticism, 'and children enjoy reading from it.'

'But surely you will own that there are more appropriate and contemporary schemes that have a greater appeal to the modern child?' He had the look of a parent disappointed by the behaviour of a wayward child.

'I'm sure there are contemporary schemes available, but I like this one,' said the teacher drily. Her cheerful disposition had disappeared. She had not been expecting to be grilled. 'The scheme has a tried and tested format and, as I have said, the children enjoy reading the stories and talking about the content. You observed that with Gareth's reading this morning. As you will no doubt have noticed, the books are about a farm. Many of the children in the class live on farms, as does Gareth, so the stories have a particular relevance and appeal.'

'Nevertheless, I think there is more suitable reading material. The language is rather stilted, don't you think?' He waited for a response, but Mrs Golightly remained tight-lipped. 'However, I won't pursue the matter,' he said in a brittle tone of voice.

Well don't, thought Mrs Golightly, getting increasingly irritated. Her heart sank at the thought that this cold, dismissive and patronising man would be the new headmaster.

'But I think reading schemes like the one you are using have had their day.'

So he *was* going to pursue the matter then, she thought.

'Well, we will agree to differ, shall we? Because I don't,' she told him, bridling.

'At Skillington we use an up-to-date—'

'Mr Smart,' interjected Mrs Golightly stoutly, 'might I ask, have you ever taught infants to read?'

He was taken aback by the question. 'Well, er . . . no, actually. My experience has been with the junior-aged children but—'

'Then I hope you will allow that I, who have taught reading for more than forty years with a great degree of success, know something about the subject. No child moves up into the juniors unable to read and what is more he or she has a love of books.' She thought for a moment of the inspector's report of 1890 in the log book from which Mr Gaunt had read, and was predisposed to repeat the remarks of HMI Mr Harcourt: '"A little experience has taught me that infants should be left in the hands of their teachers, and that the inspectors should look on".'

Mr Smart made a quick exit.

20

In Mr Cadwallader's classroom the tables had been pushed together to form one large square area in the middle. The teacher and children were busily engaged with rulers and scissors, measuring, cutting and pasting. They were chattering and laughing.

'Good morning,' said Mr Smart, striding purposefully into the room and raising his voice above the noise.

'Good morning,' replied the teacher. 'You must be Mr Smart.'

'That's right.' His lips tightened into a thin smile, which soon slipped away from his lips.

'Quiet, children,' ordered the teacher. The talk stopped. 'We have a visitor joining us this morning who, I am sure, will be interested in our project. Eddie, perhaps you might like to tell Mr Smart what we are doing.'

'We're constructing models of famous pyramids,' said the boy. 'Me and Jimmy are building the Great Pyramid of Giza, Sarah and Donna are making the pyramid of Khufu.'

'Khufu is the largest pyramid in Egypt,' Sarah told him, 'in height and volume.'

'It's the biggest structure ever built by man,' added Donna. 'Did you know that?'

'No, I didn't,' admitted Mr Smart. His face was as expressionless as a guard on sentry duty outside a palace.

'It is two hundred and thirty meters long and one hundred and thirty-eight meters high,' the girl informed him. 'The base is square and right-angled, and each side forms an equilateral triangle.'

'I have found that children have a fascination with facts,' Mr Cadwallader told the visitor. 'They have really got their teeth into this project.'

'We have to convert the meters to feet and then build our models to scale,' said Sarah.

'And what is two hundred and thirty-eight meters in feet?' questioned Mr Smart, with a note of challenge in his voice. He was not really expecting a correct answer.

'Seven hundred and fifty-six,' replied the girl.

'Impressive, eh?' said Mr Cadwallader.

'How old is this child?' Mr Smart asked the teacher.

'Old enough to talk,' said the girl sotto voce, pulling a face.

He gave a small, pitying smile.

'Do you know anything about pyramids?' Donna asked the visitor, looking at him quizzically.

'Not a great deal,' he replied, with the vacant interest one might give to a collection of insects in a museum case.

'They were the tombs of the pharaohs. Do you know how many pyramids have been found?' persisted the pupil.

'No, I do not.' Mr Smart was unused to being quizzed by children and was beginning to feel uncomfortable.

'There have been one hundred and thirty-eight pyramids discovered so far,' informed the girl. 'Do you know—'

'I shall move on,' Mr Smart interrupted, speaking to the teacher. Then, failing to convey any thanks or appreciation of what he had seen, he left the room.

'That chap didn't know much, did he, sir?' asked Sarah.

Mr Cadwallader felt it diplomatic not to respond.

'And who the hell was he anyway?' asked Eddie, speaking to his pal in a whisper.

'He'll be one of these school infectors,' answered Jimmy.

Mr Smart entered the second lower junior classroom, the seven- and eight-year-olds, unobserved by the teacher, for Joyce had her back to him. She was standing in front of the class, swinging her arms like the conductor of an orchestra.

'Remember, as I have told you before, timing is especially important, as are dramatic pauses and facial expressions. You will be judged in the competition on interpretation of the verse, tone, volume, timing, stress and clarity of delivery. There should be no fidgeting and there will be clean noses and no sniffing. I am looking at you when I say that, Nathan Barraclough. I want to hear a clear, unhurried performance. Now remember the poem is called "Hiawatha" and not "Iawatha". Remember the aspirate.'

'The what, miss?' asked Nathan.

'The "h" at the beginning of the word,' said the teacher. 'Remember we did some exercises last term: "Happy Harry Hopkinson hops hurriedly on his heels and hopes to hike to Harrogate".'

'There's a man watching us,' Nathan told the teacher, pointing at the visitor.

Joyce swivelled around. 'Oh, I didn't see you there. Do come in. You must be Mr Smart.'

'Yes,' he replied.

'As you can see, we are practising our poem. The children will be performing part of "Hiawatha" at the Clayton and District Choral Speaking Competition next week. There is a chair at the back of the room if you would care to listen.'

'Thank you, no,' he said. 'I will not be staying long.'

'I'm sure the children would welcome an audience and any constructive comments on their recitation.'

'I know little about poetry,' he said airily. 'I'm afraid it is not my métier.'

'Pardon?' Joyce felt a sudden prick of annoyance.

'I am not an enthusiast of poetry,' he confessed in a perfunctory tone.

'Children,' said Joyce, turning to her pupils, 'we will have a
short break while I speak to our visitor. Get out your reading
books and read quietly.' She had expected that Mr Gaunt's
successor would enter the room with a smile and a friendly 'Good morning', introduce himself, say how much he was
looking forward to starting at the school, perhaps mention the
bright and tidy classroom and take some time to speak to the
children. She was not anticipating the appearance of such a
cold individual with a disagreeable manner; nor was she ready
for the confrontation which ensued. She turned to Mr Smart
and lowered her voice. 'So, you are not keen on poetry, then?'
she asked, staring at him in a disconcerting way.

'To be frank, I don't think poetry has any practical relevance to the real world,' he told her pedantically. 'Very few
people read poems these days and as regards its place in the
school curriculum, to my mind it occupies a small place.'

'I don't agree,' responded Joyce.

Mr Smart smiled condescendingly, the way an adult might
smile at an inquisitive child with an over-active imagination.

'Poetry is not going to help pupils to get jobs when they
leave school,' he said. 'First and foremost, children need a
good grounding in English and mathematics.'

'So that is the point of education, is it?' questioned Joyce.
She composed her face, which disguised the annoyance building up inside.

'I beg your pardon?' A suggestion of irritation passed over
his face.

'That education is merely to help children get jobs when
they leave school?'

'Education,' Mr Smart told her with serene confidence,
'is to equip young people with the necessary skills required
for the world of work.' Joyce felt patronised like a child

being patted on the head by a condescending teacher. 'It is to prepare children for the demands of society, and I don't see poetry as being particularly helpful in that regard. Personally, I can't see the point of children chanting poetry.'

'It is choral speaking, not chanting,' she countered briskly. Her tone was glacial. 'I place great emphasis on the teaching of speech. Poetry readings, discussion groups, drama and choral speaking give children the opportunity to extend and improve the way they speak, encouraging them to use their voices effectively and converse with clarity, enthusiasm and confidence. To perform in front of others takes a great deal of self-assurance. Even the most self-possessed and practised feel nervous speaking in front of others.' She paused for effect. 'Those, therefore, who are able to overcome their shyness and self-consciousness to speak before an audience deserve our admiration. For me, every lesson is a speech training lesson.'

Mr Smart was irked at being lectured at. 'That is debatable,' he said, with the vagueness that meant she was misguided, 'but this is not the time nor the place to debate it.'

'From what you have said, Mr Smart,' Joyce replied with a small sardonic smile, 'I really don't feel that debating poetry with you would prove very productive.'

He could feel the tension and controlled anger radiating from the teacher and felt it would be fruitless to discuss the matter further so, with the sweetly damning words resonating in his ears, he departed.

'I d . . . d . . . don't like that man, Miss Tranter,' said Geraldine. 'H . . . h . . . he was headmaster at my last school, and I was frightened of him.'

I do not like him either, thought Joyce, but I am certainly not frightened of him. The days when she had been bullied by a domineering man were over.

The prospective headmaster of Risingdale School paused for a moment outside Tom's classroom when he heard laughter. He then opened the door charily and entered. The laughter stopped and all eyes centred on him.

'Ah, Mr Smart,' said Tom cheerfully. 'We were expecting you. Do come along in. There's a chair at the back for you.'

'I won't be staying long,' Mr Smart replied. 'I'll stand if I may. Do carry on.'

There was no smile, shake of the hand, no greeting and no apology for disturbing the lesson. He stood by the door, pale and poker-faced, as still and as cold as a statue.

'Perhaps you might like to tell our visitor what we are doing,' said Tom to Hazel.

'This morning we are discussing the things that make us happy,' said the girl, 'then we are to do some non-fiction writing.'

'We are having a brainstorming session,' added Tom.

Mr Smart was inclined to tell the teacher that the word 'brainstorming' was not now used in the classroom and that the term 'thought shower' was deemed to be more suitable. He recalled a directive from Mr Nettles on this very subject of political correctness. However, he desisted. 'So, children,' said Tom, 'where were we? Hands up, what makes you want to smile and feel happy?'

The children were keen to give their thoughts and a forest of hands shot into the air.

'Yes, David,' said Tom, pointing to a small, gangly boy with a squint.

'When we don't have to do maths,' replied the boy.

There was a gurgle of laughter.

'What about you, Carol?' asked Tom, looking at a pretty girl with mousy-brown hair, pink glasses and a shining, eager face.

'When my granddad wins a blue ribbon at the Clayton and District Agricultural Show, Mr Dwyer,' answered the girl. 'That makes everybody in our house happy.'

'I might have guessed that's what you would say,' remarked the teacher. 'Did your granddad win this year?'

'No,' replied the girl. 'Mr Croft pipped him at the post with a Swaledale tup. Young Mr Croft that is, not the old one.'

'Well, there's always next year,' said Tom.

'That's what my granddad said, Mr Dwyer. He said, "Blessèd is he who expects nothing, for he shall never be disappointed." He's always quoting the Bible. He does it on Sunday at the chapel when he's preaching.'

Tom pointed to a little, pixie-faced girl. 'So, Marjorie, what makes you happy?'

'I like to help my gran when she's quilting, Mr Dwyer,' volunteered the girl. 'She tells me stories about when she was young. Grandparents have a lot more time for children, don't they? They don't rush you and they don't tell you what to do, not like mums and dads.' She grinned. 'And teachers. Sometimes when my dad tells me off, my gran says, "Oh, stop mithering, Frank. You had your moments when you were a boy." It makes me laugh.'

Christopher, the large, ruddy-complexioned boy who seldom smiled, raised his hand.

'Yes, Christopher.'

'I'll tell you what makes me happy, Mr Dwyer,' he offered, pulling a face, 'it's when my dad doesn't shout at me.'

'And Colin,' said Tom, not wishing to pursue this line of thought. 'I have an idea what makes you feel happy.'

'It's when I finish painting a picture, sir,' said the lumpen moon-faced boy with the lank black hair, 'and I'm pleased with it.'

'Yes, I thought it might be,' said the teacher. 'Colin is our star artist,' he told the visitor. 'He won the County Art Competition.'

Mr Smart, who had as much time for art in the curriculum as he did for poetry, did not respond.

'What do you say, George?' asked Tom.

'I think if I 'ad to pick just one time when I feel reight 'appy, Mester Dwyer,' said the boy, uttering his thoughts as always without inhibition, 'it's when a calf is born. As tha knaas, we've 'ad a few problems on t'farm lately wi' calvin' an' mi dad gets reight worried when a cow is abaat to calve. But when it gus well, 'e's dead chuffed. It comes out all wet an' shiny an' steamin' an' t'vet rubs some 'ay on its little body an' it oppens its eyes fer fust time. Then its mother turns an' sees it an' she starts to lick it. It makes me feel . . . I don't know . . . sort o' good inside. Then I see mi dad's face. 'E's gorra gret big smile an' 'e nods an' pats t'cow on 'er rump an' sez, "Well done, old lass".' The boy giggled. 'It were same when mi babby brother were born. Mi dad telled me mam, "Well done, old lass," but 'e din't pat 'er. 'E gev 'er a kiss.'

'Do you know, George,' said Tom, moved by what the boy had said, 'That is one of the nicest things I think I have heard.'

The boy's face reddened and he beamed.

Many more ideas were shared by the class: visiting grandma and grandpa, playing with friends, being able to breathe through your nose after having a cold, drinking cocoa on a cold night, staying in bed on a Saturday, listening to a favourite record, going on holiday, having a birthday party, scoring the winning goal.

'Charlie, you've been very quiet this morning,' said Tom. 'What do you think makes you really happy?'

'It's having a father, Mr Dwyer,' replied the boy quietly.

When Mr Smart had gone, Vicky Gosling, who had remained uncommonly silent during the lesson, waved her hand in the air. She had been staring at the visitor in an inquisitive way and did not like the look of him with his deadpan face.

'Mr Dwyer,' she said, with the self-same expression of her grandmother's that Tom knew only too well. 'That man who came into the classroom, he didn't look very happy, did he?

He didn't smile once and stared like Count Dracula ready to sink his teeth into somebody's neck.'

At morning break Mr Smart, on returning to the school office, came across Tom in the corridor on his way to the staffroom.

'Might I have a quick word?' he asked.

'Yes, of course,' answered Tom.

'Regarding the lesson I have just observed,' he said, 'I think you might spend some time teaching the children about the correct use of English. The boy – George, I think his name was – spoke with such a conspicuous accent it was difficult to understand a word he said.'

'Are you saying that I should correct the children's spoken English?'

'Well, yes that is exactly what I am suggesting.'

'I must disagree,' Tom told him. 'I believe that a child's accent should be accepted and that to attempt to suppress it is irrational and neither humane nor necessary. A teacher should accept the language a child brings to school. I recall at college studying the major government report stating this very thing. In *A Language for Life* it was emphasised that the child's language should be accepted, and that to criticise a person's speech may be an attack on his or her self-esteem. And speaking of what George said, I think it was honest and very affecting.'

Another uncooperative and rebellious teacher, thought Mr Smart. I am going to have my work cut out when I become the headmaster.

'I have not the time to dispute the matter,' he told Tom, 'but I will say this. We do children no favours by allowing them to speak in a coarse accent. They need to be taught to speak correct English.' He did not wait for a response but, being keen to depart, walked away.

In the school office, Mrs Leadbeater glanced up impassively from the papers on her desk.

'Could you tell Mr Gaunt I am ready to depart?' Mr Smart asked.

The school secretary slowly removed her glasses and met his eyes levelly. She stood and smoothed the creases out of her skirt and went, without a word, to inform the headmaster the visitor was about to leave. She returned to her desk a moment later. 'The headmaster will see you before you go,' she said, before looking at the papers on her desk.

'Off so soon?' said Mr Gaunt when Mr Smart entered his study.

He did not rise from his chair.

'Yes, I have seen quite enough.'

'And I hope you have been suitably impressed with what you have seen.'

Mr Smart sat down. 'No, to be frank, I'm afraid that I have not. I feel that there are certain changes necessary to move the school forward.'

'What sort of changes?'

'The infant teacher is very set in her ways and her methods and materials are old-fashioned. The Welshman, I can't recall his name, had the pupils spending a fruitless amount of time, in my opinion, making cardboard models of pyramids. The information could easily have been found in a reference book. His room was noisy and untidy. I am very much in favour of a quiet and orderly classroom.' He raised his voice a fraction higher. 'Miss Tranter, I found a difficult woman with extraordinarily strong views and, as I mentioned to her, I saw little point for pupils spending time on choral poetry. For me poetry, art, music and drama are, of course, part of the school curriculum but they decorate the margins of the more serious business of study. As for Mr Dwyer, I thought he was far too free and easy with his class. That, I am afraid, is the way of young teachers these days; they want the children to be their friends. This leads to a breakdown in classroom discipline.'

Mr Gaunt, who had listened to the diatribe with a sinking heart, his hands joined under his chin, and his elbows on the desk as if in prayer, had heard enough.

'Mr Dwyer,' continued Mr Smart, 'also had some strange views about the teaching of English, telling me—'

'May I stop you there,' cut in Mr Gaunt with cold authority. He sat up at his desk and ran a hand through his hair in a gesture of weariness. Then he shut his eyes for a moment and breathed out heavily, as if struggling to compose his temper. 'I take exception to your criticisms,' he said, his voice firm and steady. 'I am enormously proud of this school and the teachers in it. I am amazed that you should come here and think it appropriate for you to start disparaging everything you have seen.' Then he looked down at a paper on his desk. 'I should like you to listen to this, if you would. It is from the report of HMI Miss Tudor-Williams who visited the school the term before last. Let me read you a part which you may find interesting: "It has been a great pleasure to inspect Risingdale School. The real interest shown by the children, their obvious enjoyment of the subjects they study, their thoughtfulness and intelligence as well as the accuracy of their answers, all point to the thorough and painstaking work of their teachers. The great spirit of happiness and endeavour, evident in all the classrooms, is to the credit of the teachers who should be highly commended. Children talk freely and accurately about the local countryside and its history and could write personally with rare fluency; paintings are lively and revealing and poetry well-established." I shall leave the full report for your perusal when you take over the position of headmaster here.'

'In my opinion, school inspectors are like back-seat drivers,' Mr Smart informed him. 'They are full of advice on how to drive the car but unable to do so themselves.'

'I'm sure when Miss Tudor-Williams makes a return visit next term you will no doubt apprise her of your views,' said

Mr Gaunt. Not wishing to hear any more from the man, he stood and, maintaining a polite and meticulous coldness, informed the visitor, 'Now, if there is nothing else, I hope you will excuse me. I should like to join my staff for a cup of coffee.'

Mr Smart opened his mouth to reply but thought better of it and got to his feet. And so they parted in a mood of mutual antagonism.

When he saw the black saloon car leave the school premises, Mr Gaunt left his study and headed for the staffroom. On his way he passed Mrs Leadbeater, who was sitting at her desk, typing. They exchanged glances, each knowing what the other was thinking about the visitor. As he approached the staffroom, he heard angry, raised voices. He took a breath and entered the room. The teachers fell silent.

'I am sure you will have much to say following Mr Smart's visit,' he said, 'but could I ask you to wait until lunchtime when I will join you. We will then have more time to discuss it.'

*

Mr Smart drove a little way from the school and then pulled off the road at the foot of the steep hill where before he had skidded and hit the dry-stone wall. He turned off the engine and sat back, resting his head on the back of the seat. He needed time to think. The visit to the school had been disturbing, not least his wrangle with the headmaster. It was not too soon for the man to retire, he pondered. Perhaps he should have kept his comments about the teachers to himself, but then he had been asked for his impressions and he was not one to keep his opinions to himself. As regards the school, there was so much to do. Clearly Mr Gaunt had let things slip. His easy-going, laid-back approach to management and leadership had meant that the teachers seemed to do exactly what they wished without any interference or supervision. It was obvious that they had ignored the curriculum guidelines sent to all schools by the Education Department, which set out the areas which should be covered and the appropriate resources available to use. And as for resources, where were the computers, he asked himself. Just one unused machine in the corner of a classroom and none in the office where the hard-faced secretary with the old-fashioned glasses knocked away on a typewriter. Then there were the ancient, lidded wooden desks, which would have to go. And the stuffed animals. There had been a directive from Mr Nettles, he recalled, stating that stuffed animals should no longer be used in schools, for they gave children the wrong impression about wildlife. He thought of the teachers he had met. A bizarre group if ever there was one: the infant teacher who was well past her prime with her outdated reading scheme; the self-important and dogmatic drama woman; the tiresome Welshman with his paper pyramids and Mr Dwyer, a young man who was far too familiar with his pupils. He would have to knock them into some sort of shape; and knock them into shape, he would. If they were unprepared to toe the line, then they could seek posts in other schools. He nodded. He would bring order, discipline, and direction to Risingdale School when he took over.

As he sat there contemplating where he should start on taking up his new post, he glanced up and became aware of something glinting in the road at the top of the hill. He blinked, thinking that it might be a trick of the light, and shielded his eyes. Then his mouth opened in alarm and he felt the blood drain from his cheeks. Three large, stainless-steel barrels started rolling down the incline, gathering speed and bouncing in his direction. He started the car and fumbled with the gear stick to get into reverse, but he was not quick enough. There was a sickening thud as the first barrel hit the front of the vehicle. The second barrel vaulted over the first and crunched over the bonnet, making a deep dent. The third hit the top of the car, caving it in, and then continued on its trajectory down the road. Then all was still. Mr Smart grasped the steering wheel and very nearly wept.

*

At lunchtime, the teachers gathered in the staffroom and were soon joined by a grim-faced Mr Gaunt.

'I guess I do not need to ask you what you thought of Mr Smart's visit,' he said. 'I heard you outside at morning break and can see it in your faces.'

'I cannot work with that man,' said Joyce vehemently.

'Neither can I,' said Mrs Golightly.

'The man was as cold as a corpse,' said Mr Cadwallader. 'I didn't warm to him at all. He was more like a deadmaster than a headmaster.'

Tom remained silent and stared at the floor.

Mr Gaunt sighed. 'I really don't know what to say,' he said. 'I am as disappointed as you.'

'Disappointed!' snapped Joyce. She sniffed disparagingly. 'Mr Gaunt, the man is intolerable. He's a pompous, patronising philistine, full of his own importance—'

'And rude,' chipped in Mrs Golightly.

'Yes, rude,' agreed Joyce, 'and self-opinionated and . . . and . . . well, I'm just lost for words.'

Tom hid a smile. It certainly did not sound to him that his colleague was lost for words.

'Can't you do anything, headmaster?' asked Mr Cadwallader.

'I really wish I could,' replied Mr Gaunt. 'The problem is that Mr Smart is the only head teacher in the county who needs to be redeployed. Risingdale is the only school in the county with a vacancy for a head teacher. I think it has been decided at the Education Office. I wish I had some influence in stopping his appointment. I did have a word with the Director of Education, but I fear my views fell upon deaf ears. There is the old saying that "The King is dead, long live the King." I can't imagine that anything I said will make any difference.'

'You could speak to Sir Hedley,' said Joyce, 'and tell him what Mr Smart is like.'

'Yes, I suppose I could.'

'Well, I shall tell you this, Mr Gaunt,' she declared, 'if that man becomes headmaster here, I shall resign. I do not need to teach. I am more than comfortably off. I teach because I love the job. I think I am good at it and I want to do the best for the children, but I just cannot work for that despot. There, I've said it.'

'I shall take early retirement if Mr Smart takes over from you,' Mrs Golightly told Mr Gaunt.

'I'm at a loss what to do,' remarked Mr Cadwallader glumly.

'You are noticeably quiet, Tom,' said Joyce. 'Please don't tell me that things will be all right and we should try and look on the bright side and make the best of it.'

'No, I'm not going to say that at all,' he told her. 'I feel the same as all of you. I would like to think that Mr Gaunt can do something, but I am not that hopeful. If Mr Smart takes up the position here, I shall seek another post.'

'Oh dear,' sighed Mr Gaunt.

The following morning as the teachers fretted about Mr Smart's visit, Mr Gaunt wondered what to do about the situation and Mrs Leadbeater sat at her desk unable to concentrate on her work, Mr Smart was in the blackest of moods back at Skillington School. It was not just the visit to Risingdale that had distressed him, it was what had happened to his treasured new car, which he had only recently had repaired after his skirmish with the dry-stone wall. He sat seething at his desk.

His secretary, a small, timid, bustling woman, could tell he was not in the best of moods when she found him at the desk in his office drumming his fingers impatiently on the desktop.

'Here's a nice cup of calming herbal tea, Mr Smart,' Mrs Bosomworthy cooed. 'You look as if you can do with it.'

'Get me the Education Office,' he barked. 'I need to speak to Mr Nettles.' The telephone was, after a long wait, answered by a clerical assistant who informed him that the education officer was tied up and that he would get back to him.

'Tell him I need to speak to him urgently!' he snapped.

*

Toby Croft, on that bright sunny day, was in a very different frame of mind from the teachers at the school and Mr Smart. He sat in the shade on a bench outside the farmhouse with a pint of beer in his hand, listening to the pigeons cooing on the roof, the hens clucking in the farmyard, the hum of bees, and thought that everything was right in the world. He had never had it so good. It was said of him in the village that if the curmudgeonly old farmer were to fall into a great mound of steaming manure, he would emerge smelling of roses. Toby smirked as he saw his son and two of the farm workers he had employed, repairing a dry-stone wall. They had been labouring for over two hours, their shirts wet with sweat. He considered taking them a drink but then thought better of it. It would mean getting up. He sighed contentedly. Things had worked out well for him since his son had taken over the running of the farm. He now did only the things he wanted to do. There was no pressure for him to lend a hand and Dean did not require him to do very much at all. His son was pleased his father made himself scarce.

Toby watched the slow progress of a policeman huffing and puffing like a geriatric pug dog as he made his way up the track to the farm. He quickly reached under him and pushed his pint of beer out of sight. The officer, heavily out of breath, arrived and sat down on the bench. He removed his helmet, opened the top button of his uniform, took a large handkerchief out of his pocket, and wiped his brow. He was a tubby individual with a round, pinkish face, large blue, bulging eyes and a thatch of black hair.

'I shall have to sit down,' he said, panting. He rested his helmet on his lap. 'By, but it's a walk and a half up here.'

'If it was any shorter, it wun't stretch,' Toby told him.

'I could have driven up, but I'm trying to lose a bit of weight.' He patted his stomach. 'The wife's been on at me to take more exercise.'

Toby examined the man's bulging abdomen but resisted saying anything.

'I could have sent the young bobby who's just started,' said the policeman, 'but I've put him on school crossing patrol. I know from experience what that involves.' He shook his head. 'Kids these days running amok across the roads like frightened rabbits and answering you back. In my day if a kid saw a bobby walking towards him, he'd be scared right down to his socks even if he hadn't done anything. Not now though.' He scrutinised the old farmer. 'Now then, Toby,' he said. 'I want a word with you.'

'I din't do it, Sergeant Pollock,' came the reply.

'What didn't you do?'

'Owt what thy're accusin' me of.'

'I'm not accusing you of anything. I'm here to make a few enquiries.'

'Abaat what?'

'Beer!'

'Beer,' repeated Toby. He glanced down to make certain his pint was hidden.

'Aye,' said the police officer. 'A lorry carrying a load of beer on its way to the King's Head, nearly came off the road yesterday at the bad bend that passes one of your fields and it shed half its load of beer barrels.'

'Well, theer's a thing,' said Toby.

'They managed to get most of the barrels back but there's one missing.'

'Well I never.'

'I don't suppose you've seen anything of it, have you?'

'Not a thing.'

'Are you sure?'

'Course I'm sure. I'm not likely to miss a big metal barrel o' beer.'

'How do you know it was a metal barrel?' asked Sergeant Pollock.

'Course, it must 'ave been a metal barrel. They're not med o' wood anymore. Everyone knows that.'

'Well, it's a mystery as to what happened to it,' said the policeman.

'It is that,' agreed Toby.

The officer scratched his scalp. 'Seems it disappeared into thin air.'

''Tis a bad bend is that,' said Toby. 'They ought to purrup more signs. There's allus accidents. That young teacher, Mester Dwyer, hended up in a ditch when 'e cem fer an interview fer that teachin' job at t'school. Then Sir 'Edley's lad an' that motorcyclist were killed theer. A week or so back some daft idiot cum off of t'road an' knocked daan 'alf mi wall. Now yev got lorries careerin' all ovver t'shop sheddin' barrels o' beer. Somebody cud 'ave got killed.'

'Somebody nearly was,' said Sergeant Pollock. 'Fortunately, the driver stayed inside his vehicle when three of the barrels landed on his car.'

'Bloody hell!' exclaimed Toby.

'His vehicle's a write-off. Big black saloon car it was.'

'Oh dear,' said Toby, hoping that it was the car that had run into his wall, the one driven by the obnoxious chap.

The policeman stood up, put on his helmet and fastened his top button. 'Speaking of beer,' he said, 'I could enjoy a pint of beer at this moment. My throat's as dry as dust with all that walking.' Toby said nothing. 'Well, I'd better make tracks. If you do happen to come across that missing barrel, let us know.'

'I shall get in touch straight away, you can be sure of that,' Toby told him.

He watched the policeman plodding slowly down the track and when he was out of sight, Toby reached under the bench and rescued his pint of beer. He took a great gulp and wiped the froth from his mouth with the back of his hand.

He had been examining the damaged dry-stone wall the day before when he had heard the screech of brakes and had seen the lorry reach the bend in the road, swerve to the side, then back again and discard half its load. Three of the barrels had bounced down the road; one had rolled through the gap in the wall and landed at Toby's feet. The old farmer had gazed heavenwards. He had given a rare smile. 'Somebody up theer loves me,' he had said.

21

The following evening, Tom was preparing his lessons when there was a knock on the cottage door. He found Sir Hedley on the step.

'I hope I am not disturbing you, Mr Dwyer,' said the baronet.

'Not at all,' Tom replied. 'Do come in.'

'I saw the light on and thought I might call. I believe congratulations are in order. You will, I am told, soon be a married man.'

'That's right.'

'Miss Fairborn is a delightful young woman. I have known her since she was a child. She's very clever and good-natured and a fine horsewoman. You are a very lucky young man.'

'Yes, I realise how lucky I am,' said Tom. 'May I offer my congratulations on your marriage?'

'Thank you, that's kind of you. It has certainly raised a few eyebrows in the village, but that was to be expected, I suppose. Of course, you knew of my relationship with Mrs Lister when we met that night in the garden outside her cottage,' said Sir Hedley. 'I appreciate you keeping it to yourself. There is nothing in the world that spreads swifter than rumour.'

The news had certainly caused a great deal of gossip. On a visit to the King's Head soon after the news had broken, Tom had overheard the locals discussing the hasty marriage and the revelation that Sir Hedley had fathered Mrs Lister's son. He had expected that Toby Croft would be voluble with his observations and was proved right, for the old farmer was holding forth.

'It's all daan to money,' he had given his opinion to his drinking pal. 'I mean what's hattracted an 'andsome younger woman like Missis Lister to shack up wi' an old bloke like t'squire, if it weren't money?'

'Tha'd be surprised,' Percy had remarked. ''E's not a bad-looking chap is Sir 'Edley and tha knaas what they say, "Many a rusty key can oppen a silver lock".'

'May I offer you a drink?' asked Tom now.

'Thank you, no. I am trying to cut down on the whisky,' replied the baronet. Tom had meant a cup of coffee. 'My wife thinks I drink too much.' He looked around. 'Your garden is a picture. It's a delightful little cottage.' He resisted making any comment about the far from homely interior.

'Still quite a bit to do,' Tom told him.

Sir Hedley caught sight of two paintings on the wall. 'I say, is this a scene of Marston Castle?'

'It is,' said Tom. 'It was painted for me by one of my pupils. The other one is the old barn at Bentley Beck.'

'Yes, I recognise it. These pictures are awfully good.'

'Colin Greenwood's a fine artist.'

'They are painted by the son of my gamekeeper?'

'That's right.'

'Yes, now I remember Mr Greenwood telling me that his son had a talent in art. These watercolours are excellent. I wonder if the boy might be persuaded to paint a couple for me.'

'I'm sure he would be delighted,' said Tom.

'It's just that my wife is not greatly enamoured with all the dark oil paintings at Marston Towers – lots of murky canvases in heavy gold frames. They are a tad depressing, I must admit. She wants something a little brighter for the morning room.'

'I will ask Colin, tomorrow.'

'I would appreciate that.' Sir Hedley sat in the old, cracked chocolate-brown leather armchair. 'Speaking of art, I was down in London at the Wordsworth Gallery a while ago to open the exhibition of Mrs Stanhope's work. You will recall she was the artist who came to live in the village and made such an impression. Delightful woman and quite a hit with the residents. She painted those superb scenes set in the Dales and the portraits of the people in Risingdale. I have a couple of her paintings.'

'Yes, I remember Mrs Stanhope,' said Tom. He remembered her very well.

'Her exhibition was a cracking success,' Sir Hedley carried on. 'She is in Spain now with another assignment. She asked after you and sends her best wishes.'

'Did she say how her son is getting on?' asked Tom, thinking of Leo, the small boy with his mass of golden curls, his wide, inquisitive blue eyes, and his pale face. He had been for a short time in Tom's class and had been upset at having to leave Risingdale. It had been the first place in his short life where he had felt happy and settled.

'No, she never mentioned him,' said Sir Hedley. 'Anyway, down to business. My visit this evening, Mr Dwyer, is not really a social call. I wanted to ask you about the man who will be taking over as headmaster of the school in September.'

'I see.'

'I was speaking to young Charlie last night and when I mentioned that a Mr Smart would be the new headmaster at the school he told me that he had joined your lesson.'

'Yes, he did.'

'Charlie did not take to him. He said he was not a person given to much smiling, in fact he said he resembled a man who had climbed out of a coffin.'

Tom thought of Vicky's comment when Mr Smart had left the classroom. He had found himself agreeing with his pupil.

Mr Smart, thin and bloodless, had a whiff of the vampire about him.

'Of course, I did tell him that one should not judge a person by appearance,' said Sir Hedley, 'and that the man in question was probably a decent sort, but he said that Mr Smart never opened his mouth not even to say "Good morning" or "Thank you" and looked very stern and unfriendly.' Tom didn't answer. 'They do say that children and drunkards tell the truth,' continued Sir Hedley. 'I have found that my son is a particularly good judge of character and a truthful young man.'

'Young people do tend to be honest, that's true,' said Tom. He was not inclined to discuss Mr Gaunt's successor, so changed the subject. 'In the lesson we were talking about the things that make us happy.'

'Yes, Charlie was telling me,' said Sir Hedley. 'If I had been asked, I should say that for me, four things make for a happy life: a cheerful mind, a peaceful rest, a moderate diet and a loving wife. I might add a fifth – a glass of malt whisky.'

'I asked Charlie what he thought was the thing that made him happy. He told me, "Having a father".'

'Did he really.' The baronet was quiet for a while, clearly moved by what he had heard. 'Well anyway, after our conversation, I received a call from Mr Gaunt. He feels this Mr Smart is not really the sort of man for the job. I have known Gerald Gaunt for many years and trust his opinion unreservedly. He suggested I might have a word with the staff. As he told me, he will not be there next term and it is the teachers who will have to work with the new chap.' He waited for a response, but Tom looked thoughtful and did not say anything. 'So, what are your feelings?'

'I only met Mr Smart fleetingly,' Tom told him evasively, 'and we exchanged just a few words.' He recalled his Auntie Bridget's advice that one should never speak ill of a person, particularly if you hardly know them. 'He stayed in my lesson for maybe ten minutes and then we had a brief conversation in the corridor, that's all. It is difficult for me to form a full opinion of his suitability for the post having only met him for such a short time. I also think it might be unprofessional for me to make a comment about the man who will be the next headmaster.'

'But I assume you know what your colleagues feel,' said Sir Hedley. 'You must have gleaned their opinion of the man and you do have a view of your own.'

'I think, Sir Hedley, it might be better to speak to them.'

'You know Mrs Gosling, my housekeeper, of course,' said the baronet.

'Yes,' replied Tom. 'She used to work at the school.' He was wondering what she had to do with this conversation.

'Mrs Gosling is a very astute woman, Mr Dwyer, very astute. I had a most interesting conversation with her one day and she told me she believed that it is always best to be straight with people. This is a Yorkshire characteristic, of course. I agreed with her. "I've always been a one to speak my mind," she told me, "and then people know what's what." I am sure that you will agree with me that the children at the school deserve the best. You and your colleagues owe it to them to make sure of that. It is the responsibility of a teacher. So, Mr Dwyer, be straight with me, don't beat about the bush, and tell me what's what.'

'All I will say, Sir Hedley,' said Tom, the speaker's words hitting home, 'is that should Mr Smart become the headmaster of Risingdale School, Miss Tranter will resign, Mrs Golightly will take early retirement and I shall seek another position.'

'Which says it all,' said Sir Hedley, rising from the chair.

*

It was the week before the school broke up for the summer holidays. That Friday morning Mr Gaunt had sent a note around the classrooms asking the members of staff to remain after school for a brief meeting.

Since the visit of Mr Smart, the teachers had been in a sombre mood. The staffroom, once the place for badinage, the shared joke, the relating of amusing anecdotes and gossip, the good-humoured chit-chat and laughter, was now a solemn place where the teachers drank their coffee quietly and exchanged few words. They sat in dejected silence, contemplating their future with the air of those resigned to the inevitable fact that things would not be the same at Risingdale with the arrival of the reviled Mr Smart.

At morning break Joyce, still rankling, broke the silence.

'I have my resignation in my handbag,' she told no one in particular, 'and I shall be giving it to Mr Gaunt at this afternoon's meeting.'

'I have already put my application for early retirement on his desk,' said Mrs Golightly, heavy-hearted. 'All he needs to do is sign it and I shall put it in the post on my way home.'

'I saw you looking in the educational supplement of the paper,' said Mr Cadwallader to Tom. 'Anything there of interest?'

'There's a post in Selby and one in Scarborough, but they are too far away,' he said unhappily. 'Anyway, I wouldn't be able to start in September.'

'What about getting in touch with the head teacher at the school where you trained,' suggested Mrs Golightly. 'I'm sure she would have you back. She spoke very highly of you from what Mr Gaunt said.'

'I did give Mrs Stirling a ring last night,' answered Tom. 'There was a vacancy last term at her school, but it's been filled, so nothing there I'm afraid. She groaned when I told

her that Mr Smart will be the new headmaster here. His reputation has evidently gone before him.'

'It's a crying shame that you have to move just when you're
starting your married life,' said Joyce.

'I suppose you will have to move out of Risingdale to get
another job,' remarked Mr Cadwallader unhelpfully, 'and Janette will need to find a position in a bank near where you are
teaching, and that won't be easy. You will have to sell your
cottage. It might mean you will have to delay your marriage.
It's a pretty dismal prospect.'

'Well, thanks for that,' said Tom sarcastically. 'That's really
cheered me up.'

'Not as dismal as it will be for you, Owen,' said Joyce, 'not if
you stay here and have to put up with Mr Smart Alec.'

'I *have* to stay here,' he retorted glumly. 'I don't have any
choice. I can't afford to resign, and they are not likely to give
me early retirement like Mr Gaunt and Bertha. I don't get
much of an army pension and my teachers' pension wouldn't
amount to much and it's no good me looking for another job
at my age.' He sighed loudly. 'I shall just have to stick it out
and put on a brave face.'

At lunchtime, Tom was on playground duty.

Vicky approached arm-in-arm with Carol and Marjorie.

'Mr Dwyer, what's up with all the teachers?' she asked,
blunt as ever.

'What do you mean?' asked Tom.

'Well, something's up. You are all going round with faces
like the back of a Clayton bus on a wet Monday.' Tom could
hear the girl's grandmother speaking.

'You haven't been yourself, Mr Dwyer,' ventured Marjorie
quietly. There was concern in her voice. 'You keep looking out
of the window in lessons as if there's something on your mind.'

'There's something up,' stated Vicky decisively. 'Have you
broken it off with Miss Fairborn?'

Tom laughed. 'No, I've not broken it off with Miss Fairborn,' he told her. 'Anyway, who told you about me and Miss Fairborn?'

'Things get around,' said the girl.

'Well, you should be really happy, Mr Dwyer,' said Carol.

'It's nothing for you to worry yourselves about,' Tom told her. 'Now run along, girls.' As they ran off, he noticed Mrs Leadbeater sitting on the bench in the shade to the side of the school. She looked wretched with red eyes and pinched cheeks. He went to join her. She had a cigarette between her fingers. It had burned down, slowly turning to ash.

'I didn't know you smoked, Beryl,' he said.

'I don't,' she replied. 'Well, I do, but only when I get stressed. The last time was just after my mother died.' She nipped the end of the cigarette, which she then put in her bag. 'I just don't know what to do, Tom.' He couldn't think of a time when she had used his first name. It had always been, 'Mr Dwyer this' and 'Mr Dwyer that'. 'Bob and I can't stay here, that's for sure. I cannot stand that Mr Smart. He makes my flesh crawl.' She shook her head. 'The school won't be the same. I shall so miss Mr Gaunt, I really will.' It was only when she sniffed that he realised she was crying.

Tom put his arm around her. 'It will be all right, Beryl,' he told her with a lack of conviction in his voice. 'Things have a habit of working themselves out. "Every cloud has a silver lining." That's what my Auntie Bridget is forever telling me.'

'In this case every silver lining has a cloud, and that cloud is Mr Smart,' she said. 'I don't see how this is going to work out. Come September he will be in post and everything will change.'

Tom agreed, but said nothing.

*

After school the teachers, gloomy-faced, waited in the staffroom for the meeting to begin. Mr Gaunt had asked Mr and Mrs Leadbeater to attend.

'If he's asked that Mr Smart to join us, I'm out of here,' said Joyce.

'So am I,' said Mrs Golightly.

'We should all walk out in a show of solidarity,' said Mr Cadwallader. 'If the Education Authority sees fit to foist this man on us, we should make our feelings plain.'

'Yes, Owen,' said Joyce, 'I think you are right.'

'So do I,' added Mrs Golightly.

'You can count us in as well,' said Mrs Leadbeater.

'Are you with us?' Mr Cadwallader asked Tom.

'I think that we should hear what he has to say,' he replied, 'that is, if Mr Smart *is* joining us. To do as you suggest, Owen, would make us as rude as he has been with us and I am sure such an action would upset and embarrass Mr Gaunt.'

'There is nothing Mr Smart can say that will placate me,' said Joyce.

'Nor me,' stated Mrs Golightly.

'And I do not wish to see him,' added Mr Cadwallader.

The door opened and Mr Gaunt entered, accompanied by Sir Hedley Maladroit. The teachers were pleased to see that there was no sign of Mr Smart with them.

'I appreciate that you have been kind enough to stay behind,' said the headmaster. 'Sir Hedley is here to speak to you.' He turned to the Chairman of Governors.

'Thank you,' said the baronet. 'Firstly, I should like to congratulate Miss Tranter.'

'I'm sorry,' Joyce said, jumping up in her chair as if she had been flicked in the face with icy water. She imagined it had something to do with her husband's death. Was it about her inheritance? 'You wish to congratulate me on what, Sir Hedley?'

'Mr Gaunt has just told me that your talented youngsters have won the Choral Speaking Competition for the second time. This is quite an achievement.'

'Oh yes. Thank you.' She gave a forced smile.

'You must feel very happy. Well done.'

My state of happiness depends on what is to follow, she thought.

'The main reason for wishing to speak to you,' said the baronet, 'concerns the future of Risingdale School.'

The teachers all sat up and listened with absorbed interest.

'Now, I am well aware that you are concerned about the appointment of Mr Smart. Mr Gaunt has expressed his reservations to me, and I gather that the teaching staff is also, what shall I say, less than pleased. As the Chairman of Governors, it is my responsibility to ensure that the school is a happy, productive and thriving place where teachers work as a team, respect the head teacher and give him or her their full support. This, I fear, is unlikely to be the case were Mr Smart to be appointed. With this in mind, I have spoken to the other governors and had a candid conversation with the Director of Education and with Councillor Wayne Cooper, the Chairman of the Education Committee, acquainting them with the situation.' He paused for effect. The teachers sat on the edges of their seats. Mrs Leadbeater craned her neck. 'It has been agreed that Mr Smart will not be appointed as the headmaster of Risingdale School and will be found a suitable position elsewhere.'

'Yes!' cried Joyce. She could not have put more passion into a single word. She then slapped her hands over her mouth before resting them on her lap. 'I'm so sorry,' she apologised, her face becoming red with embarrassment, 'it just slipped out.'

Mrs Leadbeater, in a rare show of affection, reached out and held her husband's hand and muttered, 'Thank God for that.'

'Splendid news,' said Mr Cadwallader, drawing in a long, contented breath.

Tom remained silent but thought of the poor teachers at another school who would have to work with Mr Smart, a man who would go on to spread discord and despondency.

'So, you are staying on, Mr Gaunt?' asked Mrs Golightly, beaming.

'No, no, Bertha,' he replied. 'When you busy folk are slaving away at the chalk face in September, I shall be sailing around the Mediterranean on a cruise ship.'

'Now the fact is,' continued Sir Hedley, 'that this situation does present us with a bit of a dilemma. We will need someone on the staff to temporarily take the reins, as it were. It is too late now to find anyone for the start of the next term, so it will have to fall upon one of you to assume the position of acting head teacher.'

'Don't look in this direction,' Joyce said quickly. 'I have quite enough on with my theatre work and lecturing and I also have a business.'

'And you can count me out,' said Mr Cadwallader. 'I couldn't possibly take it on. I know my limitations and being a head teacher is one of them.'

'And I can't do it,' said Mrs Golightly firmly. 'I'd be out of my depth.'

Sir Hedley looked at Tom. 'Well, Mr Dwyer, it looks like you have drawn the short straw.'

'Oh no,' said Tom, shaking his head. 'I've only been teaching for a year. I don't have the experience. I couldn't possibly . . .'

'Yes, you can,' Joyce called out.

'Of course you can,' echoed Mr Cadwallader. 'You're the best person for the job.'

'Yes, Owen,' said Mr Gaunt, 'I think you are right.'

'You'll be fine, Tom,' said Mrs Golightly.

'It seems you have the endorsement of all your colleagues, Mr Dwyer,' said Sir Hedley, 'so it doesn't appear you have much of a choice.' Tom was clearly stunned and was lost for words. 'So, in my capacity as Chairman of Governors of the school, I hereby appoint you as the acting headmaster come September.'

'I don't know what to say,' said Tom.

'Say yes,' said Joyce.

'Well, it's only temporary, I suppose,' he said, 'and when Mr Gaunt's replacement arrives, I can return to my classroom where I belong, so I guess I could try and make a go of it. There are, however, three conditions.'

'Which are?' asked Sir Hedley.

'Firstly, that Miss Tranter doesn't resign and stays on at the school.'

'Easily done,' said his colleague reaching into her handbag, taking out an envelope and tearing it in half with a dramatic flourish.

'Secondly, I should like Mrs Golightly to withdraw her application for early retirement and agree to remain too.'

'Of course,' she said.

'And I'm not going anywhere,' announced Mr Cadwallader.

'And thirdly?' Sir Hedley asked Tom.

'That Mr Gaunt continues to be part of the work and life of Risingdale School and is there to give me his advice and support when I need it.'

Sir Hedley turned to the headmaster. 'Well?' he asked.

Mr Gaunt nodded. 'Of course, I should be pleased.'

'Then I accept,' said Tom.

*

'I would open a bottle of champagne to celebrate,' said Mr Fairborn, 'but you don't want to go drinking if you are driving.'

'No,' Tom agreed.

He was at Fairborn's farm at Saturday lunchtime. Janette was upstairs getting ready for their visit to Tom's Auntie Bridget.

'It's quite a feather in your cap, being made the headmaster,' said Mr Fairborn. He was standing in his favourite position by the fireplace with his hand on the mantelpiece.

'Acting headmaster,' Tom corrected him.

'It's quite something the way you have shot up the ladder with this promotion. You've not been in the job two minutes and now you're running the school.'

'It's only temporary,' Tom answered. 'I shall be back in the classroom once a new head teacher is appointed.'

'When will that be?'

'For next January, I guess.'

'Course, it will take a big man to step into Gerald Gaunt's shoes.'

'Yes, I'm aware of that.'

'He's a legend in these parts. He's been at the school as long as I can remember.' Tom said nothing. 'Aye, but it will look good on your CV, having run a school.' He thought for a moment. 'I reckon it won't be long before you get a head teacher's job and move out of the village, taking Jan with you. I shall be sorry about that.'

'I'm very settled here,' Tom told him. 'I've no ambition to leave.'

'For the time being,' muttered Mr Fairborn.

'So, how are things on the farm?' he asked, wishing to change the topic of conversation.

'Fair to middling,' said Mr Fairborn. 'I've bought a couple of Friesian cows and some sheep at the Clayton Auction Mart. Prices aren't what they were, so I didn't do too badly.' There was a pause. 'I'm thinking of doing up one of the out-buildings. It would just suit a young couple.'

'I think you've had this conversation with Janette.'

'What conversation?'

'About us living on the farm when we get married,' said Tom.

'Who's talking about you and Janette. I'm just saying that I'm thinking about doing up one of the outbuildings.' *He* now changed the subject. 'You will never guess what I found outside my gate this morning.'

'I've no idea,' said Tom.

'An empty barrel – a big, empty, stainless-steel beer barrel. It had been dumped right outside my gates. Now, how did it get there and who put it there, that's what I'd like to know? I mean if it had been full of beer, I wouldn't have minded, but there wasn't a drop inside. It's a mystery.'

Janette came into the room looking prettier than ever. Tom gave her a loving look. She gave her father a quick kiss.

'We won't be late,' she told him.

*

After the young couple had gone, Mr Fairborn picked up a silver-framed photograph from the dresser and sat on the sofa. The picture in the frame was of his wife dressed for the hunt in a black jacket and white cravat. He stared at it for some minutes.

'I wish you could see our daughter now, love,' he said to the picture. 'You would be so proud of her. She's turned out well, found herself a nice young man who will look after her. He's not a Yorkshireman, more's the pity, but he's a decent enough chap and I know he will make her happy. I will no longer be the man in her life. I'll miss her so much when she gets wed and leaves.' He stroked the glass in the frame. His bottom lip trembled. 'I wish you were here, love,' he said, wiping away the tears with the back of his hand and sniffing. 'I wish you were here.'

*

'You really shouldn't have gone to all this trouble,' Janette told Tom's aunt.

Mrs O'Connor had set out the table with afternoon tea. There were plates of salmon and cucumber finger sandwiches, scones with clotted cream and strawberry rose jam, meringues and fairy cakes, lemon curd tartlets and shortbread cookies and a large Victoria sponge cake with redcurrant jam and vanilla buttercream. The table groaned under the weight of so much food.

'Sure, it's a pleasure,' replied the hostess. 'I don't get the opportunity to bake for anyone any more. I used to be a cook at "the big house" in Ireland. Barrenscourt would be called a stately home here in England, but in Ireland it was always known as "the big house".'

'I didn't know that you were a cook, Auntie Bridget,' said Tom.

'Sure, there are a lot of things about me, Thomas, that you aren't aware of,' she replied. 'I'll have you know, I was the cook for Lord and Lady Staithes for five years and I enjoyed every minute, so I did.'

'When was this?' asked her nephew.

'I started at Barrenscourt as a girl. When I was about to leave school, I was sent for by the headmistress of the Mercy Convent, Sister Augusta. I was educated by the Little Sisters of Misery, as we pupils used to call them, but they were not a bad lot and did their best for us. Sister Augusta had a bit of a soft spot for me and arranged with Mrs McCrudden, the cook at "the big house", to take a look at me because there was a vacancy for a kitchen maid. I can remember the day I had to go up to this great stone mansion with parkland, a lake and a summer house, twice the size of our cottage at home, to be interviewed by Mrs O'Flaherty, the housekeeper, and Mr Power, the butler. I was so frightened, so I was. The house belonged to Viscount and Lady Staithes. They were of an

Anglo-Irish family, not proper Irish.' She chuckled. 'Brendan Behan, the writer, said the definition of an Anglo-Irishman was "a Protestant with a horse".' Once Mrs O'Connor had got an audience, there was no stopping her. Tom eyed the banquet before him and felt a twinge of hunger in his stomach. He exchanged a glance with Janette.

'Anyway,' continued his aunt, 'I got the job and joined the household. I was told by the housekeeper that I had to be humble, inconspicuous and obedient, and not talk to Lord Peregrine and Lady Staithes unless I was spoken to. You would never believe the number of servants there were: all manner of maids, footmen, valets, chauffeurs, and groundsmen. There was a governess and a nanny and a tutor. There was even a man whose only job was to wind up all the clocks. It was another world entirely, so it was.'

'What a fascinating life,' said Janette.

'Oh, I could write a book,' said Mrs O'Connor. 'In the 1920s the IRA had come to Barrenscourt and told the old Viscount, Lord Hubert – he was Lord Peregrine's father – to vacate the house and then it would be set alight. The family had a week to get out. He was a crusty old invalid was Lord Hubert and used a wheelchair and did a lot of shouting. Anyway, he was not a man to mince his words and used a few choice expletives, sending them on their way. When they returned to set fire to the place, Lord Hubert told them he had no intention of leaving and they would have to burn down the house with him in it.'

'Whatever happened?' asked Janette, fascinated by the account.

'They departed and never returned,' Mrs O'Connor told her. 'It was just after the last war when it all changed. Lord Peregrine's son and heir was killed in the fighting and his grief-stricken father died a month after he received the news. Then the daughter passed away with pneumonia. Lady Staithes never got over the loss and became a sort of recluse. Many of the servants left and most of the house was closed up. By this time, I was the cook, housekeeper and companion rolled into one. She was such a sad and lonely figure was Lady Staithes. She used to come down to the kitchen to talk to me. Well, I did all the talking to be truthful, so I did. I think she enjoyed me chattering on with all the news and the village gossip.' Mrs O'Connor smiled. 'It was Oscar Wilde, I think, who said that "If one could only teach the English how to talk, and the Irish how to listen, society would be quite civilised." Oh dear, and here I am doing all the talking and you two doing all the listening. I've not asked a thing about yourself, Janette, so come along, tell me about the young woman who's captured my nephew's heart.'

The afternoon went quickly by and soon it was time for Janette and Tom, stomachs full to bursting, to leave.

'Before you go,' said Mrs O'Connor, 'I would like to give you something, Janette.'

She opened her handbag and brought out a small, red, leather-bound box. Inside was an intricate gold necklace. 'This is called a Celtic Knot eternity necklace,' she said, 'and was given to me by Lady Staithes when I left her service. I should like you to have it.'

'Oh, I couldn't,' protested Janette.

'Yes, you can. I shall be offended if you refuse.' She pressed the necklace into Janette's hand. 'You might like to wear it on your wedding day. You must have something old. That's the tradition.'

'Oh, I will definitely wear it,' said Janette, fingering the necklace. She went over to Mrs O'Connor and kissed her on the cheek. 'Thank you so much.'

'I know,' said Tom's aunt, 'that you two will have a very happy life together. I can see how much you are in love. Love is like the wind: you cannot see it, but you can feel it. It can sometimes be painful and sometimes it can make fools of us, but it breathes meaning into life.'

'God bless you, Auntie Bridget,' said Tom.

22

It was the last day of the summer term at Risingdale School. In the afternoon, lessons were suspended and the children were allowed to read, paint or play games while the teachers cleared the classrooms. In Tom's room the children emptied their desks, and some helped take down the wall displays, tidy the books, put the shells, coloured stones and fossils into boxes and the stuffed animals away in the cupboards. The teacher's desk was heaped with all the cards and presents Tom had received from his pupils: ties and handkerchiefs, after-shave and cufflinks, pens and books. Marjorie had given him a brightly coloured patchwork cushion cover, Colin a water-colour of the school and Vicky a coffee and walnut cake baked by her grandma, which was rather worse for wear and minus the walnuts, having been carried half a mile to the school.

At afternoon break Vicky, arm in arm with her two friends, walked around the playground in the bright sunshine.

'Teachers are funny onions,' she declared. 'I mean, one minute their faces are like the back end of a donkey and the next they're as happy as pigs in muck.'

'I'd like to be a teacher,' declared Marjorie.

'I wouldn't mind,' said Vicky. 'It must be nice to be able to boss people about all day. I'd quite like to be a vicar though, like Mr Pendlebury – living in a big house, not much to do all week, telling people how to behave and paid money for saying a few services one day a week. Mind you, I wouldn't want to wear black all the time.'

'I don't want to leave,' Carol told her friends despondently. She had been listening to her friend half-heartedly.

Vicky sighed. 'I know what you mean,' she said. 'I'll miss Mr Dwyer, too. I hope I get a dishy young teacher up at the secondary school and not some old battle-axe.'

Mr Gaunt stood with Mrs Leadbeater in the corridor, staring at a cardboard box that contained the few things he wished to take with him. He was leaving the oak desk with the brass-handled drawers, the antiquated swivel chair, the battered grey metal filing cabinet and the heavy dark wood bookcase now empty of books.

'I'm taking the children's paintings and the Victorian sampler,' he told Mrs Leadbeater, 'but will leave the alpenhorn; I'm sure Tom will make good use of it when winter sets in.' The school secretary began to sniffle. 'Now come along, Beryl, none of that. You've not seen the back of me. I shall call in every now and then to see how things are going. I'm leaving the school in good hands.'

Five minutes before the bell sounded to indicate the end of school, Tom asked the children to sit at their desks.

'Before you all shoot off to start the summer holidays,' he started, 'I would like to say a few words to you all.' He studied the sea of expectant faces. 'I wanted to tell you how much I have enjoyed having you as my pupils this year. I could not have asked for a better class of children. You made me feel welcome from the very beginning, you have worked hard, behaved yourselves and it has been a pleasure to teach you.' He noticed that some of the girls had started to cry; a couple of the boys looked at the floor, rubbing their eyes to stem their emotion. Tom felt a lump in his own throat. 'Good luck in your new schools and do come back and tell me how you are getting on.' The bell rang shrilly. 'And thank you for the cards and the presents.' The children remained in their seats. Then Colin got to his feet and began to clap. He was soon joined by all the children. When the applause died down Tom held up a hand. 'Thank you,' he said, his voice quavering with emotion. 'Now, off you go and have a lovely holiday.'

He stood at the door of the classroom and shook each child's hand in turn as they filed past him. Vicky gave him a hug. 'If you'd have waited for me, Mr Dwyer,' she told him, '*I'd* have married you.'

Charlie was the last in line. Tom smiled at the plain-looking, thin little individual with the wide mouth, dark eyes, large ears, the spit and image of his father. The bruises on his face were now faint and the cut on his forehead had healed, leaving a small scar. It had been such a pleasure to have taught the boy, with his ready smile, enthusiasm, and curiosity. Tom would miss him.

'Thank you for all you have done for me, Mr Dwyer,' said the boy, 'I shall always remember you.'

The teacher watched from the classroom window as the children hurried out of the school gate, scattering wildly – running and skipping, shouting and laughing, freed from school and lessons for six weeks. A moment later, Miss Tranter and Mrs Golightly could be seen heading for their cars, keen to get to the hairdresser's, and Mr Cadwallader off to collect his dinner jacket from the dry cleaner's. That evening Mr Gaunt was taking the staff and Mr and Mrs Leadbeater out for a meal at Le Bon Viveur. The teachers wanted to look their best.

The deserted school became eerily silent. Tom sat at his desk and gazed at the empty classroom. He thought of Mr Gaunt, who had really made him feel how important is the role of the teacher. Who would have thought, he asked himself, that within the space of one year he would have made such close and caring friends in the staffroom, been made to feel part of the village, bought a cottage, been asked to manage the school and fallen in love? He thought of the lesson where he had asked the children what sort of things made them happy. As he continued staring at the empty desks, he felt his was a profound happiness.

Mr Leadbeater, a rare smile lighting up his craggy features, appeared at the classroom door, jangling a bunch of keys. 'Well, that's another term over,' he said chirpily. 'I hope I can get a cleaner in September.'

'I'll get onto it as soon as I can,' Tom assured him.

'Have you finished in here, Mr Dwyer?' he asked. 'It's just that I need to lock up. I'm going to leave the cleaning until tomorrow.'

'I'm just off,' replied Tom, getting up and looking around the bare and silent room. 'I'll be seeing you and your wife this evening.'

'Yes, that's right,' said the caretaker, 'we're looking forward to it.'

'I'll see you there,' said Tom, heading for the door. 'Well, good afternoon, Bob.'

As he walked down the corridor Mr Leadbeater called after him.

'And a very good afternoon to you too . . . headmaster.'

*

The following week, Sir Hedley and Lady Maladroit hosted a luncheon for the governors and staff of the school to celebrate Mr Gaunt's retirement. The drawing room was crowded and noisy when Tom arrived for the celebration at Marston Towers. He stood at the door, unnoticed at first by the assembled guests, and glanced around the room. There were the school staff with Mr and Mrs Leadbeater and several of the governors: the Reverend Michael Pendlebury, Dr Entwhistle, Mrs Sidebottom and the Reverend Robert Cockburn, all holding glasses and all in animated conversation. Mr Gaunt was standing with Moira, Sir Hedley and Lady Maladroit before the carved white marble fireplace bearing the Maladroit coat of arms with its Latin motto. When he saw Tom, he beckoned him over.

As Tom made his way through the throng, he was congratulated on his appointment as acting headmaster. People shook his hand and patted him on the back.

'Congratulations, Mr Dwyer,' said Moira as he approached. 'Gerald speaks very highly of you. He tells me you are a born teacher.'

'That's very kind of him,' said Tom, colouring a little.

'And may I add my congratulations,' said Lady Maladroit. 'Your appointment is well deserved.'

'Thank you,' replied Tom. 'Quite unexpected.'

'I am sure you will rise to the occasion,' she assured him. 'Thank you so much for all you have done for Charlie. He will certainly miss having you as his teacher.'

'I imagine he is getting excited at starting at his new school next month.'

'Oh yes,' she said. 'He is keen to learn Latin of all things. They teach the subject at the grammar school.'

'How is *your* Latin, Mr Dwyer?' asked Sir Hedley, listening in to the conversation.

'Non-existent,' Tom replied. 'Brother Dominic, who tried to teach me Latin at school, despaired in the end. I was much keener on football than learning a dead language.'

'I was just mentioning to Mr Gaunt that my family motto –' he pointed to the coat of arms above his head – 'is most apt for those of you in the education business: *Docendo discimus.*'

'I'm afraid you will have to translate for me,' Tom told him.

'"We learn by teaching",' Mr Gaunt informed him.

'That is true enough,' said Tom. 'I have certainly learnt a great deal from teaching the children in my class this year. I have become something of a farming expert, even if I do say so myself. I can tell a Texel sheep from a Scottish Blackface, a

Wensleydale from a Leicester, I can recognise the finer points of a Belgian Blue bull; I know about breech births in cows, artificial insemination, sheep scab and scabby mouth, how to snare rabbits with a ferret and tickle trout and can just about understand the Yorkshire dialect, and all of this taught to me by the children.'

Sir Hedley chuckled. 'Well, if you are to marry a farmer's daughter then that sort of thing will come in very handy and if the headmaster's job doesn't suit, then you could always become a vet, like Miss Macdonald here.' Seeing Mrs Gosling gesticulating at the door, he raised his voice. 'Excuse me. Ladies and gentlemen,' he said in ringing tones, 'luncheon is served.'

The long polished mahogany table in the dining room was set out for a formal occasion with crystal wine glasses, shining silver cutlery, china plates and starched napkins. In the centre were two over-elaborate ormolu candelabra with twisting branches. Sir Hedley sat at the head of the table with his wife, Mr Gaunt at the bottom facing him. Tom was placed between the rector and the Methodist minister.

'The meal this evening is in honour of our distinguished guest,' Sir Hedley announced. 'The choice of the date will not have escaped your notice. This being August the first – Yorkshire Day – we are to have a truly Yorkshire feast. I think you will find the caterers, aptly named "Yorkshire Fare", have done us proud.'

Tom glanced at the menu. If the word 'Yorkshire' was mentioned once, it was mentioned rather too many times: 'Parsnip soup infused with Yorkshire honey' to start, 'Yorkshire beef with Yorkshire pudding and vegetables' as the main course, followed by a choice of 'Yorkshire desserts – Yorkshire curd tarts, Yorkshire rhubarb crumble or apple pie made from Yorkshire cockpit apples from the Maladroit estate orchard'. To finish there was 'Wensleydale and Swaledale cheeses with Yorkshire oatcakes'.

'Mr Pendlebury, you might like to say grace,' said the host. 'You perhaps know an appropriate Yorkshire blessing.'

'Oh, dear me,' said the vicar, 'I am afraid I only know one Yorkshire grace, which might be considered a little . . . how shall I say . . . unseemly. I recall the historian Professor Penn-Bailley once using it at a dinner at the Merchant Adventurers' Hall in York, when he spoke about the Wars of the Roses. He was an enormously proud Yorkshireman, was Professor Penn-Bailley.'

'Do share it with us, Mr Pendlebury,' said Joyce. 'You have whetted our appetites.'

'Well,' said the clergyman, 'if you insist.' He put his hand to his mouth and cleared his throat. '"Thank you, God, for the repast before us, the food we eat and the wine we drink, and may your hand of righteousness rise up and smite the Lancastrians".'

There was a ripple of laughter.

'Perhaps, Mr Cockburn,' said Sir Hedley, 'you might know a more fitting Yorkshire grace? I would not wish to offend Dr Entwhistle, who hails from the other side of the Pennines.'

'Oh, do not trouble yourself on that score, my dear sir,' said the doctor, with a polished smile, 'we of the Red Rose County are well used to the Yorshireman's taunts. Everyone knows, of course, that the best thing that came out of Yorkshire is the road to Lancashire.'

There were groans of good-hearted disapproval.

'Let us not start the Wars of the Roses again this evening,' said Sir Hedley, laughing.

'I do know a Yorkshire grace,' said Mr Cockburn, bowing his head.

The diners followed suit. The minister put his hands together. '"God bless us all, an' mek us able, ta eyt all t'stuff 'at's on this table".'

This was accompanied by a voluble, 'Amen.'

Following the lively and cordial meal, the guests withdrew to the drawing room where champagne was being served by a waiter.

'It falls upon me to say a few words,' announced the baronet, taking up a prominent position before the fireplace. 'When the Yorkshire author and poet, Oliver Goldsmith, wrote about the village schoolmaster, "And still they gaz'd and still the wonder grew/That one small head could carry all he knew", he might have been speaking of Gerald Gaunt, a man of great erudition who could have gone on, I have no doubt, to become headmaster of a large school or one of Her Majesty's Inspectors, but he loved being a village schoolmaster. It has been his life. Shrewd, warm-hearted, generous, and dedicated, he is a passionate advocate of education and the preservation of the small village school. He is a man who holds the strong conviction that classrooms are places where there is grace, humour, warmth, and compassion and, of course, hard work. At Risingdale School he has—'

'Please, please, Hedley,' interrupted Mr Gaunt, holding up a hand. 'This is most kind of you, but I am finding this acutely embarrassing.'

'I must say,' remarked the vicar turning to Tom and lowering his voice, 'it does smack rather of an obituary.'

The baronet, who had not heard, smiled. 'Fancy being told to be quiet in one's own house,' he said good-naturedly.

There was laughter.

'Well, I will shut up,' he said, 'but not before I ask you all to raise your glasses and toast our guest of honour. I give you Gerald Gaunt, OBE.'

'Gerald Gaunt, OBE,' chorused the assembled guests.

'Do you wish to say a few words, Gerald?' asked Sir Hedley.

'Merely to thank you,' said Mr Gaunt, 'and to wish my successor as the headmaster of Risingdale School—'

'Acting headmaster,' cut in Tom.

'To wish my successor, every good wish. I know that he will be a great success.'

'Hear, hear!' shouted Tom's colleagues.

'As regards a gift for you, Gerald,' said Sir Hedley, 'we considered a silver tankard, a painting, a gold watch, a clock, but none of these seemed to us the right thing. Then we asked ourselves, what would be an appropriate present for someone intending to develop his smallholding when he retires? Now, I have it on good authority, that each year you borrow Mr Midgley's tup to serve your ewes when it is time. If you would make your way to the window you will be able to see that you will not need to bother again.'

All the guests crowded around Mr Gaunt as he headed for the window. On the lawn, standing solid and proud, was a majestic ram with off-white wool, great curled horns, and a black face, marked bright white around the nose and eyes.

'He thinks he's the bee's knees, now he's the winner of the blue ribbon at this year's Clayton and District Agricultural Show,' said Sir Hedley. 'Full of his own importance, isn't he? You should get a fine flock of sheep from him, Gerald.'

'But I heard that Dean Croft's tup won the blue ribbon,' said Mr Gaunt.

'He did,' replied the baronet, 'and it took a bit of persuading for the young man to part with him.' He winked in the direction of the teachers. 'There are people here tonight who know how persuasive I can be. When I told young Dean it was to be a gift for you, he readily agreed, but only on the understanding that he would be able borrow the tup from time to time.'

'I'm overwhelmed,' said Mr Gaunt. He knew that fine pedigree rams like the one on the lawn could sell for over a thousand pounds.

'Now then, Mr Dwyer,' said Sir Hedley, 'let me see if you really know your sheep. You were telling me earlier you consider yourself something of a farming expert. What breed is this fine specimen do you think?'

'It's a Swaledale,' said Tom without a moment's hesitation.

'It is indeed,' said the baronet. 'You certainly know your stuff.'

'By the way, Sir Hedley,' said Tom, grinning, 'I also know that Oliver Goldsmith was not a Yorkshireman, he was Irish.'

Mr Gaunt waited until the clapping had come to an end before he spoke. 'Thank you all so much for the splendid gift,' he said. 'I've now got to find a suitable name for this self-important-looking creature.'

'Why not call him Cuthbert!' Joyce shouted out.

*

Janette and Tom were married at the end of August at St Mary's Church. On that bright summer morning, the sun shone through the perpendicular west window bathing the whole of the building in subtle colours of reds, blues and golds. Brightly coloured images of saints in the stained-glass windows gazed down benignly on the congregation. The great burnished brass lectern in the shape of an eagle with its brooding stare and sharp beak towered over the congregation. It glistened in the bright light. The church was bedecked with extravagant arrangements of lilies and orchids, carnations and daisies, hydrangeas and tulips, all creations of the members of Mrs Golightly's flower-arranging group. On either side of the altar were two wrought-iron pedestals with elaborate displays of white roses. At the front of the church, in the ancient, polished oak-panelled pew, which had been reserved for members of the Maladroit family for many years, sat Sir Hedley in a pale linen suit and striped navy silk bow tie. A hand rested on his wife's arm. The new Lady Maladroit was dressed decorously in a pale blue cotton dress. She was in whispered conversation with Mrs O'Connor, elaborately hatted and attired in an emerald-green suit. Mr Gaunt and Miss Macdonald sat on the pew behind next to Mrs Golightly, who sported an unbecoming straw boater with small flowers arranged around the wide brim and Mrs Gosling, dressed in a voluminous canary-yellow ensemble and a peacock-blue hat with ostentatious coloured feathers. She resembled some large exotic bird. Behind were Mrs Mossup and Leanne with Dean and baby Marcus. Most of the villagers had turned out, so the church was packed. When Toby Croft and his pal arrived, there was not a seat to be found, so they had to stand at the back, much to the old farmer's vexation.

Outside, the pupils who had been in Tom's class had gathered, waiting for the arrival of the bride and groom. When their former teacher was spotted walking with the best man towards the church, there were cheers which signalled Mr Pendlebury and Father Daly to take their places before the altar. Eyes turned as Tom and Owen, dressed in grey morning suits and pale blue waistcoats, each with a white rose in his buttonhole, took their positions before the altar to await the entrance of the bride.

'He scrubs up well, does Mr Dwyer,' remarked Mrs Gosling, turning to Mrs Golightly.

'He does indeed,' agreed her neighbour, dabbing her eyes. 'I'm getting all weepy and the bride hasn't arrived yet.'

Moments later the organist struck up with the Trumpet Voluntary in D major, the Prince of Denmark's March. The congregation stood. All eyes turned to see the entrance of the bride. Janette, holding a small bouquet of white roses, wore a delicate organza white dress and veil and around her neck was the necklace Tom's aunt had given her. She walked slowly down the aisle of the church on her father's arm towards the altar where Tom and Owen were waiting. She looked exquisite. Behind her was Joyce, the matron of honour, in a coral-coloured silk dress, and then the two little bridesmaids in matching outfits.

Mr Fairborn kissed his daughter lightly on the cheek and taking her hand, he placed it in Tom's and the service began.

'May I welcome you all to this ancient church of St Mary's to celebrate and bear witness to the marriage of Tom and Janette,' intoned the vicar. He smiled with benign pleasure. 'God is love, and those who live in love, live in God, and God lives in them.'

'Marriage is a serious matter and the words in today's ceremony remind us that it is not to be taken lightly,' stated Father Daly, with ministerial solemnity.

'A wedding is one of life's great moments,' said the vicar, 'a time of serious commitment and a time of joyfulness. St John tells us how Jesus shared in such an occasion at Cana and gave there a sign of new beginnings as he turned the water into wine.'

The ceremony proceeded without a hitch. Then came the vicar's homily.

'Oh dear,' whispered Mrs Golightly to Mrs Gosling as she saw the clergyman ascending the stairs to the pulpit, 'I do hope he won't go on too long.'

'Now, I do not intend to go on too long,' started Mr Pendlebury, echoing her words.

'Thank the Lord for that,' said Mrs Golightly under her breath.

'And I, being unmarried myself,' resumed the vicar, 'do not feel qualified to offer the new couple the benefit of any advice on matrimony. What I would like to do, is read the words of the Victorian writer George Eliot and then a verse composed by Shakespeare.' He coughed theatrically.

'"What greater thing is there for two human souls, than to feel they are joined for life – to strengthen each other in all labour, to rest on each other in all sorrow, to minister to each other in all pain, to be one with each other in silent unspeakable memories at the moment of the last parting."'

'Well, I hope the poem is a bit more cheerful,' whispered Mrs Gosling to Mrs Golightly. 'I'm sure the happy couple won't feel particularly cheered by the mention of "sorrow" and "pain" and "the last parting".'

'The verse is Sonnet 116, called "Let me not to the marriage of true minds" by William Shakespeare,' continued Mr Pendlebury. He looked at the bride and groom and then began to read.

> '"Let me not to the marriage of true minds
> Admit impediments. Love is not love
> Which alters when it alteration finds,
> Or bends with the remover to remove.
> O no! it is an ever-fixed mark
> That looks on tempests and is never shaken;
> It is the star to every wand'ring bark,
> Whose worth's unknown, although his height be taken.
> Love's not Time's fool, though rosy lips and cheeks
> Within his bending sickle's compass come;
> Love alters not with his brief hours and weeks,
> But bears it out even to the edge of doom.
> If this be error and upon me prov'd,
> I never writ, nor no man ever lov'd."'

Joyce, with tears in her eyes, recalled Mr Smart's words that poetry has little relevance in the real world, that it is impractical and idealistic, and she thought of Julian. Mrs Golightly bowed her head and thought of her husband. Sir Hedley squeezed the hand of his new wife.

To the vibrant strains of Sortie in E-flat major by Lefébure-Wély, the newly married couple walked down the aisle and into the bright sunlight to be welcomed by a cascade of confetti and the cheers of the children. Tom and Janette climbed into the pony and trap, which was festooned with flowers and ribbons, and they were driven off at speed, for the driver, Mr Firkin, was keen to be away. He had a big funeral that afternoon.

Toby and his pal waited until the church had emptied and then they sat at a pew at the rear of the church.

'They mek a gradely couple,' remarked Percy.

'Aye, I reckon,' replied his friend.

'Puts me in mind o' mi own marriage.'

'Does me an' all,' said Toby, grimacing. 'T'wife's mother wun't be in t'photographs, 'er dad got drunk, best man lost t'ring an' there were a feight at t'reception. An' I'll tell thee this, Percy, married life's not all it's cracked up to be. It's a long dull meal wi' t'pudding served fust. Most people live ovver t'brush these days, anyroad. I've allus thought marriage is ovverrated. For me, an 'appy marriage is between a blind wife an' a deaf 'usband.'

'Gi'oer,' replied his pal. 'Tha's not done too badly. Thy wife's a martyr to purrup wi' thee. How long 'as thy been wed?'

'Too bloody long. It's a fact that t'chains o' marriage are 'eavy. Every year thy adds another link. It used to be that wives were created fer t'comfort of their 'usbands an' do what they were telled. A woman wi'out a man is like an 'orse wi'out a bridle, that's what mi owld dad used to say. It's all changed now, an' not fer t'better. It's all this hemancipation. My missis teks no notice of what I say.'

She is not alone in that, thought Percy.

'I sez to 'er t'other day, when tha'r deead, weer dus't tha want to be buried. "On top o' thee," she sed.'

His pal gave a gravelly laugh. 'Well, tha's got to hadmit, it were a champion wedding,' he said, bringing his pal back to the point. 'They were like love's young dream walkin' down t'aisle today.'

''Appen,' said Toby, grudgingly, 'but I've said it afore an' I'll say it agin, that Mester Dwyer 'as landed on 'is feet an' no mistake.'

'Tha's telled me,' grumbled Percy. 'I'm sick o' 'earin' it.'

Toby carried on regardless. 'Not been in t'village above a year an' 'e buys hissen that nice little cottage what Arnold Olmeroyde 'ad 'is eye on fer years, gets well in wi' landlady at t'King's Head, t'squire, t'vicar an' t'MP, then weds t'daughter o' one o' t'biggest an' richest landowners in t'area 'an 'er a bank manager to boot. 'E'll be rollin' in it. Then, if he dun't land t' 'eadmaster's job at t'school.'

Percy sighed.

'An' then, blow me, 'e dun't 'ave one vicar at 'is weddin', 'e 'as two of 'em. It's a wonder Harchbishop o' Canterbury or t'Pope weren't doin' t' 'onours. T'luck o' t'Irish, that's worrit is.'

'Come on, Toby,' said Percy, nudging his pal, 'stop thy mitherin'. Kind words are worth a lot and they cost nowt. 'E's a decent enough chap is Mester Dwyer an' tha knaas it. I fer one wish t'lad an' 'is new wife hevery 'appiness.'

Toby gave a nod and smiled, with a playful gleam in his eyes. 'Aye 'appen I do an' all,' he replied. ''Appen I do.'